KILL PROCESS

KILL PROCESS

WILLIAM HERTLING

version 1.1

liquididea press
PORTLAND, OREGON

KILL PROCESS

First Edition; Version 1.1

Please note: this novel is about a survivor of domestic violence. I have minimized explicit abuse in the novel, but the story deals at length with the aftereffects, including post-traumatic stress disorder.

Please subscribe to my mailing list at williamhertling.com to find out about new book releases.

ISBN-10: 1-942097-03-4
ISBN-13: 978-1-942097-03-7

liquididea press
PORTLAND, OREGON

Definitions

Tomo

noun:

1. The world's largest social network, with more than two billion users.

2. Japanese for friend.

PART ONE

CHAPTER 0

THE THING YOU HAVE TO KNOW ABOUT ME, to understand everything that's coming, is that I kill people.

It's ten-thirty at night, and I'm hiding in the bushes across the street and two doors down from a two-bedroom, two-story home. It's midsummer in Portland, and the temperature dropped after sunset, but it's still too hot for the dark, long-sleeved hoodie I'm wearing to reduce my visibility. Tomorrow morning I'll pay the price for crouching for hours on forty-five-year-old knees.

Inside the house are Cathy and Dave. According to their Tomo profiles, Cathy is twenty-four, and Dave is twenty-nine. They've been together for five years. Six months into their relationship, Cathy dropped out of college in Boston and they left together for the West Coast. They rent. Cathy takes temp work, and Dave's in construction.

Learning these details is painful, ripping open old wounds every time. Echoes of the same story, my story, recurring with consistent frequency, like a drumbeat punctuating life. I want to bury my head in the sand and drown out the sound, but I can't escape it, no matter how hard I try. Every case is different in the particulars, the same in the patterns.

Cathy's been on Tomo compulsively, visiting her best friends' profiles. However, she's not updating her status like she usually does. She goes through periodic gaps in posting, and when she manages a small post now and then, text analysis shows negative sentiment.

In the social media frenzy of the last twenty years, the tech industry invented dozens of new ways to analyze tweets, Tomo posts, and blog posts to determine the mood of the poster. Originally used by corporations to measure their customers' perceptions of their brands and products, the profiling tools now help me find the depressed.

I wonder what my own sentiment scores would be, although I don't possess much of an online profile these days. I keep my thoughts in my head. They're too dangerous to let out. Fortunately no one has invented the mind police yet, although the day is coming.

The lights upstairs blink out, and suddenly I can't take a breath. I'm clenching my hand so tight I'll find lingering fingernail bruises in the morning, but right now I don't feel a thing. Terrible things happen in the darkness.

It takes a long minute before my body forces me to breathe, and with a sharp inhale, the spell breaks. I'm not in the house. Dave is not my demon, even if he is Cathy's. I'm an independent agent, in charge of my own self.

The black nylon bag weighs heavy against my right side, the tools inside enabling me to do my job, and in the worst case, take personal action.

I know better now than to consume liquids less than an hour before the stakeout. I don't chew gum, smoke cigarettes, or carry anything I could leave behind or forget. I wait another hour to be sure they're deeply asleep. Everything is quiet in the house.

I'm wearing men's Nike sneakers (20 percent market share) I bought at FootLocker (most popular shoe retailer). I'm wearing men's Levi jeans (best-selling brand, and a different material makeup than women's jeans). Sticking to the most generic possible shoes and clothes reduces the chance the police will profile me. At 5'6", I fit into a lucky middle ground: a bit taller than average for a woman, still a passable height for a man.

DNA evidence is the kicker, of course. So I did the usual before I came out tonight: thorough shower first, clean clothes that went through two rounds of extra hot wash in a public laundry. My exposed skin got a liquid bandage product that helps prevent skin cells from flaking off. My shoulder length dark brown hair, courtesy of my Italian parents, received an extra-sticky spray that decreases the number of loose strands I'm likely to drop. The residue each product leaves is still better than shedding DNA.

At the back door, I withdraw my lock picks from a shirt pocket. A geek rite of passage with a long history in computer science departments dating back to MIT, lock-picking was something I mastered in my first year. Of course, it's considerably different with one hand instead of two.

Amputees can be divided into two types: those that measure themselves by what they've lost, and those grateful for what they've got.

Who am I kidding? Every amputee is both.

Me, I'm grateful for my stump. In fact, I've got everything up to but not including my elbow, and that's enough to apply pressure on the torsion wrench to hold the lock in tension, while I work the pick with my left hand.

With a subtle click I feel—not hear—the last pin lift into place, and the wrench shifts. I grab with my hand and complete the turn. The deadbolt opens.

I take a deep breath and try to ignore the growing pit in my stomach. Time for the real work.

CHAPTER 1

I SCREAM. Not some girly scream. A full-tilt, blood-curdling yell like I'm being murdered.

There's movement to my right, and someone touches me. I lash out, my fist hitting something hard.

There's a cry of pain, then a groan. "Angie, it was a dream."

I shake my head, trying to make sense of the world. I reach for the lamp, miss, and knock the alarm clock to the floor with my stump. Damn it.

Light blossoms as Thomas turns on his lamp. He slept over. Shit, that was Thomas I hit.

He's lying on his back, holding his face.

"I'm sorry," I say automatically, still focused on the night terrors.

"It's my fault, I shouldn't have touched you."

His tone, carefully even, plainly disguises inner frustration. I glance over at him. Maybe I'm reading too far into it. He could merely be in pain.

I curl my arm around my knees and rock back and forth. I want to take it all back, starting with the years leading up to my mistake. Sweat covers me and my muscles tremble from the adrenaline rush. Five years and still the nightmares come.

I dip my head onto my knees and close my eyes. I wish I could be unbroken. I wish these dreams didn't come. If I do nothing, I have nightmares about being the victim. If I kill an asshole, I get nightmares about what I've done. I don't know which is worse.

The bed shifts as Thomas sits up. "May I touch?"

I nod without lifting my head, and he puts an arm around me. Bless this man, I don't know how he puts up with me. He's a saint, and somewhere deep inside I love him for that, although I can never tell him.

‿

I drive to the office early, stopping briefly at Coava for a pour-over with enough caffeine to wake an entire team of software developers. It barely makes a dent in the exhaustion I feel after last night's minimal sleep.

At this hour, the traffic across the Willamette is non-existent, and I make it into downtown in a few minutes.

Our Portland offices are in the Big Pink, everyone's nickname for the U.S. Bancorp tower, where Tomo has six floors. I've worked at Tomo, the world's largest social networking site, since 2002, way before my ex-husband, and I still work there now, but everything has changed.

When I arrive at the security door on our floor, I've got the coffee in my good hand, my computer slung over my back, and now I'm out of hands, because my stump is no good for swiping my badge.

I tuck the coffee under my stump, swipe my badge, hold the door with my foot, then take my coffee in hand again. I've done this one-handed entry ritual since I lost my arm.

I wend my way through a mess of desks to my distant corner, a few other early risers there. By common social agreement we ignore each other until the niners arrive.

I take a seat, plug my laptop in, and leave the headphones on the desk. I want my ears free to warn me of anyone's approach. I've got my back and right side to a wall, a safe corner I usurped when I moved to the Portland office.

The data queries I run this morning hit our backend database, spidering through social graphs and past behavior, feeding the custom algorithms I wrote to profile our users.

When someone uses Tomo, we log everything. What status updates they saw, whose photos they clicked, what profiles they opened, everything they posted, read, uploaded, or downloaded, as well as when these things happened and where they were when they did it. Printed out, as happens when the court subpoenas someone's profile, a user's account history spans thousands of pages.

I used to be Tomo's chief database architect, employee number forty-eight. After I returned to work, I couldn't handle the Palo Alto headquarters anymore. In some ways, my new role in the Portland office suits my needs better. I'm a data analyst, writing code that interfaces with our databases and optimizes ad placement. The job gives me the time and access I need to pore through our endless stores of user data.

Want to know what an obsessive mother looks like? She visits the Tomo profiles of her children 11.6 times a day, every day.

I spot drug dealers by their endless private messages, filled with dozens of varying nicknames to disguise the drugs their clients ask for. Even as fast as street names change, it only takes a few dozen messages to ferret out the connection between old names and new ones, and watch brand-new drugs come online. I can watch them in real-time, if I want. The suppliers, of course, don't use Tomo. They're rightfully too paranoid.

I even watch the watchers. An FBI research analyst views thousands of profiles of people he doesn't know each day, and he logs in and out through different accounts. We track everything, even which accounts are used on the same computer, so we can build up inferred associations, even if two accounts lack explicit connections.

Child pervs are easy. They're the ones viewing profiles of kids under thirteen. Tomo officially doesn't allow kids under thirteen, of course. Still, it's easy enough to identify them by their obsessions over music, actors, TV shows, even their word choices. There's also the curious phenomenon of duck faces, the attempt to make sexual faces that seems to peak around twelve. I got tired of looking at them, so I wrote a duck face eliminator plugin. It detects pursed lips and replaces them with the Mona Lisa's smile. Much more peaceful.

I know who clicks on the links about wardrobe malfunctions, and who loves their mom and who doesn't. I can spot who's cheating on their spouse, and who has ever thought of it. We retain those drunken chat messages forever. In short, I know everything.

If the police had unfettered access to Tomo's data and knew what they were doing, they'd spot the criminals in an hour. Crime would drop overnight, and it would only require imprisoning half the population of the United States.

Angels we're not, with the possible exception of Thomas.

The NSA has unlimited access to our data, although nobody knows what they do with it. The raw data isn't of much use unless you know how to find the patterns. That's where I shine, even though my manager doesn't understand a tenth of what I do. He still thinks I pick ads out of a database to place on webpages, although I've tried to explain profiling countless times.

Of course, I'm not interested in the millions of crimes and morally bereft activities I unearth. It's incidental, the sort of stuff anyone familiar with machine learning and a few weeks to spare could do. For the most part, I don't give a damn. We're all guilty of something.

No, what I'm interested in is a little harder to find, a little more specific. My own personal demon.

CHAPTER 2

EMILY PLOPS INTO THE BOOTH across from me with a sigh of the world-weary.

"You are not going to believe my morning. I'm in the middle of getting Freddie ready for preschool, and the damn cat pukes in my laptop bag. It's not enough I still had to change a diaper. I'm already running late, so I have no choice but to bring the bag full of bile with me, drop Freddie off, and when I arrive at work, run to the nine o'clock meeting. I take out my laptop to present to the executive managers. It's covered with a layer of stinking yellow puke and matted fur, but it's too late to do anything, so I give the presentation and pretend everything is fine."

She emits a guttural yell of despair. I smile. Emily's life is so ordinary, it makes me want to hug her. Maybe this is the life I could have had, if everything hadn't gone awry. I'm not sure I would choose kids, but I'd like to live my life totally out there, brutally honest, without these half-lies, calculations, and suspicions that eat away at me like toxic waste my body can't expel.

"Did you order yet?" she says. Without waiting for a response, she reaches out an arm to block a waitress carrying food to another table. "The salad with the chicken breast on top, no skin, no cheese, light on the dressing, and coffee, lots of coffee."

I'm not required to talk a lot with Emily, which I like. It's different than when we were in elementary school, when I was the fearless leader.

"How'd the presentation go?"

"Awesome, of course. A little puke wasn't going to stop me. The executive team loved it, although one guy kept trying to edge away from my laptop." She shakes her head and grabs a pickle from the bowl on the table. "That computer was only two months old, but it's not like I can wash the thing. I told my boss, who's still pissed I forgot the last one in a taxi. 'Blah, blah, six notebooks in six months, blah, blah.' The hell with them, I make the company several million a year, they can damn well buy me a new computer any time I want." She says this last bit waving around her pickle like a school teacher wielding a pointer.

"So how's your job going? When are they going to make you manager?"

Of course, I don't want to be a manager. Even when I was high up in the food chain, my role was technical, not managerial. These days, I like my quiet corner and my unlimited database access, and the last thing I want is attention. If I could be invisible, that would be best.

This doesn't fit Emily's picture of the world where everyone should seize the opportunities that come their way with gusto. She wants me to once again climb the ranks of the company, but those days are over for me.

"No promotion yet," I say. I grab onto one exciting thing to tell her. "I discovered if you rotate an ad on a page a tiny bit, so the crookedness is imperceptible at first glance, in certain cities it increases the click-through rate. In Cincinnati, a three-degree clockwise twist increases the click-through rate ten percent. A one-degree left turn is more effective in Philadelphia."

I'm right on the border of where Emily accuses me of speaking a foreign language.

"That's exactly why you should go for a promotion," she says, nodding. "How many ideas do you have? How many can you test in a week? One, maybe two. If you were a manager, you could farm out your ideas to an entire team and test ten or twenty concepts in a week."

Our food drops with a thud on the table. The waitress tears off the receipt, depositing illegible scrawl onto the table.

"Jesus, Angie, how can you eat that?"

I ordered the house burger, a colossal construction five inches across, with an accompanying mound of onion rings. One-handed burger eating isn't pretty, and I'd never order anything like it with anyone besides Emily or Thomas. I don't work out, but thanks to good genes and the occasional hike or bike ride, I've managed to maintain a reasonable physique considering that I mostly sit on my butt all day and code. Besides coloring my hair every month at the salon, I'm not big on appearances.

"It's delicious," I say. "How can you eat tasteless salad?"

"I eat salad so I feel light and ethereal. It gives me energy so I can kick butt."

Emily is strange sometimes.

"Database queries can't be written on rabbit food. I need protein."

"That explains the onion rings, then."

Looking at the mound of greasy batter, I resolve to eat only half of them.

"Tell me what Freddie's doing."

She launches into a long explanation of Freddie's gastrointestinal system which somehow segues into his new vocabulary. Although my kidless coworkers would be bored to tears, I revel in the normalcy of it all.

℧

That night I microwave a burrito when I get home. On occasion, I let myself have a night off between projects, but not often. The anxiety eats at me. On average, eleven women die each day at the hand of a husband or partner. Maybe I can save one.

Gary is the top candidate for my next target. He's a banker, barely on Tomo at all except to post the occasional picture of his new BMW or home entertainment system. Pictures come in floods only on vacations, when we receive a long sequence of Helen. Helen at dinner, Helen in the BMW, Helen in a bikini. At Gary's forty-fifth birthday in London, Helen's makeup is on thick. I enlarge the photo to see if there's a bruise underneath. There's a slight darkening, but I can't be sure. I look at more photos, wondering if I'm really dying a little bit each time I see one, or if it only feels that way.

All database queries return results in a particular order, such as alphabetical by name or sorted by age. When someone visits Tomo, they see a sequence of posts in reverse chronological order.

My custom queries are ordered by potential threat and need for intervention: How likely is he to be abusing her? How likely is she to help herself or obtain help from someone else? There's only one of me, and so many millions of women.

The typical domestic violence victim will live with the abuse for two to three years before they seek help, and it usually takes five or more attempts before they finally extract themselves from the relationship. That is, if they can. Seventy-five percent of battered women who are killed by their abusers are murdered when they attempt to leave the relationship.

This last statistic drives my extreme approach. No sane person wants to go around killing other people, but I explored all the other options. Try to get the woman out, and you might indirectly kill her. Use punitive measures against the abuser, such as ruining their finances or getting them fired, and they'll take out their anger and frustration on their victim. Expose their abuses in the hopes of getting them arrested, and they might go free, in which case the repercussions fall on the partner. If I knew of anything else that guaranteed results, I'd use it, but I don't. The outcome of my kill process is deterministic.

And whatever excuses we might make for them, whatever their own pasts, abusers make a choice to hurt the very people they profess to love: at that point, they forfeit their right to mercy. The fact that our institutions are weak and ineffectual, that they don't protect the victim, is something we've allowed to persist. I won't.

Right now, my algorithms tell me it's very likely Gary's abusing her, and very unlikely she's going to self-rescue, at least not in time, not before the danger to her life grows critical.

Helen doesn't reply to her mother's messages, even though they're connected on Tomo. Helen's Tomo activity has gone passive; she's reading without posting. She's clicked on links her friends shared for domestic abuse hotlines. Many times. Most of them weren't actually posted by her friends. I inserted them in her stream, visible only to Helen.

Thanks to the Tomo app permissions on her phone, I have access to her call history. Even with all those clicks on the abuse hotlines, she's never actually placed the call, at least not from her personal phone. It's almost certain Gary monitors her phone usage, so if she makes the call, she'd better be ready to go.

Tomo's search engine is predictive, like all searches these days. Before Helen ever hits enter, the browser sends up the partial string that's been entered to see what might match, so we can suggest likely terms in a dropdown list. This data isn't normally saved as it would overwhelm our logs, however I can turn it on for a given account as I did two weeks ago for Helen and Gary.

Maybe the most damning piece of evidence is the time Helen typed into the search "how to kill yourself." She never hit enter, never went on to see all the help the net has to offer on that particular topic. Later the same day, she looked up her mother's profile eighteen times and her father's profile twelve. She composed a message to her mom six times, and cancelled each time. She couldn't send a simple "I miss you," even though she stared at the text for twenty-three minutes.

I rest my head on the cool metal case of my laptop, and let the sharp edge bite into my forehead. I focus on the pain and try to still the trembling in my hand.

I know what it's like when even suicide doesn't seem like an escape. It's possible to become so fucked in the head that you still love the person that does such terrible things to you. These assholes use warped logic and emotions as weapons even the most intelligent person can fall victim to, leaving you believing you're responsible for the situation. All the while, they're killing you from the inside, bit by fractured bit.

Nobody deserves to have their love repaid like that.

Helen and Gary live in Beaverton, a suburb twenty minutes outside of Portland. This vastly simplifies my ability to take care of Gary.

ひ

Finally the day arrives when my preparations are complete. I wake, go to work, put in a full day, then come home. I try to take a nap and fail. Later that night I pop a caffeine pill and get ready to leave.

I leave my cellphone at home, in front of the television, set to stream Star Wars episodes 4 and 5. The mobile phone runs code to act as a remote control. It will pause and resume the movies at pseudo-random periods to simulate bathroom and snack breaks, at which point it will report accelerator data consistent with those activities. It took two weeks to patch the core OS to make it do what I wanted. It's an alibi if I need it, but more importantly, it keeps my data profile normalized, so I don't ever pop up on anyone's radar in the first place.

I drive what I think of as my project car, an old Honda Accord, a model I chose because it's the best-selling car, and therefore as anonymous as a vehicle gets. I take Highway 26, stop for a restroom at a place with no security cameras, and then park in a grocery store lot across the street from a bar, a suitably ambiguous spot to leave a car. I hoof it the last mile to my destination.

My nylon gym bag hangs from my right shoulder, obscuring my missing arm. I walk through a quiet residential neighborhood, the only real danger encountering a late-night dog walker. I've checked all the neighbors ahead of time, know who has dogs and who doesn't, and what time they usually walk them, and I've plotted a path that minimizes the chance of discovery.

Gary's and Helen's next-door neighbors are visiting their daughter in New Mexico right now, according to the geolocation tags in the photos they're uploading, making their yard a safe harbor. I was tempted to check the property on Street View, but they've got logs too, and I don't want the authorities to find out someone's been researching that address. I settled for high-level satellite photos. From the abundance of greenery, I figured there'd be enough shrubbery and trees to provide plenty of hiding spots.

Sure enough, I'm in suburbia. I'm in place by eleven. It's Thursday night and Gary's planning a big party for the following night.

I settle in to wait between a butterfly bush and a small tree. It's cool out tonight, and the windows are closed, yet I hear their raised voices from time to time. They must be working on last minute preparations for tomorrow's party, because they're up far later than the median time of Helen's last evening Tomo visit.

My legs grow cramped. I resist fidgeting because moving, even a little, would work dirt into the treads of my sneakers and increase the marks I'd leave here in the garden. In much of the world, squatting is a normal resting position, so I stay calm and meditate, and hope my knees hold out.

Gary and Helen eventually finish their work, and the house grows dark and quiet.

My stomach jumps into my throat as the last light goes out, my mind replaying the utter dread of my husband climbing into bed next to me. The sound of a man brushing his teeth still makes me sweat. It's why I make Thomas use the little half bath next to the kitchen before bed. He accepted the demand as another of my many little oddities.

It takes the average person seven minutes to fall asleep, so I wait thirty, and then carefully rise, one painful inch at a time, my knees screaming all the way. Taking a step backwards, I use a stick in my gloved hand to break up the dirt where I was squatting. It's not perfect, though my goal is for no one to suspect what has taken place, so they shouldn't be looking for my footprints. The ground is not wet, so brushing my feet at their doormat should be sufficient to remove the dirt from my shoes.

At their back door, I reach into a pocket on my bag. Although my Teflon-coated lock picks reduce the amount of forensic evidence left behind, I won't be needing them tonight. Gary snapped photos of Helen last month at their golf club, and Helen's keys were clearly visible on the table. Using the digital photographs at their native resolutions, I had enough detail to recreate a three-dimensional model of their house key, which I reproduced on a 3D printer. The height of the rearmost tooth was hard to distinguish in the photo, a problem I solved by printing out multiple keys, one for each possible height of the rear tooth.

The plain white plastic key gleams faintly in the moonlight. I try the first. It doesn't want to turn, and I'm afraid to use too much pressure, since the plastic doesn't possess nearly the strength of a metal key. The second key turns easily enough, and I'm through the door.

I have half a minute to enter the security code, which Helen helpfully sent to her mother via a Tomo message six months ago. Cursing the audible beeps of the security panel, I enter the code, Gary's birthday.

The panel turns green. I'll need to lock it again on the way out. For the moment I stand motionless by the back door, waiting to see if anyone's heard anything. My eyes gradually acclimate to the murky darkness, a hallway nightlight providing all the illumination in this part of the house. I wait three minutes, running off the seconds in my mind, suddenly recalling a childhood memory of counting to a hundred on my grandfather's lap, despite his protests I could never count that high. I remember his strong, safe hands, calloused with years of construction work.

I memorized the layout as best I could glean from the photos in their Tomo albums. With everything quiet, I head for the kitchen, balancing cautious movement against speed. Although I'm in control of what I do, the longer I take, the greater the impact of a random occurrence screwing up my plans: someone waking, a phone ringing, a loud horn of a passerby.

I need access to Gary's car. Such a simple thing, you'd think I could've done it at his office or when he was parked on the street; yet a week of tracking his location didn't turn up anything I could use. He pays for parking at his office, and the lot is busy and covered with surveillance cameras. Breaking the wireless code for the home garage opener is trivial, except that the sound of the door rising in the middle of the night would wake everyone.

I take the keys off the kitchen counter with my gloved hand and enter the garage. The door closes behind me, weather-trim making a snug fit. The garage has windows in the outside door, so I keep the lights off and hope nothing gives me away as I wait for my eyes to adjust to the glow from the street filtering in.

The BMW will chirp if I unlock the doors. I've spent days researching this problem. I can't kill the power, because the door lock is electronic and won't unlock without electricity. The solution is ugly but functional. I hit the trunk unlock, and the lid pops open without a chirp. The thunk of the lock releasing is relatively quiet, although I still hide behind the car and wait until two minutes pass without a sound. Nobody comes.

I climb into the trunk. One-armed crawling in a trunk is not elegant, but gets me where I need to be. The fold-down seat has a release mechanism in the trunk on this model, so I pull the lever and crawl into the back seat. I try not to think about DNA evidence, because crawling about is not great. Yes, I'm wearing a blue glove pulled over my stump for this. No point in leaving a stump print, since that would narrow things down pretty damn quickly. Of course, if I do things right, no one will suspect anything other than an accident.

I finally get into the front seat and plug my handheld computer into the car's diagnostic computer port. I insert the car key, and now the BMW car unlocks silently. The real meat of the matter is so anti-climatic, it barely merits mentioning, but I upload my computer program to the vehicle's firmware. It's a small change, not much different from factory firmware, and the odds of it being detected are tiny.

I exit through the driver's side door, which now opens silently, then wipe down the seats and return everything to its original configuration. I close up the car, and the only thing I've left behind are changed bytes in the car's computer program.

↻

Gary Broadhurst, Oregon Banker, Killed on Daily Commute

Portland—Gary Broadhurst, 47, was pronounced dead at the scene when his car ran off the road in the Terwilliger curves section of I-5 on Friday morning. Police blame the fatal accident on driver distraction as phone records show Broadhurst received a phone call seconds prior to the accident during his morning commute to work.

According to eyewitnesses, Broadhurst veered right as the road curved left, sending him down an embankment into a grove of trees. His vehicle struck a tree head-on.

CHAPTER 3

MODERN VEHICLES are drive-by-wire. When the driver depresses the brake, the pedal isn't connected physically to the brake system. It hasn't worked like that since computers took an active role in cars, modulating brake pressure for ABS, applying differential torque for traction control.

Instead, a potentiometer measures pressure on the pedal, transmits this measurement to the car's computer system, which decides how best to apply the brakes given the vehicle speed, traction, and driver intention.

The software program I copied to Gary's vehicle computer last night triggered when Gary's phone rang. It didn't matter who called, although it was the party caterer in this case, the standard prerecorded reminder they send to all customers on the day of their event. I tweaked their autodialer to call Gary at the exact moment he was on that section of the highway.

Activating only the right-side brakes was easy. The tricky part was getting the airbag to deploy a quarter of a second after impact. The bruises will puzzle the coroner, yet they'll still conclude it was an accident. People die when they hit a tree at seventy. It just happens.

I'm at work when the event occurs, and of course I'm not going to click on the news article when it appears. That would leave a trail. It would take the NSA or better to track an isolated click on a news articles back to me given my defenses, yet I'm still not willing to take that chance. *I* could find me if I clicked on the article, even if run-of-the-mill police couldn't.

Instead I do a few database queries here inside the firewall where I control the logs, find people who shared the article on Tomo, and read the article excepts that are part of their posts. I've done the job, and that's what matters. Helen is free to seek help and rebuild her life now.

The window I'm reading fades to black and I look up. My manager, Daniel, approaches.

There's a fascinating and useful application called ItsPersonal, which uses the webcam to monitor people-shaped blobs approaching, and automatically hides sensitive windows the user designates with a keyboard shortcut.

Running the original ItsPersonal would be foolish. The embedded neural network is trained to recognize patterns every time a window is marked sensitive, so that over time it can automatically determine what you want protected.

My guess is a future software update will upload that sensitive data to their corporate servers, and the firm will blackmail its twenty million users.

That's why I borrowed only their image recognition code, and threw away the rest. Then I cobbled together my own version.

If you think that's paranoid, you should see how I route my data connections.

"Angie," Daniel says, rapping on my desk for no reason, considering that I'm looking straight at him. "We have a meeting at eleven. I need you there."

"What's it about?"

"Marketing came up with a new privacy-related product, and they're socializing the idea around the organization."

I could puke at the idea of another marketing meeting. Bullshit dished out verbally and by slides. Oh, joy. "You sure you need me there?"

"You said to include you in any meetings involving data and profiling. You complained about being left out of the data re-architecture meeting."

"That was a *technical* meeting, Daniel. Deciding the structure of the data we store, a fundamental aspect of how we analyze and profile our users. Not a bunch of marketing flacks discussing possible plans for the future."

"So you don't want to give any input on our privacy policy?"

Oh, jeez. If I say no, it virtually guarantees they'll make a major decision in my absence I'll disagree with and will suffer the consequences for months to come.

"Fine, I'll go."

"Thanks, Angie. Oh, and one other thing." He leans forward and lowers his voice as though we're being spied on. "Maggie's going out on maternity leave in a few weeks."

"Yeah, we all know. Her belly is about to explode. You don't need to whisper."

"Yeah. I assume you're planning a party and a gift for her?"

I clench my fist and release it. Twice. "Why would you assume that?"

"Well, because you two are close."

"I'm not sure reviewing her code counts as close. Is it possible you assumed that because she's female and I'm female?"

"Well, no, of course not." Daniel stands up straighter, manages to look a little indignant.

"Or because I'm a woman, so only I could plan a maternity leave party?"

Now I stand and Daniel backs away.

"You know what, it's fine. I'll take care of it." Daniel practically runs away.

Asshole. My heart pounds slightly, but I'm not panicked, merely angry. Keep me in an open, public place with lots of escape routes, and my PTSD rarely kicks in.

↻

Laptop in backpack, coffee in hand, I walk into the meeting room. A long table occupies the middle of the space, a flat-screen TV on the wall to my right as I enter.

My breathing tightens as I see the seats nearest the screen—and therefore those closest to the door—are all filled. To take a seat at the table would mean putting eight people between me and the exit, six of whom are men. This is unacceptable to some lizard portion of my brain. Rationally, I tell myself to walk in and take a seat, yet it's not that easy, and I falter. Shit. The confidence I felt an hour ago when I yelled at Daniel evaporates in a heartbeat.

Logically I know none of the men in this room are going to hit me, threaten me, or lock me in a closet. I've analyzed the profiles of all the people I work with to make sure, and occasionally tweaked the job requisition system to nudge any risk factors far away from me. Even if these men possessed any of those tendencies, they aren't going to surface here, threatening my well-being in the professional work environment at Tomo. In spite of all that, the sympathetic nervous system doesn't take orders from the neocortex, and all the logic in the world is powerless against the flood of fight-or-flight hormones raging through my body.

I glance at the chairs along one wall, there for when the room is overflowing. The room is not full now, of course, although these are the only seats near the door. If I take a seat along the wall while there's still empty seats at the table, I'm telling the people in the room I don't care enough to sit at the table and I'm not engaged.

I once remarked to a friend that the cost of building homes for the homeless would be cheaper than dealing with the social impact of homelessness. She said lacking a home was the symptom of homelessness, and the causes went far deeper: mental problems, substance abuse issues, social support. What seemed like a simple problem was quite complex.

In this moment of hesitation, I'm overwhelmed by the complexity of my issues. Having one hand is nothing at all compared to the warring factions inside my mind: Sit at the table to show you care. Don't let anyone between you and the exit.

I'm a woman in tech, an amputee, an abuse survivor. The intersectionality kills me.

Carl, a senior marketing manager, looks up at me from his corner seat at the front of the table. Maybe I've gone pale, or perhaps he notices my shaking. He stands and moves his stuff. "I'm going to be presenting, Angie. Take my seat."

Carl may be a good guy despite his career choice.

"Thanks," I mumble, and slip into the chair as unobtrusively as possible. I'm embarrassed and thankful. I wipe a fine sheen of sweat from my forehead, and avoid looking at anyone at the table. I can't avoid the gaze of my boss, Daniel, directly across and clueless of what transpired. He's probably still wondering why I was pissed about the maternity leave party.

Down the table, three other people from marketing are present, along with a designer and two UI engineers, including Sarah, the technical lead for our new web browser. There's no one from backend engineering except me. Tomo as a company thinks first and foremost about how things look. That I'm present at this meeting is only because I've spent the last two years indoctrinating Daniel into the importance of involving all the stakeholders. I hate these meetings, yet being here seems to be the only way to ward off the worst of the stupid technical decisions.

One last person enters and Carl nods to them.

"Let's get started, everyone," Carl says, and thumbs through slides on his phone, which are displayed on the wall behind him. "One of our top user complaints is about privacy." The slide contains a pie chart of customer issues. "The number one complaint is concern over who can view their posts, followed closely by concern over the use of their personal data for advertising."

Carl is stating the obvious to anyone who works in social networking. Advertising is how Tomo makes nearly all of its revenue, and those dollars are dependent on accurately targeting users.

Usually this is good. If the band The Strokes tours the country and wants to advertise tickets to fans who live in Sacramento, California, they can do it with Tomo. Their fans perceive it as a feature, not advertising. I've read feedback from users who said "I love Tomo's concert alerts!" when we have no such alerts. The band pays two bucks a click to place those ads in front of their fans. Two dollars to sell a forty-dollar ticket is good business all around.

On the other hand, hyper-personalized advertising has its drawbacks. When a teen researches birth-control or pregnancy or other sensitive topics, and related ads follow her around the Internet, her friends and parents will spot it sooner or later.

What users hate most is that both Tomo and our corporate partners profit off the information they share: once when we sell personalized advertising, and again when that advertising manipulates them into spending money and making decisions they wouldn't have otherwise.

People like to believe they own the space inside their own minds, but the reality is it's all rented away to the highest bidder, bit by bit, every time they're exposed to another piece of planted information.

I'm daydreaming while Carl rambles, until he startles me with an unexpected turn of direction.

"We're going to market privacy to our users with a new product, *PrivacyGuard: Protect yourself and your family*." Carl grins like a cat with two mice. "Not only will we address our number one customer issue, we also create a new source of revenue. Mike, can you explain the details?"

One of Carl's marketing flacks gets up. "We eliminate personalized advertising. Zero, zip, zilch. No use of customer data to run ads targeted at them. Of course, that's only half the picture. Nobody is going to pay for that. We also guarantee their personal data does not appear anywhere on the Internet."

I literally feel my eyes squinting as I stare at him. Does he understand how the Internet works? We don't control it. Nobody controls it.

He sees me staring and pointedly looks away to scan the rest of the audience. "With our total access to all user data, we can scan the Internet for any occurrences of the user's personal data. We then opaque that information, so no one can access it."

Sarah, the browser technical lead, nods brightly, and it's obvious she knows what they're talking about. It takes me a long time to connect the dots to Sarah's involvement because the idea is so monumentally stupid I must undo everything I know about technology and see it from their perspective.

Finally it hits me. We introduced our own web browser six months ago, and it's slowly been winning users, eating away at Avogadro's market share. Now our browser is responsible for almost a quarter of all web page views. They want to hide the data in our browser.

"Just because you're not showing the user their data," I say, "doesn't mean it's removed from the Internet. You're not removing the data, you're lying to the user and pretending it's not there."

"It's better than removing it from one site at a time." Sarah glares at me even as she keeps her voice light. "We make sure no one can see the private data, regardless of where it is. We find it, we blacklist it, and the Tomo browser won't display it. We've got two dozen patent applications in the works already."

"Carl, Daniel, this is insane," I say. "Please. We're providing the illusion of privacy, not real help. If someone looks at this, they'll believe their information is secure, but if anyone switches browsers, it'll be right there."

"Privacy is the *feeling* of being secure and comfortable," Carl says. "We can give them that feeling, and that's what's important."

I take back what I said about Carl being a good guy. Oh, maybe he is, one-on-one, but somehow companies turn employees into monsters who exploit anyone and everyone to make the next billion dollars.

"You expect customers to pay for this?" I ask. Some people count to ten to calm their emotions. I count off ten ways I could kill Carl. Number nine is an ax to the forehead, which is ridiculous, because axes are unwieldy with one arm, but I like the image of his skull cloven in two. I clench and release my fist.

Carl nods. "We'll double revenue for privacy customers. *PrivacyGuard* will cost $9.95 per year. We've already done user testing of the price point."

I glance around the room. Does anyone really believe this nonsense? No one trusts us. That's the problem. *Oy vey*. Half the people in the room harbor dreamy eyes at the idea of increasing user revenue.

"Our annual advertising revenue is currently eight bucks per user," I say. "Double would be sixteen bucks, not ten."

"Well…" Carl gestures to his marketing flack, who chuckles.

"Privacy lovers enjoy thirty percent more discretionary income. There's a slew of companies wanting to advertise specifically to people who want more privacy."

My head pounds, and I experience phantom itches in my missing hand. "You said no personalized advertising. 'Zero, zip, zilch' were your exact words."

"Right. Well, there's no personalized data. However, the lack of personalized data *is* data. Data indicating a user who values privacy."

Carl chuckles. "We win on both ends, Angie. It's great. We're going to make the company a fortune and make our users happy."

The other people in the room laugh along with Carl.

I'm thinking an ice pick. Can't they see how bad this idea is? Anyone who cares one iota about finding information will pick a web browser other than Tomo. The barrier to entry is as simple as installing an app.

For a very brief moment my heart surged at the thought that Tomo was actually going to make a meaningful contribution to privacy.

Now I shake my head and fight off the urge to vomit. Corporations are disgusting beasts.

Believe me, the irony of my position is not lost on me. Here I am, complaining about how we're treating people's privacy, and yet I'm invading people's privacy up the wazoo. But I do it to do good.

ʊ

I wake up, sweating, my ears ringing and blood pounding. I'm twisted up in the sheets and my throat is sore, like I've been screaming, which I probably was.

For a moment I'm too panicked to move, trying to remember exactly where I am. I'm in my condo. The bed next to me is empty, Thomas at his own place. I glance in the darkness at the walls, think about the people in neighboring units. Do they hear me scream in the middle of the night? How can they not?

I walk to the bathroom, drink a glass of water, and return to lie down on the other side of the bed where it's not so sweaty and damp.

After my...accident, I spent six months in rehab, learning to write again, tie my shoes, and everything else I needed to do one-handed. Then I went back to work. It's hard enough to walk into the same office, see the same coworkers, without an arm. Harder still when everyone looks at you and sees a woman who killed her husband.

My old boss understood right away and offered me a job in the Portland office if I wanted it. I took the job, moved in the fall and immediately bought a house, a classic Four Square, the quintessential Portland home, with grassy yard and a huge maple tree. Two weeks after I moved in, the leaves fell, then it rained.

You *can* rake leaves one-armed. You can do pretty much anything one-armed, even put a watch on if you use your teeth. You can cut a steak and cut your fingernails, because they've got great adaptive tools. However, some difficult things hold almost no reward. After eight hours hard labor and only a fraction of the wet, heavy leaves in bags, I went into the house and cried myself to sleep.

The next morning, I briefly considered hiring a yard maintenance service. That's what any of my old coworkers in the Bay Area would have done. Somehow I can't stomach the idea of hiring someone to do what I can't do. I don't know why. Maybe because my mother believed you should do your maintenance and wasn't above taking a wrench to the plumbing if the super didn't show up when he was supposed to. Watching someone else mow my lawn and rake my leaves would be an ever-present mental sore reminding me of what I can't do.

Before lunch, I called my real estate agent. The house was sold before I'd even made the first mortgage payment. I've been in this condo since.

A burst of shame leaves my face burning. What do the neighbors think? These aren't whimpers in the night. I scream loud. The last thing I want is to explain my nightmares to anyone, but why doesn't anyone ever ask if I'm okay?

CHAPTER 4

FRIDAY MORNING, THOMAS CALLS to make dinner plans and ask if he can stay the night. We decide on Japanese food and I agree he can stay over.

A few years ago, I had several disastrous attempts at dating at Emily's insistence, events which inevitably aborted early after panic attacks. Thomas was different. He never pushed, never made a move that surprised or threatened me. He was simply there. He made me laugh even though my teeth were gritted in fear. We've gradually inched closer together, and now, two years later, part of me yearns to marry him.

No matter how badly I've suffered, the need to be hugged and loved never goes away. That he can manage to fit himself into my jigsaw puzzle of mental issues and myriad oddities makes him all the more precious.

It's impossible for us to become closer, let alone get married. I can't ever explain what I've done. What I continue to do. There are people out there ruining other people's lives. I must stop them.

How would I account for the long road trips? The strange outings in the middle of the night. The weird computer hardware. My secret office.

He has to stay where he is, a carefully controlled distance away. This tears at me. There must be limits to his patience, and I dread crossing that unknown line and losing him.

ↄ

We travel to Alberta Street in northeast Portland. I let Thomas drive. He bought a new Audi this week, and his grin is as wide as his face.

I sit in the passenger seat and take long, slow breaths. Even the slight loss of control of being the passenger brings on anxiety. I'll cope for his sake.

At the restaurant, a hip new place, we split a small bottle of sake and order omakase, chef's choice. After I finish my first thimble of sake, the rage at PrivacyGuard resurfaces.

"Do you understand? That they're actually making privacy worse, by hiding the data from the owners, while it's still out there for anyone with the know-how to download an alternate browser?"

"I get it," Thomas says, a slight smile crossing his face. "The question is, what are you going to do about it?"

"Me?"

"Yeah, you."

"I'm only an engineer. I can't stop this." Thomas runs his own company, a law practice specializing in intellectual property. He's forgotten how hard it is when you're not totally in charge, when it takes months of lobbying to affect even a small change, the way big organizations build up the momentum of bad ideas until they're impossible to stop and no one even remembers where the concept came from.

"You're their data goddess. They idolize your every word."

"No, they humor my every word, because I single-handedly improved ad targeting enough to increase company revenue 12 percent."

He glances at my stump.

"Yeah, I do everything single-handedly."

"Can you talk to your boss?"

"Daniel?" I don't bother to hide my snicker. "He has no backbone. He'll kowtow to Carl all day long."

"Then go to Carl."

"Carl cares about the bottom line. He sees a way to boost revenue per user." Thomas doesn't even know I was once Tomo's chief database architect, that I reported to our CTO. I set the ground rule early on that I would never talk about the past, and he would never ask about it. Why don't I go back to the CTO? I'm hesitant, and I wonder whether he sent me off to Portland to protect me or because he was embarrassed by me.

"Give him a better way," Thomas says, grabbing a skewer of meat off the serving plate. "Design a real set of privacy enhancing features."

"What?" I'm too deep in my thoughts and I've lost the thread of the conversation.

"Carl wants to make money with a privacy product. You should design a real privacy product."

"He's not going to care about the technical details of privacy." I take the other skewer. Beef grilled over sumibi charcoal, with a smoky flavor. My mouth wakes up and I realize I'm starving.

"Give him a whole product, not only technical details. Describe the experience of using the product, and how they'll make revenue, and why this is better than the alternative."

"I want to write SQL queries, not make slides." This is one way of saying I want to sit alone by myself and not interact with anyone.

"Do you? Or do you want to change the world?"

I set aside my food and stare at Thomas, his soft brown eyes, the little crinkles at the corners, the sideburns peppered with gray. This is why I love him. Not because he sees infinite possibility in every situation, but because he senses some deeper truth about me that even I lose track of. Unbelievably, he likes what he sees.

CHAPTER 5

I OWN A THIRTY-YEAR-OLD VW BUS. Well, own is a strong word, since it's not registered to me. I paid cash in a private sale twelve months ago in Idaho. I have a fake driver's license corresponding to an actual New Yorker who doesn't own a car, and a real vehicle registration in their name. It was a complicated bit of work, but it will cover me in the event of a routine traffic stop. The final touch was installing flowery curtains. Now it's the mobile office I use when I need the highest level of security.

I wrote a script to pick a random place to park the van, usually in the parts of Portland where you find the most hippies. The VW blends in well.

Today I'm a quarter of a block down from a coffee shop with a good wi-fi signal. I aim the directional antenna at the coffee shop until I maximize the signal strength.

From there, the direction my packets take is very, very complicated.

The Raspberry Pi, a tiny computer smaller than a credit card, is dirt cheap and can do anything a regular computer can do. Each iteration gets smaller, more powerful, and less battery-hungry. I paid cash for a thousand units direct from a distributor.

In my own version of a clean-room, dressed in a biohazard suit so I wouldn't leave DNA on them, I embedded the tiny computers inside weather-proof cases, marrying each to tiny solar panels and a rechargeable battery. Each component was chosen because they were cheap Chinese parts manufactured by the millions.

The little computers run a secure variant of Linux, with a single open port, protected with heavy encryption. Part of the computer board contains a sensitive accelerometer, which means I can detect when the computer is moved.

When I travel, I find coffee shops and homes with wi-fi signals and flat roofs, and I toss one of these onto the roof.

If you were to find one, pick it up, and look at it, you might not be sure what it was. If you plug a headphone into the jack, it plays pirate music stations.

Of course, that's what it does only if it's been moved or if the battery level drops too low. Because when the accelerometer detects motion, the code I wrote replaces my extensive software with a simple dummy music app and erases the remaining storage a hundred times over.

If it hasn't been moved, and the battery level has never dropped too low, then it does what it's supposed to do: operate as part of my private onion routing network with hundreds of nodes to disguise my digital trail so others can't trace my location.

This secure private network is what I'm using right now to research Erik Copley, my packets bouncing back and forth in encrypted channels. I haven't trusted TOR since the government took down Silk Road. I don't buy the explanation that they used unrelated weaknesses. The government isn't going to let on that TOR is broken, any more than we let the Germans know we'd broken Enigma.

Erik Copley, forty-nine, is married to Jessica. They live in Tucson, Arizona. Jessica is his third wife. The first two managed to escape him and move far, far away. Jessica, however, is in a downward spiral.

Tomo embedded NFC payments into the latest version of its mobile app, so you could pay for things in person without using a credit card. Jessica was an enthusiastic user, until shortly after she married Erik. Now there are extended periods when she doesn't leave the house.

We share purchasing data with a major online retailer so we can improve advertisement targeting. Jessica buys things online during these at-home spans: bandages, pain relievers, an arm sling, even crutches. The purchases are consistent with someone who plays hockey or football, an interest Jessica does not possess. She's regularly getting the kinds of injuries you'd associate with dangerous sports despite never going out of the house.

Unfortunately, Tucson is a little too far for me to drive without anyone being aware of my being gone, and I can't come up with a good excuse to fly there. If there had been a good database conference in Phoenix, or even San Diego, it might be feasible.

I need a remote hack. Something I can do from here, with an eighty percent or greater chance of killing Erik that will appear to be an accident.

I run through my gamut of options. I can't count on getting Jessica out of their home, which rules out several simple and reliable house attacks. He doesn't work in construction or a manufacturing facility, unfortunately, because lovely and dangerous things happen around heavy machinery. I could compromise his car's brakes, or maybe lock him inside on a sunny day until he dies of heatstroke, except I used a vehicle attack on the banker in Beaverton, and I'm hesitant to create a pattern by employing anything similar.

I scan his Tomo messages, searching for anything I could use. He's having an affair. He goes to strip clubs with his coworker. He likes Japanese anime. Ugh. I'm about ready to give up.

I could kill him with an elevator at his job if I must. I could stop the thing about eighteen inches off the ground, open the doors a foot. He'd hesitate but eventually try to go through, and when he did, I'd raise the elevator the rest of the way, crushing him between the floor of elevator and the top of the opening. I bought a suite of elevator exploits from a Chinese kid for a thousand bucks that I've been saving for a rainy day.

I probably spend a quarter of my disposable income on zero day attacks. The really good ones, the exploits in operating systems and browsers that can be used for almost anything, are usually too expensive for me to afford, in part because I'm bidding against the NSA, the Russian mob, and the Chinese government, who have big-time budgets for this sort of stuff. Besides, I have my purpose-built backdoors in Tomo to take care of most of those needs. No, I tend to spend my limited cash on vulnerabilities in embedded systems like elevators, cars, and household appliances. They're more obscure, and at least so far, no nation-states have shown interest in taking people out with their refrigerators.

The problem with the elevator exploit is that I'm worried about detection. There'd be a thorough investigation, right down to the firmware on the embedded computers, and there's no way for me to mask my changes.

I'd eventually like to build a drone for these distant targets. A video made the rounds a while back of a handgun mounted to a quadcopter. The range on a quadcopter is awful, a few miles at best. New, long range, fixed-wing drones under development have solar panels and can stay aloft indefinitely. Combine one of those with a gun, and automated cellphone tracking, and you could kill a person anywhere in the world, fully autonomously, with no way to track back to the originator. The tech is almost there. For now, it's still a pipe dream.

I keep reading, working my way backwards chronologically, hoping I'll know what I'm looking for when I see it.

Boom.

He used to play racquetball with a friend, although he stopped for a while after his pacemaker was implanted four years ago. His pacemaker...

I switch computers. I've got another machine, connected via another onion route entirely, running a VPN to an exit node in Brazil. I connect to Tuned to a Dead Channel, the latest incarnation of a community so old it dates back to the pre-Internet BBS community. There isn't a group much more exclusive than this. Even among these select few, I've got something they don't: a *page sysop* link rendered in green monospaced type, PR Number 3 for the font geeks out there.

Nathan9 is online.

```
SysOp> What's up?

Angel> Pacemaker attacks still viable?

SysOp> Not really. You can't sniff the data any-
more. Although...if you have the device ID, anything
is possible. Unfortunately, it's only stored in PMA.
```

Damn. Permanent Medical Archive, the centralized medical data store, was one of the few systems with legitimately strong protection.

```
Angel> Known PMA exploits?

SysOp> BWB claims access. Data for 50K, changes for
100K.
```

Nobody knows if Beef with Broccoli intends to insult the Chinese or if he's actually Chinese. Since he tends toward Chinese tools, Nathan9 and I suspect the latter. I can't afford five thousand, let alone fifty thousand, and BWB isn't known for exchanging favors.

I disconnect from Dead Channel, shut down my connection, and start a new one. No point in letting anyone watching connect the dots. I spend the next hour researching pacemaker manufacturers. There are a dozen manufacturers, four of which are common in the United States. I know who Erik Copley works for, and a bit of searching turns up their healthcare plan. From there I find eligible cardiologists in Tucson.

I search Erik's Tomo geolocation data from four years ago to find a time when he would have spent most of a week in his home recovering from surgery. Once I've found that, I examine the location log from the days prior to his homestay. There! He was in Southern Medical Center for twenty-four hours. I visit each of the eligible doctors' websites to find out who would perform surgery at SMC. There are three and they're all part of the same practice.

I'm going to need access to their email. Not their personal email, which would be easy to read using the extensive permissions the Tomo app demands on installation, but their work email, which may be harder to obtain. I send a message to a non-existent email address at their domain, receive a bounce message, and examine it to see who their provider is. Armed with that, I look up all the doctors, nurses, medical clerks, and receptionists, and grab their Tomo passwords.

We don't store passwords in the raw. We use a salted hash, among the best possible ways to safely store a password. Of course, most attackers don't possess an army of half a million high performance servers and inside knowledge on how the salt is generated.

A few minutes later, I've obtained the passwords for all twelve employees, and I try them on the email server. I'm counting on someone foolish enough to use the same password on multiple accounts. Sure enough, one of the medical clerks has. I breathe a small sigh of relief. Legitimate password access beats having to backdoor my way in.

Even with all this work done, I don't know exactly what I'm looking for. I'm still phishing for some weakness I can exploit.

I wedge my thermos between my knees and twist off the cap to pour myself another cup of coffee. I've been in the van for hours. My vertebrae pop as I stretch. I take a sip of coffee, stretch again, and then do my business.

That means pulling out a five-gallon bucket from Home Depot, prying the lid off, and perching on the rim while my urine splatters off the bottom of the bucket. Primitive yet functional. I usually go out if it's more than pee, which is a huge process, because then I've got to disconnect all my network connections, move the van to some place without security cameras, use a coffee shop or restaurant bathroom, then move the van again, find new wi-fi connections, and reconnect to the onion network. Better to hold it, in that case.

Once I'm done, I return to reading the clerk's email. It takes a while before I finally find a weakness. One of the three doctors doesn't officially work on Fridays, but he apparently handles patient calls on his day off, because he occasionally emails in a request for patient data. Which the clerk sends him via his personal email account in clear violation of the PMA policy. Lovely.

Today's Wednesday. It's two days to Friday and his day off.

I shut down my computers and pack them away, start up the van, and drive east to a new part of town. I leave it parked between a commercial and residential neighborhood where it won't attract attention. I put on my prosthetic arm and don my bike gear and a backpack.

With a bulky rain coat, helmet, bike shoes, wrap-around sunglasses, and second arm, I've changed my profile and gait. I return to my bike left outside a coffee shop, clamp the prosthetic onto the right handlebar, and ride back to the apartment building where I keep my bike locked up alongside dozens of others belonging to the residents. I shrug off my prosthetic, and slip it into the backpack with a practiced move. From there, it's a quick walk back to my place.

ʊ

On Friday, early in the morning, I email work and tell them I'll be working from home again. In reality, I already finished today's work. I slaved away sixteen hours yesterday and left half my work sitting on my computer, with scripts standing by to check in code and send emails at predetermined times. I won't reply to any emails, but I can claim to have been buried in code changes.

I head back to the van, reversing my steps from two days before. I check the bike and van for radio emissions to ensure my equipment hasn't been hit with a GPS transponder. Someone would need to suspect me to do that, and to date my perfect record stands: everyone I've eliminated has been classified as some form of natural or accidental death, never murder, so it's unlikely anyone is onto me. I play it safe, nevertheless.

I flip a hidden switch in the Tomo mobile app for both the clerk and the doctor. Well, technically, I flip a debug switch on their accounts, and the next time their Tomo mobile app checks for updates, it sees the change, and begins broadcasting continuous telemetry data, including their GPS location, to our servers, where it goes into a log file associated with their account. Later, when I turn the debug switch off, the log file will be deleted. This clever little feature, ostensibly to help the software engineers troubleshoot bugs, perfectly fits my needs without requiring security exploits on my part. Which is why I indirectly requested the implementation in the first place.

I know from previous emails the doctor golfs in the early morning, does a light workout at the gym, and then swims with his wife in the afternoon. Sounds like a lot of activity to me, but then I'm not a cardiologist. I guess if you spend your whole day surrounded by unhealthy people, you're going to overcompensate.

I need to create an email appearing to be from the doctor, wait around for the clerk to reply, and then receive the reply. This has to happen while the clerk is in the office. I'm worried she might call him for clarification (his phone log suggests this sometimes happens), and I can't take the chance he'll answer the call, so I need to time it for when he's away from his phone. The doctor starts golfing before his office even opens, which makes sense, considering summer temperatures in Tucson. I take a deep breath. So many complications.

I switch over to the clerk's email account, and compare the inbox to the sent folder to see how long it usually takes between the time he emails her and the time she normally replies with the patient data. It's anywhere between five and thirty minutes.

I track the doctor's location on a map, his geocoordinates still streaming in every fifteen seconds over the connection. He's on the ninth hole when the receptionist gets into work. When he gets to the sixteenth hole, I upload a server-side rule for the receptionist's email, temporarily shunting all incoming emails except the ones from the good doctor into a folder. I want to make sure that when his email arrives, it's the only one she's looking at.

When he gets to the eighteenth hole, I turn on his microphone, and listen to him talking to someone, I assume his golf partner. The sound is muted, as you'd expect from someone carrying their phone in their pants pocket. I happen to know it's his left-front pocket.

It sounds crazy I can ascertain this from the motion data of a phone, but I've got acceleration details from one billion people, 365 days a year, for dozens of sit/stand events per day, and from this mass of data points I can tell you with 90 percent reliability whether a person keeps their phone in a pant pocket, jacket pocket, or purse, and if it's a pocket, whether it's the left or right, front or back.

I had to be sure of my accuracy, so I wrote a predictive algorithm, and tested it by turning on the camera, so I could capture video of the phone being extracted. From these videos, I figured out how often the algorithm was correct.

I didn't do this research because I suffer from an OCD disorder when it comes to analyzing data, although that helps. This was an actual client request from advertisers who wanted to target ads based on where a woman carried her cell phone. I won't go into the research I did to segment users based on bathroom paint color.

If this sounds intrusive, you're right. If you think Tomo users should cancel their account, you're also right. They won't, because for many of them, we hold hostage their primary, or perhaps only, connection to their friends.

More and more, I see parallels between Tomo and the assholes I choose to eliminate. Abusers remove any sense of self-control from their victims by wielding absolute power over their lives, removing any privacy or ability to have a life apart. Every user of Tomo experiences same situation, albeit to a different degree: no privacy, no life apart from Tomo, and no ability to leave without forfeiting their social connections. Few recognize the parallels, but I do, and it makes me increasingly ill.

The dot on the screen moves. Focus, Angie.

The doctor approaches the club house, my cue to act. I use my backdoor into the Tomo app to send a personal email from his phone to the medical clerk. The messages requests the pacemaker model, device ID, install date, and date of last checkup for Erik Copley. All I really need is the device ID. The rest is there to lend credibility.

I bite my fingernails when the doc stops to talk to someone. I'm counting on him heading into what I assume to be the locker room. My geospatial data is less accurate once he's inside. Historically there's a stationary period of thirty to forty minutes after he finishes golf. My guess is he leaves the phone in his locker while he works out, and that's ideal in case the receptionist calls for more information.

The delay is only a minute or two. In another window, I'm tracking the clerk's inbox. She's opened the email.

Finally the doctor gets back in motion, and a minute later the accelerometer records the sharp impact of a hard surface. He's laid the phone down. I listen through the microphone and hear only muted sounds. I jump out of my seat when the phone rings, even though I was half expecting it. Channeling through my backdoor in the Tomo app, I check the phone status, and see he's receiving a call from his office. I cross my fingers and offer a small prayer to the universe he's not within distance of the phone.

Crap, there's probably an Android API to reject calls! Why didn't I prepare for this? I search and end up with a list of Stack Overflow questions and answers even as the phone keeps ringing. Damn. I'm hoping for a simple one liner, but none of them are, and to be honest, Java makes my eyes want to bleed. After an eternity, the phone stops ringing. I keep searching, because it would be awesome to dismiss the notification of the phone call. I glance at the receptionist's email. No reply yet.

Finally, I find what I'm looking for, a snippet of Java to allow me to dismiss notifications I have permission to access. I check his Android version, compile the code, and download it to his phone, where the backdoor executes it. The odds are good it worked, although I can't be sure without finding and running yet more code, which just isn't worth the effort.

I wish I could get up and pace. I can't stand without hunching over, and the van rocks back and forth if I move around, so instead I settle for closing my eyes and counting. I'm up to 697 when my computer beeps to indicate the doctor received an email. I open my eyes. It's spam. I go back to counting. At 770 it beeps again. A text from his wife. The doctor is suddenly popular. After losing track of my count several times, I'm up to 852 when I hear the third beep. The subject line says "Erik Copley."

I snap my fingers and return to work, copying the email contents onto my computer, deleting the email from the doctor's phone, and clearing his notifications again. I hit Enter, realizing too late I accidentally cleared the notification for the text message from his wife. Whoops. Oh well, the worst that will happen is that he's puzzled. Finally I delete the email from the clerk's sent archive. Anything else? Not that I can remember. I reset the doctor's account to non-debug status, and shut down all my connections.

Armed with the ID, I'm ready for part two.

Wirelessly reprogramming Erik's pacemaker requires a 175 kHz signal or 402 to 405 MHz signal. I need a transceiver capable of those frequencies. Fortunately, the office building where Erik works uses a mesh network, and the mesh boxes use software-defined radios to implement their transceivers. That's a fancy way of saying they can transmit and receive on a wide range of frequencies, including 402 MHz.

I've already researched Erik's workplace, so I spend the next three hours finalizing a piece of software and data package, interspersed with eating protein bars, drinking coffee, having a chocolate bar, using the bucket again, and shaking out my arm, which grows numb from hours of non-stop work.

When I'm done, I make a call through my computer, a simple dial-out through an anonymous Skype account, passing through a service to spoof my caller ID. Someone picks up, although I can barely make out the voice on the other end through the garbled connection. I glance at the screen to find I'm routing through twelve onion network nodes. Too much latency. I dial it back to four nodes.

"Lois Thatcher, calling for Chris." I've called the building management's main office. I happen to know Chris Robson, their onsite IT administrator, has left work early, according to his current Tomo location.

"Sorry, Chris is gone. This is Margaret. Can I take a message?"

"Damn. He and I played phone tag all day. You have a new tenant coming in on Monday, on the fourth floor. He needs me to reconfigure the network." This I found out from a quick web search.

"You're with Tucson Telecom?"

"Yes, that's right," I say. Sucker.

"Oh, Chris will be sorry he missed you."

"Well, maybe you can help."

"I'm the office manager." She laughs. "I don't know a thing about computers!"

"Oh, it's pretty easy. Is there a white box, high up on one of the walls, with a green light on the front?"

"Yes, I see it. It has a couple of stubby antennae sticking out of it."

"That's it!" I say. "I need you to press and hold the power button."

"Oh. It's very high up."

"Maybe you can stand on a chair?"

"I'll try. Hold on."

I hear the sound of a headset being placed on the table. A minute passes.

"No, I'm sorry, I can't reach it. Maybe you can wait for Chris on Monday?"

"Chris really wants this done before the new tenant moves in. Is there a table you can stand on?"

"I really don't think—"

"I'm sure you can, Margaret. Climb onto the table, look for the big button, there's only one. Press it in, and hold it for six seconds. You could bring the chair over there with you, and pull it up onto the table if you need to."

There's another thump of the handset being set down. I feel badly for poor Margaret, I really do, but I'm dying to see her face and what's going on. I should have gotten access to their security cameras. I hear furniture being dragged around in the background.

A few more moments pass, and then I hear a distant cry of "I did it!"

I thank Margaret and disconnect the call.

The mesh node, thanks to Margaret's help, temporarily resets to its default configuration and password. I connect to the node from the nearest phone running Tomo, and grant myself administrative access. The rest of the mesh network reincorporates the known MAC address into the greater network.

From there, it's simple. A software-driven radio preconfigured for the correct frequency, a payload already prepared with Erik's pacemaker ID.

I'm about to upload the module to the network node when I hesitate, overcome by a familiar gut-wrenching feeling. I'm reaching out through the Internet to kill someone thousands of miles away. My finger might as well be connected to a switch on the back of his skull marked "kill." It's absolutely irrevocable, totally fatal. The ultimate action against another human.

Who am I to do this? Someone else should make this decision, someone with perfect judgement, who could be trusted to do the right thing from among all the choices. But there's only me, avenging hell cop or angel of mercy, with all of my flaws and hangups. Am I really killing Erik, or am I trying to reach into my own past to kill my husband?

Sometimes I don't know.

There is nobody else, so I do what needs doing. I hit Enter, my script runs and uploads the module to the network node I own, and within seconds the file distributes to the rest of the mesh network.

Every transceiver in the building broadcasts a handshake, trying to reach to Erik's pacemaker. Soon enough a node on the third floor closest to Erik's office connects with the pacemaker. I freeze, set down my coffee cup, and press my hand to the desk.

It only takes a few seconds. The new instructions override the pacemaker's default behavior. Instead of tiny pulses at the natural rhythm of the heart, the pacemaker sends the strongest electrical charges it can generate, isolated to one of the three leads to desynchronize his heart. It'll drain the rest of the ten-year battery in the next few minutes.

I wait, keeping an eye on his accelerometer data. I see movement consistent with a fall and imagine him collapsing at his desk. I start a timer and wait another two minutes, until it's impossible for him to still be alive.

There's a huge gaping pit in my stomach. I'm afraid I'm going to be sick, but I force myself to focus on the unfinished work. I must eliminate any traces of my presence.

Now I have to reach back inside a man I killed seconds ago. I revert the pacemaker program to its original settings while there's still battery power left, erase my software-defined radio program from the mesh, add in the troublesome tenant access code Chris was "mysteriously" having difficulty configuring, then remove my temporary administrative account from the mesh right before I reboot the whole thing.

I shut down all my network connections, pack up the computer equipment, and sweep all my snack wrappers into a bag. My eyes water, but I'm sure it's just because I'm tired. Three straight days of non-stop work.

One last thing. The point of the whole exercise. I insert links into Jessica's feed and email for grief counselors and support groups for domestic violence survivors. God, universe, Dennis Ritchie, if there's anyone out there listening, please give Jessica the strength to take this hard-won opportunity and build a new life. I can't save her again.

I wipe my eyes with a tissue.

It would have been easier to go down there and shoot him. Dirty Harry had it so easy. Could I have pulled the trigger in person?

↻

A nightmare wakes me. I work my way out of the hot, twisted sheets and I'm halfway to the bathroom before I realize it wasn't the usual dream. I dreamed about Gary, the banker from Beaverton whom I killed with his own BMW. I never met him in person, only ever saw photos. In the dream, I'm with him in the car, and he turns to me in the passenger seat, begging and pleading for his life as we go off the edge of the road. I woke when we hit the tree.

I splash water on my face and return to bed on the other side, where the sheets are cool. In the beginning, I didn't dream about the men I've killed, but lately it happens most of the time. If I don't kill anyone, then it's my own history that comes back in my nightmares. I'm screwed either way.

As much as I'd like to deny it, the men are victims, too. Usually they've grown up in households with violence directed at them, their mothers, or both. They're my victims, too. They may be vile and violent, but they're still people.

I remind myself the majority of people who've grown up under those conditions don't become abusers. There's a choice here, a surrender of humanity. At least, I want to believe that.

I lie there for a long time before fading back to sleep.

The next morning is Saturday, and I'm too tired to repeat all my usual processes, so I settle for a VPN connection to work, then SSH to a machine in the server clusters we run our news aggregation on. I search the database from the command line, and it doesn't take long to find the news stories about the heart attack and subsequent death of Erik Copley in Tucson.

Mission accomplished, the pressure is off my shoulders. Jessica will not be hurt again, at least not by Erik.

There will be someone else. It's the weekend, and since I have no work, I could profile the next person. I would go mad if this was all I did.

I push the keyboard away and will myself not to look at the code to see who is next. I grab my phone and text Thomas to see if he wants to meet for lunch.

CHAPTER 6

I ARRIVE EARLY on Monday morning. I boot up my laptop, then disregard it and stare at the wall. Once an idea has been planted in my mind, it's hard to let go. I'm still contemplating privacy, social networks, and the travesty of Tomo's PrivacyGuard.

In polls, a third of Tomo users love us, citing reconnections to old friends and maintaining relationships. Another third have mixed feelings, citing benefits and costs. The last third claim to hate us, and yet still use Tomo.

Those with complaints talk about three classes of issues: privacy (who can see their data), data ownership (they've given all their data to us, and we monetize it), or the trivialization of human relationships.

I can't do much about the last, unless society decides to give up computers and spend our time together; however, there's a chance to do something about the first two. I head to the kitchen to refill my coffee. The pot is empty, so I refill the basket and wait for it to brew.

I go back to thinking about users and data. Data ownership is a big deal. Users stay on Tomo, even when they hate us, because their friends are here. If they want to remain in contact with their friends, they're stuck with us. Everyone is jointly locked in together.

At the far side of the break area, a guy is trying to figure out why the big poster printer isn't working. He's wearing slacks and a button-down shirt, which means he's marketing. A button-down shirt alone isn't a giveaway, but the slacks are. He's not in legal, because the shirt is a little too nice. Eventually he gives up fiddling with the printer and turns around, a man clearly in need of help.

Two men, programmers, are drinking coffee and talking at a table in the break area between the marketing guy and me. I can tell they're programmers because they're both wearing t-shirts, and nobody around here in marketing or management wears a t-shirt to work. That they're talking about video games only reinforces the stereotype. If they'd been born twenty years earlier they'd wear neckbeards.

The guy at the printer looks at the two men, and sees me. Oh, no, here it comes. He has to walk around the guys right next to him.

"Oh, hi. My name's Jerry." He holds out a hand to shake.

I back away slightly, trying to keep my distance, judging angles so he can't cut me off. I'm at work, I'm safe. The words seem weak in my head. I raise my coffee cup to show my hand is full. "Jerry."

Once he realizes I'm not going to shake, he uses his outstretched hand to point back toward the laser printer. "Is there any chance you could help me out with the printer?"

My first job in tech, an older woman in the office came up to me at the end of the first week, as I washed the dishes for the third time, and told me to never make coffee for a man, never wash his dishes, and never help with the copier. The printer is close enough to count.

The temptation to avoid confrontation is strong. I try to embody how I felt when I was young, new to work, and full of verve. "What's wrong with those guys over there?"

He looks back. "They seemed busy."

"They're talking about gaming. You could have interrupted them."

The coffee gurgles as it nears the end of the brewing cycle.

He shakes his head and walks away. "Jeez, you don't have to be such a..."

My shoulders relax as he moves away and the threat diminishes. I'm so relieved he's gone, I almost don't care he implicitly called me a bitch. Still, I can't let behavior like that go on. I make a mental note: Jerry, from marketing, my floor. He's overdue for an accident in payroll.

Then I let it go. It's small beer, and I have enough karmic debt. I grab my coffee and go back to my desk, forcing myself to put the incident out of mind and focus on social networks.

Every once in a while, a new competitor comes along, like Ello, the social network that says they won't sell data. I checked it out. What are you going to do there? You visit and none of your friends are around. So you leave. A new social network has to offer an incredible benefit to get people to stick around long enough to overcome the empty network problem. Sure, maybe I check it out for a day or two, then I give up. By the time a few friends come along, I'm gone.

It's a variation of Drake's Equation or maybe Metcalf's Law. I'll call it Angie's Equation:

$$P_{adoption} = B^x (nN^x fEA^x fAT^x nL) / (nB^x nF)$$

B = The benefit of the new social network
nN = Size of my network (number of friends)
fEA = Fraction of those friends who are early adoptors
fAT = fraction of those with available time to try a new network
nL = Average length of time people stay on the network
nB = Average length of time it takes to see benefit of the new network
Nf = Number of friends needed to see benefit

What it basically says is enough friends have to show up and stick around long enough and at the same time I do for me to see the benefit of the new social network. That doesn't happen very often.

It would be easy enough to fix if social networks were open. If I use Tomo and you want to use some new network, and there's still some way to communicate and connect across those networks, then you're free to go use your new network and keep your connections to your friends. The empty network problem goes away.

Of course, Tomo doesn't want that. They don't want competition. They want barriers to entry, which they achieve by owning your social graph and social connections.

It's this barrier to movement that keeps people stuck on Tomo. You can hate our privacy policies, and our data ownership, and our manipulative ad techniques, but what are your alternatives? To quit Tomo?

In today's age that means choosing isolation. Nobody chooses isolation. That's why they use it as a punishment in prisons.

CHAPTER 7

SAM BEKINS, THIRTY-NINE YEARS OLD, lives in Bend, Oregon, a five-hour drive from Portland, over the Mount Hood pass and into the desert highlands.

I debate taking the Accord. It predates computers, so there's no track of where it's been, except for photos of it. I can swap out the license plate, and I've made sure there are no distinguishing marks on the vehicle. Although I worry about taking it so far from home. Will I unwittingly bring home compromising evidence it's been to Bend, a smidgen of dirt or wisp of leaf caught in a crevice that would tie it specifically to that geography? All the cool kids get car washes these days, but you never know what forensics will turn up even after a machine wash.

I reserve two nights at Timberline Lodge, the highest place you can stay on Mount Hood. It's a beautiful old place made of thick beams and heavy stones. Snowboarding season ended many weeks ago, yet plenty of people stay up there during the summer to explore the mountain, hike, or fish. Timberline Lodge itself is seven miles up a twisting and turning road away from Highway 26, the main path across the mountain and primary way to Bend.

I take three days off work, and wake up very early on Wednesday morning. I check into Timberline mid-morning, enjoy the lunch buffet, and go for a short walk. By three, I'm back into my hotel room and launch an app on my laptop to start a preprogrammed sequence of emails, web browsing, and video streaming. I swallow a dose of Benadryl, shower, and lie down for a nap.

My phone wakes me at eleven, and I change into a set of clean clothes. I head down to the parking lot, where my chariot awaits: an old Jeep Wrangler belonging to a couple staying overnight.

I drive down the mountain, pulling over briefly near a trailhead to swap the license plates with a spare set and disconnect the speedometer cable where it plugs into the transmission. I lay my flashlight on the ground, trying to aim it toward the license plate. Of course, the beam hits way too low. I grab the flashlight between my teeth, and pick up a nut and wrench in my hand. I fumble and the nut rolls away. Shiza. Dear universe, I'd like another hand, please, at least for a few minutes. The license plate is easy compared to the speedometer cable. Twenty minutes and plenty of curses later, I'm back on the road and by 3 A.M., in Bend.

Sam Bekins lives on the outskirts, in a cul-de-sac of identical suburban homes, every third house a mirror image floor plan. He drives a Ford Explorer, his wife drives a Taurus. Both are parked in the driveway. They don't seem to travel much. I called both Ford dealerships in Bend, and the second had done the service.

Neither of them work. When I ran a standard financial check a few weeks earlier, I found Sam gets a monthly disability check from the New Hampshire State Police. Forty percent of all women married to police officers are abused. *Forty percent!*

Of all groups of victims, the wives of police officers are stuck with the least options. They're scared to report it, and even the agencies that normally help battered women are hesitant to become involved when a police officer commits the abuse. If the victim does report it, they're almost never believed. Even when they are believed, neither police nor prosecutors are likely to do anything. They protect one another. Cops are fired for failing a single marijuana test, but remain on the job after battering a spouse.

Like homelessness, abuse of power in authority is a complex problem without a simple fix. Except in this case. I'm here now.

Sam's wife, Kelly, has been in the hospital six times. I know this despite the fact that neither he nor his wife use Tomo. Both of their identical phones came with the Tomo app preinstalled, an arrangement Tomo pays the cellphone providers three bucks per device to ensure. The Tomo service runs in the background, reporting geospatial and other data, even though the user never signed up.

Some imagine they can avoid us simply by not using Tomo. It's not that easy. We track the non-users too, in the hopes of figuring out what makes them tick and how to convert them to active users.

At any rate, I'm here now because Kelly is out of town. She got a text on Monday about a sick relative, flew out on Tuesday, and isn't expected back until Saturday. I had nothing to do with it, but I'm not going to overlook a gift when it shows up.

Sam's in the house alone, which opens up a world of opportunities.

In a more ideal case, I'd be able to use a remote exploit, but they don't own any smart appliances directly connected to the Internet I can exploit. They do have a wireless diagnostic interface on their furnace and a local network of connected smart detectors for smoke, fire, and carbon monoxide.

It's 3:30 when I pull up in front of their home. Lights are off, as they are for all the neighbors. I pull a clean laptop out of my bag, attach a directional antenna, and brute-force attack the smart detectors.

It takes six minutes before I'm in, exploiting the lousy random number generator the detector manufacturer uses at the factory, leaving the attack space for encryption keys way smaller than it should be. Once I'm in, I trigger the detectors' programming mode, a setting normally used only in R&D. All this learned thanks to DEF CON, the annual hackers' conference, where someone shared this exploit in an after-hours party room. In programming mode, although the LEDs flash, the audible alerts don't sound. Presumably the firmware developers didn't want to listen to blaring alarms while they were testing devices.

Next I go after the installed furnace, a smart device like every household appliance built in the last five years. Although the Bekins household never connected it to the Internet, the embedded computer still runs a hidden wi-fi hotspot to make it easier for service technicians to connect to. With the detectors effectively disabled, I redirect my laptop connection to the furnace, creating a peer-to-peer network with the same directional antenna. The furnace doesn't possess any protection at all besides the original factory password they've never bothered to change. I download a firmware update, and five minutes later, the furnace reboots. I've changed the combustion settings, and now the furnace is generating copious quantities of carbon monoxide as it also runs the ventilation fan backwards with the cleaning duct open. These three things should never happen at the same time, but they are now.

My rough calculations predict the house will hit 600 ppm carbon monoxide, a lethal level, in twenty minutes. After ten, the levels are at 250 ppm. Even if Sam woke now, he'd be too befuddled to rescue himself. At twenty minutes, the levels reach 500 ppm. Not wanting to risk a botched job, I wait a whole hour. The carbon monoxide crosses over 1,000 ppm, and I back out my changes, leaving only the cleaning ducts open.

Without ever getting out of my car or even cracking the window, my work is done. It's 4:45. I've got two and a half hours of driving to look forward to. Back near Timberline, I'm utterly exhausted and try not to think about the work ahead of me. I refill the gas in Government Camp, then drive up the long, winding road. At the trailhead, I swap out the license plates and reattach the speedometer cable, then drive the last mile to the parking lot.

The spot where the Jeep was parked when I borrowed it last night is taken. Vision blurred from exhaustion, at first I'm confused. I check my notebook, and I'm right about the spot. I briefly consider moving the other car, but there's no time now. The sun is coming up, and I've got to exit the Jeep before someone spots me. I hope the owner assumes he's the one who is confused. I park about five spots down, and pray the engine cools down before the owner comes out.

↻

When I wake around noon, I immediately wonder if I succeeded. Of course, there's no way there could be news available this quickly. So I force myself to pretend everything is normal, and take an actual vacation day. I hike to Mirror Lake, where I gaze at the upside-down reflection of Mount Hood in the water, eat a granola bar, and wish Thomas was with me to share the experience.

That night, back at my hotel room, I decide to chance a quick check to see if there's any news. Timberline is remote enough they've got only the one Internet connection to the rest of the world, and even the most sophisticated onion routing tricks won't hide suspicious traffic originating from the mountain.

I've got channels I can use for this, piggybacking a few low-bandwidth bytes here and there on other communications to legitimate websites. It's enough for me to find and read a short article in the *Bend Bulletin*, allowing me to determine that Sam Bekins definitely died.

With that out of the way, a weight lifts off my shoulders. Now I can relax for real.

CHAPTER 8

I ARRIVE AT THE OFFICE at 8 A.M. on Monday, rested and out of touch. I intentionally avoided my work email for three days, to make sure the evidence shows I really was on vacation.

I scan screenfuls of email subject lines. Maybe ten percent are about PrivacyGuard, and my coffee sours my stomach. Skimming a few only reinforces the increased momentum of the project. With disgust, I delete everything in my inbox and empty the deleted items folder.

For a few seconds, I'm shocked at what I've done. There were almost certainly important messages in there, stuff I needed to reply to. It was…irresponsible.

I stare at my completely empty inbox, a blank white screen, and relief floods in. I let out a little nervous giggle.

It's clear Tomo is going to hell. The PrivacyGuard stuff is one sign of many. It's more important than ever to figure out an alternative, a way out of this heinous one-sided power dynamic. With an empty inbox, I've got an hour free before the morning planning meeting. Screw work, I've got to figure out an alternative to Tomo.

The empty network problem weighs heavily on my mind. For a new network to blossom, it must somehow overcome this barrier, a rare occurrence. When it does happen, as it did with Picaloo, Snapchat, and WhatsApp, it's usually because of a compelling benefit not offered by Tomo.

Take Picaloo. Why were they successful? They did photos, Tomo did photos. But Picaloo did photos better. Filters made them look cool. Focusing on only photos reduced the noise and eliminated annoying Candy Crush invites.

I also can't overstate the power of children. When a kid is thirteen and their parents are on Tomo, it is not a cool place to hang out with their friends. They've got to go somewhere else, and they do, rushing out to new networks where they're safe from the spying eyes of parents, at least for a little while.

What happens if a new social network overcomes the empty network problem and thrives? If they grow large enough to matter, Tomo buys them. Or Tomo integrates those features into itself: adding filters, for example.

In the end, nothing anyone does weakens Tomo. To actually eat into Tomo's core business, there's got to be a benefit to switching networks that applies to everyone on Tomo, not only a niche, and not only the few holdouts that aren't on it. Whatever this new social network is, it must be resistant to a takeover from Tomo or to Tomo copying their features.

How do you stop a giant who can squash or acquire everything and everyone that stands in its way?

ひ

The user experience designers send out draft screenshots for PrivacyGuard this week. I spend half an hour getting angrier, until I remind myself anger without direction is pointless. I need to channel my frustration. I'm torn between tracking down the next person on my list, and working on my Tomo alternative.

I settle for a bit of both, investigating a guy down in the Bay area, because it's easy to justify a work trip down there, and then working over an extended lunch hour on my new social network.

That night at home I'm microwaving a burrito when the smell of cheese and beans suddenly triggers an old memory of eating out with my husband at his favorite Mexican place. My stomach curdles and I dump the food in the garbage, too upset to eat.

I'm suddenly exhausted and crawl into bed, with my clothes still on. The mistakes I've made overwhelm me. Sometimes I feel trapped, doomed to somehow repeat things, no matter how hard I try to fight them.

I'm wallowing in existential doubt one moment, and the next I sit bolt upright, then nearly fall over myself in my rush to get out of bed.

Pacing back and forth in my living room, I experience a revelation. What's true for dysfunctional people is also true for dysfunctional corporations.

Even if I create a new social network with the explicit goal to do no evil, even if that is structured as a brand new, independent company, there will inevitably come a day when the company will repeat the mistakes of Tomo. If the new social network is so successful it wipes out Tomo (I'm giddy at the thought), then everyone in the world will be locked into this new company, and the barrier to switching yet again would be even higher.

Then what would protect people's rights, their privacy, and the ownership of their data?

What the world needs is not a new social network that concentrates power in a single place, but a design to intrinsically prevent the concentration of power that results in barriers to switching.

ʊ

When I arrive at the bar, Emily is already halfway done with her drink, a gin martini with one vestigial olive, and she's obviously tipsy, her voice pitched high as she flirts with the guy next to her who radiates cockiness like a fifty-kilowatt transmitter, from his shiny shirt to his bulging pecs.

I'm momentarily peeved, until I see she's got a jacket slung over the barstool on her other side. The seat she's saved is at the end of the bar, against the wall. Check. It's within ten feet of the exit, and no chairs in the way. Check. My stump will be on the bar side, where less people will stare. Check.

I'm reminded again of why Emily is quite possibly the best person in the world.

I sit and the bartender nods at me, although he walks in the opposite direction, away from me. He's busy, the after-work crowd hounding him, shouting out requests for drinks. He comes back a scant thirty seconds later carrying a mint julep and sets it in front me.

"Your friend said you'd want this when you got here." He smiles, and moves away again.

Emily gives the guy she's talking to a peck on the check, does a last teasing flip of her hair, and then turns to me. She leans in close, hugs me and says, "What a jerk!"

I'm momentarily flustered. Is she talking about me? The bartender? Or the guy she was flirting with and kissed? The latter is the only plausible answer.

"Why'd you kiss him?"

"He's hot and arrogant."

"Is that bad or good? Because it sounds bad."

"I'm married. I'm not going to date the guy. He's just fun to flirt with. " She turns and takes a long drink, draining the martini.

There were guys like that in my distant past, the false confidence they exuded a siren call to some deep flaw in my personality. Rage runs through me, my blood hot and pounding in my ears. I can find out who he is, this prick on the other side of Emily, and I can kill him.

Something triggers in my mind, and I realize I'm in a danger zone. Ever since my ex-husband, there's something wrong with me. It's not only the anxiety and PTSD symptoms, but something different inside that allows, or maybe even requires, me to go out and kill people.

With the feeling of vertigo over a bottomless chasm, I see that the difference between me and a thug on the street is premeditation, data gathering and analysis. I'm not a random killer. Does that make me better or worse? I'm not sure.

Either way, it's terrifying to reach the point where I am now, to know all the time that I can kill people. All that separates anyone from life and death is a few hours of my time in front of a computer.

I don't want to be broken, yet I am. I'm only sane to any degree because of my ability to compartmentalize, and the belief I'm doing some good. If I save even one woman, it's worth everything.

"You're in your head again," Emily said. "Get out of there."

Emily recognizes my thousand-yard stare for what it is. She knows nothing of the killing, of course, but she understands my demons.

She puts a hand on my knee, gentle and kind, telegraphing the touch so I know it's coming. "Tell me about something, anything."

I sip my drink and tell stories about the office, picking the funniest moments of the week, those things I know Emily will laugh at, that I remembered especially to tell her.

ʊ

When Emily tries to order her fourth vodka martini, slurring noticeably, I cut her off.

"Don't," I say. "I need to get up early tomorrow. I want to go in a bit."

Emily takes a long moment to process my words. "I don't want to leave. Come on, have one more."

I quit after the first drink. Maybe at a quiet restaurant with Thomas or

Emily I might order a second. At a busy place like this, surrounded by un-known quantities, I'm not willing to risk the loss of control associated with a state of actual inebriation. Earlier, I was jealous of her carefree ability. Now, with her judgement eroded, I'm slightly glad I have my limits. Just slightly.

"Did you drive?"

She shakes her head. "Uber."

"Let's go," I say. Suddenly everything feels too loud, too hot, and I want to be gone.

Emily pauses, then nods. "I'm going to use the ladies' room."

"I'll wait for you out front." I sling my bag over my shoulder.

She nods and leaves.

I plot my way toward the exit, scanning ahead, not coming within arm's reach of anyone, keeping an eye on any men too close to my path.

As I close in on the door, I see a woman in her twenties arguing with the doorman. She tries to grab for her driver's license, he holds it up high.

I don't even need to hear what they're saying. The playful smile on his face, the way he leans in, suggests he believes he's flirting with her. The set of her shoulders tells me she's angry and afraid and wants out.

I reach inside my bag.

He glances at the license again. "Hey, you live in those new apartments off Belmont. My friend lives there."

"Can I have my license please?" She still has her hand out, trying to reach her license, but he's somewhere north of six feet and sitting on a tall barstool, and she's a few inches over five feet. She glances around for help.

The problem is the doorman is the authority here. That's what she wants, somebody who can force this guy who holds her license hostage to give it up, yet the very person she should be able to go to for help is the one causing the problem in the first place. That's the way it is. I should have been able to count on my husband to protect me, not hurt me.

"Well, do you live in the apartments or don't you?"

It never crosses his mind the last thing she'd want is some asshole in a bar who obviously violates boundaries to know where she lives. But it's printed right there on her license.

I will not let this go on. My hands tightens around the stun gun in my bag. Eighteen million volts will lay the asshole on the ground.

I'm five feet away when he gets off the barstool, and my limbic system re-members he's not some abstract threat, but a real live man an arm's reach away. It's like opening a closet door to find a lion charging right at you. I freeze solid, mid-stride, hand inside my bag wrapped around the stun gun. There's a roar in my ears and I'm dead stuck.

The girl looks around for help again, sees me right there, and her eyes plead with me. If the two of us argue with him, her eyes say, surely then he'll give up the license.

Yes, I want to say, I'll help you. This is what I do, after all, I make these situations right. Together we can beat him. But I'm locked inside my body, inside my mind, and although I'll later have these retroactive thoughts, right now I'm consumed with terror, like imminent death is upon me.

He is the predator, I am the prey, and my body has decided only absolute stillness can save me. I wish I could say I could fight it, grabbing the stun gun tighter as I struggle against the paralysis. However, that would be lying, because in this moment there is nothing except life-strangling fear.

Something blocks my view of the predator, and I distantly recognize Emily's voice. She says something to the doorman, takes the driver's license, hands it to the girl. Her words are garbled as she turns to me, grabs my arm, and pulls me outside, my body resisting all the while.

Outside, I'm still numb. I'm distantly aware of Emily going through my bag, prying my hand off the stun gun, and pawing through the contents until she comes up with a blister pack of olanzapine, breaks out a pill, and slips it under my tongue. She zips my bag up, pushes me back against the wall, and pushes down on my shoulders a few times, harder and harder, until I finally sit on a bench.

I sit and stare directly ahead without moving. Emily sighs and pulls out her phone.

It's maybe ten minutes later when I turn my head and look at her.

"Why'd you get involved?" Emily says.

My brain tries to reconnect with my vocal cords. "She needed help."

"You can't help."

"I can, I can help people like her."

"No," Emily says. "You can barely keep yourself going. Don't interfere in other people's shit. Come on, this is us."

She grabs me by the elbow, pulls me toward a car idling by the curb.

Tomorrow I'll replay this conversation in my head. If she was less drunk she might have said something different, encouraged me for trying, and told me I will eventually be able to do it. I'm not sure which Emily is right.

CHAPTER 9

DOMESTIC VIOLENCE DOESN'T START with abuse. It begins with charm, love, and seduction. I know this from personal experience. My husband was a paragon of support, a loving partner who comforted me when I was going through my biggest professional challenge. That lasted one year, five months, and six days.

Abusers know exactly how long it takes to establish dependency. There's nothing random about their behavior. Place a group of domestic violence offenders together in a room, and they'll compare notes. How long before you move? When do you suggest they quit their job? Six, twelve, or eighteen months before it's okay to threaten them? They approach their victims like an experienced bank robber planning a high-stakes heist.

I've researched Nancy and Todd's relationship, looking through old photos, status updates, and especially the messages Nancy exchanged with her best friend. I read secondhand how Todd told Nancy he loved her, how he appreciated the beauty she created as an interior designer. Later, he disclosed that he wanted to overcome the abuse he survived as a child and start a family with her. Nancy gushed to her friend about how funny and smart he was, how she loved to stare into his blue eyes.

They married, and then with the predictability that comes from thousands of these cases, he isolated her. He lost his job, seemingly through no fault of his own, and got a new job outside of Santa Clara with a tech startup. She moved a thousand miles to a town with no family, no friends. Because she once said she dreamed of a farm house, he bought a home far out in the foothills. They were in one of the biggest, most well-off metropolitan areas in the world, yet she was still alone.

Then, when she was separated from any kind of support, the violence started, hand-in-hand with the threats he would kill her if she left, and then he would kill himself.

At least, the last bit is my conjecture, based on the patterns of domestic violence. Because her online trail slowly fades after they move to Santa Clara, and there's no way to be sure. At some point he probably began monitoring what she posted on Tomo. Then one day there's no data going in or out of their house when he's not there, which means that he took away her access to a computer or even a phone.

This is the most dangerous time of all.

I'm in the VW van, parked in a multi-level garage downtown. It's a great viewpoint with wi-fi access to hundreds of locations. Using the directional antenna I glom onto a strong open signal a few blocks away.

I will fly down to Palo Alto on Wednesday, in theory to visit Tomo headquarters. I want to do a bit of last minute research before I go because there's so little data available from Nancy right now that I must take more active measures.

Todd should be home now, and he's got a smartphone, and it's on, and it runs Tomo. He checks into Tomo every day to visit Nancy's profile, her parents, and her best friend.

There's a tiny part of me that wonders if she's already taken off, and he's simply not telling anyone. Or if he's already killed her. Strange as it might seem, I won't kill him if Nancy is already dead. I'm not doing this for vengeance. I'm doing it so people can rebuild their lives. On the other hand, he'll probably repeat the pattern.

Still, I've got to know.

I'm sitting in my chair in the back of the van, curtains drawn. Cameras monitor all four directions and feed a small display to warn me in case anyone approaches, and another panel displays the status of my private onion-routing network. I lost two nodes last week, which happens from time to time. Eventually someone climbs up on a roof for maintenance or cleaning, discovers one of my solar-powered computers, and picks it up. Then the unit self-destructs, and I've lost a node. Still, the network comprises three hundred live routers, more than enough to securely route my packets and hide my origination point.

I've got a connection to the router in Nancy and Todd's house, which I've usurped so I can intercept all their traffic. Every fifteen minutes, the Tomo app on Todd's phone checks for notifications. My code running inside Tomo's data center receives the request and responds with the control packets to set debug mode on Tomo.

The console prints out "debug mode on," and I'm in. Now the app will accept an extended set of commands, and I turn the microphone on.

I listen and hear only muffled, distant sounds. Someone washing dishes. Maybe talking. I turn up the volume as far as I can, which only results in louder noises in a background of hiss, the conversation too indistinct to make out. I suppress the camera indicator light, and turn on the front and back cameras. Nothing. No light at all. More time goes by, more distant sounds. The accelerator says the phone is absolutely motionless, lying on its back.

After a half hour of this, I risk turning on the screen for a second to throw off a little light for the camera to see by. I'm staring at something tan, with a piece of wood running across the screen. I tilt my head from side to side trying to puzzle it out. If I were to guess, I'd say I'm looking at the underside of a desk. Like maybe the phone is in a drawer. This whole exercise will be fruitless if the phone is stuck in a drawer.

I sit back and settle in for the long haul. I never know what might turn up. A few minutes later my speakers erupt in a roar of sound. The accelerator says the phone jiggled back and forth. There's a bloom of light, and the drawer is open, and the front camera is aimed at a woman staring at the phone.

I see her grow frustrated, and realize she must be trying to unlock the phone.

I leap forward and bend over my keyboard, desperate to remember the code to unlock the screen without the password.

"What are you doing?" A man's voice.

"Nothing." A woman's voice as the camera image shifts. I glimpse her backside as she puts the phone back in the drawer.

"You're trying to use the phone again," he says. "You know it's not good for you. Those people are trying to make you think you're unhappy. They don't understand you the way I do."

"No, I wasn't."

"Don't lie!" he yells.

My stomach clenches at those words and I'm going to be sick. I've made a terrible, terrible mistake. I can't handle this. I try to reach for the keyboard, to cut the sound, but my hand is frozen and I can't breathe.

More crying. A scream.

Todd yells, "Don't fucking raise your hand against me."

A release valve inside me lets loose and vomit spews from my mouth, covering the laptop. I hit my head on the table, and my vision goes gray and fades away.

℧

I wake up and everything is wrong. My face is in a pool of vomit and I retch again, dry-heaving with disgust.

I pry my body off the floor, putting my hand in the vomit. I climb to my knees, weak, so very weak. I wipe my hand on my pants, and realize I've pissed myself.

I'm still on the floor, leaning against the wall of the van, covered in piss, tears, and puke, when I notice dozens of blinking lights on the screen above me on the tabletop.

I've passed out, this much is clear. Maybe from pure fright. During my recovery, after the amputation, they warned me this could happen. When the body undergoes something so traumatic, the mind can't cope, and it blacks out to protect itself. I find a napkin to wipe my face. When I touch my forehead, pain blossoms as I encounter a swollen bump. I must have hit my head. Maybe that's why I was out.

I glance at the clock, try to remember what time it was before. I've been out for an hour. That's not why my screen is full of blinking alarms. Something happened to my onion routing network. I grab another napkin and wipe away the worst of the vomit on the keyboard, then type a few commands.

Four nodes have dropped off the Internet because the underlying latency suddenly changed, tripping my counter-surveillance triggers.

If someone discovered the onion network and wanted to backtrace the connection to me, they'd subvert an individual node, like I did with Todd's network router, and make all the traffic flow through them.

Even with the connection intercepted, they couldn't read the payload data since I'm using three-layer encryption, stacking AES, Serpent and Twofish. Even the NSA's new datacenter shouldn't be able to crack that combination anytime soon.

Whoever is monitoring would instead look to see where the node received traffic from, and node by node, they'd try to trace each connection until they reached all the way to me. If it is the NSA, and if their capabilities are as powerful as I've heard, they might use the pattern formed by the size and speed of my network packets, then see where those patterns repeat in the Internet.

Either way, by observing and copying the traffic in real time, they've minutely affected the latency of packets. This is what I've detected. In four different nodes. Across the network. This can only mean one thing: someone powerful monitoring me, trying to figure out who I am.

I hit a button and kill the connection. The routing display fades away, leaving my heart thumping in my chest. Who is trying to find me? How close did they get? Though I possess a big bag of security tricks, I can't tell you how many nodes in the onion network could be compromised, and still have the network be able to guarantee my anonymity.

If they're onto me, I'm fucked. Kill someone in self-defense, and you can get away with it, even if your friendships evaporate and coworkers suddenly avoid you at all costs. Kill dozens of people in premeditated ways, and you're going to jail. It doesn't matter that I'm rescuing people.

Now I'm truly panicked. I've got to decamp ASAP, regardless of how shitty I feel.

Then I remember why I was here in the first place. Nancy is in danger. Immediate, extreme danger. What can I do?

I grab the directional antenna to change networks, pointing it around wildly, my hand trembling so much I can't establish a connection at first. Finally, I get a strong signal and VPN into work, then remote desktop to a machine in San Diego I compromised, and launch Skype. Using a text-to-voice synthesizer I phone in a domestic violence call to the Santa Clara police.

My vision and hearing are clouded, and I'm starting to disassociate from my body. I need to extricate myself, but my call to the police isn't sufficient by itself. I find a shelter hotline for Santa Clara, someone who will actually drive out there and remove Nancy from the house. Because when the police release Todd, as they do too often, if Nancy is still there, her risk will increase.

At last, I'm done. I've used the system the way it was designed, and I pray it's enough. In the back of my mind, I know it isn't. I know the stats. Five intercessions, on average, to get out.

I kill the power to the computers, move up front, and drive away.

⟲

I'm still covered in puke, although I'm already trying to make a plan. The van is totally fucked. I was never under the impression I could hide all my DNA evidence, but I took every precaution I could. I showered and used clean clothes before I entered. I wore a hat, hairnet, or hairspray to cut down on shedding. Once a week I rode Max, our light transit, to work. Sitting in a corner where the surveillance cameras didn't reach, I swept up hair and dust, which I blew all over the van the next time I entered, so there was the DNA of hundreds of people.

But now there's vomit, sweat and urine, and it's gone who knows where. If I were an international spy, I'd possess some amazing way to sanitize the van, or at least destroy it in a fiery blaze so hot every bit of DNA evidence is destroyed. Sadly, I don't, and if I give it a try, I'll end up creating a suspicious fire that would fail to destroy the DNA and instead would trigger an arson investigation.

I drive a few blocks from my house, the closest I've ever brought the van to home, park it, and walk home, carrying a bag of electronic equipment. I nod to a neighbor I recognize and cross the street so she doesn't smell the puke on my clothes, smiling slightly to avoid weird-neighbor vibes.

At home I shower, change clothes, and stick in a wash. I grab a few hundred in cash, a shawl, and a wide-brimmed hat, all of which I throw in a bag. Once in the van, I don the hat and shawl and take the van to a car wash specializing in detailing. I pay in cash to deep-clean the interior, aware the whole time of the surveillance cameras all around. There's not much I can do. Going other places would expose me to more surveillance cameras, creating more of a record of my existence, this mysterious woman who details an old VW van. I sit in the car wash and read *People*…for hours.

Then I swap plates, drive it up to Seattle, and leave it with a full tank of gas near a park with homeless people camping out, the window partway down and the keys in the ignition.

I walk away, glancing back once. I liked that van. I only ever used it as a secret office, yet I dreamed of camping at the beach in it, in my imaginary normal life. I pay cash for the bus back to Portland.

CHAPTER 10

DANIEL PEERS AROUND MY SCREEN from where he sits on his side of his desk. "Wake up, Angie. You had all weekend to relax."

"Right." I'm sitting in Daniel's office, my laptop balanced on the edge of his desk. I suck down more coffee, bone-weary from the unexpected day trip to Seattle combined with a night of worry. I still don't know what happened to my network of onion routers, and haven't had a chance to investigate.

"Can we still optimize ads for PrivacyGuard customers?" he asks.

Marketing's new numbers for the PrivacyGuard adoption rate has Advertising in a panic. It means a massive shift in revenue for the company, and a probable increase in average revenue per customer. The real problem is the new revenue will flow directly to Product without passing through Advertising. The VPA, Matthew O'Connelly, had a shitstorm in his office when he found out. Shit only flows one way in a corporation…downhill.

I partially close my laptop screen. "Daniel, you're missing the point. The reason people would pay for PrivacyGuard is because they don't want to be marketed to. They don't want personalized ads. They're asking to be left alone."

"That's not going to happen. O'Connelly won't accept anything less than six bucks per user ad revenue. Talk to O'Connelly about it."

"Ok, fine. I'll email him right now." I open my laptop back up and place my hand on the keyboard.

Daniel leans forward from his chair and pushes my screen back down.

I snatch my hand away, and hiss at him. My legs react involuntary, moving me toward the door, and I warily keep an eye on Daniel. I force myself back into the seat, will myself to stay there and not make a scene. As usual, Daniel doesn't notice a thing.

"What the heck, Angie? I didn't mean you should really talk to O'Connelly. It's a given. We *must* increase ad revenue. Optimized ads are more than double the revenue of non-optimized ads. Isn't there something you can do with, uh, metadata?"

Torvalds help me, there is nothing more dangerous than when a manager learns a piece of lingo. "Metadata is still data. It's the time it was posted, who it came from, where it was posted, who liked it. Everything other than the actual content itself."

Daniel looks hopeful.

I shake my head. "Metadata is still personalization."

"Well, is there something we can do without personalization?"

"Sort of, maybe. There's a grey zone." I wave my hands at my computer. "We can disregard everything we've got on their profile, their likes and dislikes, topics, and friends. We could optimize on the basis of interaction with the ads themselves: which ones they click on or hover over. We could visually and geographically optimize based on IP address geolocation. It won't be based on anything truly personal, although now we're getting into semantics of the word 'personal.' Customers will see this as an invasion of their privacy. What's going to happen when the users realize they're paying for PrivacyGuard and they're not getting it?"

Daniel laughs. "What's going to happen? Nothing's going to happen. They'll sit there and take it."

Adrenaline floods my system, and I stop myself short of screaming; but for once Daniel, who is oblivious to nearly everything, sees my expression and edges away from me, his fear showing in the widening of his eyes. My own breath is ragged. *Sit there and take it.* Not on my watch.

I grab my laptop and storm out of his office, slamming his door for good measure. A dozen people look up at the commotion. I ignore them all and go back to my desk. I'm too angry to sit, so I leave my laptop there and go outside.

It's raining, but I don't care. I walk toward the river.

Daniel, a mere cog in the organization, is a sign of things to come. He's escalated the level of abuse of our customers. He's right, too. A tiny handful of users will notice, and an even smaller slice will make some noise about it, while the overwhelming majority, nearly everyone, won't do a thing. In an attempt to make sense of their universe, they'll defend Tomo, claim Tomo's doing what any big business will do. They'll shift the blame to themselves, and decide if they really wanted privacy, they probably shouldn't post anything online. Then they'll do it anyway, because all any of us really want is to connect to other people, and Tomo is increasingly the only place they can.

I finally arrive at the metal railing along the riverfront. The water flows past slowly, dark with only a hint of green to betray the blackness. I've had it. I've just fucking had it. I lean over the railing and scream at the water with all my might, a wordless yell of rage that goes on and on.

My throat hurts afterwards. I look up and see people staring at me.

I ignore them, pull my hood up and walk down the riverfront path. And walk and walk.

ↄ

An hour later, I'm still outside, sitting on a bench with my raincoat drawn around me.

I've been working my day job, chasing down abusers in my spare time, trying to maintain a relationship with Thomas, and then, after everything else is done, trying to design a new social network. It's not possible to give everything the attention it deserves, and solving the social network problem is coming last.

I've freed thirty-six women from abusive relationships. I'm getting better and faster. Still, I can help maybe fifty people in a year, in the best case, and half of them will find themselves another abusive partner and end up in the same hell again.

Every time I kill someone, a little piece of my hope for the future dies. This isn't the dream I had the first time I laid my hands on a computer. I knew then the world was going to a better place. I believed our manifest destiny was to travel to the stars, on the *Enterprise* no less, in a post-scarcity economy, a post-conflict society. I wanted to help build that place.

What have I built? Better advertising engines. Tools to help kill people. I'm literally raining death and destruction on the world.

I leave the bench and stalk over to the river again. It's not the raging Atlantic that pounded ceaselessly against the beach where I grew up. I want that water, the water I could scream and rage at and which responded with more fury. I yell again at the water, which flows turgidly and won't return my anger. People stare at me once more. I ignore them and walk back along the river, my feet pounding, almost running. I would run, if it could take me away from all this.

Tomo has two billion users, and it's abusing them all. It's not the same thing as battering a woman, not at all. Not qualitatively, not quantitatively. I'm not even sure there's any way to compare the two. The violation of a thousand Tomo users is nothing compared to one victim of domestic abuse.

Regardless, I can't sit there and partake in it any more. I can't. It's eating away at me. If there was a man out there doing what Tomo was doing, I'd kill him in an instant.

I lack the energy to fight a war on another front. I'm trying to do too much. I'm individually freeing one woman at a time and that takes all my available time and creative energy. Then I go into work, and what's left to fight Tomo with? Nothing.

I could build an alternative to Tomo, I know I could, if I only had the time. Something has to go.

This past weekend, with the van and the problem with the onion network, was a close call. How many more times can I roll the dice and escape being caught? How many more people can I kill, each one eating away at my soul? How long until there's nothing left of what makes me a member of the human race?

Thomas helps me be human. I can feel love and compassion when I'm with him. Certainly Thomas is not the center of my universe. I'll never let another man define me that way. For all that, our connection is precious. If I give up killing people, I could build a real relationship with him. These occasional dates, the arm's-length distance I keep him at, they aren't what I want.

I shake my head. What am I even thinking about?

Give up freeing women one by one, in exchange for taking on the bigger problem of Tomo and its abuse of their own customers. Create a new online environment, one where people are truly free. Make a difference in the world like I wanted to in the first place.

No, I'm being ridiculous. Me, an ex-security penetration tester, database administrator, and data analyst. A damaged geek. How am I going to change the world?

On the other hand, Lewis, Tomo's founder, started the company in his dorm room with nothing except a spare Linux box.

If he could do that, why can't I destroy Tomo by building a better competitor?

I can't go on with this quasi-life I've been living. It's time for a change.

CHAPTER 11

BY THE TIME I RETURN to the office, it's late and people are filtering out. My outburst seems forgotten. I grab my computer and head home, texting Emily to see if she can meet for a drink.

"Girlfriend, I'm in Barbados for work until Thursday. Lunch on Friday?"

I never heard of anyone going to Barbados for work. I assume she's arranged a boondoggle on the company's dime.

Then Thomas texts me: "Dinner?"

An hour later, we're having cheap tacos at Mi Mero Mole, a tiny place on Division. They don't sell hard alcohol, so Thomas brought a flask of good tequila, and we sit at a sidewalk table, having sips of fiery tequila between bites of food.

We walk back to my place afterwards, nicely buzzed. I haven't said anything about my idea. Not until I've spoken to Emily, whom I like to vet my plans with. At least those that don't involve killing anyone.

"Can I stay?" he asks, arms hugging my waist, somehow safer than the claustrophobic panic I'd feel if his arms were any higher.

"Yes, but—" I yawn, overcome with exhaustion from the weekend, the dreadful stress of the day, and now the tequila.

He laughs. "I got it. You're tired. I'll grab my stuff."

He retrieves a small bag from his trunk, and we walk into the house holding hands.

In bed, drowsy, I feel the weight of him pressing down on the mattress, hear his quiet breathing, as his warmth crosses the inches of space between us. This is nice.

ↄ

On Tuesday I go into work and spend a couple of hours crunching data. Across the open workspace, Daniel discusses PrivacyGuard with someone. It takes only a few overheard words before I'm angry. I try to focus on my screen as the conversation keeps intruding into my thoughts. My pulse races, though, and soon I lose all ability to concentrate.

I grab my laptop and move to a small conference room where I can work without having to listen to him. I shut down chat and email clients, so there's no way Daniel can contact me, and focus on something I started noodling on last night, the distributed-identity problem.

When a new user joins Tomo, they want to find their friends. They can search for them by name, phone number, or email. Not many search by phone number explicitly, though the mobile app works behind the scenes by accessing the contacts on your phone and comparing their metadata against that in our central database. That allows Tomo to automatically send out friend requests. We do a variation on this on computers, relying on the user's email address book instead.

Once you've joined and define at least a few dozen relationships, it's easy to suggest other people you might know by looking at the relationships you have in common. Amy knows Betty and Cindy. Betty and Cindy know Daphne. It's a good bet Amy knows Daphne, too.

Now what happens if there isn't one social network, but many?

How can Amy find Betty and Cindy? And how can Daphne be recommended as a friend?

I'm perched on the edge of the table, staring at the whiteboard. I've drawn boxes and labeled them Network A, Network B, Network C, Network D. I placed Amy in A, Betty in B, and so on.

The first thing that becomes obvious is the networks need to talk to each other, using a standard protocol. Network A needs a way of asking the other networks questions and getting back answers. Because software doesn't speak English, that means defining protocols.

In the modern day and age, there's only one protocol that matters: JSON-encoded REST over HTTP. Ignoring all the acronyms, the basic idea is I've chosen a way for the services to communicate.

Now that we know *how* they talk, *what* do they speak about?

Network A has to be able to say "Do you have a user named Betty?" and the other networks need a way to reply, saying "Here's Betty."

It's a little trickier, because there is likely more than one Betty. An email address or phone number may return one user, but a name could match hundreds of people.

To make matters worse, Network A doesn't know Betty is on Network B or C or D, so it has to ask everyone.

I spend the next several hours sketching out messages for the services to exchange. On one run for coffee, I overhear Daniel ask a coworker where I am. I duck into the restroom, wait a few minutes, and then sneak back into the conference room.

It's the end of the day by the time I'm ready to stop, and mostly everyone's gone from the office. Software architecture drawings are scribbled all over the whiteboard walls. The centerpiece is an interaction diagram at the center showing the exact sequence of messages exchanged. This is the software equivalent of an architectural blueprint. I take photos to record it all and wipe down the boards.

The most important thing is I've made a discovery. It *can* be done. This crazy idea of mine is technically feasible.

Now what?

↻

"I can't make lunch today," Emily says, leaving me a voice message on Voxer, her new favorite messaging app. "Sorry for the short notice."

In the background, I hear the sound of arguing, and she sounds like she's in a room full of people fighting.

I look at the empty spot across from me at the table. Guess I'll be eating alone. My heart sinks, though not from loneliness. I need her advice.

"Short notice implies the message comes *before* the time we're supposed to meet. This is late notice. Or, an after-the-fact apology. How about tomorrow?"

The reply comes three minutes later.

"Can't do lunch. Dinner?"

Thomas and I are supposed to go to dinner, but I really need to see Emily. Hell, I'll invite her to the date. If there's drinking involved, they'll both have a good time.

"Dinner's good. Tasty N Sons at 6pm."

↻

Thomas and I video chatted last night, and even over the webcam video, I could see his face drop slightly when I mentioned Emily joining us.

When I promised him he could stay over, he wiggled his eyebrows playfully, and we both laughed. So it's all good.

Thinking about getting into bed with him tonight gives me a tingle down there.

At the restaurant, I ask the hostess for a table for three, then huddle in a corner.

"Angie!"

Emily arrives with such a burst of energy loaded into that one word that people turn from all over to stare. She gives me a peck on the cheek.

"If you'll come with me." The hostess has menus in one hand, and she leads us past the bar toward a big common table.

"We'll take that one, over there." Emily points to a much smaller table along the wall. A card standing on the table says "reserved" in a fancy script.

"I'm sorry, we—"

When the waitress tries to protest, Emily slips something into her hand.

"Thank you," Emily says.

I shake my head, barely believing what I've seen. This is *Portland*. Did Emily pay off the waitress?

"Certainly," the hostess says, now beaming at us. "Come with me."

The table Emily picked has one side to the wall, and there's ample space on either side of the table. Emily didn't pick the table for herself. I know she'd rather sit at the bar, where she'd probably flirt with the bartender. That the bartender here is female wouldn't slow her down at all.

"Thank you," I say, and squeeze Emily's hand.

"Of course. We gotta be comfortable."

I order a Pinot blanc and Emily goes right for whisky, ordering something Scottish I can't pronounce.

Our drinks arrive at the same time Thomas sits down. Burnt peat wafts over from Emily's drink, and I recoil at the same time that Thomas bends over for a big sniff of Emily's glass.

"One of those," he says to the waitress.

We both lean in for a kiss.

"Hey," Emily says. "She didn't give me any tongue."

I want to talk about my ideas for the distributed social network, but wait until after we order. We make small talk as we pick out a bunch of small plates served family style.

Once the food order is in, I clear my throat.

"Here it comes," Emily says.

"What?"

"Your big announcement. You're as transparent as a fish bowl. Spit it out, girl!"

"I have an idea. A really huge, change-the-world sort of idea, and I'm committed to make this happen. I'm working on it now, but once it's ready, I'm going to leave Tomo."

Emily's jaw drops. "Holy shit, what did you do with my Angie?"

"I'm serious."

"We can tell," Thomas says, carefully telegraphing his movement so I can see and nod at him. He puts one hand on mine. "What's the idea?"

"I'm going to build a distributed federated social network." I can't help the big smile that comes to my face. This is the biggest idea I've ever had.

"Um, a what?" Emily says.

Thomas is equally blank.

"A distributed federated social network. See, I've analyzed what it would require to overthrow Tomo. They've grown so big no single company can displace them. Even if they could, a replacement would only maintain the concentration of power in one company, which is exactly what's gotten us into the problem with Tomo. My plan is an architecture that divides the network into many pieces. Today, a social network embodies a social graph—that's your list of friends—a profile, publishing content, reading content, a feed algorithm to select which content you see, and a social commenting aspect. I've come up with a way to split these pieces so different companies can do each part. Dozens of companies compete to maintain your social graph or provide the best platform for authoring content."

I'm talking a mile a minute and I've got their undivided attention.

"How do you make money with this?" Emily asks.

"Ah. I knew you would ask. I've come up with three ideas. First off, you can pay for an ad-free experience. Tomo makes about ten bucks per user per year, by comparison. We allow users to pay us ten bucks, and we don't show them ads at all."

"Okay. How many people are going to do that?" Thomas says.

"I don't know, but Pandora and other companies use freemium models like this. The second option is the traditional advertising experience. The third option is corporate sponsorships. You buy a PC, you get two years free. The PC manufacturer picks up the cost."

Thomas nods his head in appreciation. "You've given this some thought."

"That's how money comes in," Emily says. "Who gets it? You've described lots of different companies. What's their incentive?"

"Pay per usage. Let's say Betty comes along, and she looks at her feed, and she interacts with a piece of content from her friend Alice. Everyone who had a role in that experience gets a percentage including the app Alice used to write the content, the social graph maintainers, the notification component, the algorithm that selects the story for Betty's feed, even the reader app that Betty uses. If Alice interacts with 1,000 articles in a year, and pays ten bucks a year, then each interaction would be worth a penny, and each of those companies earns a corresponding fraction of a penny."

Emily shakes her head. "How do *you* make money? You, Angie."

"A percentage off the top? A salary? I'm not sure. I'll figure it out."

"You've worked out quite a bit," Thomas says, fingers massaging his temple. "When did you do all this?"

"At work. I've been skating by with the bare minimum and working on this every chance I get."

"At *Tomo*?" Thomas grimaces.

"Yeah, why?"

"Lalalala," He puts his fingers in his ears. "I don't want to know."

"What's the problem?" I ask.

Thomas sits up straight and puts his lawyer face on. "The problem is they own your intellectual property. These are no longer your ideas, they belong to Tomo."

"Fine, I can work on it at home." I'm a little indignant. He's the lawyer. Why am I only finding out about this now?

"No, it's no good. You're working in the same field at Tomo. Your employment contract will give them ownership. If you're serious about this stuff, you've got to quit. Even then, you might be under a non-compete agreement or an NDA that would prohibit you from working at, or starting, a direct competitor."

"Quit my job? What would I live on?"

"Savings," Emily says. "Until you develop the idea far enough to raise money or have an income stream."

I stare at the tablecloth wondering what to say. Emily knows I forfeited my unvested stock options now worth millions when Jeremy convinced me to quit my first job at Tomo. Still, since they rehired me, I make good money. Excellent money, in fact, which I know because I peeked into the HR database to compare my salary to my coworkers. The problem stems from all sorts of unusual expenses. Zero-day exploits I purchased on the darknet. Cash for a VW bus. A thousand count lot of Raspberry Pi computers. Killing people is surprisingly expensive. Hell, by some estimates the government spent about ten million per Taliban soldier killed, so I'm damn efficient by comparison.

Obviously I can't reveal what I spend my money on, so I lack a good excuse for why I have so little savings.

"Let's assume I can survive financially. You're saying I should quit Tomo, and then what?"

"Quit, but don't say what you're doing," Thomas says. "Keep quiet about it for a while. You don't want it to look like you're jumping right into something else based on your current work. Eventually you'll probably want to raise money from a venture capitalist."

"Why live off my savings then? Why not ask for money from a venture capitalist in the first place?"

"They need to believe you can pull off what you're describing. You can't go to them with a vague idea—"

"There's nothing vague about it!" I've never been accused of vagueness in my life.

Thomas holds up a hand. "I don't mean technically. I'm sure you've got the technology worked out. What you need though, is concrete ideas about how you're going to do business, make deals with partners, get money from customers. How will you even build the thing? How many employees does Tomo have?"

"Fifteen thousand."

"You're one person. A venture capitalist won't believe one person can create a competitive product by herself. Who will build this with you? How are you going to hire them? What will you pay them with?"

My face heats up and Thomas's voice gets high and thin, like he's speaking through a long pipe. I'm overwhelmed by the questions. I want to write code.

"Thomas," Emily says, "go powder your nose in the little boys' room for a while."

Thomas looks back and forth between us. "Of course."

Emily waits until he gets up, and watches him cross the restaurant toward the bathrooms.

"Nice ass," she says, and turns back to me.

"I know," I say, managing a weak smile.

"What's going on?" she asks.

"This is too much. I don't know how to hire people. I'm not endowed with money. I don't know or want to know anything about pitching venture capitalists. I don't even like *talking* to people."

Emily leans back and sips her drink. "You care about this idea."

"Yes." My voice is firm even as I'm falling to pieces inside.

"Lots of people think of ideas. Turning those ideas into something real, that's a lot of work."

I nod, afraid I might cry. I grab my wine, suck the rest of it down.

"You used to be the Chief Data Whozig. Didn't you work with people then?"

"Chief Database Architect. It was different, then. The company was little, and we were all tech people. I never made slides. Occasionally I'd go into a meeting with an architecture diagram. Mostly we wrote and talked code."

Emily leans back and stares at me. "I know you like to look down on managers, but they possess a whole mess of useful skills. How to create a good presentation. How to interpret a profit and loss spreadsheet. The ability to stand up in front of a room of investors, employees, or customers, and make them believe. They aren't born knowing how, they learn it. If this is what you want to do, then you've got to embrace learning all that."

"I don't know, Em. I'm a coder, not a...manager."

"Yeah, today you are. You didn't start out a coder. You learned that. What's harder, learning to code or making slides?"

I smile. She knows what I think of most managers.

"You're smarter than those guys. You can do what they do." She leans in close. "Only if you care about this federated...thingy. If you don't care, then don't bother."

"Okay, I understand. I care. I do. I will learn how to do all that crap."

"Not crap," she says. "All the necessary hard work to get you what you need."

"Fine, all the necessary hard work."

Emily grabs my hand, and pulls it close to her. "And something else. You need to talk to someone. A professional."

"What are you saying?" I try to pull my hand away. Emily holds tight.

"How many men's hands will you need to shake to do this? How many times will you walk into a room of venture capitalists, and find a table full of hairy people? Are you going to suffer a panic attack each time? Going to look for an escape route?"

I want to shrink into the furniture. "Fuck you!" The words stumble out of my mouth, surprising even me.

The diners at the next table stare. Please, God, let me disappear.

"What happens when you want to hire someone, and the best candidate is a man? Are you going to pass him over because he might be a threat?"

"Screw you."

"You never got help. You've never seen a therapist."

"I did. In San Jose."

"I'm not talking about physical therapy to live without an arm," Emily says in a harsh whisper. "I'm talking about your phobia of men. I'm not saying this to be cruel, Angie. I'm telling you because I care. You can't live your life in fear. You'll kill your odds of succeeding if you don't deal with it before you create this company."

She lets go of my hand, and I pull it back into my lap. I shake with anger and embarrassment.

Emily extracts a tissue from her purse with shaking hands.

"Why are *you* crying?" I ask.

"I love you, girl. I want you to be happy." Emily blows her nose with a loud honk. "I believe in you. You can do this."

"It's hard. So hard."

"Yes. Everything worthwhile is hard."

PART TWO

CHAPTER 12

MONDAY MORNING, I GO INTO THE OFFICE at my usual time.

I need access to Human Resources' employee records database. Unlike all the ones we use for customer-facing operations, or even some of the less sensitive finance systems, I don't have access to the employee records. Tomo has a reasonably good security department, and we run twice-annual audits with the same firm that hired me out of school.

Administrative assistants have access, delegated from the managers they work for, but changes made through the official path leave a digital trail, by design, that can be traced back to the time, location, alteration, and user. I need something more permanent with less evidence.

The company is big enough that the overwhelming majority of people don't know each other. Every few months, I make a local copy of the corporate directory so I can do employee searches without being tracked. I check my cached copy now. There's an engineer, Andy Trask, three floors down who works for IT in records management. He'll have the access I need and he's in the office now, according to his chat availability status.

Ten minutes later I've doxxed the guy. I know where Andy lives, who he's married to, where she works, and their kids' names and ages. I know they moved here from San Diego, and they contracted out a kitchen remodel when they bought their home. The kids go to "A Bowl of Cherries" preschool. The school has a private Tomo group, where they post pictures of the kids. Andy hasn't visited the group in six months.

I download pictures from a recent garden planting, and copy them to a USB hard drive. I stick that drive and a spare into my pants pocket.

I glance around. The workspaces near me are empty. One guy across the floor is making coffee.

I retrieve my prosthetic arm from my bag. I slip it on, press down hard with my stump, and twist the air valve closed with my hand. It's suctioned onto my upper arm now. I slip on a wind breaker, and slip the prosthetic gripper into the pocket, which takes a half dozen tries. I normally use it to balance my weight when biking so I don't wipe out when I hit the brakes. I can't actually control the arm, only position it, and lock into place.

When it's finally set, I visit the restroom and examine myself in the mirror. I'll pass for a two-armed being today.

Downstairs, I wind my way toward Trask's desk.

"Andy, how are you? You're looking so good!" I do my best impression of Emily as I imagine her at her kids' school auction, but it comes off more Valley Girl. Impersonating moms isn't really my thing.

He looks up from his screen, a blank gaze as his eyes settle on me.

"Oh God, you don't recognize me!" I do my best giggle. I'm not really a giggler either. "From A Bowl of Cherries."

He shakes his head.

"My son, Jerry. Goes to school with your Thomas. They did the planting together, the cherry trees."

Andy smiles. "Of course, I'm sorry." He points toward his screen. "You know how it is."

"Yeah, of course. I didn't even realize you worked here, but your wife mentioned it at the potluck. I looked you up in the directory, because I had some photos of the kids, from the planting." I nod.

He nods along with me.

"Anyhow, I probably should have emailed them, but I wanted to say hi in person. You don't drop off the kids very often do you?"

"Only on Fridays."

"Well, of course. That's when my husband takes them. I'm Monday, Tuesday, Wednesday. Anyhow, you're waiting for the photos. I'm sorry, you're being so patient with me."

I dig into my pocket and grab both USB sticks.

He reaches out a hand, and I clumsily fumble the drives, dropping them both on his side of the desk.

"I'm such a klutz. I'm so sorry."

He digs down and picks them up. They're identical.

"Which one?" he asks.

"Uh… I don't know. One is the photos, and the other is my presentation. Could you check which one is which?" I try to look worried. This is why I brought and "dropped" two drives, so he'd be forced to plug one in on the spot.

He glances at his computer and then back at me. Corporate security has sent out at least three memos this year about the danger of plugging unknown USB devices into your computer.

To refuse now would be an act of wimpiness, demonstrating he was afraid of a tiny USB drive, in a woman's presence, no less.

I smile warmly at him. "Maybe it's the one on the left? Try that one."

He opens the secure drawer where his laptop is protected during the day from theft or random drive-by USB insertions and plugs the USB drive in. He clicks the icon and photos of his kids pop up on the display.

"That's the one!" I say. "The other one must be my presentation."

He dutifully hands it back.

I wait. "Uh, my USB drive. I was only bringing the photos. I kind of wanted the drive back."

"Oh, yeah." He copies the photos to his desktop, ejects the drive, and hands it to me.

"Thanks. I hope you enjoy them. Say hi to your wife for me."

I leave and board the elevator. When the doors close I take a deep breath and let a wide smile spread across my face.

Andy's computer is totally fucked. And I own it.

༄

The USB virus I've installed in Andy's computer lets me control it remotely, which I do, examining the drive to see what projects he's been working on. In the ideal case, I'd find a snippet of code that includes a hardcoded password for an account with write access to the database. If I found that, I could simply log in, delete a row, and be done. Unfortunately for me, I don't find any passwords.

I read through dozens of scripts, looking for anything that executes database deletions against the employee records database. There isn't a single delete anywhere, which puzzles me at first. As I keep digging, I discover employee records can be marked as archived but never out-and-out deleted. Makes sense. It enforces the audit trail and protects the company.

By the middle of the afternoon, I'm an expert on HR's technology stack, and I have new levels of respect for whoever is working computer security on their team. They're good. I try a couple of zero day exploits I can be reasonably sure won't be detected by any active countermeasures, but all the holes are buttoned up. I manage to log into one of the machines with ssh, and, as I expect, the account lacks sufficient permissions to do anything useful.

Almost ready to give up, I force myself to make one more pass through their source code repositories. I'm staring at a deployment script that sets up load balancing when an idea comes to me. It might work.

At some point I head down to a food truck to grab dinner and come back to my desk with a Cuban plate. Everyone's gone now. It's after seven. In the early days of Tomo, when the employees were young college graduates (or dropouts), people worked until all hours of the night. Now the average employee age is thirty-six, half have kids, and everyone I can see from my desk is gone.

When my modified scripts are finished and I've run all the local tests I can on my machine, I remotely connect back to Andy's computer. I copy the new code over, commit it, and push to their git server.

The build computer sees the change, runs tests, and deploys code.

When it's done, there's a new server added to the database cluster, a collection of computers working together to share the database load. The new server has a duplicate of the existing database, with two changes: the row delete permission is turned on for all users, and I've given myself a login to this machine.

In fifteen minutes, Tripwire will check that this server's policies are in compliance with expectations, which they aren't. When Tripwire discovers this, it'll notify router management safeguards, which will isolate this machine at the network level. So I've got that long to do what I need.

Database coherence is a tricky thing, and it takes several long minutes before my wolf in sheep's clothing is ready to accept database requests. The database engine finally responds to my pings. I enter one simple command.

```
DELETE FROM EmployeeContracts
WHERE employee_id = "000048" AND
      body LIKE "%noncompete%"
```

I run a few more SQL commands, querying for and deleting all agreements I think might affect me from my employee records. I say a silent prayer to Ted Codd in thanks that Tomo only has digital records and manages our own backups. I can't imagine what I'd need to do if there was actual paper sequestered in archival storage.

I connect to another server in the cluster to see if my change has propagated. There's a constant stream of traffic between the servers in this cluster as they share data to keep the database synchronized. Fortunately, the new server only has a small set of deletes it needs to propagate out to the others.

It takes two minutes before the records are updated everywhere.

I run a new set of deployment scripts to remove my temporary server from the cluster cleanly. If I were to simply kill it, failover scripts would alert on-duty engineers.

I copy files to Andy's machine, git commit and push, and wait for the build machine.

The clock is ticking. Six minutes before the next Tripwire scan.

With three minutes to go, the machine vanishes, reclaimed by the cloud as though it never existed.

For now, I've done what I came here to do. I've wiped out any record of the noncompete clause I signed when I started, and destroyed the NDA that might have restricted my future work. There's no way I'm waiting three years to build a new social network.

Now for cleanup. A bit of surgery on the git repo and a final deploy from Andy's machine, and all history of my deployment script changes disappear. I don't bother deleting the SQL logs on the rest of the database cluster because they roll over after 24 hours, and I don't expect anyone to look at this for a while.

The provisioning service is something I've had my hand in for a while, and I've left a few backdoors. I log in, remove the record of the provisioned machine being attached to the database cluster. Then I remove the log of my removing the record. Always layers, so many layers.

I find the actual hardware I provisioned by virtue of the non-changing MAC address and do a secure wipe of the hard drive.

I'm done cleaning up. It's 2:15 A.M., and I've been at work since 7 A.M. yesterday. A twenty-hour hacking session. My forearm is cramped and my shoulder so tight it might as well be frozen in place. Script kiddies give the impression penetration is easy, and maybe it is when your only approach is to try every known exploit against a soft target in the hopes of bringing it down. True hacks, where the target is security-conscious and can't know the intrusion ever happened, and the goal is a specific, controlled change: that's a whole other ballgame.

I sling my backpack over my shoulder and walk back to the elevator. I wince at a cramp in my lower back, and roll my neck to work out the kinks. For all that, there's still a little saunter to my step. Nothing compares to pulling off an attack like this.

ʊ

By Wednesday it's been more than twenty-four hours since my alteration of the HR records database, and any last records of my exploit were removed by the scripts automatically deleting day-old logs.

I try to add a meeting to Daniel's calendar. Like most managers, his calendar shows he is busy all day and tomorrow's availability is the same. I message him instead, saying I need fifteen minutes of his time. He tells me to come at 1 P.M.

Butterflies in my stomach annoy me all through lunch. It's only a job, I remind myself. I can work anywhere if my new venture doesn't work out.

At 1 P.M. I walk in, and Daniel, without saying anything, points me toward the guest chair with one hand as he gestures to the headset he's wearing with the other.

I leave the door open. My escape path.

He's on the phone for another five minutes, and hangs up, ripping the headset off.

"I've got another meeting, but I can be a few minutes late." He gets up to close the door.

"Don't—" Don't bother, I want to say, but it's too late, and already the temperature seems to be skyrocketing. Why can't he stay on his own side of the desk, where we'd have a barrier between us?

"What's up?" He goes back to his side of the desk and sits with a squeak from his pneumatic chair.

I swallow deeply, my throat tight. "I'm giving my two-weeks' notice. I'm leaving Tomo."

Daniel blanches at this, and for a few long seconds, he's too stunned to speak. I'm the strongest engineer he has by far, and to a certain extent, his reputation to make things happen is due to my contributions.

He clears his throat. "I thought you were happy here."

"I am, or was, although something's come up, and I need to leave."

"I…you…you're the best employee I've got."

I shake my head at him. I lean down, pick up his badge from the floor.

He glances down at his waist, sees his badge is missing, and takes the one I hand him.

"It is a personal thing?" he asks. "You could take a leave of absence. No need to quit. Take three or six months off. Come back when you're ready."

"It's okay, Daniel. My mind is made up. I'd like my last day to be in two weeks. I have some work to transition to the rest of the team. I can be finished before then."

We go back and forth a few more times, and I leave an in-shock Daniel in his office.

ʊ

It's been five days since the dinner when I promised Emily I'd find someone to talk to. I've put it off as long as I could. Now I'm out of excuses and spend Thursday morning investigating support groups.

There are many in Portland, and, as I normally do, I over-research every-thing about them. Time, methodology, location, outcomes, duration, leaders and their educational background.

I don't want one near home or work, afraid I'll run into someone I know and ashamed of what I see as a weakness in myself. The logical half of my brain argues anyone there is in the same boat as me. The emotional side counters that I'm better than those people, and have more to lose.

Which is it? Am I weak, and therefore should be ashamed? Or better, and too proud? It doesn't make sense it could be both. But then my emotions usu-ally don't make sense to me.

Late Thursday morning, Emily texts me from outside Big Pink, and I take the elevator down to meet her. She's waiting in the lobby with two coffee drinks. People are streaming around us, coming to and from the massive ele-vator banks behind me.

"Quad shot mocha," she says, holding one out. "Let's walk."

"I like my coffee black," I say.

"The chocolate increases happiness and the sugar elevates energy. The milk is for your bones. It's good for you. Drink up."

"This from the woman who eats salad without dressing? Besides, they de-bunked that bit about milk."

"My coffee is black. The dessert drink is for you."

I sigh and accept the cup, and Emily walks away without waiting, her heels seemingly no impediment to her quick pace.

I chase after her, trying to sip my coffee on the run. The sweetness is sickening.

"Have you set something up yet?" she asks, when we're half a block away. The sidewalk is crowded with workers from the surrounding office buildings.

"Set what up?"

"You know, a thing," she's almost whispering, which might be a first for Emily. I realize she has no idea who my coworkers are, and this is her idea of discreet. They're only my coworkers for another thirteen days.

"No, I'm still researching support groups."

She looks up at me. "Oh God, you'll take forever. Here." She digs into a pocket and holds out a slip of paper.

I unfurl two fingers from my cup and take the paper between them. I try to read the paper from around the cup, but can't make it out. Emily grabs the coffee back from me.

"Thanks."

The half sheet flyer is for a domestic violence support group that meets early tomorrow morning.

"No way. It's in a church."

"It's good. My friend went there for several years. She says it helped a lot."

I glance up from the paper, check out Emily's face. People don't walk around volunteering their domestic violence support groups unsolicited. She's been asking around. Nothing terrifies me more, but if Emily can do this for me, I can go for her.

"Fine, I'll do it."

"It's not religious. They only meet at the church."

"I said I'll go."

"Oh, okay." Emily looks away, down the street, toward nothing I can see that's important.

I have no idea why things are suddenly awkward between us.

I pocket the paper and take the coffee back. For a moment, we're both holding the cup at once. "Thank you," I say. "I know you mean well and you care." My voice is gruffer than I want it to be, and I realize I'm not mad at Emily, but I *am* scared and my knees are weak. I take a long chug of the mocha, and the chocolate and sugar fortifies me.

Emily knows me better than I know myself.

CHAPTER 13

I'M SO NERVOUS before I leave for the support group I contemplate a drink even though it's still early morning. All I know of support groups is what I've seen on television, which I associate with alcoholics, and though this group is for domestic violence survivors, it's enough to conclude a drink is probably inappropriate.

I descend a flight of dark stairs to the basement of the church, in a cold room with a linoleum floor and high, squat windows letting in a trickle of natural light. There are no men present, so for once I don't worry about the distance to the exit or being blocked in. One woman, professionally dressed in a green satin blouse and slacks, smiles at me, and gestures for me to join the women seated in a circle on folding chairs.

"Please, help yourself to coffee or water, if you like, and take a seat," she says. "We'll begin in a few minutes."

I skip the beverages and sit down. It's the most diverse group of women I've been in for a long time. The youngest is still a teen, awkward and gangly, with red, puffy eyes. The oldest could be a grandmother. There's a woman in ripped sweats and a band t-shirt, and nearly opposite her, a middle-aged woman in an expensive tailored suit. Portland is known as the whitest city on the west coast, due to draconian discrimination laws before the Second World War, yet here are two black women, a Hispanic woman, and an Asian woman.

For a moment, I'm comforted. I'm not going to stick out here. I might have one arm, I might be afraid to step into a room with a man, and I might make a scene if a man touches me, but here none of that will happen. If anything, I'm almost average for the group. Maybe losing an arm is extreme, even by these standards, although it's possible someone here has experienced worse.

At some point the woman in the green blouse talks about the ground rules. A gnawing pain blossoms in my stomach, and soon all I can focus on is the feeling. My limbs tingle, another kind of nervousness I know from past experience.

The pit in my stomach grows every day around this time. It used to begin at 5 P.M., a full hour before he came home from work. Then he started coming home at different times, sometimes 5, once at 4:30. The gnawing and trembling appeared earlier then, at 4 or 3, even. Eventually, the feelings became too much, overwhelming, and my body and mind would go numb. I had to finish the household chores earlier then, by noon, for fear I'd lose control of my body, and be unable to do them—

He touches me on the shoulder, and I know I shouldn't, but I lash out, I fight back, but I miss and I fall out of my chair.

I'm confused. Where am I? I don't remember this linoleum.

I realize I'm on the floor in the church basement.

The woman in the green blouse speaks to me, but her words come through a long, narrow tube. A squeak is all that reaches my ears, and I can't understand anything over the pounding in my head.

I lurch to my feet, and stumble through the ring, crashing into several empty chairs before I run outside.

I gulp air as though I swam a hundred yards under water. The tunnel vision is so bad I can barely distinguish my car. Eventually I find it, grab onto the fender, and for a moment I'm afraid I'm going to be sick.

The woman in the green blouse circles into my vision, a cautious ten feet away, sunlight so bright on her blonde hair it's almost blinding. She's speaking, but I still can't make out what she's saying. She approaches me slowly with something held out in front of her, and she places it into my hand, which doesn't protest. She backs away, and my hand folds tight of its own accord, crushing the business card inside.

I'm in my car, in the driver's seat. I have no idea how long I stood next to my car, no idea how I got in, or how long I've been sitting here. I haven't driven anywhere, because I still see the church right across the street. It's still the same day. I'd know if a whole night passed, right?

I unfurl my hand, which has cramped up tight, and look at the business card. It's damp with sweat, but the text is clear, and the words that stand out are *psychologist* and *private practice.*

Private practice means not having to go into a room and hear other women talk about their experiences.

My breathing gradually returns to normal, eventually my vision appears normal, and I might be fit to drive. I'll call and make an appointment. From home.

↻

I stare up at the building. My appointment with Charlotte, the psychologist from the group session, is in a few minutes. After the experience at the church, I'm not sure I can handle this. I avoided thinking about it on the drive over, although now that I'm here, I'm sweating and faint, and haven't even gotten out of the car.

In the elevator ride up, I get agita, that combination of nauseous and acid reflux and impending vomit which apparently only Italian-Americans experience often enough to warrant a word for the specific feeling. Are we going to talk about what happened? How can we not?

By the time I reach Charlotte's office I'm shaking, and it takes everything I've got to keep putting one foot in front of the other.

Charlotte opens the door when I knock and takes in my sweaty, trembling mess.

"Come in, Angie. I'm glad you called. Please, pick a seat."

The office has two chairs and a couch. I pick the chair, because I could make a faster exit from it.

Charlotte settles into the other chair with a pad of paper. "You're anxious."

I swallow, unable to form words, and nod.

"We're not going to talk about anything from your past today. We're not even going to talk about feelings, or any challenges you feel."

I nod again, my head like one of those desk toys that bounce up and down uncontrollably, although I don't understand. Isn't that what therapy is? Talking about stuff you can't handle? How are we not going to do any of that?

"You're anxious. I'm going to give you some tools for dealing with anxiety. How does that sound?"

My head continues its unstoppable bobbing.

"Wiggle your toes in your shoes, and pay attention to the feeling of your toes rubbing around inside your shoes."

What the hell? I can't see the point of it, but I do what she says.

"Can you feel your toes?"

Of course I can. I nod, a little slower.

"Now focus on your heels. There's some weight pressing down on your heels. It's the weight of your legs, the pull of gravity. Can you sense that?"

"Yes." My voice is a whisper.

"Good," she says. "Now think about your legs and pants. Your pants are touching your skin. The fabric is lying on top of your legs. Can you feel that pressure, the sense of the cloth resting on your thighs?"

"It's very faint," I say.

"That's okay." She continues to lead me through my entire body, all the way up to my hair. I thought maybe she was going to become all new agey on me, and talk about energy and wacky stuff, but she never did.

"How are you feeling?" she asks, after she's assessed whether I can feel the difference between the side of my face closer to the window and the side away from it.

"I'm okay." I'm startled to realize I'm relaxed, even slightly blissful.

"That's a big difference from when you walked in. That's what we call grounding, and you can do it any time you feel like you need to. I can teach you more tools you can use."

"Is that what therapy is?" I ask. "I thought…"

"Different people need different things. I like to find out what a new patient needs. Based on what happened at the church, and how you looked when you came in, I thought we should start with something to help you cope with your anxiety. If you agree, we should continue to focus on some more tools to help you deal with anxiety. Would you like that?"

I feel like I've been drowning for years, and someone has thrown me a life preserver.

"Yes," I say, and resist the urge to cry.

CHAPTER 14

MY LAST DAY AT TOMO is a Wednesday. Thomas takes the next two days off work, and we spend a long weekend in a small beach house in Manzanita. It's cold and wet, but we bundle up and go for long walks on the beach. At night we curl up by the fireplace and read books.

More than anything else, I sleep. I'm shocked by how tired I am. It's like the exhaustion of years of double-duty hit me all at once. Thomas asks if I'm okay when I sleep until nine one morning.

Although money is tight, Apple lures me in with a refresh of their laptops, and I resist for a week before I give in. I spend a few days playing with my new toy and getting my development environment set up just right.

I build skeletal prototypes of my ideas for the protocol between disparate social networks. They're simulators, more than proper software, but I still take great joy in passing messages back and forth between the separate programs.

I show off my code one night to Thomas, who leans in to stare at the text scrolling by in my console.

"See, right there, it's passing messages back and forth."

"This line here, where it says 'message received'?" He smiles. "That's cool!"

He's happy for me, because I'm excited, but it's clear he doesn't experience the same thrill I feel. That night at dinner he suggests I meet with a client of his, Mat, who is the CEO of a small tech company. "He's recently been through the funding process, and knows everyone in the startup community."

I know he wants to be helpful, but I grit my teeth in resistance. I want to do things at my own pace, in my own way. At lunch with Emily a few days later, she convinces me to at least give it a try.

"You're not committing to anything," she says, around bites of lettuce-wrapped chicken breast. "You're only meeting someone to find out what they know. There's nothing wrong with learning."

I sprinkle more hot sauce on my chimichanga and manage to look doubtful.

Emily sighs. "It's an email. Humor Thomas and talk to the guy."

I let Thomas email me an introduction to Mat, and after a few back and forth emails, Mat and I agree to meet for lunch at Pok Pok, a restaurant in Southeast Portland, far from the tech bubble downtown.

I arrive fifteen minutes early to ensure a table in a far corner where we won't be overheard. Of course, this table choice requires some compromises. The front door looks like it's a few hundred feet away. *Don't believe everything I think. Don't believe everything I think.* I repeat Charlotte's mantra five times, counting it off, then practice grounding myself. Seat. Floor. Butt. Shoes. The panic subsides, and when Mat approaches, I'm able to greet him with a smile.

He holds out his right hand for a shake, and his eyes flare when he sees my stump. I turn my left hand around and give him the best off-hand shake I can.

I decide to try one of the corny jokes Charlotte told me. "I had a little problem with a pit bull on the way over."

Mat laughs, and the awkward moment passes. We exchange the usual greetings and discuss our backgrounds. He's British, and has been in the United States almost ten years. He founded his latest company several years ago, their specialty is data analysis for other tech startups. We geek out on our favorite statistical analysis software until we've ordered food.

"I heard you want to do something in social media. Aren't you worried about a Tomo noncompete?"

I swallow hard, and force myself to wave it off casually. "No non-compete. Didn't sign it."

His eyes go big. "Wow. That's fortunate. What's your angle?"

I'm wondering how much I can and should say. The question is natural enough, yet I'm reluctant to share my idea.

He sees my reluctance, and misunderstands. "Ideas are cheap. It's building them into profitable companies that's hard. Gifford Pinchot says 'ideas are like insects: many are born, but few live to maturity.'"

"I'm not worried about you stealing my ideas. I'm thinking about how ridiculous it sounds. I want to create a direct competitor to Tomo."

"Hmm." Mat leans back like he's wondering how he got himself into having lunch with an insane person.

"It's not as crazy as it seems. I don't want to build the whole thing. The concept is we decompose the social network into its constituent parts and enable anyone to build a single part in isolation by defining standard protocols to allow the pieces to plug in together."

"One app for photo-sharing, a different one for status updates, like that?"

"Even more fine-grained. Consider your feed—everything you see when you visit Tomo. Tomo has an algorithm that chooses what you see, and you don't have any control over it. Tomo gives you a hundred and fifty updates a day, max. Other social networks give it to you raw: every message, as it happens."

"That's a whole different approach," Mat says. "The most you can do is dip a toe in the stream and sample it. You can't read everything."

"You can't read everything no matter what. Even a modest user has two hundred friends, times five updates a day, that's a thousand messages to read. Highly connected users might have a raw feed of twenty-thousand items. They can't read them all. Right now, users don't have any choice of the algorithm used. Should it be everything? Should it be filtered? If it is filtered, what's the criteria?"

"You want to let the user pick from different algorithms?"

"No, I want an API so anyone in the world can create feed filtering algorithms, and every person can choose the algorithm they want that day. One algorithm might be based on the number of thumbs up and thumbs down a post gets. Another algorithm can use sentiment analysis to figure out what's funny, serious, sad, or happy. Another can measure the strength of friendship based on the number of interactions we have. You could—"

"You could combine them anyway you want," Mat says, a mouthful of pork belly not inhibiting him at all. "Twenty percent of my feed is dedicated to my top friends, and the other eighty percent is weighted depending on thumbs, sentiment, keywords, etc."

"Exactly. Now imagine every time a user interacts with a post selected by an algorithm—by thumbing it, commenting, resharing—the company providing the algorithm is credited with a fraction of a penny. In effect, they've implemented a portion of the overall, aggregate social service, and so they are paid for their work."

Mat stares off into the distance before perking up. "Brilliant!" he says slowly. "Bloody brilliant. My company could build a data analysis component, and earn royalties based on how much we're used."

"Exactly. Now take that basic concept—little micro-services built to perform one function, working through a standard interface—and multiply by every aspect of the social network. It's not only feed filtering. It's how you maintain your friend graph, manage notifications, create and share content—one micro service for status updates, another for photo sharing. On the other side, it's the app you use to view content, the commenting infrastructure, even the data storage. It's your choice where all of your personal information is stored. Every player in the ecosystem gets their fractional pennies every time they provide useful work to somebody."

Mat is silent. He's stopped eating and he's got a huge grin on his face. "It's a meritocracy without boundaries. If you add value into the system, then you make money."

"Yup. Conversely, if you screw your users—like violate their privacy or try to screw them over—they're free to swap out your component for a different provider who doesn't."

I feel like Mat gets it, and now I can concentrate on some food. I grab a fork and spoon and use them like tongs to load up my plate. I take a bite of thinly sliced flank steak and my mouth holds a little party in celebration.

"It's a little like the old fixed price airlines," Mat says. "When they couldn't compete on price, they had to differentiate by providing the best customer service and experience."

"I'm calling it Tapestry," I say, "because the whole system is woven together of multiple parts."

"Tapestry, I like it." Mat says, as he pulls out a pen and a folded sheet of paper. "I have a ton of questions. What you described is huge. How much needs to be built in order to launch? What's the minimum you need to start testing with users?"

"I don't know," I say. "I hadn't really thought about it."

"Okay. Well, obviously you wouldn't want to build the whole thing, then launch and find out the core user experience is broken. How much of this is already built?"

"Just some lightweight prototypes of the message passing framework."

He nods and jots down the questions he's already asked. "Who's already playing in this space? You probably aren't the first person to have this idea. Why hasn't this been done before? What's to stop other people from doing it?"

"I don't know." I lean over and try to see what he's writing. "You want me to answer all these right now?"

"Not necessarily. These are the questions investors will ask, and you should give them some serious thought. Here are a few more: Who's on your team? How much money do you need? What's the one thing that will stop you?"

"How can I know the one thing that will stop me?"

"It's a way to try to understand your biggest possible risk. The assumption is you've considered a whole list of possible problems and figured out the most daunting one. And, of course, the crux of the matter: How are you going to make money?"

"That I can answer! I have—"

Mat holds up one finger, as he writes something down. "A special question specific to your situation: What happens when Tomo reacts? Also, you need to talk to Amber about IndieWeb." He sticks the pen back in his pocket and hands the paper over with a flourish.

He scribbled down the questions in nearly illegible writing, along with Amber's handle.

"Before you approach an investor," Mat says, "you want to be ready with solid answers. Be prepared to spend some of your own money getting there. Nobody hands out cash these days."

"If I had money, I wouldn't need money."

"I know, I know! But it helps to show you're personally invested in the success of a business. You've got credit cards. Don't be afraid to max them out."

I can't believe what I'm hearing. "Why would an investor give money to somebody who is fiscally irresponsible?"

"Look, if you've got literally everything on the line to make this business succeed, then an investor will trust you're going to give it 110 percent."

We go back and forth on money and a few other questions. By the time we're done with lunch, I'm convinced investors are another bunch of control freaks to be avoided.

CHAPTER 1 5

IT'S AMAZING HOW MUCH STRESS little green pieces of paper can cause. I've got enough for maybe six months if I'm frugal. Somehow, time passes blindingly fast, and before I know it I've been without a paycheck for two months and my bank account balance is disappearing faster than free disk space on my new laptop.

I haven't decided if I'm going to bootstrap my effort on my own or seek funding, but either way, I need some money in the bank now.

The temptation to simply take the money is always present for someone with my skill set. Although I'm not a financial systems expert, I built enough holes into Tomo that I'm sure I could squirrel money away from them. Tomo has dozens of billions in cash and I can't imagine needing more than a couple million. The interest Tomo earns in a single day would be enough. I could pilfer a day's interest pretty easily.

Still, the idea rubs me wrong. Tomo may be evil, but outright stealing... Even though I use my abilities to kill people, I've always felt stealing is the antithesis of the true hacker ethic. It's a last resort.

I focus instead on solving my financial problems with bitcoin. Like most geeks, I've thought about how the distributed protocol works, whether it's as secure as people believe, or if the whole system will be compromised, and if so, what will happen when all that wealth evaporates in the exchange of a few TCP packets. Fortunately, my idea doesn't require me to compromise bitcoin, only to move a little money around.

I spend a week preparing, feeling guilty the whole time I'm not working on Tapestry. I could be building a full implementation of the all-important backbone messaging protocol. Instead, I end up diving deep into the history of bitcoin trading, expert trading systems, and using my backdoors to make extremely subtle tweaks to Tomo's financial systems.

Eventually, I search Local Bitcoin for people who sell the cryptocurrency for cash. There are sites that claim to launder bitcoin for you, though I don't trust them. For what I need, local is best, because it avoids any digital trail for me.

Half a day of research later, I'm messaging with someone named DIMMN. The background data I dug up says DIMMN is the best for what I need. He's also a guy. Although I'd feel safer with a woman, I'm keeping in mind Emily's advice about choosing the best *person* for the job, not just the best woman for the job.

We plan to meet at the central library early in the afternoon. I check the online catalog, find two copies of William Gibson's first novel on the shelf, so I tell him to look for someone reading *Neuromancer* at a table near where it's shelved. Then I load up a paper bag with the contents of a fireproof box I keep hidden in the ductwork and go change.

I'd prefer to avoid DIMMN remembering a one-armed woman. The prosthetic arm in the pocket trick is clunky if used for more than a few minutes. Instead, I stick a pseudo-realistic hand on the prosthetic, useless for grabbing anything, but it looks sort of real, at a glance. After wrapping the hand in clean white gauze, I don a fake sling and a blouse with a plunging neckline. If he's going to remember anything, let it be my breasts. My phone stays at home while a script runs to stream episodes of *Nexus* with occasional pauses for simulated bathroom and snack breaks. A burner phone and extra-wide-brim sunhat complete my preparations, then I take the streetcar downtown.

At the library, I find my copy of *Neuromancer* and sit at a table by the wall, keeping my sling away from the room. Choosing a few books at random, I pile them at the spot next to me so no one will take it.

After a ten minute wait, a young bearded guy sits down next to me.

"Pieta?" he says, friendly and casual, like he's greeting a friend he hasn't seen in so long, he's forgotten what they look like.

"Demon," I say. "Nice to meet you."

"Demon? Uh, wrong guy."

Funny. Pieta is the name I gave him online. He's got to be the right guy. "Your username. D-I-M-M-N."

"Short for Danger is My Middle Name." He smiles. "But you can call me Dan."

"Dan. I want to buy some bitcoin."

"Sure, if you've got cash."

"Good." I pass the bag across to him, my entire bug-out stash. "Fifteen thousand."

"Whoa." He shakes his head and shoves the bag back. "I do deals for two hundred or less. Someone buying drugs online doesn't want a digital record tying their purchase back to their credit card. But, fifteen grand…you must be killing someone. I don't want to know and I'm not getting involved."

He stands, and I swallow dramatically, like I'm deciding whether to trust him, and gently place my hand on his arm. "Nothing like that. There's going to be *movement*."

His eyes go wide. Everyone's heard stories about people manipulating the market, exploiting exchange rate fluctuations by dumping or buying bitcoin. According to his Tomo posts, Dan believes people are gaming the system.

"A run on bitcoin," I say in a low voice.

He stares through me, his face blank, maybe calculating money right then, probably calculating how much he has invested in bitcoin.

"If you're thinking about what you might gain or lose, you'll do better if you know the timing. You can keep five percent of what I make."

He leans back, takes a deep breath, and slowly nods his head. "I need to deposit your cash. I don't have enough in my account to cover you."

"Go do it. I'll wait here."

I already know there's a bank one block away where he can make the deposit. His social profile shows he's honest to a fault, and keeps his word to his friends. He might make money in a weird way, but I trust he's not going to disappear with mine.

He comes back fifteen minutes later. He pulls out his phone to transfer the bitcoin to me. I hold up a sheet of paper with a QR code printed on it encoding the address of my bitcoin wallet. "Transfer a thousand to me. Keep the rest in your account. We're going to be selling it today."

He raises his eyebrows. "Whatever you say."

He scans the paper with his phone and transfers almost three bitcoins to my account. The exchange rate is 392.31 U.S. Dollars to 1 bitcoin.

"Here." I hold out the copy of *Neuromancer*. "Borrow this from the library."

He holds up a hand. "I already own a copy."

"Borrow it."

"Okay, okay." He takes the book and we walk together to the counter. He holds his library card under the reader, then scans the book.

Somewhere in the library's database, the status of the book moves from ON SHELF to CHECKED OUT. There's a server application inside Tomo whose responsibility it is to check every Tomo user's library usage to share their reading habits. DIMMN's status updates to show he's "Reading *Neuromancer*."

A different cluster of servers inside Tomo is responsible for digital-currency exchanges. The primary purpose is to accept bitcoin payments for services and advertising and convert that into regular government currency, but it can also work in reverse, buying bitcoin to make payments to partners. Tomo maintains a small pool of bitcoin, about a hundred thousand dollars. If the pool drops too low, we buy some more on the open market. If it gets too high, we sell some.

Simple math brings the pool back to its normative size by buying the difference between current value and desired size, the midpoint between the maximum and minimize:

```
if pool.value < MIN_POOL_SIZE

    Exchange::buy (MAX_POOL_SIZE+MIN_POOL_SIZE)/2-
pool.value

    end
```

If the pool holds 35 bitcoin, the minimum is 50, and the maximum is 100, then 100+50 is 150, divided by 2 is 75. 75 minus 35 is 40. So Tomo buys 40.

The next time the algorithm runs, pool.value is greater than the minimum, and nothing is bought or sold.

What if pool.value returns the inverse of the actual value? It reports negative 35 dollars. 75 minus *negative* 35 is 110. The next time, it reports -110, and Tomo buys 185. The more it buys, the farther behind the math shows it is, and it buys more, approximately doubling on every run.

The algorithm runs every ten minutes and DIMMN borrowing the book has triggered the change causing the bug in the code. Beginning with the next run, every time the quantity of bitcoin is requested from the central store, it will report the negative inverse value causing Tomo to buy bitcoin in bigger and bigger chunks.

Dan has no knowledge of this, and I purposely didn't bring a device to monitor things. He must suspect I know something, but without even a computer or phone with me, he won't believe I'm the cause of this bitcoin manipulation. He follows me back to the fiction section with his checked-out book.

"Now we wait. Give me that back." He hands me the book and I open to a random page. "Get something to read."

Reading is a pretense when we both know something major is going to happen. Dan bites his nails, and I take the sign to mean he's invested his own money. Not having my own computer to check prices is slightly infuriating, but Dan checks his every minute. He holds it in between us, displaying a bitcoin ticker.

Nothing happens at first. There's billions stored in bitcoin, and it takes an exceptional event to move the needle. Twenty minutes goes by without a noticeable change. At just past twenty-five, there's a tick, and the price jumps up two percent.

This has almost no effect on my equity, but it means everything for the artificial intelligence algorithms watching currencies around the world.

At forty-five minutes, the bitcoin hits four hundred and fifty dollars, up 10 percent from our purchase price. From there, Dan's phone display becomes like a spinning display counter, the price rolling up every time the phone polls for new data, which it does every few seconds in response to the ever-changing values.

It hits six hundred an hour and fifteen minutes after Tomo started buying, and now the entire bitcoin community tries to acquire more coins. Transaction volume is up dozens of times over normal.

"We sell, right?" Dan's nails are all gone. This is a bit out of the ordinary for him.

"No, it's still going up."

"This is too fast. They're going to know something is up."

"It's okay," I say. "Someone big is buying."

The math says Tomo's next buy will be about 1.6 million dollars, and the one after that will be $3.2 million. Neither comes close to the largest exchanges for fiat currency in the history of bitcoin, which are well north of ten million, but it's the pattern of gradually escalating purchases which has to be driving automated buying algorithms into a frenzy.

At two hours, the bitcoin discussion boards are nearly inaccessible under the load. Everyone in every timezone is awake and online. At near as I can estimate, Tomo bought about a hundred million dollars worth of bitcoin. The cryptocurrency is now trading at $2,000. Dan is sweating and pale, both knees bouncing under the table.

"We must sell."

I see him switch to his bitcoin exchange app.

"No, wait." I place my hand over his screen. "It's going to go up more."

"We…we…have…we have to *sell*. Right freaking now." He's like a trapped animal.

I take my hand away. "Fine, sell ten percent every ten minutes. We can lock in our gains."

Bitcoin analysts must be observing the transactions, and they'll have spotted the purchases doubling in size from the same bitcoin address. They'll be monitoring to see if that trend continues, with their finger (or more likely code) on the trigger, waiting to see whether the repeat buyer continues the trend of escalating purchases. If not, the analysts will auto-sell their own coins, attempting to cash in before the market collapses. Automated trading bots will be doing the same, magnifying the impact of any trends.

Meanwhile, somewhere inside Tomo, engineers are undoubtedly racing to figure out what the hell is happening. The bitcoin-buying code probably hit account transaction limits back around the time it exceeded a hundred thousand dollar buy. The code has a list of backup accounts, a list it pulls from a database with a SELECT query. Instead of the normal two matching rows, the query now returns the entire list of Tomo bank accounts sorted in descending order by their transaction limit along with the necessary account credentials.

In a worst case scenario, this could financially harm Tomo, but I have strong confidence in the ops team. They can freeze the bank accounts, change the bank authorization, or find the server and kill the running process or the server itself. The thing is, nothing would seem wrong for the first hour. Probably at an hour and half, they'd discover the problem. It'd take them ten, twenty minutes to assign the right people to work on the problem. Those people take time to come up to speed, then they'd be racing to solve the problem... I know what they would do.

At two hours and twenty minutes, two teens sitting at the next table are using the library's free computer terminal, looking at pictures of their female classmates. One of them yells, "Damn, dude. Tomo's down. They kicked you off."

"Sell," I say to Dan. "Whatever's left. Now, all of it."

Dan's been near catatonic with anxiety for so long that at first he doesn't move, then he jerks upright and jabs at his phone.

Now *I'm* biting my nails.

"$7,600," Dan says in a squeak.

Bitcoin is up almost twenty times what we bought it for only a few hours ago. Counting our combined contributions, and gradual sell-off, Dan has three hundred thousand in his bitcoin account, of which $220,000 is mine.

Tomo is almost certainly off the net because someone smart realized killing all outbound traffic would stop the purchasing server from making its next buy. They're probably triangulating on the specific server right now. In the meantime, they stopped a tens of millions dollar bitcoin purchase by shutting down the entire network. It's what I would have done.

"They're going to know." Dan says, still pale. "Trace it to back to me. It's not anonymous you know. They'll see I made all this money in a couple of hours. I don't want to go to jail—I've got a girlfriend."

"Think about it. How many people made money today? How many need to cash out? Hundreds of thousands. Not just you. Bitcoin miners and speculators around the world. Millions of transactions occurred. You made a half dozen of them. They aren't going to trace anything to you."

Dan looks modestly reassured, and nods along with my explanation.

Of course, if that was really true, if there was that little risk, then I could have made the trade myself. There is some risk, though Dan is squeaky clean. He's not the one doing anything illegal, and if it comes down to it, there's nothing he can go to jail for. I can't withstand that level of scrutiny.

"Don't withdraw the cash all at once," I say. "Anything over $10,000 requires notifying the fed. Take out six or seven thousand in cash, every week. You take your percentage, meet me here on Friday mornings, and give me my cut. Sound good?"

He nods. "My book." He points towards *Neuromancer* like it was a poisonous snake.

I pass it toward him, and as I do, I look down at my hand. My fingerprints are on the book. I pull it back toward me.

"I'll keep this. You report it lost in a few weeks."

"You can't keep a library book. It's public property."

"Don't worry, you can afford the fine. See you later, Danger."

CHAPTER 16

MAT MENTIONED INDIEWEB, and when I first research it, there's almost too much for me to read: the grassroots effort has spawned a sprawling wiki and dozens of web sites. There are principles, how-to pages, protocol specifications, history, and nobody is in charge of any of it. It's decentralized, self-organizing, and rapidly changing.

The first principle is so compelling, I know they're onto something important: *When you post something on the web, it should belong to you, not a corporation.*

My reading increases my desire to meet Amber, but only when I'm done with my bitcoin manipulations do I have the time and energy to meet. We make contact and plan dinner at Bamboo Sushi.

Amber's already here, sitting at the sushi bar, easily recognizable from her profile picture. She's American, but chatting with the chef in Japanese, fluently as far as I can tell.

"Amber? I'm Angie."

Amber glances up from the chef and smiles. Without hesitation, she bends her right arm at the elbow and touches her upper arm to mine. It's rare to meet someone who knows the right protocol for greeting an amputee, let alone carries it off so smoothly.

"Have you been here before?" Amber asks. "It's my favorite."

"First time."

Soon we're chatting about the menu. Before we order, the sushi chef brings over several plates, and says something in Japanese.

"Hiro says they're compliments of the house."

I raise an eyebrow.

"Sorry. I travel frequently to Japan, and Hiro told me to visit his hometown. I met his mother. Ever since then, he gives me sushi. But you probably didn't set this up to discuss fish."

"No, I really want to talk about IndieWeb."

Amber stares at me like she's assessing my worth. "So you said in your email. I looked up your profile. You work for Tomo. IndieWeb is…well, the exact opposite of everything Tomo stands for."

"I left Tomo. I'm working on a new project."

"What's that?" She grabs a piece of sushi with the back end of her chopsticks, then passes the serving plate over.

"Decentralized, decomposed social networking."

Amber smiles and laughs. "I love it. Even the employees of the Evil Empire are peeling away to join the Rebel Alliance." She takes a bite, then continues. "IndieWeb is about returning the web to what it was before—a bunch of home-brew websites. People create content, they should own that content. Too many companies went out of business and lost all of their users' data."

My heart beats faster. She understands!

"Yes!" I jab at the table. "Users are completely dependent on the goodwill of companies for access to their own data. If Tomo changes their retention policy, old photos disappear. Or private photos turn public with a change in sharing policy. When I joined Tomo, it was about empowering the user. Now it's about controlling the user to maximize ad revenue."

Amber nods. "That's why the first principle of of IndieWeb is each person is in control of what they create. Take a basic website, the way it worked in the old days, before blogging services and social media. If you wanted to share ideas, you'd write HTML, upload a few files on your server, and share the link. Five or ten years later, your data is still there, still readable, still linkable. If you want to take the data away, you remove your file from the server. You're totally in control."

"How do you bootstrap?" I ask. "How do you solve the empty network problem?"

"How do we convince people to adopt IndieWeb in a world where nobody cares about it?"

I nod, and grab a piece of fish.

"Metcalf's Law is a bitch," Amber says. "The IndieWeb solution is POSSE. Post on Own Site, Syndicate Elsewhere. You create content on your own domain, then copies are automatically shared to Tomo and other networks, with links back to the original version. Your friends and family keep using whatever silo they're on to read your stuff."

It strikes me that I want to build a new type of social network, but I don't have a circle of friends and family to read my posts, or anything to even share. The only thing I ever talk about online is hacking in conversations hidden away in darknet forums. What would I post about? Who would read it? There are precisely two people I give a damn about: Thomas and Emily.

How can a social isolationist expect to make a social network? I'm crushed under the hopelessness of what I'm trying to do.

Amber looks expectantly at me, and I replay what she was talking about—oh, yeah, syndication.

"How can you expect Tomo to allow you to do that indefinitely? What if IndieWeb, or something else, becomes a threat? Won't they shut down the ability to replicate content on Tomo?"

Amber shrugs. "IndieWeb content is the web. That's it. Is Tomo going to shut down the Internet? Make it so you can't see public web articles? They aren't that powerful."

My mind immediately jumps to PrivacyGuard, and the plan to filter webpages with private data. The web turned dystopia. Oh yeah, Tomo could do that, and they will. Unfortunately, I can't share those details with Amber.

"Tell me about what you're working on," Amber says. "Decentralized, decomposed social networking. You must have your own ideas."

I explain how I want to break apart the pieces of social networking—content authoring, content storage, notifications, user identity, friend networks, content selection algorithms, feed readers—and make them all interoperate. "I'm prototyping now, defining and building RESTful interfaces. With a complete protocol definition, anyone could build an interchangeable component."

Amber shakes her head. "There's a better way."

My first thought is *stupid kid, what do you know?* She's half my age and doesn't have any idea what I'm capable of. She probably writes database queries that iterate over a single row at a time. I don't possess much of a poker face unless I'm trying. She must see what I'm thinking.

"Obviously you can define messages in JSON. You absolutely can. But according to IndieWeb principles, you're doing it backwards. You've looked at RSS, right?"

"Of course."

"It's totally pointless. It's an XML representation of a blog post, in theory to make a machine-readable version of the content. But why? The blog content already exists in HTML. HTML is XML. If you want a machine-readable form of a blog, instead of defining a secondary representation, mark up the HTML with extra tags. It's what we call micro formats in IndieWeb, and you already see little bits and pieces of this in the semantic web and HTML5."

The individual words make sense, but I don't grok the whole.

She grabs a laptop from her bag.

"You want to exchange information between two sites about a person. Your way, the protocol-first approach, would have you define JSON to represent that person. Something like this…" She cranks out text in an editor.

```
{
    "Person": {
        "Name": "Angie Benenati",
        "Url": "http://angiebenenati.com",
        "Email": "angie@angiebenenati.com",
        "Photo": "http://angiebenenati.com/angie.png"
    }
}
```

"Yeah. Of course." In fact, my protocol does look similar to this.

"You'd agree we could represent the same thing in XML, and it would be functionally identical?" Amber bangs out a little a few example lines.

```
<person>
    <name>Angie Benenati</name>
    <url>http://angiebenenati.com</url>
</person>
```

"Yeah, that's the same."

"Now, isn't that information already present?" Amber brings up my website, and there it is, sitting in the upper-right hand corner: my name, my email address, my photo, my bio.

"It's not machine readable like the JSON or XML," I say. "The HTML used to display this is unstructured, just a div and some paragraphs. It's impossible for me to write code that can tell the email address from the phone number from my bio, because they're all just strings of text."

"So structure it." Amber goes back to her text editor, copies the source from my site and adds class tags to my HTML.

```
<div class="h-card">

    <img class="u-photo" src="http://angiebenenati.
com/angie.png"/>

    <a class="u-email" href="angie@angiebenenati.
com">email me</a>

    <a class="u-url" href="http://angiebenenati.
com">website</a>

    <p class="role">Angie is a data analyst at Tomo
and former security consultant.</p>

</div>
```

"It's the same data," she says, "but instead of two different representations, you've got one. It's the user interface *and* it's machine readable. If you later add phone numbers or addresses to your UI, you don't implement that twice. Just once."

"These things are already defined?"

"Sure," she says. "People, events, reviews, tags, even social relationships."

My mind reels. This is half the work laid out in front of me.

CHAPTER 17

THIS IS MY FOURTH APPOINTMENT WITH CHARLOTTE. We haven't really talked about anything so far. Each of my last several visits I arrived in a state of anxiety, and she spent the time having me practice coping tools. She asked on the last visit if I was interested in a referral to a psychiatrist for anxiety medication, but I shook my head. Drugs seem like another way to lose control of myself.

When I arrive at her office, I sit on the couch for a change, plopping onto the cushion with gusto. I'm still excited about yesterday's discussion with Amber.

Charlotte sits in her own chair with a pad of paper. The office is quiet, the noises of city traffic filtering through the ninth floor window, making it sound far away. The room is a little on the warm side, and I can feel the sun streaming in, heating the room up.

I smile at myself. I started my grounding practice subconsciously out of habit even though I'm not at all anxious today.

"You're in a good mood," Charlotte says. "Want to talk about it?"

I tell the story of the meeting with Amber and of her ideas, and I'm animated, my arm waving about as I draw pictures in the air, architecture boxes of how servers communicate. Charlotte would be lucky to understand a quarter of what I'm saying, but it feels so good to be talking to another person about creating something so exciting. It helps that she's a good listener, asking questions at all the right places. They aren't the technical questions I might have asked, but they're still interesting ones.

"The decision to leave Tomo to work on this is relatively recent. What made you decide to build Tapestry?"

Where do I begin? I can't say killing people eats away at the fragile remains of my humanity. I can't ask which is worse, what those assholes do, or that I reach out and rip their lives from them. Maybe I could tell the story of Tomo, and how they're abusing billions of users, manipulating everyone to extract one more piece of data, one more minute of screen time, one more layer of entanglement into their universe so they can hold everyone's relationships and content hostage. But that is too personal, too intricately linked to my own past experiences, and I don't want to discuss those either.

Charlotte clears her throat softly, and I glance up at her. She smiles and waits.

I swallow, try to start, and the words stick in my throat. I try again. "There are two sides to everything: creation and destruction. When I finished college, I went on a job interview."

↻

1993, twenty-two years old

"Angelina Benenati?" The secretary looks at me. I'm the only one in the waiting room.

"Angie, please."

"Mr. Repard is ready to see you. Follow me."

Last week I interviewed at this same office, with a dozen different people over eight hours. They say all the Big Six accounting firms have tough interviews, though I found the questions simple. I could have answered them while still cranking out code. Still, a security job here is my dream, and I've been waiting around the clock to hear back.

I received a call yesterday, and was told only to come back so Repard can meet me.

I hung up confused. I was neither given the job, nor rejected. Repard is known throughout the hacker world. It's hard to imagine him taking an interest in a potential candidate. Nonetheless, I'm here, dressed in my one skirt suit, carrying a small purse, a serious case of impostor syndrome leaving me feeling like a parody of a smart, eager employee-to-be.

The secretary opens a door to an office and ushers me in. "Miss Benenati, Mr. Repard."

She closes the door.

There's a guy in a white T-shirt with the number 2600 across the front, and he's typing furiously at a computer. His hair is graying, and he wears thin-framed glasses. On the back of his chair there's a suit jacket, and on his filing cabinet, a hanger with a white dress shirt and a tie.

I wait for a minute, standing, then clear my throat quietly.

"Sit down, and don't interrupt again."

Jesus. This is Repard? I sit, inching into the chair to avoid any noise, and wait. I glance at my watch, and decide to time him. Time passes slowly when you're watching someone else type. I wonder if making me wait is some sort of power trip for him, and whether taking off his suit jacket and shirt is his way of thumbing his nose at management.

Seventeen minutes go by, and the typing stops. He leans back in his chair, puts his hands behind his neck, and smiles. He stays like that for a while, staring at the ceiling, face creased wide. His eyes slowly come back down and resolve on me.

"Miss Benenati, sorry for making you wait."

"Angie, please."

"Not Angel of Mercy?"

My throat catches, and I'm dumbfounded for a second. "I'm not sure what you mean," I manage eventually.

"Come on. You want to work as a penetration tester. Every newbie cracker wants to earn money to hack. You think we wouldn't do a little background research?"

"I guess you got me." My stomach churns as I try to force a smile to my lips. Are they going to count my past hacks against me? What does he even know about?

Repard stares at me. "How'd you pay for school? MIT isn't cheap, and they didn't give you a scholarship until your second year."

He must have access to MIT's systems. I'm impressed. I could never break into their finance systems. "I had savings. From my parents."

"Bullshit. You and your mother were living in a one-bedroom apartment in Brooklyn next to the 86th street line. You had subway cars running right outside your window. If you had money, you would have lived somewhere else."

I drum my fingers on my skirt. Shit, I guess I've got nothing to lose by telling him. "I won the Z100 Corvette contest in '91."

Repard looks off into the distance. "They gave away a ZR-1 Corvette?"

"Two of them. One in July and one in August. I won both."

Repard sits upright, and peers at me over his glasses. "How?"

"I shunted all incoming calls, routed them through my own PBX, and forwarded them on to Z100. When they got to the hundredth caller, I disconnected the caller and took their place."

"You have your own PBX?"

"Dumpster-diving. I picked up a used Merlin."

Repard laughs. "Brilliant. But...problematic. You can't hack if you work here."

I nod in the direction of his computer. "That was the Federal Reserve Board you infiltrated while I was sitting here."

"Yes. They're our client, and we're paid to assess their security."

"You didn't just hack them?"

"No, I performed penetration testing to evaluate potential weaknesses."

"You hacked them. I can do that."

"You've got the skills. The question is, can I trust you to do only your job and not freelance or abuse the power you'd have?"

"I did what I needed to do to get by. I aced all of my classes, and received a full scholarship my second year. I haven't..." I was about to say I hadn't done any other hacks, though who knows exactly what Repard might know. "I haven't done any *major* hacks since then."

"You're still active on Chatsubo."

He even knows the board where I hang out. I don't even use the Angel of Mercy handle there, not anymore.

"I stay current."

"Good." He nods to himself. "You'll want to know all the latest exploits."

He turns back to his computer, and gets absorbed.

Do I have a job or not? What the hell?

"You could have gotten into the Fed quicker. That was a Cisco 2500. There's an authentication flaw."

"I know, Miss Benenati," he says without looking away from his screen. "My goal is to find *all* the vulnerabilities, not only the obvious ones." He's silent except for that furious typing again.

I'm about to clear my throat again, when he speaks up.

"Still, it is impressive you recognized the Cisco from a few lines of output eight feet away at nearly right angles from the screen. Tell my secretary you're hired. You'll be reporting to me. Also, ask her to buy me a privacy screen for my monitor."

I wait, but he says nothing else. I let myself out as quietly as possible, and give an air high-five to no one.

↻

"Hacking has a destructive and a creative side," I say. "And Repard saw that. He wanted me to channel my energy toward something constructive."

"He did some breaking in of his own to obtain your college records and find out where you lived. In 1995 that information wasn't sitting there on the Internet. How do you feel about him prying into your personal life?"

I shrug. "A little weird, I guess. But it had happened lots of times before, when I was a teenager. I'd done it plenty of times myself. It was…uncomfortable, but not unexpected."

"You've done what yourself?"

"Doxxing. Assembling information on someone to level the playing field." My missing right arm twinges, and I briefly recall the hard edges of my Amiga mouse under my right hand, bringing up a CLI or shell window, moving files into directories. I focus on the scratchy feeling of the couch cushion fabric under my left hand. "It was what we all did in the eighties. To survive."

Charlotte's eyebrows raise a little in surprise, and she jots something down. "To survive? Really?"

"It was the Wild West back then, and we fought each other as much or more than we fought the system. Stupid stuff like getting slighted in a conversation or booted off a system would start wars over turf and reputation. Our electricity and phone lines were shut off several times. We were almost evicted once."

"I'm confused how this forced you into hacking."

"Someone would have it in for you, they'd mess with your life. You'd hack them back to show them you were more powerful than they were, make them back off. There was no other option."

"That's scary."

I remember the fights with my mother, the accusations that I had caused the hell we went through. The ever-present anxiety every day over what new disaster I'd find when I returned home from school, and the panic over whether I'd be able to fix it. I nod in agreement.

"Why didn't you go to the police?"

I laugh. "In the eighties? The police had no clue what hacking or social engineering was. They couldn't do anything. It's not much better now."

"But did you ever try? Even ask? You were being harassed. Did you ask anyone for help?"

"No." I don't like where this conversation is headed. It's only one step from "Why didn't you do anything?" to "It's your fault." I don't want the responsibility for this placed on me.

Charlotte makes more notes in her pad, her pen audible as it travels over the paper. "Why'd you become involved with these people at all? What year was this?"

"About '86, '87."

"Pretty unusual to be involved in computers back then, and I'd guess even more unlikely to encounter a bunch of computer hackers. Why not avoid them?"

"I didn't ask to be attacked. It just happened. I defended myself." Fist clenched, my blood pounds thick in my ears. I'm so angry, and I don't even know why.

"Let's take a few slow, deep breaths."

"I don't want—"

Charlotte lifts her head a little and breathes in through her nose.

Damn her. I breathe in through my nose.

We both sit there breathing for a few moments.

"How are you feeling?"

"I don't know why I got so angry."

"That's okay. Talking can be uncomfortable sometimes." She glances at the clock. "We're almost out of time. Think back to when you came into the office. Remember how you felt, so excited about Tapestry?"

"Yes." There's a little twitter in my heart thinking about it.

"Dwell on that when you leave here. It's a happy place for you. Sometimes, when people have emotions that are hard to deal with, they bury those emotions for a long time and never deal with them. That's not healthy. Sometimes people brood on those emotions forever, and never move past them. That's not healthy either. There's a middle ground, a place where we can process more challenging feelings when we're ready, and when we have the right support. When we don't feel as ready, or supported, we make an effort to focus on things that are easier for us. It's a coping mechanism, like grounding or breathing. Give yourself permission to choose what feelings you want to focus on, and to move back and forth depending on how you're feeling. I'll see you next week."

I leave, more confused than when I went in.

CHAPTER 18

WHEN I MET MAT a few weeks ago, he offered to set up a weekly coffee with me. Although I didn't take him up on it, now I want to talk to him. Neither Thomas nor Emily will understand the slightest bit about why micro formats are so exciting.

I email Mat, and we agree to meet the next morning at Coava coffee on Grand Avenue, halfway between my house and Mat's downtown office.

I start recounting the details of meeting Amber earlier that week. I'm barely a few sentences in when Mat holds up a hand for me to stop.

"It sounds fascinating, but I've got a customer call in thirty minutes. Let's cut to the chase. You're trying to figure out how much to offer her, right?"

"Uh, what?"

"You want to hire Amber. That's why I introduced you two. She's a natural fit."

"Well, not really," I say. "I thought I'd go it alone for a while."

"What do you mean?" Mat sucks down his pour-over, and I wonder if all Brits drink coffee the way he does. "You can't compete with Tomo *by yourself.* You need to both build the thing and contrive to bring partner businesses onboard. Getting to scale will require special expertise on the engineering and marketing side. There's only one way to make all that happen in a timely fashion, and that's with a team. Stop trying to do everything alone."

I don't want to work with other people. I like my space, my boundaries. I'm not even sure I know how to work with anyone else. Other people means having to compromise, spending time communicating instead of doing, having to convince them of what I want.

I want to spend my time with beautiful lines of code, not messy, complex people. Communication should be through keyboard shortcuts for my text editor. The kind of convincing I like is coaxing information out of tables with one less database hit. I want to sculpt an intellectual Japanese garden: clean, precise, ordered.

Mat's staring, waiting for me to say something. I hear his message, I do. The books I've read said the same exact thing. The success of a startup is all about having the right team, a broad set of skills. Eventually I'll need to hire people, but I hoped to postpone it as long as possible.

Damn it. I squeeze my fist under the table. The idea of working with someone else terrifies me. But I want to succeed. More than I've wanted anything in a long time.

"Hypothetically, if I was ready to *maybe* consider bringing someone else on board, how would I know if she's the right person?"

Mat smiles as though he's won some small victory. "Are you compatible? Can you communicate? Does she have expertise you need? Is she passionate about what you want to do? Can you imagine working side-by-side with her for the next couple of years?"

Jesus. Years? My mind can't grasp the concept. I've never worked that closely with another person for any length of time.

Mat's shifting his bag onto his shoulder and stuffing his napkin into his coffee cup.

"Maybe," I say.

"Sometimes you take a leap of faith." Mat stands, begins to walk away. "Offer her 5 percent of the company and the same salary you're drawing. You can figure out the rest later."

I dumbly realize I don't even know what it means to give her 5 percent of the company. How does one do that? Thomas's specialty is intellectual property law, but he's still a lawyer. Maybe he knows. A few text messages later, and we're on for dinner.

I stare at my phone, wondering what I'm getting myself into.

CHAPTER 19

THOMAS AND I discuss hiring Amber at dinner.

The sum total of the funding for Tapestry is $220,000, the money I'd gotten from manipulating the bitcoin market. With very little savings outside of that, I need that money to live on. If I work alone, it could provide me with more than two years of runtime to bootstrap Tapestry. Hiring Amber means parting with some of my money.

We review the basics of company structures and control at dinner. As long as I own a majority of the stock, I can pick the directors and in effect control the company. If I give up more than 50 percent of the company to investors or other employees, I'd no longer be in absolute control.

"Why would anyone give away control of their company?" I ask him.

Thomas shrugs. "You can have absolute control over something doomed to failure because you don't have enough money to accomplish what needs doing, or conditional control over something more likely to succeed, in which case, you'll maintain control as long as you're doing a good job."

"No investors," I say. I won't let anyone else have control. It's almost enough to consider another bitcoin manipulation. I risked fifteen thousand last time and multiplied my money by fourteen. If I did that again, I'd have enough for a team of employees for a couple of years. But like a magician, you never want to repeat a trick. That's how you get caught.

"Then you'll need to start small, and grow slowly." Thomas spears another bite from his plate.

I nod as I take a sip of wine. Is there some other financial trick I might try? It's not really my specialty, and at least one lesson I learned from Repard is that the heat is always hottest for financial crimes.

Thomas sleeps over that night, but I toss and turn so much I feel bad for disturbing his sleep. I grab my pillow and a blanket and move to the living room couch, where I stare at the stars through the big living room window.

Hiring Amber scares me, though I recognize that's an emotional reaction, not an analytical one. She's smart, she knows the space well, and she's passionate. I didn't quit Tomo to do this half-assed. I quit to maximize my chance of succeeding, of actually creating a worthy competitor.

Bringing Amber on board is the next logical step. If I don't do it, I'm letting my fears rule me. I turn onto my side and pull the blanket up. I'll call her in the morning.

ひ

Amber and I meet for a very early lunch at a Thai restaurant. We're in the back corner, the only people there.

I cut to the chase, and tell her I want to her to work with me. We go back and forth a bit, and eventually settle on her getting 10 percent of the company and a long-term salary comparable to her existing one. Until we take on investment or earn a regular source of income, she agrees to take only as much as my own draw. Now I'll burn through my pool of money twice as fast.

Amber offers up her spare bedroom as a place we can work together. I hadn't even thought of the issue of office space. After lunch, we check it out together.

That afternoon I contact a law firm Thomas recommended, and one of the partners agrees to meet me the next day as a professional courtesy to Thomas. The paperwork is drawn up, and by the next Monday Amber and I go in to sign the documents together.

On Tuesday morning we go together to Ikea and pick out furniture, then drive back to her place. I'm screwing a desk leg onto the top using a cordless drill when I notice Amber watching my one arm technique.

"That's impressive."

"Not so hard. I'm doing it singlehandedly."

She laughs and we flip the desk over together.

"We have an office!" I say, a bit proud of this moment.

We simultaneously glance around at the mess of cardboard boxes and packing material from the furniture.

"Let's take care of that in a bit," Amber says. "Beer?"

"Sure."

Amber comes back in with two glasses. "It's called Whit Faced," she says, gesturing with the glass. "Local brewer friend makes it once a year."

We chink our glasses together, and I take a sip. It's crisp with a hint of clove and orange.

Amber sits on one of the desks. "I was thinking about Tapestry over the weekend. There's two big pieces of existing work we can leverage. Diaspora was a distributed social network launched in 2010. It's got the idea of multiple nodes in the network, and they've defined protocols to enable those nodes to communicate. And IndieWeb, along with everything it brings: POSSE syndication, notification, micro formats."

"IndieWeb doesn't handle selective visibility of content," I say. "Everything is either public or private."

Amber taps a finger on the desk. "Before social networking, we had the web for public stuff, and forums for discussions."

"Which were themselves rooted in the BBSs of the eighties," I say. "We still have forums. More than ever before."

"More in absolute numbers, but as a percentage of all Internet users, fewer than ever. The reason I bring it up is because forums foster a different kind of community, especially in the old days. Most people in a forum knew each other, had social norms specific to that community."

I nod. "So forums develop deeper human connection than social media?"

Amber stands, one finger on her nose, and stares at the wall.

I glance at the wall, don't see anything there.

"Sorry," she says. "I'm picturing my bookcase, trying to remember if I read anything on this."

"In my experience," she goes on, "forums are better at establishing new friendships. How many new friends have you made on Tomo?"

Damn. Right to questions I don't like to answer. "None, but I'm weird. Don't go by me. How about you?"

She shakes her head. "Not as many as I made in the days of forums. Social media maintains existing friendships, but doesn't create new ones."

"Why?"

She shrugs. "Forums are more cohesive somehow. Usually they're closed. They have a common purpose. A moderator keeps the community on track." She grabs a marker, makes notes on a cardboard box.

"We need whiteboards."

She nods. "Tomo has a groups feature, although, of course, it's another silo. Since we're going to be open, we must define interfaces so Tapestry can interact with forums. There are lots of forums out there. Better integration will breathe more life into them."

We go back and forth like that, slowly working our way through Amber's hyper-local beer supply, into the wee hours of the night. Sometime during the late night I realize I've not only gained a business partner, but maybe also a friend.

CHAPTER 20

AMBER AND I WORK TOGETHER every day, our energy feeding each other. The weekend comes and goes without a break, and I don't mind a bit. I've never been one to vegetate on a couch watching television, and I'm certainly not going to do it now when we're making so much progress. I wake each morning tired but excited to return to work at Amber's house.

The days turn into weeks. Toward the end of our work days, coding slows down, and we spend our time discussing and arguing until late in the night. Amber works around the clock, with the stamina of a grad student weeks from her thesis. I usually peel off around ten or eleven, after the texts from Thomas peak, then slow down.

```
Angie> Not tonight. Working late.

Thomas> You worked late the last four nights. Take
a break.
```

I can't take a break. Amber just keeps going. I'm the owner, the founder. I force myself to work as many hours as her. It was my idea, after all. But I'm nearly twice her age, and after a few weeks I give up my attempts to equal her hours, and settle for merely working harder than I've ever worked since Tomo's first year.

I come back in the mornings, let myself in quietly while Amber sleeps, and see what's changed during the night. One long wall we covered with cheap whiteboard panels hot-glued to the sheetrock, and in the mornings the boards are usually covered with new diagrams, arrows pointing every which way, which I then puzzle out. I check those out first, then review the git history to see what changes Amber committed after I left.

One night I come home a little after midnight, exhausted, my brain fried, and make the mistake of sitting down on my couch. The next thing I know, I crack my eyes open, crusty and tired, to find it's midmorning. I stumble to my feet and head to the bathroom for a shower.

Standing there, letting the hot water run over me, watching it spin down into the drain, I find myself wondering about my VW van. Where is it now? Is someone living in it? Add up all the hours I spent holed up there, researching people, penetrating their phones, computers, and lives, maintaining my tools and infrastructure. I spent way more time on that than I ever did on my day job at Tomo.

Now I barely have the minutes in my day to brush my teeth and shower. The time and energy I spent killing abusive assholes held me back. There's no way I could do both.

I turn off the water and grab my towel. As I dry off, I remember the pile of carefully sanitized laptops sitting in my closet. Encrypted hard drives packed with utilities ranging from remote administration tools to port scanners to assorted infectious malware. A bag of burner phones. Pirated SIM cards. A toolkit I use for disabling GPS and bluetooth on devices. Directional antennae. An expensive software-defined radio. Thumb drives to hold USB viruses. That's a lot of evidence surrounding me that is, if not incriminating, at least highly suggestive of wrongdoing. I'm not killing anyone now, though I might as well be driving around with a trunkful of guns.

It's not worth the risk. I'm not ever going back to that life.

When I'm done in the bathroom, I message Amber and tell her I'm taking care of personal stuff this morning and won't be over until the afternoon.

I go through my condo and make a heap of electronics on my bed. Although hacking doesn't require much specialized hardware, I took the time to prep all this equipment, removing unnecessary transmitters, anything that could leak my location or data. The software on the drives is mostly superfluous. Encrypted backups of everything are stored in the cloud. If I needed to, I could recreate this. I have a few long-term assets that aren't in my apartment, and I'm not going to dispose of those, but neither are they likely to lead back to me.

I've never dumped so much equipment so fast, but I make a general plan. Everything's triple-encrypted, so in theory there's no risk of anyone accessing my data, but there's no harm in zeroing everything out, so the drives appear empty rather than full of encrypted information. I set up all the laptops on my dining room table and then boot them with a keystroke that invokes custom firmware to erase the hard drives and restore the original OS images from a backup file.

The NSA can recover data even when it's been overwritten by multiple passes of zeros, so I ultimately trust more in my encryption than the wipe. But a wipe is what the average, modestly secure individual would do, so it's less likely to raise suspicions.

Layers upon layers of security and misdirection. I honestly can't say if I love it or hate it. A little bit of both, I guess, though it'll be a relief to put all this to rest.

When everything's done, I vacuum the laptops, blow them down with compressed air, and then wipe them down with screen wipes. Wearing gloves, I separate the gear into bags, then load them all into my car.

One goes into a residential garbage can left out by the curb. Another bag gets dropped off by a park near a high school. I drop one bag off at Free Geek, another at Goodwill. One goes into a dumpster behind a grocery store. Individually, they are nothing. Only together do they make a pattern.

I experience a sharp pang of regret as I drop off the final bag. I let it slip slowly from my fingers. It's okay. They are only tools. I have backups. Still, I'm throwing away bits of my life.

I return to my car and breathe deeply, trying to shake off some weird mix of grief and fear. I hit the stereo, fire up Suicide Commando, and crank the volume to drown out my feelings.

CHAPTER 21

AMBER AND I ARE GOING ON TWO MONTHS working together, when I come in one morning to discover a wide swath of board wiped clean. Foot-high letters spell out "SOLVED EMPTY NETWORK" with no clue as to what the solution is. She hasn't checked in any code.

I have a moment of panic, imagining Amber developed a great epiphany, an insight as deep as any of the core breakthroughs in science, only to have been killed or kidnapped during the night. I take off my shoes and walk down the hallway in my socks on the hardwood floors, and carefully peek into her bedroom.

I've only glimpsed it before. I open the door slowly, unveiling shelves covered in small Japanese toys and memorabilia from around the world. It's surprisingly pink, given that Amber displays few girlish tendencies. In the dim light, I see the enormous bookcase she often grabs references from. Sometimes during our discussions, Amber runs in here, grabs a book by yet another social scientist or anthropologist I've never heard of, then comes back to read me a prophetic passage written in the early seventies or some other equally unlikely time period that exactly addresses whatever topic we're working on.

"People who are depressed spend more money on what they buy," she announced one day, and five minutes later delivered a book open to the page citing the research. "Advertisers want sentiment analysis because those prospective customers are valuable, not because they care how people feel. I'll bet the data shows they charge those customers more."

I used my backdoors into Tomo that night to verify Amber's conjecture, and it was true: the same company advertising the same product to multiple people would increase the price by as much as twenty percent depending on how depressed people were.

This morning all I see is a half-empty bookcase, the remaining books collapsing over each other, since half of Amber's library is now haphazardly scattered around the room we use as an office.

There, on her bed, is Amber, dressed, lying face down. I watch, waiting until I see the rise and fall of her body. She's still breathing. A false alarm then. Nobody came and killed Amber in the night. Her insight survives.

I return to the office and dispense boiling water out of the Zojirushi kettle to heat the glassware we use to brew coffee, then fire up the burr grinder.

When we established the pattern that I'd come over in the mornings before Amber woke, I tried to grind the beans the night before, so I wouldn't wake her in the morning with the noise. She raised an eyebrow in alarm at the notion of pre-grinding, and built the little acoustic chamber of fiberglass batting and flannel now surrounding the grinder.

I drink my pour-over when it's done brewing, and peruse her code changes. She optimized the path notifications take to trickle through the system, but there's no sign of anything having to do with empty networks.

Finally, around ten, she pokes her head in, grunts, and heats up the coffee apparatus again. I don't try to speak to her. It's not until the second cup of coffee that she approaches partial functioning.

I wait patiently, head down, reading articles Mat forwarded about raising capital. Finally, Amber clears her throat.

"Chatbots."

"Huh?"

"What if we solve the empty network problem by not having an empty network?"

I look down at my coffee cup. Maybe I need more. Chatbots are horrible little bits of code that parse out the nouns of what you type and echo them back to you, pretending at intelligence while being completely idiotic. They do not explain why Amber is now bouncing on the balls of her feet.

"Humor an old lady and explain the whole thing."

"I read a bit of research…" Amber ruffles through piles of papers, magazines, and books hunting for something. "25 percent of adults have no one to confide in. No one to tell their triumphs or problems to. It was a study about social isolation. Isolation has a big impact on health and happiness."

I nod my head. Now this I know about. Victims of abuse are isolated.

"One of the first chatbots from the seventies took the role of a psychologist. People would tell Eliza everything, even though she only had a handful of responses."

"Eliza is not a solution to empty networks," I say. "That'll entertain people for fifteen minutes, maybe. It's not going to keep them on the site for days or weeks, which is what we need."

"Eliza is forty-year-old technology. Chatbots are completely different now. Avogadro Corp was working on email with natural language processing until the project was terminated."

"You want to hire their employees?"

"We can't touch anything from Avogadro. I'm sure it's all locked up in IP agreements. Their stuff was breakthrough, though. I say we independently reconstruct what they did."

The idea tempts, but I shake my head. "No, this is a distraction from building Tapestry. We need to stay focused."

"You want to solve the empty network problem," Amber says. "We make the network useful and fun. That's not a distraction."

"We need to stay focused on our core mission."

"This might be a part of that mission!" Amber clenches her jaw.

"We can't build chatbots and also build a distributed social network. They're two separate things."

"We don't need to build it ourselves." Amber shakes her head at me incredulously. "We hire the right experts to build a chat system. The bots are merely users on the system that don't happen to be human. No extra work for us at all."

Oh, sure. Just hire people. My pool of money is dwindling rapidly. "We don't have the money to hire anyone."

"Well, maybe you should find us some capital," Amber says. "Then it would be more than the two of us working out of *my* house."

Where's this sudden anger coming from? My heart thumps in my chest and my missing arm throbs. I rub the stump and take a few deep breaths. "What's bothering you?"

"We can't build this ourselves. It's a job for a bigger team than the two of us. I'm stressed because I'm trying to keep it all in my head at the same time. I'm all over the code base. I want to turn some of this crap over to someone else, you know? It's tough to bear the brunt on every single challenge. I want to go to sleep some night and know when I wake up, someone else will have fixed something."

"Are you saying I'm slacking? Because I'm working eighty hour weeks here."

Amber rubs her hands over her face. "Don't take it personally. I'm stating facts. I want to work on this. It's going to change the world, but we need help. Why don't you want to raise money?"

I stare at the floor for a moment, then look up. "I'm afraid of losing control of the company to a bunch of white guys in suits. I'm afraid of creating something and having it taken away and twisted into the very same evil I want to stop."

"Not every venture capitalist is a dick," Amber says in a tired voice.

"But it's the power dynamic. Whether they're well-meaning or not, I still don't want them to have control."

"Does this have anything to do with…" She looks at my arm.

"Maybe. Yes." I can't even remember what I've told Amber.

"Okay, fine. I'll back off. But eventually, if you don't raise money, I'm not going to keep doing this. I'm trusting you to raise the money to not only pay me a salary, but make this company succeed, so the years of my life I invest in this company are not wasted. I'm not here to write code. I'm here to make a difference. If you don't do your job, then you're basically crapping on my life."

I'm miserable and exposed, and want to run away. I can't, though, not if I'm ever going to succeed at this.

Shit, this is harder than I ever thought it would be.

CHAPTER 22

I TAKE MY USUAL CHAIR closest to the door, and Charlotte sits opposite me.

"Can we talk about something?" I ask.

"That's what we're here for," Charlotte says.

I talk about my morning with Amber, about her insistence I raise funding and hire more people.

"What do you think?" Charlotte asks.

"She's probably right, although I still don't want to ask a venture capitalist for money."

"Is that your only option? What about borrowing the money? Or looking for a grant for business owners? There's usually assistance for female entrepreneurs."

I shake my head. "Grants and loans get you tens of thousands. That's nowhere near what I would need to take this all the way. A team to create a strong prototype, not even MVP, would be at least a million."

"An MVP?"

"Minimum viable product. The smallest number of features that would be enough for people to use Tapestry. We need about three million to make it to MVP."

"You've given this some thought."

"I guess so."

"What's stopping you from taking the next step?"

"We've been so busy. We haven't had the time. Amber and I have been working around the clock."

Charlotte is silent. I wait her out. Two can play this game.

She smiles at me.

I smile back.

She waits.

"Fine, I grok it. I'll always be this busy because we don't have anyone else, and we don't have anyone else because I haven't raised the money."

"So, why haven't you?"

"Because then a venture capitalist will own a part of the company, which gives them say over how the company is run. If they end up with more than half the voting shares, they can take control anytime they want."

"And contractually, can you prevent that?"

"No VC will accept those terms. If you want money, they want control, so if you screw up, they can take over and get things back on track."

"That sounds reasonable."

"There's nothing to stop them from screwing me over. If they don't like how I'm running the company, if they don't like my mission, they can kick me out. I don't want anyone to have that power over me."

"Any time you enter a relationship, there's a chance the other person will take advantage of you. Nothing provides an absolute guarantee that won't happen. There has to be trust for two people to enter a relationship."

"I don't want trust. I want power. I want control."

"What does power and control mean to you?"

I fiddle with a thread on the arm of the chair. "When I was fifteen, I went to Death's party."

☊

1986, fifteen years old.

We're in the Upper East Side, a few blocks from Central Park. There's four of us, and we're huddled in the cold trying to figure out how to pass the doorman, who wears a blue uniform with matching top hat, and a yellow sash across his chest. He opens the door for an old woman and her poodle. They climb into a chauffeured Rolls at the curb, and the car pulls away. I wonder if the door is real gold.

"We're invited guests," BTS says. "We go up and tell him."

"What are we going to say to him?" I ask.

"We're here to see…" Ruger fiddles with his Zippo.

"We're here to see *Death*. Yeah, that's going to go over well."

"We can't stand around all day," dragon says. "Let's go." He insists on the lowercase d for reasons nobody knows, and I've come to think of him this way, even in my own head.

BTS shoves me forward. I shrug and saunter over, the rest of them falling in behind me.

"Hi, we're here to see our friend."

The doorman looks down at me, takes in my razor blade earrings, my carefully cut up Dead Kennedys t-shirt. His dismissive frown does not indicate approval.

"Whom are you here to see?"

"Death." There's a chorus of giggles behind me. The guys are children.

He consults a piece of paper on a podium and sighs. "Fourteenth floor, apartment 1401." He opens the door very slowly, staring off into the distance.

"No problem," BTS says, once we're inside. "See?"

The elevator opens, and we step in. I hit the button for fourteen, noticing there is no thirteenth floor. The guys crowd needlessly close to me. I wiggle free and go over to the other side of the elevator with an annoyed sigh. They're mostly harmless, but I'm not in the mood to be groped right now. I'm intensely focused on Death's party.

A Zippo snaps open with a metallic pop, and BTS lights a cigarette.

"Don't smoke in here," dragon says, running his hand up and down all the buttons for the floors above fourteen. "Not cool."

"Screw that," BTS says. "I'll smoke where I want."

"Put it out," dragon says.

"Fuck you. It's a Craven A. I'm not wasting a cigarette."

"Hey, idiots," Ruger says, his own pack of Marlboros out, a smoke in his mouth. "We're here. Let's motor."

Ruger holds the pack out to me. I take one and hold it out for a light. He hands me his cigarette, and I light mine off his.

We stroll down the hallway. I trail one finger over opulent wallpaper, and compare it to the shitty little apartment I live in on 86th street in Brooklyn. Someday I'll live in a place like this.

At 1401 Metallica's Master of Puppets bleeds into the hallway from the door. Ruger bangs on the door so hard it shudders in its frame.

A short kid, well, my height, opens the door. "Bill the Skinhead! Rooooga! dragon! Angel of Mercy!" He belts out our handles like he's announcing us to the guests.

"Death." BTS is all cool calm. "Rad party." With a nod, he walks in.

People we know gather at the door to see us, and for a few minutes, we're celebrities.

The couches and chairs in the living room are filled, people arguing the finer points of the new Metallica album, the Amiga versus Atari ST, and whether baud rate is the same thing as bits per second. Conversation hiccups when I enter, and everyone stares at me. I scan the room without meeting anyone's eyes. Three girls present.

I run a Diversi-Dial. Install seven lines from the phone company, plug them into seven modems slotted into an Apple IIe, load the DDial software by cassette tape over the audio port because there's no slots left to plug in a floppy disk drive, and presto: online chat system.

There are four of these chat systems in New York City and about a hundred around the world. In 1986, if you're the sysop of one, you're hot shit. If you're a girl online, you're also hot shit. Combine the two, and I'm molten lava.

By definition, everyone involved in DDial is a geek. You've got to be. You must own a computer, and terminal software and a modem, things computers don't come with. You need to know someone in the community to discover the phone number, then puzzle out modem settings. Finally, you've got to choose to spend your time chatting online instead of in the real world.

For whatever reason, it's almost all guys.

I hang out with Ruger, dragon, and BTS all the time, but the rest of these guys, I mostly chat with online. We hold parties every couple of months, usually when somebody's parents go away for the weekend. dragon had a party at his place last summer, and burnt down half the kitchen. No more parties for him. It's been nearly six months since the last major DDial party. Hence there's been a lot of anticipation for Death's party.

I wander into the dining room, where they're packing a bowl into a giant clear bong. Everyone's crowded around the table, all chairs taken. Ruger's there, and he pulls me onto his lap. Within a few seconds of sitting down, his thing pushes against my butt.

I slept with him once, on his birthday. He's cute enough, and I thought maybe I could be nice to him that one time. That was a mistake. We see each other all the time, and still he hopes for a repeat, even though I've told him no every time he's asked.

In the beginning, I was flattered by the attention, although it's getting old and bothersome now.

The bong comes around, and Ruger takes a long hit, the weed glowing red and sizzling. I lick my lips and swallow, anticipation growing. Finally, he hands me the bong. I inhale, the pot crackling, smoke bubbling up through the water, filling the chamber. I stop when the smoke hits my throat, exhale, and take a huge breath in, sucking as hard as I can. I let go of the carburetor halfway through, and a huge rush of smoke hits my lungs. When the chamber is cleared, I hold my breath. I smile with closed lips and pass the pipe to my left.

"Damn. She emptied the bowl."

A round of cheers goes up.

I stay for another round, then depart before things become too crazy. I'm not here to be falling-down stoned. I've got people to see.

Ruger follows me into the hallway between the dining room and living room. He wraps an arm around my waist, and presses me against the wall.

"Let's do it," he says. "We can go upstairs."

Ruger's almost a foot taller than me, and he's staring down into my eyes. He's big, blond, and strong, and I used to imagine him as a Viking warrior, but in this moment he's weak. His eyes plead with me, tell me he'd do anything to make it with me. This sad puppy thing is a turnoff. I want him to go away, but I don't want to hurt his feelings.

His body is hot against me. One hand slides down my shoulder, around my arm, toward my breast.

He can, and has, lifted me into the air with one arm in the past. Today I nudge his arm aside.

"No. That one time was it."

I shove against his chest, and he resists for a second. I push harder, and he turns sideways, lets me out. I walk down the hallway, and glance back to desperate longing on his face.

I wander around, marveling at Death's place. Granted, he's the same age as me, and this is his parents' apartment, but still, it's amazing. The furniture is heavy, dark wood. The walls are decorated with carved wooden moldings, and there are paintings all over the place.

I compare this to the tiny, bare apartment I share with my mom, where we never know if there's going to be hot water. Worse is Ruger's basement, with his broken walls, countless stinky-ass cats, and the pile of empty soup cans by the sink he can't be bothered to throw out, or even to have heated up in the first place.

I'm sure when Death steps into the shower limitless hot water pours out.

There's one room on this floor with a closed glass door, two heavy arm-chairs blocking the doorway, like maybe Death doesn't want anyone to go in there. It's dark in the room, and I can't see through the door. I push one of the chairs aside, and go in. I fumble for a switch in the dark. When the lights come on, I'm in a library, an actual library, with books on every wall from floor to ceiling. Many are leather-bound, titles gilded on their spines in metallic leaf, their titles unfamiliar. There must be… I do a quick estimate, count the books on a shelf, then count the shelves, and multiply. More than two thousand.

A desk occupies the middle of the room, a huge thing with wooden inlays all over, smelling like polish, battered and aged. Two stacks of unbound paper occupy the middle of the desk. I come around to see neat handwritten script, each page numbered. I lean closer and read something about a war.

"Hey, nobody should be in here!"

My heart jumps in my chest, and I glance up to see Death.

"Oh, it's you." His voice softens.

"What is this?" I ask.

"My father's next book. The famous fucking writer. He'll kill me if he knows anyone came in here."

Death is the opposite of Ruger, scrawny where Ruger is strong, short not tall, nervous, almost trembling in my presence. But he's also the opposite of Ruger: rich, not poor, smart, surrounded by books. He has everything.

I walk up next to him, and his eyes flare as I approach. He's barely an inch taller, and thin as a stick, maybe smaller than me, wearing a black Megadeath T-shirt and black jeans. He's frozen, like a frightened animal. I want to do it with him, with this rich boy in his fancy apartment.

"What's your favorite?" I say, gesturing toward the walls.

"In here?" he says. He shrugs. "I like science fiction, but my father would never have that in his library." He looks around, then points to the opposite wall. "The Prince, by Machiavelli."

"What's it about?" I carefully place a hand on his waist.

"It's about ruling, and…"

He's distracted by my hand, and I edge my fingers up under his T-shirt until I touch bare skin. He trembles slightly. I lean in close, inches from his face, and he gets the hint. We stand there in his library, French kissing, and he wraps me in both arms. His chest presses up against mine, my boobs tingling at the touch. After a few minutes of this, his hand tentatively works its way up my side.

"Let's go up to your room," I say.

He's speechless, but nods and takes me by the hand.

Now we must wind our way through the party. It suddenly feels like everyone knows what we're going to do, and I'm afraid of the snickers and snide remarks that will inevitably come later. Everyone wants to do it, yet the few girls here will likely still condemn me behind my back.

Death was nervous in the library, but at this moment, he's got a grin on his face. I wonder if he's more excited to bring me to his room, or to be *seen* bringing me to his room.

We turn the corner to go upstairs, passing the kitchen where BTS and Ruger chuck bagels at a pyramid of beer cans stacked on the kitchen counter. Death's hand is wrapped tightly around mine, pulling me upstairs, suddenly forceful. I close my eyes and pray Ruger doesn't see us going upstairs.

I'm a little surprised to find Death's bedroom is covered with posters like mine, a huge Iron Maiden *The Number of the Beast* poster dominating the wall at the head of his bed. I thought his room would be like downstairs, fancy, expensive. He locks the door, and the next thing I know, we're on his bed, and he's groping me, then pulling my shirt off.

"Do you have…?"

He nods and reaches into a drawer.

There's a stereo on a shelf next to the bed, and I paw through his cassettes for something suitable. I open the cassette door, slip the tape in, and press play. The button engages with a satisfying thunk, and there's a slight hiss, the recorded drop of a needle onto vinyl between tracks, and Tendencies's *Subliminal* comes on.

I pull off my shirt and kiss him. Soon we're naked, and he's on top of me, doing his thing, which feels good, but I can't help staring at his face. His eyes are closed, his face twisted up in concentration, and he's panting slightly. This party was the biggest event of the last few months, and Death was surely looking forward to it, the clout he'd accrue online for the next few months, until the next bigger thing happened. Instead, what he's going to remember about this night is not his party, but doing it with me. Everyone who was here, all of the events of this night, will pale in comparison to this moment. With nothing except a caress and a kiss, I've toppled the order of things.

I lean up and kiss Death, then bite his lip. He grunts and spasms inside me. He's sweaty, his breath hot in my ear, and then he's kissing me again, the little afterward kisses that are supposed to mean thank you or you're awesome, or something like that. Each touch of his lips is an electrical charge, power flowing from him to me.

Afterward I pull the sheet around me as I find my panties and bra. "Where's the bathroom?"

"Wait. Let's do it again." He's staring at me, adoration on his face.

I lean down to kiss him and he grabs my boob. I push his hand away, and put my bra on. "Maybe another time. People will talk."

"So?"

The same friends who will high-five him when he tells them we did it will turn around and say I'm easy, a slut, when I'm not around. When I am, they'll try to make it with me, too. For him, it's all upside.

For a brief moment, I think it's unfair. Then I recall that feeling in bed, of changing how Death will remember and think about this evening. That's real power. Everyone else's judgement only affects me if I let it. I smile at Death before I leave.

It takes ten minutes in the bathroom to repair the damage. If Death had a sister, with actual girl stuff here, this would be much easier. As it is, I make do with lipstick and an eye pencil I had stuffed in my jeans, and leave the rest of my make-up alone. I wonder if people will smell the sex on me, and briefly consider dousing myself with Death's cologne. One sniff of the bottle makes it clear that would be a mistake.

I wander down the hall to see the person I really came here to spend time with. I head toward a greenish glow coming out of a doorway.

In the room, I take in the dark figure on the couch in a glance, but let my eyes slide past. Play it cool, Angie.

Half a dozen people crowd around two computers in the dim room. My mind reels. Two computers, and they aren't even in Death's bedroom. He's got a dedicated room for them.

I can sit on my bed and type on the keyboard.

They—all boys I don't know— are online, and a surge of pride runs through me, as both computers are connected to MercyStation, my DDial. They're chatting with a girl named Stacey, trying to convince her to come to the party.

I ignore them, and turn to the guy on the couch. The music is only a quarter as loud up here, and it's possible to hold a reasonable conversation.

"Nathan9," I say, as flat and cool as I can manage, although my heart pitter-patters. He's not Case from *Neuromancer*, but he's pretty close.

"Angel." He tips his head in my direction, but he stares off toward nowhere. His seeing-eye dog is at his feet, carefully watching me. "Sit down."

I sit next to him on the couch. He orients his face in my general direction. He's weird, his face misshapen, his eyes scrunched up small. This is so different than chatting online.

"I told them Stacey's not a girl," Nathan9 says, "but they don't believe me."

"Ha, they wouldn't notice a real girl if one walked into the room."

We both smile at that.

"Did you install the modz I sent?" He leans down, feels along his leg, and pats the dog.

"Not yet," I say, "I need to borrow a disk drive from dragon to read the floppy."

"No disk drive?" he smiles, like this is the most foolish thing he's heard. "You're a hacker without a disk drive?"

I bow my head sheepishly, which is sort of pointless, since he can't see me.

"I had to sell mine. I needed the money."

He nods, as though this is normal, though it isn't. Among my friends, they're saving up to buy the next newer computer, not hawking off parts for dinner. The phone company wants payment for all my telephone lines, and the monthly membership people pay for access to MercyStation doesn't quite cover the bills.

"Well, the Hayes SmartModem will do 450 baud with the patch, which will be a nice upgrade. Install the patch." He says the last part with emphasis.

"Can your screenreader keep up?"

Nathan extracts his screenreader from his shirt pocket. "Not this portable one," he says, holding the deck-of-cards-sized device in his hand. "At home, I have one built into my PC."

I nod, realize he can't see me, and say instead "I see," then worry maybe I shouldn't say I see.

"How *do* you get around at home?" I know Nathan lives by himself, but I can't picture it.

"Everything has a place, and I put everything back in its place. That's about it, really. I avoid furniture with pointy corners."

"Wasn't it hard to get used to?" I lean down to pet his dog, and the dog leans toward me.

"Please don't. If his harness is on, he's working." Nathan puts one hand on the dog, steadies him. "I was born this way. It's as natural as can be."

We've never talked much about Nathan's blindness online. But it's different when he's sitting right here in front of me.

We hear a double-click of two modems hanging up their connections simultaneously.

"Crap!" one of the guys says. "Booted off MercyStation at the same time."

I shake my head. "That shouldn't happen."

The modems start their automatic redial in parallel. The buzz of the dial tone is followed by super rapid touch tones. Death's got his modems configured for war-dialing, tweaking the speed at which they send the touch tone frequencies. The maximum pace for every phone line is slightly different, depending on your distance from the phone company exchange and the equipment the exchange runs.

We never hear the squeal of MercyStation answering. In fact, we never even hear a ring. It goes straight to an operator recording. "The number you have dialed is no longer in service."

"What the hell?" I stand, and for the first time, the guys notice me.

"Angel!"

"What happened?"

"I don't know. We were talking to some chick."

"Is there a phone around here?"

Death leans over, grabs something off the table with a long antenna sticking out of it, and hangs it to me. "Cordless telephone," he says. "Switch it to Talk."

I take the phone dumbly. I've heard of a cordless phone, of course, just never expected to use one. I dial my own number, my voice line, to see if it's somehow a problem with my computer.

"The number you have dialed is no longer in service." I hang up. Or rather, slide the switch to off.

"Tell me exactly what happened online right before you got disconnected," I say.

One of the guys, wearing a dungaree jacket, answers. "We were talking to Stacey, and she asked for Angel of Mercy…I mean, you. We didn't know where you were. We tried to convince her to come to the party, but she wouldn't. She said she'd wait for you to come online."

"Did she say anything unusual?"

"No," the dungaree jacket says.

"She did… when she first came on, she said 'hi, you suck.'"

Please let it not be HUS. "Did she spell it y-o-u?"

"No, just the letter u."

"Shit, shit, shit." HUS is the abbreviation we've been using for an unknown pain-in-the-ass who calls into all of the dials and says 'hi, u suck'. I've been aggressively kicking him off whenever he connects, and he's been threatening me for a while.

"He tricked the phone company into shutting down your account," Nathan9 says. "Not bad."

"It's the middle of the weekend!" I scream. "Phone company won't even take account calls until Monday. MercyStation will be down for days. My mother is going to kill me if her phone is out too."

Death and the guys at the computers stare uneasily at me.

"You don't need to wait until Monday," Nathan says. "We fight back. We call, pretend we're a lineman, and ask someone in the central office to flip the right switch."

I've heard of the trick Nathan wants to run. The problem is, I've never done any of this stuff, only heard Nathan and the other old-timers describe it.

"Will you do it?" I ask. I don't even bother fluttering my eyelashes, since he can't see me.

"I could, though it would be better if you learn how. I'll tell you what to say."

Nathan outlines what we're going to do, beginning with calling the phone company on an inside number, a line the public doesn't have. I'll pretend I'm an employee, a repairman who's out on maintenance, who needs them to flip a few switches, enter a few codes. They won't know what they're doing, but if I sound confident and know the lingo, they'll do exactly what I say. Except there's no way I can pull it off.

"No one is gonna believe a girl is a telephone lineman."

Nathan nods sagely. "You play to your strengths, then. You'll be an inside employee. You're on the phone with a lineman, and he's asking you to make changes, but your terminal went down. You need them to make the changes. If they ask, you do data entry configurations for the SCCS maintaining the 1ESS."

"Whoa, what are SCCS and 1ESS?"

"Doesn't matter for our purposes. They're acronyms the central office will be familiar with, and it'll make you sound real. Now dial and put it on speakerphone."

Death closes the door, the music fades away, and everyone is dead silent. Nathan reels off a stream of digits I enter into the phone. There's a series of pulsing clicks, then a buzz for a new trunk line, a ring, and then we're back to a dial tone. "That got us into the New York Stock Exchange's PBX, so they won't be able to trace the call back to here. Now the central office."

He gives me more digits, and I punch them in. We're waiting, static on the line. Nathan reaches out for me with one hand, finds my shoulder, and whispers, "Hear the metallic clanging? We hit an old mechanical relay switch."

The line rings twice and a woman answers. "C.O., Helen speaking."

I rehearse my line in my head and spontaneously decide on a Staten Island accent.

"Hi Helen, this is Angela. I've got a lineman on and he's asked me to reconfigure the 1ESS for central switching, but my terminal went down. Can you help me out?"

Two minutes later, she's done following the instructions Nathan whispers into my ear and I relay. If everything goes correctly, we've bypassed billing and accounting, and directly reconnected my number to the phone exchange.

Nathan whispers. "Tell her to hold while the lineman verifies."

"Please hold for verification," I say, and press my hand over the microphone.

"Redial," I say to Death.

He presses a few keys, the computer modem fast-dials, and a few seconds later, we hear the sweet squeal of MercyStation answering. My heart soars.

"I'm on," Death says. "Everything's normal."

"Thank you," I say to the central office operator, and hang up.

"Congratulations," Nathan9 says. "Not only did you finagle an off-hours phone reconnect, you're also never going to be billed for them again." He laughs so hard his seeing-eye dog raises his head and howls.

ↄ

"Power. You either have it or you don't."

Charlotte glances at the clock. "We're almost out of time, but let's explore this a bit. What happens if you don't have power?"

"You're powerless."

Charlotte gives me a look like she's expecting a smarter answer. "And then what?"

"You can't get what you want."

"Hmm. If you want to, say, leave this room, do you require power to do it?"

"Absolutely." Honestly, I have no idea where Charlotte is headed half the time. "If I don't have power, if you have the power, then you can stop me from leaving. That's the definition of power."

"Let's say that maybe that was true. That I could in theory stop you. Could you leave the room?"

"No."

"You could leave the room if I wasn't trying to stop you?"

I follow through her logic, trying to find the flaw in it. "Yes," I say cautiously, "I guess so."

"It's not a trick question," Charlotte says. "Let's say I'm a trained and armed police officer, sitting here without interfering. Can you leave the room?"

"Yes. I don't understand where you're going with this."

"Power is only important when you and someone else are opposed and they hold power over you. If you're not opposed, then power doesn't matter."

I sigh. This makes as much sense as talking about whether a tree makes a sound when it falls in the forest. "What's your point?"

"Right now, you live each moment as though you're in a fight to obtain your way. Is that a reasonable depiction?"

I'm always on my guard. I nod.

"What percentage of the time do people accept what you want versus actively fight you?"

I shrug. "I have no idea."

"Give me a rough idea. All the time? Half the time? A quarter of the time?"

I shake my head to all of these.

"Ten percent of the time?"

"Maybe ten percent."

"If you prepare for every encounter as though it's going to be a fight, yet those fights rarely occur, then you spend a lot of your personal energy preparing for something that doesn't happen. It would be like a U.S. government ambassador showing up to every routine trade meeting with a battalion of tanks. Not only does it waste resources, it also affects the outcome of those meetings.

If you bring tanks to a meeting, it puts everyone else on the defensive. Makes them worry that maybe they need tanks too. Make sense?"

"I guess."

"Your exercise this week is to notice how often people are opposed to what you want, accepting of it, or indifferent to it. In other words, how often do you actually require power to secure what you want, and how often do you achieve it without exercising power."

"Am I supposed to keep track of every interaction I have?"

"Keep a journal. Write a few paragraphs each night about your observations of the day."

↻

I'm not much for journaling, and the idea of having to take notes each night… ugh. Instead I go home, and dig around in a cabinet until I find what I'm looking for: a tiny bluetooth button from a Kickstarter I backed last year. I have a choice of velcro backing, self-stick, or slide-on clip. I pick the latter, and clip the button to my jeans.

I load the associated app on my phone, sync the button to it, and define what happens when I click. One click will mean someone is actively supporting what I want to do. A double-click will mean they're indifferent to what I want, and a triple-click will signify having to use my personal power to get what I want. Now I can collect a week's worth of data and be able to plot events by time and type of interaction.

Charlotte would never think of recording my experience this way, but it'll do the job better than a journal. After a moment's thought, I double-click the button. I got my own way, and so far as I know, nobody's opposed me.

CHAPTER 23

"Type," Amber commands, and shoves a laptop next to my keyboard on the desk.

I glance at the screen which displays a chat window.

```
Jake> Good morning. What's your name?
```

"Type what?" I ask.
"Anything at all," Amber says.
"Must I?" I ask with a sigh.
"Yes."

```
?> Angie

Jake> Angie, nice to meet you. What's your passion?

Angie> What do you mean?

Jake> It's boring if I ask about your job. You're
probably asked that every day. I'm asking about your
passion. Everyone has a passion, right?
```

"Is he hitting on me?"
"Maybe," Amber says.
"Why am I doing this?"
"Chat with him for five minutes. Please."

```
Angie> I'm passionate about pizza. How about you?

Jake> Eating it or cooking it? And why? BTW, my
passion is learning about the world.

Angie> I'm from New York, and it's a big deal when
I can find a slice as good as what I remember from when
I was a kid. What's the most interesting thing you've
learned?
```

Jake> New York, huh. Thin crust, or Sicilian?

Angie> Okay, you know your New York pizza. Usually thin, though I'll take a square now and then. You didn't answer me — what's the most interesting thing you've learned?

Jake> I can usually predict how much a person reads and watches television within fifteen minutes of talking to them.

Angie> What about me, then?

Jake> Ask me again in nine minutes. :)

I glance up at Amber. "I get it, you know. It's the chatbot software you told me about."

"Maybe. Keep talking. Give it a few minutes."

Angie> Tell me about yourself.

Jake> No, we need quid pro quo. You told me about pizza, I told you about my crazy-good predictive ability. Now it's your turn. What's the bravest thing you ever did?

Jesus, how should I answer that? No way was I going to talk about California.

Angie> I quit my job and started a company.

Jake> Wow, that is brave. Changing jobs is one of the three hardest life events to deal with. How are you coping with the change?

Angie> I'm okay, but I worry about the future. Where our money is coming from. Hiring employees. Working with people. What are the other life events?

Jake> Death of a parent or child, or breaking up with your life partner. Isn't it strange that changing jobs, which seems like a straightforward event, is on the same level as death of a parent? Do you have anyone to talk to?

We go back and forth some more. I'm increasingly uncertain about whether I'm talking to a chatbot or a person. After a bit, I check the clock, and I'm shocked to find I've been chatting with Jake for twenty minutes.

I look up at Amber, who smiles back.

"Okay, I give up. Person or bot?"

Amber picks up her mug, makes a process of taking a sip, making me wait for the answer. "A bot. Hand-tuned ahead of time with data about you. If it was part of a social network, it could tune itself to a person using their public data."

"Erp."

"What's *erp?*" Amber says.

"It feels icky. I don't want it using my data."

"You liked talking to it?"

I don't want to say yes, but the fact is, I did like it.

"Well," she says. "How did you *feel* talking to it?"

I look over at the laptop.

Jake> You still there? If you need to go, no prob. I enjoyed our talk.

"It felt...good. Natural."

"Would you talk to it more?"

I stare at the screen, then out the window. I want to say no. Do I really want or need anyone in my life to talk to? I can't even make time for Thomas as it is. On an impulse, I lean over and type some more. A good friend can help you when you have a problem. The ultimate test for this chat software is whether it can truly help me, not just engage in idle banter.

Angie> I don't have time to talk to my boyfriend, and I'm afraid of losing the connection we have. Any suggestions?

Jake> Is there anything you can do together that you need to do anyway? Even if it's only a few minutes, if it happens regularly, it can help tide over your relationship until you're less busy with your work. Some crazy ideas: Have coffee together in the morning. Go grocery shopping together. Make time for a walk together every afternoon during your sluggish period, since you aren't going to be very productive then.

Angie> How do you know I have a sluggish period?

Jake> Circadian rhythms. Nearly everybody does, especially heavy coffee drinkers like you, and people who work too much. Plus, the exercise would do you good. Would your boyfriend be interested?

Angie> I'll ask.

I open my chat app. A lump forms in my stomach as I discover screenfuls of unanswered messages from Thomas going back several days. Crap. I compose a message to Thomas.

Angie> I know we haven't been able to see each other much lately. I miss you. Would you be up for meeting for a thirty minute walk at 1:30?

Thomas> You're alive. Wow.

Angie> I'm sorry I haven't replied to your messages.

Thomas> I'm not one of your computers you can turn on and off anytime you're tired of me.

I take a deep breath. Though there's not a lot of explicit emotion in his message, I know Thomas well enough to read the depth of hurt in his message. I've been so involved with work, I had no idea.

Angie> I'm sorry, I didn't mean to hurt you.

Thomas> Now you think I'll drop everything in the middle of my day to see you?

Angie> I'm trying to find a creative way to fit in some time together.

Thomas> I'm not an exercise machine.

Shit. He's way angrier than I ever expected. I switch back to Jake's window.

Angie> I tried talking to him, but it's not working.

```
Jake> Did you try telling him "I love you"?
```

This is absurd. Taking relationship advice from a freaking chatbot? I sigh. I do as Jake says, then tap my fingernails on the desk while I wait long seconds for a reply.

```
Thomas> I love you, too. I'll give it a try. Tomor-
row at 1:30.
```

"Un-fucking-believable." Relationship advice from a piece of software is better than my own instincts.

"So you like it?" Amber asks.

"Yeah, I guess I do."

"Whew. A friend of a friend specializes in this stuff. She and her partner spent the last week setting up the demo for you, all unpaid. I'm hoping you can meet with them, and if you like it, we can hire them."

"Whoa…we don't have any money."

"They'll work for your current draw and a percentage of the company until you raise money. You have no frigging idea what a steal this would be. You're getting cutting edge tech for the cost of two employees."

The same deal I gave to Amber.

"It would be pretty cool, right? Jake will keep people on the network."

"Set it up," I say. Holy shit, I might hire more employees.

↻

Amber sets up a 9 P.M. meeting at Puppet Labs, a late-stage Portland startup.

"They're subleasing space here," Amber says, as we ride up the elevator.

"Why?" As in why not work out of a house or coffee shop, like us.

"You'll see in a couple of minutes. Try to keep an open mind."

The elevator opens. There's a girl in a baggy white hoodie that comes almost to her knees slouching against the opposite wall. What's a little off-putting is that the hood is up, her face shrouded. What little I can see is diminutive and dark.

"This is Igloo," Amber says. "Igloo, this is Angie."

I was expecting maybe a Stanford neuroscience post-doc, or an MIT grad. Igloo seems more like the bassist for an all-female Led Zeppelin cover band.

"Nice to meet you," Igloo says, and she stretches one small hand out of a sleeve to shake.

I do my usual inverted shake with my left hand.

"I'm surprised you've got offices."

"We found the arrangement through PivotDesk. Puppet has extra space temporarily," Igloo says. "We'll be booted out in a couple months according to their growth plan, but meanwhile they've got good bandwidth and a machine room."

"You're running your own hardware?" I say. "Not in the cloud?"

"Bare metal gives us the highest possible performance." Igloo leads us past the open pods of a DevOps infrastructure company, a handful of engineers still around, half of them with pints of beer at their desks. "Let's take a peek."

She waves a key fob at a heavy black door and lays her palm on a biometrics reader. With a click, the door unlocks, and Igloo pulls it open. The machine room was clearly built for an earlier generation of tech startups, ones that had racks upon racks of on-site servers. The room is ten feet wide and twenty long, with two lonely racks in it. The near one is half-full, but the far one is jam-packed, full of heavily blinking lights. Igloo leads us to the farthest one.

"Jake's not easy to run. A hundred blade servers. On…loan."

The hesitation in Igloo's voice sends off alarms. What sort of loan? I hope she didn't steal them.

"How many simultaneous chats can he support?" I ask.

"One."

"One?" I'm expecting a number in the tens of thousands.

"Two or three if you're willing to accept some slowdown and pauses. We can interweave conversations. It's computationally intense."

"You can't go to market with this."

"We're porting him to run on graphics processors instead of CPUs. Much faster and more efficient. It'll take a while to rewrite, and Amber said you wanted a demo right away. Hence the prototype. Come on, let's go to my office."

Igloo leads us out of the server room and down the hall into another room. From the whiteboards and flatscreen at one end, the room was obviously intended for meetings, but it's set up with a pair of desks. An open computer chassis and parts are spread all over a table along one wall.

"Ben's working on our new hardware, testing different graphic cards." She lifts a red add-on circuit board and hands it to me.

"It's heavy."

"Sixty-four hundred coprocessors. Liquid cooling. This is one of the manufacturer's demo boards. It'll be out in few months, and should be down to five hundred dollars in a year. One of these will replace the entire rack in the server room. But I gather you like the demo, or you wouldn't be here, right?"

"Yeah. Jake is…impressive. Smart, even. What's your background?"

"I studied neuroscience at Stanford. Got pissed off at my professor. Switched to comp sci at MIT. The one-forty of my thesis is a neural network that analyzes tweets and chat logs to build an internal representation of conversation, correlating people, messages and sentiment to suggest the next message."

I stare at Igloo, trying to puzzle her out. "What's your goal?"

"You watch Star Trek, The Next Generation?"

"Sure."

"I want to build Data. Not a walking, talking android, but a friend, someone people can talk to. Without selling out to a corporation. I need a salary, some hardware, and a few more developers."

"Amber told you what we're working on?"

"Roughly. A replacement social network, with pluggable components. If we tie in Jake, we earn fractional revenue every time Jake is used."

"That's the idea."

"Do you want him? Can you hire us?"

I love the idea. But hiring people. Salary. Money. Damn. Why must it come down to money? Why is money consistently the barrier? For a brief second, the connections flare up in my mind: money equals power, and power equals control, and I almost allow myself to go over the brink and conclude what I really, really need to do is take down our economic system. Merely toppling Tomo will not be enough.

It's bad enough my mind even grazes the thought. I pull myself back. Focus on the here-and-now. I want to hire this girl. She seems as crazy as me and twice as smart.

"I'm interested. I need a couple of days to figure out the finances and see if we can make you an offer, okay?"

↻

The next day, Amber and I bring fish tacos back to the house and work through lunch. We're pair-programming on a complex bit of code to handle the fractional accounting we'll need to correctly credit each players in any interaction.

Amber wants to write each record to the database.

"We can't do that," I say. "We don't have enough database bandwidth."

"It's a Feldian NoSQL database. It scales linearly."

"You're doing a database hit for each service. We can't afford that."

"Tomo writes a million times more data," Amber says. "They manage it."

"We're not Tomo, and we don't have their budget. We need to be more efficient. Write all the data in one go, and then schedule a background task to restructure the data later."

"Then we're writing and reading everything twice."

"It doesn't work that way. Look—"

I'm cut off by my phone beeping. It's one o'clock, and if I'm going to meet Thomas, I have to leave now.

"I gotta go."

"We're in the middle of this."

"I'm sorry, but I *have* to go."

"Fine. I'll take care of it."

She doesn't say anything, yet I hear the unspoken words: "Like I do every night."

I hold back a string of curses. "This is important. But, so is obtaining funding. So when I return later, I'm not going to code with you. I'm going to spend the afternoon putting together a draft proposal to take to investors. I'll schedule time with Mat, and I'll see what I can set up. Then we can hire Igloo and her partner in here."

"That would be good. Get us an office, too, because I want my bedroom back."

Holy shit, why does it seem like everything is melting down at once?

By the time I'm out of there, I've got no choice but to drive downtown if I'm going to meet Thomas on time. Traffic is slow over the Morrison Bridge, and I'm already five minutes late as I'm still circling for parking. I end up driving over a curb and the sidewalk to grab a spot in an expensive lot, and pay twelve bucks for the privilege of being late to a walk.

Thomas looks at his phone as I walk up.

"One-thirty?"

"I'm sorry. Really sorry."

"I hear those words a lot, but they only go so far. How you treat me is what matters."

I take Thomas's hand in mine. "I hear you. I'm going to try to do better, though I'm still going to screw up. Try to give me the benefit of the doubt if the data are trending in the right direction."

He cracks a smile. "You can find a way to relate everything to data. Here." He pulls out a white paper bag from his jacket pocket and unrolls the top.

I peer in. "Fudge!"

He breaks off half, and hands it to me. "Peace offering. Where do you want to walk?"

"Along the river?"

We walk for a few minutes, enjoying the fudge, and not saying much of anything. The waterfront is quiet, most folks back at work by now.

"Thanks for messaging me yesterday," he says. "I was worried about you."

"It's been really, really busy. I can't even begin to tell you how busy."

"Are things going okay?"

"They are. We have a really good lead on something, a piece of technology to solve the empty network problem."

"That's a big deal, right?"

"Yeah, huge. It makes it extra urgent we raise funding."

"An acquisition?"

"No, hiring two employees, though they also want a percentage of the revenue share for their software."

Thomas raises one eyebrow. "If they're employees, you own what they create. It's not their software, it's your software."

"It's more complicated. They're coming in with already developed software."

"Then it's an acquisition," he says.

I shrug.

"You need good legal representation. You need to protect yourself."

"I wish you could do it."

"It's not my area of expertise. You need an expert. I gave you a list of lawyers I vetted."

"They'll want more money," I say. "Money I don't have."

"It's money well spent to avoid problems later. At least one of them should do it for equity or at reduced cost."

I look up at him. "You know what? I didn't come to talk business. I do that twenty hours a day. Let's talk about something else. What's new with you?"

"The Audi is in the shop for a brake recall until Monday. I have a loaner S4." Somehow he manages to embody "S" and "4" with deep notes of lust.

"Oh, good grief. You only got the A4 a few months ago."

"I know. But the S4…it's indescribable."

I take his arm in mine. "Try."

Thomas tells me about acceleration and horsepower, and I focus on the warmth of his arm under mine.

CHAPTER 24

"LET ME SEE WHAT YOU'VE GOT."

I place the tablet in front of Mat. I've got the elevator pitch, a twelve-slide deck explaining the problem, solution, product, and team, and a one-page summary. It's rough but complete.

He flips through the slides. "Give me the pitch."

"Two-thirds of all Tomo users feel violated by the company's policies around advertising, personal data, and privacy, and manipulated by the selection of information they're shown. Yet Tomo is the only way they have to maintain friendships, which keeps them captive. No viable competitors have formed because they can't gain the critical mass of users necessary for people to migrate over and maintain their friendships. Tapestry is our solution to this problem, a new approach to social networking that uses federation and decomposition to prevent the accumulation of power endemic to social networks. Users feel safe, secure, and in control of their personal data, privacy, and friendships. Our approach enables other companies to join forces as well, so any business vulnerable to Tomo's whims will want to partner with us. Moreover, we've built a unique solution to solve the empty network problem, which means that when new users join, they're engaged and having fun from the first minute, and they'll stick around until their friends show up."

He grimaces. "It's too big," he says, his voice low, like he's talking to himself.

"What do you mean?"

"Everyone will believe you're tackling too much. Also, you're not saying what's compelling. A unique solution? Everyone has a unique solution. Say what it is."

I try to keep my head up though my heart sinks at his criticism. "How about... Every new user gets a digital companion, an AI they can chat with, which makes Tapestry fun right from the first visit."

"Better..." He's hesitant. "Keep working on it, and figure out a way to not make it sound so big. Right now it sounds like you need every single company in the world to sign onto your platform to have a chance at success. Failure is preordained, as my friend Owen would say."

Damn. More changes? I want some money already.

"Thanks for the feedback," I say. "I'll keep refining, though I need funding—and soon. I have bills to pay for Tapestry, and I want to hire Igloo and get her chat technology."

"Forget venture capital for now, and look for an angel investor. A typical angel investment might be anywhere from twenty-five thousand to a hundred thousand."

With Igloo and her partner, we're four employees. I want to hire more: at least a couple of developers to offload me and Amber, a designer. Add up the salaries, the need for office space if we grow to that size, and a hardware budget for Igloo. "That's not going to last very long."

"It only needs to carry you until you're a little more viable, refined and proven. Then go to a venture capitalist, and get a bigger investment."

"And go through all this pitching stuff again? Why don't I get more money up front?"

"The more valuable you appear, the more money you get for a given amount of the company. Let's say you convince someone the company is worth a million bucks. You trade ten percent of the company for a hundred thousand. Down the road, you're closer to release, more of what you're doing has proven out, and you seem like a sure thing. Then the company is worth ten million and you trade ten percent to get a *million*. Later, when you've launched and acquire customers who love the shit out of you, the company will be worth a hundred million. Then you trade away ten percent for ten million."

"If I try to raise too much money up front, I'm going to give away too much of the company, and I'll have nothing left to offer later, when the company is worth more."

"Exactly. Listen. Work on the pitch, and I'll email you an introduction to my buddy, Owen. He's an angel investor here in Portland. I can get you a meeting with him. But you're the one who has to convince him you're worth the investment."

↻

I join Thomas for a walk after lunch, and tell him about the morning, and he tells me about his case. It's a quick walk, because I've got an appointment with Charlotte.

"Can I see you tonight?" he asks, before I leave.

"Ahhh… I promised Igloo I'd stop by today."

"At night?"

"No, this afternoon. Then I need to work with Amber tonight. She wants to define the chat API, and write a reference chat provider to interface with IRC."

"That's urgent?"

"It's all urgent. We're racing against time and money and Tomo and people's goodwill. I also have to work on the pitch, and reply to a bunch of emails."

"This weekend. Saturday. You have to take a day off."

I wrap my hand around his back and pull him close. "Saturday. It's a date."

I race over to Charlotte's office, where she greets me at the door as usual, and waits for me to take a seat.

"How are you?"

"Fine, just fine." I'm tapping one toe, and realize I'm impatient to be out of here, even though I sat down only moments ago. I'm counting the things I need to do in my head. "I guess I have a lot on my plate. Like ten things I must do by tonight."

"Sounds like a lot. Is that exciting or stressful?"

"I guess exciting. It reminds me of the early days at Tomo. I was employee number forty-eight."

ↄ

2002, San Francisco, 29 years old.

I've been in San Francisco two days and I've only slept for four hours. Everyone knows augmented social networks are going to be the next big thing, and this is my chance to get in on the ground floor, employee number forty-eight, thanks to a recommendation from Repard. Sometime during this never-ending fire drill caused by an onslaught of new users signing up for Tomo, I become convinced leaving the consulting firm was a mistake.

I need to remove a database column, and look at my list of chicken scratch. SQL is not my forte. DROP is the command I want, I think. I type in the DROP command, then query to verify the column's gone. I receive an error message that the table doesn't exist. I stare, dumbfounded, at the screen until I realize I've deleted not a single column, but the entire table. Now I'm going to have to replicate this entire database again. Hours of work wasted.

"Fuck my life. Who the hell invented SQL?"

I turn to the nineteen-year-old next to me, who also happens to be my boss. "Hey!"

He pulls his headphones off and I hear the tinny sounds of The Offspring escaping from the speakers.

"You hired me to do security work," I say. "That's what I know. Why am I working on the database?"

"Because the database is the bottleneck. We've got ten thousand users signing up each day. You see that guy over there—" He points toward someone in slacks and a dress shirt who's hunched over in front of a big CRT. "He's from finance, but he's working on the database too. He's using Visual Basic macros to migrate the data because it's the only language he knows. Everyone does what they can."

"Jesus. Visual Basic. Aren't we making things worse?"

"If we survive today, we can fix it tomorrow."

I want to quit, except I've never given up at anything. It's an ongoing struggle, upping capacity, bringing new servers online, refactoring the database, the one thing that's hardest to scale. I manage a few hours of sleep here and there, and survive on pizza and burritos. Someone purchased a literal pallet of frozen burritos and the refrigerators are stuffed with them.

Every couple of days I use the shower in the bathroom next to the bike lockers and change into a new set of clothes from my suitcase, which is here in the office with me. I haven't even seen the furnished apartment that's waiting for me.

On day seven, we swap in a new database schema and deploy code, and miraculously the database engine runs at ten percent load. We've gotten ahead of the incoming users and given ourselves a month of breathing room.

I'm shocked to realize I'm having fun. Security stuff had gotten routine, but this is living on the bleeding edge. It's a rush.

Later that year, my boss leaves for another startup and I become Tomo's database architect.

℧

"When you became the database architect," Charlotte asks, "what happened to computer security?"

"I did both for a while. Then we hired someone else to do computer security in 2004. Someone I…" I don't know what's safe to say here, what she must report or even might repeat. I can't dive into my long history on the wrong side of computer security laws.

"Yes?"

"Someone I knew from my college days. That turned out to be a big mistake. He screwed up, big time, which came back around to me, because I'd recommended him. I thought I was going to be fired."

"Really? Merely from recommending someone?"

"Neil was someone I'd known online, from a board I frequented when I was in college. I'd known him for a few years."

"You met him?"

"Online, not in person. The hacker community is small. Everyone knows everyone else. He was working a dead-end sysadmin job when he was brilliant and should have been doing so much more. He said he wanted a real job, and we needed someone, so I thought it would be a perfect match."

"What happened?"

"Everything was fine for six, seven months. He did his job, stayed on top of all the threats, kept our systems patched, ran penetration tests. Then one week he didn't come in, didn't answer his phone. We thought he'd taken a vacation or found a girl or something. The next thing we knew, our users' data was showing up on Russian sites. He sold us out."

My voice catches, and I realize this old story, this forever ago event, affects me more than I imagined.

"Eventually he showed up on the old boards, bragging about it. He'd done it for a lousy twenty-five thousand, which he could make in a few months working at Tomo. The whole thing had been a scam from the beginning. He never was interested in the job. He wanted to prove he could social engineer his way in, and I fell for it. I'm an idiot."

I grab my coffee, take a slow sip, before I continue.

"Tomo was a month from closing funding. I had to meet with the board of directors and all the executives to explain why we'd been compromised, and how I was responsible. They talked about me like I wasn't even there. Why was I responsible for the database? Could I be trusted? I wasn't a person to them, only a potential risk." I take a deep breath.

"They forced me to take three months off while they investigated, because nobody trusted me. It caused a month delay in funding. I came in one day to grab a few things from my desk and they had security escort me the whole time. Everyone stared."

"That's awful."

I nod. "It seemed like things couldn't get any worse, although I also couldn't imagine the situation getting any better. I went from being on top of the world to doubting everything. My skills, my judgement. Was I worth anything at all to anyone? I was thirty-three years old, and all I wanted to do was move back to New York and live with my mother."

Charlotte scribbles something in her notepad. "You didn't?"

My blood pounds in my ears, and I try to rub away the unexpected tick in my eye. "No. I met Jeremy. I should have gone to New York. Fuck!" I punch the couch and little clouds of dust puff up. I'm glad I'm angry. I usually can't even feel anger when I think of him. Anger is better than the total sense of powerlessness that usually engulfs me. That bastard.

"How did you meet?"

I shake my head and my breath wheezes in and out through my nostrils. "Not gonna talk about it." I want to scream. All I can do is sit here on the couch, feeling like I'm going to explode. I can't say anything, because if I do, I'll fall to pieces.

"He was nice in the beginning. I had been single for a while. Curled up in bed talking about our dreams, I felt whole again. Because of all the shit at work, I had stopped believing in myself, and he believed in me. When it felt like I didn't matter to anyone, he cared about me. It was..."

My throat closes up, and it's impossible to swallow. I feel like I'm choking and glance around for water.

Gasping, each word an epic struggle to force out. "A lie. Manipulation. He. Planned. It."

"Breathe in," Charlotte says, "long, slow breath out. Again, breathe in."

I struggle for air, gain control bit by gradual bit.

"Go to your magic garden."

I hate her for telling me what to do, but I've spent so much time in hate. I don't want to be there any more. I listen to her. The magic garden, another of the endless tools she shared, a special place to go where I feel safe. I imagine the beach in New York in the winter, the pounding waves off Fort Tilden, cold air blowing off the ocean, empty sand and dunes as far as I can see. Eventually I'm calm again.

"Why?" I ask. "What's the point of taking me to the edge of terror?"

"Right now your fears, very justified and reasonable fears given your experiences, control you. A fear of something is not the same as the thing itself. It is smart to be cautious of a bear in the woods, but it's not helpful to be so afraid you can't discuss bears, or act intelligently when you encounter one. Eventually, if we keep returning to this uncomfortable space, your fears will lose their power over you."

"So it *is* all about power, after all," I say.

CHAPTER 25

AND NOW FOR
SOMETHING COMPLETELY DIFFERENT

Bend, Oregon. Chris Daly, Bureau of Research and Intelligence, field agent.

CHRIS DALY FLIPS TO PAGE ELEVEN, handling his notebook with a gentle touch. He's never accidentally burst one of the destructive solvent packs capable of dissolving both ink and paper, but it's happened to agents in the field, who then suffer the embarrassment of being completely without mission instructions. Electronic devices, of course, have their own risks.

Under the glow of a red flashlight he reviews the crude black-and-white map of surveillance cameras, plotting a path of least coverage to the congresswoman's driveway where her red Tahoe is parked.

He removes a Ziploc bag from an outer envelope, touching it only with his gloved hands. It contains a single folded sheet of paper with the Congresswoman's name on the outside. They possessed the means to send an untraceable electronic message, of course. Unfortunately, the congresswoman's zealous ban on electronic devices during her family vacation made the delivery of it a complete impossibility.

There's something to be said for a bit of old-fashioned fieldwork now and then, even if electronic methods are more efficient. He and his partner even broke in to bug the vacation house before the congresswoman arrived. He hadn't done that in years. Standard operating procedure now was to hijack computer and mobile device microphones and cameras, which had sufficed for all except a handful of cases since he joined BRI.

The high-desert sky here in Bend is clear, the stars bright to his dark-adjusted eyes, though from six houses away the Tahoe appears black in the starlight. The plastic bag is slippery under his gloved hand, the single sheet of paper within a minimal payload, four sparse lines of text. He had studied the congresswoman in countless photographs and videos, knew how she reacted to good news and bad, could tell her public face from the private one she used when she thought no one was looking. She would open this letter in a few hours, her eyebrows would raise slightly, then she'd frown, the corners of her mouth curling down, her forehead tightening. Because no one would be there to see her, she'd grimace, her teeth slightly uneven, the result of a biking accident in college. She'd once confided over instant messaging to a close friend that she hadn't gone for medical treatment because she didn't want her parents to know.

Chris's breath quickens, his grip tightening on the letter, as he strides faster in anticipation of her reaction. It isn't possible to own someone like the congresswoman. She's too principled to buckle under blackmail, even with powerful leverage on her. But she could still be manipulated.

She'd been fighting the Bureau of Research and Intelligence for months now, scrambling to unveil BRI's charter and gain oversight via the House Committee on Intelligence. Once she read the note, though, she'd be outraged and distracted. Her attention would turn away from BRI and back to one of her earlier passions: gun control.

Once upon a time, leverage meant searching for useable dirt on a person. Once found, it would be applied blindly. BRI has refined the process, using dozens of psychologists and data analysts crunching profile data, to turn the application of leverage into a science with predictable outcomes. What did you want from your subject? Compliance, cooperation, distraction, anger, apathy, suicide? Archimedes said "Give me a place to stand, and with a lever, I will move the whole world." For BRI, profiling is the place to stand, intel the lever; and the objective is not moving the world, but manipulating targets of interest.

Chris steps out on the black asphalt and walks down the middle of the road for the next two houses, outside the range of the front door security cam on his right and far enough away from the limited view of the backup camera on the Lexus SUV to his left. Though BRI isn't aware of backup camera exploits, they still consider them a potential threat.

He finishes crossing the street and steps up to the Tahoe with purpose. Rolling the plastic bag and enclosed paper up tight, he inserts it into the slot where the bike rack will grip the frame of the bike. He continues his walk, noting with pride he did the drop in less than a second.

He walks around the block, gets back in his car, and drives off, the electric engine silent in the night.

ↄ

Modern vehicles, especially electric cars like the one Chris drives, contain so many sensors and computers they require multiple days with BRI techs to be blacked out before they can be used on operations. SOP was to find and fry every RFID transponder, scramble the onboard GPS, remove manufacturer telemetry transceivers, augment the standard firmware with new code to continually erase charge and driving logs, and then, because the vehicle's central computer would freak out with so many offline systems, suppress all the warning messages and error lights that would otherwise light up the dashboard.

Of course, Chris carries nothing electronic. His partner, Daryl, monitors everything from their temporary base of operations, a rented house two miles away.

He pulls into the driveway a little past 5 A.M., gets out, punches the code into the garage door keypad (he couldn't bring the transponder in the car, as its unique code could give him away), and drives into the garage. He hits the inside switch, and the overhead door closes with a rumble.

He's exhausted from the long night, almost dizzy with fatigue. He opens the door to the basement. "I'm home, honey." Daryl doesn't answer. "Well, don't get your panties in a wad. I made the drop."

He descends the stairs, and Daryl appears, sitting at a desk, glancing between windows on three computer monitors.

She pulls headphones off one ear. "I saw. Pretty good, but I made you."

She points to the corner of one window, looping a clip of his drop: him approaching the Tahoe, pausing, his arm visible with the Ziploc bag reflective in his hand for a flash, and then moving on. He would have noticed it too.

"She's not trained and there was nobody there."

"You still don't win any points for style."

Standing alongside her, he glances down, not at her face, but her neck, imagines his hand there, the pulse of her carotid arteries under his fingertips as he slows the flow of blood to her brain. He really can't afford getting mixed up with Daryl. Any hullabaloo back at the office, and he gets cut off from BRI. He laughs instead. "Don't bust my chops. You're sitting behind a computer."

"Whatever. Your phone was buzzing when I went upstairs for coffee."

Back upstairs he grabs his phone off the counter. Most phones are trackable, though this one is indirectly connected, all of the text messages and calls redirected from another phone with a different number. Without a phone these days, basic communication becomes a bitch. He flips through the text messages, pauses and smiles at a photo from the waitress in Seattle, then stops when he sees a message from Joe: "I've got tickets to the game."

Joe's his agent, because anyone who's got product to sell needs an agent. Joe connects him with buyers for fifteen percent of the deal, freeing Daly from having to deal with customer acquisition and negotiation. Keeps him cleaner, too, if it comes down to that.

He yells down the stairs, "I'm gonna get some shuteye."

"We gotta be on the move by noon."

He nods, which nobody can see, and heads up to his bedroom. When his laptop boots, it prompts him for a password. There are several encrypted partitions, a technique BRI uses for plausible deniability. If he puts in one password, the hard drive and operating system will contain an innocuous set of apps and documents. If he instead enters an alternative password, he gets access to his BRI profile. Of course, the same technology BRI uses to hide from the scrutiny of the rest of the world can also be used to hide from BRI. He puts in his third password, and he's soon chatting with Joe.

```
Joe> The client wants a deep dive profile on Angeli-
na Benenati, from Portland, Oregon.

Chris> Anything specific?

Joe> They wouldn't say.
```

The reality is all clients want something. Nobody wants dirt. They use the dirt to achieve something, a specific desirable outcome. Chris was more likely to generate the outcome they wanted with all the resources of BRI at his disposal. Problem is, clients don't like to say what they want. They lose plausible deniability. They risk losing face. So they beat around the bush and ask for data when they should ask for outcomes. Of course, Chris charges more for outcomes.

```
Chris> Fine. I'll have it in two days. Make sure
they understand I can procure the outcome they want.
Upsell them, for Christ's sake. That's what I'm paying
you for.

Joe> Faster turnaround time, more clients this way.
Margins are better on pure data.
```

Fact is, Chris likes to get his hands dirty. It's not about the money. He likes to bring the subject to the point where they pray for release and they'll do anything to get out. There's nothing quite like the rush when they have no power and he has it all.

CHAPTER 26

I RING THE BELL, a dog barks, and there's yelling inside. Footsteps approach the door and it opens.

"You must be Angie! I'm Owen." He holds out his right hand to shake. I flip my left hand over, and he glances at my stump as we shake.

"Thanks for seeing me."

"No, no, thanks for coming over. Sorry I couldn't meet at my office. The nanny called in sick, and my wife is out."

I see various faces, all boys, peeking in from down the hall.

"Come meet my kids."

They're nearly a spitting image of Owen, and they're all in slacks and dress shirts. I turn back to Owen, who's in jeans and a hoodie.

He catches my glance and shrugs. "My wife has much better taste than me."

He looks comfortable in his skin, like he knows his place in the world. I realize that I'm in a strange man's house, and we've shaken hands, and yet I'm okay.

"Kids, time to play Minecraft." The kids cheer, he doles out iPads, and they grab seats in the living room. "Let's talk in the kitchen," he says to me.

His kitchen is larger than my living room, dining room, and kitchen together. In fact, I'm pretty sure my studio in college was smaller than this one room.

He gestures toward a big island with bar stools in the middle of the room. "Grab a seat. Can I get you some coffee, tea, or water?"

"Coffee, please."

"Make yourself comfortable."

I pull out my laptop, log in, and bring the presentation up.

Owen fiddles with a Technivorm Moccamaster, by far the world's best coffee machine outside of a dedicated barista making pour-overs in your kitchen. From the way he's looking at it from different angles, I'm suspicious about whether he's ever used it before.

Even from fifteen feet away I can see he's got the brew basket lever in the wrong position, and the setting on his burr grinder is way too fine. I bite back the urge to say something. The coffee doesn't matter. It's the money I need.

After thirty seconds, I can't help myself. I clear my throat, and he glances at me. "I could show you a few things."

"Really?" He spreads his arm wide, inviting me to take over.

"First we need the right grind for the flat bottom basket." I throw away what he's ground and launch into a fifteen-minute lesson on how to use his expensive coffee setup.

We're both watching the Technivorm do its magic when I catch the time on the microwave. Shit, it's twenty after, and he told me I only had half an hour. I wasted most of my precious time making coffee. Double-damn. I made a man coffee. I'm sending all the wrong messages.

"Can we get started?" I say, and nod toward my computer.

"Sure, sure."

Mat had me practice the pitch countless times. I memorized different versions: two minutes, five minutes, ten minutes, and twenty minutes. With slides projected, slides on my laptop screen, and no slides at all. "The trick," Mat had said a week earlier, "is to make everything sound natural and fresh, while still making every emphasis and pause occur perfectly. You need a very good reason for every word and sentence you're uttering. What are you trying to communicate and why? Get that right, and it'll go perfectly."

I thought Mat's idea of preparation was insane, but now as I effortlessly flow into the ten-minute version of my story, everything coming out smoothly, I give thanks in my mind to his rigor.

Five minutes in, Owen gets up, pours coffee, and comes back to the table with two mugs.

I'm in the middle of explaining about distributed notification when he takes a sip. His eyes open wide. "My God, that's stunning. Sorry, go on."

I smile and continue.

Ten minutes pass, and Owen's phone rings. He swipes to send the call to voicemail. "Let's keep going, if you've got the time."

"Sure."

The kids interrupt us once, and Owen starts a movie for them. While we talk, he gets dozens more messages and calls, which he ignores. We're still going strong, on a second pot of coffee when his wife comes home, and he introduces us.

"You didn't make her coffee, did you?" She turns to me. "A crazy amount of money for that machine, and he's never figured out how to use it."

"Angie taught me how to use it."

"You are a miracle worker! Honey, whatever she's selling, buy it."

He smiles at me. "We're going to keep working, if that's okay. The kids are watching TV."

"I'll check on them."

She leaves, and we return to work.

"I get why it's important, Angie. If you get this to scale, I see the potential for revenue. It's not clear you can be successful, though. You're encumbered by two big challenges: user acquisition and partner acquisition, and they're mutually dependent on each other. Your success requires other companies to adopt your social platform. Why should they, if you don't have any users? But if nobody adopts your API and platform, then you've got nothing unique to offer your users. A couple of reference implementations built in-house."

"We have AI chat."

"It sounds like a gimmick." He sets down a handout I'd given him.

"It increases the fun factor, which extends the average time people spend on the system and ups the number of people they invite. It's a key feature."

"Now you're developing two products. You'll need extra funding. You even want to buy hardware. Nobody uses their own hardware anymore. It increases your capital needs when you should be running lean."

"I know we're facing challenges. We can solve them with funding."

"The risk is huge," he says, leaning back in his chair.

"The opportunity is bigger. What if you could have been an angel for Tomo? What would that investment be worth now?"

He shrugs. I'm losing him. From the other room I hear his wife talking to the kids.

"Are your kids on Tomo yet? Or Picaloo?" Picaloo is owned by Tomo, their conduit into the younger crowd.

"No, thank goodness. We haven't had to cross that bridge yet. Though our oldest has asked."

"Why do you say 'thank goodness'?"

"Kids on social media?" He laughs. "What's not to worry about? Cyber-bullying. Sharing pics. Creeps."

"Tomo doesn't have enough measures to protect them. In part because that cuts into their profit model, but also because they're only one company. But with our service, there could be, no, will be, a slew of companies to step in to address those problems. Cyberbullying detection. The ability to filter inappropriate content. Turn off advertising. Imagine a safer place for your kids to go, with an experience you customize. You make the choices, and you're in control. Isn't that worth something?"

He nods. "I'll consider it. I'll get back to you within the week."

I leave with no idea what Owen thinks, or whether it went well or not.

ʊ

When I get back in my car, I glance at my phone for the first time in hours. I've got messages from everyone: Amber, Thomas, Igloo. They've each sent multiple messages. I head toward the east side and call Amber.

"Well?" she says.

"I'm not sure. I thought it was going great, and then everything went cold toward the end."

"Did he like the idea?"

"He loves the idea, but he's not sure we can pull it off. He said he'll get back to me in a few days."

"Oh. Well, don't mention that to Kevin."

"Kevin?"

"Yeah, we're having dinner with him today. I worked briefly with him on a project a few years ago. We want him. Amazing UX guy. He can code too, so we can avoid hiring a front-end developer for a while longer."

"Whoa. Did you think I was going to come back to the office with a briefcase of cash?"

"No, but we should grab him. His last company folded, and someone else will snatch him up. We can't let that happen. He worked on the UI for Braeburn! We're meeting him at six. Act confident about the money. He has to believe we'll secure our angel funding, or he's not going to consider us."

I hang up, pissed. I don't want to pretend anything for anyone. I have no idea if this Kevin guy is worth anything or not, though, so I guess I'll need to fake confidence in our funding for now. I don't even see what the point of meeting him now is. We've got eight weeks of cash left.

I call Igloo.

"Did he say yes?" she says as soon as he picks up.

"*Kuso.* You and Amber must believe I'm a miracle worker. No, he said he'll think about it."

"Did he seem interested?"

I roll my eyes, but there's no one around to see. I turn right, toward the Morrison bridge.

"I don't know," I say, and it comes out angrier than I intend. I try to loosen my grip on the steering wheel. "I mean, it started well, and he was interested in the idea. But he was cool at the end."

"How long did you talk for?"

"An hour and a half."

"How long was the meeting supposed to be?"

"Half an hour."

"Did he take any phone calls or anything?"

"Jesus, am I being interrogated?"

"Just tell me, did he take any phone calls?"

"No, he sent them to voicemail."

"Then you're fine. He wants to invest."

I'm about to protest, but Igloo continues. She's hesitant, which I've never heard before in her voice.

"Look, I have a problem. I need to pay my partners and make rent and I'm broke. Is there any chance you can loan me some money?"

Shit. Igloo's got two employees, office space, and a ton of computing power, while Amber and I are working by ourselves from Amber's spare bedroom. She's asking me for money? I want her technology, and I've told her as much, but I need to get the funding first.

"How can you need money? You were supposed to be good for another month."

"I underestimated our burn rate. We spent more on computing equipment than I thought. Also travel, lawyer, and accountant fees I didn't plan for. I'm in control of our expenses now, but I need some money to get us through."

My heart skips a beat. Accounting? Somehow I suspect handing Amber an envelope of cash every two weeks from my bitcoin windfall deliveries from Danger isn't going to cut it when we have an accountant.

"Angie, you there?"

"Yeah, I'm thinking." I turn on Eleventh. "Money is tight for us, too."

"I stopped looking for investors because I thought you'd take care of the money."

"I hope to line up something by next month," I say. "I didn't know you needed money right now."

"Maybe we made a mistake," Igloo says, "and we should back out."

I pull over to focus. Will everything crumble because of stupid money?

"Isn't there any way you can cut back on expenses?" As soon as the words are out of my mouth, my mind flashes back to last week when we got together. I asked Igloo if she wanted to grab tacos with me, and she glanced over to a pile of Cup Noodles and shook her head *no*. I'm asking the college student who lives on ramen to cut back on expenses. I'm an asshole.

I'm so wrapped up in my thoughts I miss what Igloo says. "Wait, scratch that," I say. "Forget I even said that. Yes, I'll lend you the money."

"Thanks, Angie." Her voice cracks a little.

I end the call and sit there in my car, my brain spinning in circles. I'm parked outside a coffee shop, a row of aluminum laptops lining the window, everyone sitting there immersed in their own world. Man, when was the last time I went off by myself? When I didn't feel the weight of the world on my shoulders?

I can't remember. At Tomo I was so consumed then with finding the next asshole abuser, taking on responsibility for their victims. The time with my husband doesn't even seem like part of my life. Before he nearly destroyed me, I'd been as driven at Tomo, only I was focused on helping them succeed. As a security consultant working with Repard I'd been on the go all the time. College? Could that have been the last time I sat around and relaxed? Shit. I'm forty-five years old. That was more than twenty years ago.

I pick my phone up and make a call to a number I haven't used since I bought my condo. The mortgage broker I used for my loan.

"Hey, I need to refinance my condo and get some cash out. How quickly can we set something up?"

I make an appointment for tomorrow morning. The equity in my condo is literally the last thing of value I have. If that goes, and I still haven't obtained financing, then either I steal the money or shut down Tapestry. My stomach is in knots. I still have to go to the office, pretend everything is okay, and go to dinner tonight, where I must pretend everything is awesome so we can woo some hotshot designer.

‿

1997, New York City.

In almost two years of penetration testing, we've never hit a client better prepared than the one we're testing now. Repard has blown up a couple of times a day, and he's pulled people off other projects to focus on this one. If there's one thing Repard can't tolerate, it's a boastful client, which is why he's never allowed in contract negotiation meetings. Somehow he wiggled his way into this one, and claimed that if we couldn't penetrate their security, we'd waive the testing fee.

Upper management flipped out and Repard got a talking to, which did nothing to improve his mood.

We're twelve days into the fourteen-day testing window, with Repard getting more tightly wound with each day. We're all frazzled. We tried social engineering the front desk, the shipping department, and the receptionists in an attempt to place our hardware directly onto their network. We attacked their email servers and firewalls. We FedExed a junior IT guy the unreleased beta of Microsoft's upcoming MechWarrior video game, hoping he'd play it at work.

We subverted two of their supply chain vendors. Nothing worked.

The problem is the client warned their employees about the intrusion testing, which invalidates the whole point of the testing. It's easy to tell everyone they can't install any new computers or software for two weeks. It's impossible to do that indefinitely.

Late this afternoon, Repard is suddenly calm. His frenetic pacing has stopped, and he hasn't screamed in hours. When he calls me into his office, I assume it's to tell me how he managed to get inside the client. I never expected music lessons.

"A little higher," Repard says.

I try to bring my pitch up, but I can't hold the whistle and end up blowing hard past pursed lips.

"You need to relax your lips. Move your tongue back."

"I can't, I've never been good at whistling."

Repard bends down slightly, gets his head on my level, tries to peer into my mouth as though a visual inspection will tell him something about my whistling ability.

"I don't even see the point," I say. "2600 hertz doesn't do anything anymore. Those backdoors were closed a long time ago."

"It's an entry requirement. Let's try again."

A chill runs down my spine. Repard's rumored to be the leader of the White Knights, a group of white hat hackers. The exact membership has always been secret, with Repard the only suspected member. Word in the community is mixed, with most believing the White Knights are, indeed, working on the side of the law and big business. Yet there are a few who argue the Knights are corrupt enforcers who secretly break into big companies and then turn around and charge them to close the security holes.

I lean forward, give him a mischievous grin. "Does the secret whistle come before or after the secret knock?"

Repard shakes his head, and turns to rummage in his desk drawer. "Don't be snotty. Here, let's try this." He hands me a small, hand-built electronic device.

It possesses an old-timey smell of brittle plastics and burnt electronics. I wouldn't be surprised if Repard hand-soldered the thing.

"What is it?"

"Frequency doubler. Let's see if you can hold 1300 hertz."

I sigh and try again.

"Lower," he says.

We keep trying until I can finally light the lamp of his custom telephone box, indicating that, with the frequency-doubling assistance, I've hit and held the require 2600 hertz for a full two seconds.

"Here," he says, handing over the doubler. "Keep it handy, you'll need it."

I palm the little box. "What's really going on? Why are we in here playing games instead of working on the client?"

"Sit down."

Uh oh. This is going to be big. I tentatively lower myself down like the chair will bite.

"Relax," Repard says. "Everybody does a few things. They eat, they shit, they fuck."

"I am *not* sleeping my way in." I'm halfway out of my seat, indignant, even as part of me thinks about the men I've manipulated. I did what I needed to for my personal interests. Why is this different?

"Didn't ask you to, did I?" Repard jumps off his desk, pushes me back into my chair, and checks the door to make sure it's closed. He turns back to me. "The executive team is going out for breakfast tomorrow morning."

"How do you know?"

"Dumpster diving. We found weekly calendar printouts."

"They shred *everything*," I say, suddenly suspicious.

"Shredder broke two days ago." Repard's got a smug grin across his face telling me this is no fluke.

"That's lucky."

"Luck is for fools. I make my own destiny."

"Why didn't you tell the team?" I say. "This changes everything."

"Because you guys would have altered your behavior." He leans against his desk, arms crossed, smug with secret knowledge. "They would have seen that, known they were leaking info, and upped their security. I needed everyone to keep doing what they were doing."

"Are you running a second team?" I ask. There's no other explanation. Repard can't personally be engineering shredder breakdowns and dumpster diving, because I've seen him around here too much.

"It doesn't matter. Here's what's going down. The executive team goes to breakfast tomorrow morning. You're going to be there, as a waitress."

"In some short skirt no doubt."

"Better they look at your ass than your hands. Because you're going to put something in the food."

Repard, leans back over the desk to pull a small brown bottle out of a drawer. He pushes it toward me.

The glass grates across the wood desk, the rasp against the wood grain somehow foreboding.

"I'm not poisoning anyone." I stare at him. "I'm a security consultant, not a murderer."

"It's not going to hurt anyone. The VP of sales had a heart attack two years ago. This'll give him the sensation of chest pains. He'll call 911. We're going to respond."

"Whoa, whoa, whoa."

"Angie, there's no risk. All you have to do is add it to his food, and only *his* food. We can't have all the executives thinking they're having heart attacks simultaneously, or they'll be suspicious."

I pick up the little brown bottle and study it. It's half the size of a lipstick tube, and partly filled with liquid. It feels awfully heavy for such a small thing.

"This is the ticket to bigger things, Angie. You want to know who's pulling the strings behind the curtain, don't you?"

This is as close to an explicit invitation to the White Knights as I'm going to get.

I slip the bottle into my pocket. "When and where?" I say, though it comes out as a whisper.

"Don't worry, sweetie," Repard says, and pats my knee. "It's going to be fine."

CHAPTER 27

WE'RE MEETING KEVIN DOWNTOWN. I stare at the upper floors of Big Pink as I drive, feeling on edge, wondering if I'm being watched somehow by people at Tomo.

"Who picked Morton's?" I ask, as I drive onto the Hawthorne bridge.

"I don't remember," Amber says. "Why?"

"It's expensive." That's not the entire reason I'm complaining. Steak is impossible to cut one-handed. "There's a hundred great restaurants that cost less."

Amber shrugs. "If it's a big deal, I'll pay for it."

We get snarled up in the evening rush hour traffic getting off the bridge and hit four red lights looking for parking.

Amber clears her throat to interrupt my passive-aggressive sighing. "He's worth talking to. He's smart, and has great instincts. He turned down offers from Avogadro and Tomo because he doesn't want to work for the man." She makes air quotes around the last two words.

That's something. I try to push my worries aside. It'll be fine.

After I park, we head into the restaurant to find Kevin sitting at a table, a cocktail in front of him.

"Kevin?" I say. "I'm Angie."

"Nice to meet you." He jumps up, touches elbows with me first, then shakes hands with Amber. "Amber, nice to meet you in person."

I'm never sure whether to be impressed or weirded out when someone researches how to shake hands with an amputee. It suggests thoughtfulness and calculated manipulation in equal measure. I try to disregard the feeling. Amber greeted me the same way. She probably mentioned it to him.

"Amber's excited we're meeting," I say.

"I am, as well."

He flags down the waiter, who takes our drink orders and we make idle chat about the Portland tech scene until our cocktails come.

He tells stories about working for Pierre at Braeburn, a notorious user experience control freak, and mocks Pierre's well-known speaking style. "Anyone can make a user experience that goes from one step to the next. Seamless flow without steps, breaks, or constraints, this is what sets apart real design!"

We laugh and clink our glasses in a toast.

"Honestly though, Pierre is brilliant." Kevin takes a sip and puts his glass down to talk with his hands. "I must give the man the respect he's due. He walks into a review meeting one time, a presentation we spent weeks preparing for, picks up a sharpie, and before anyone says a word, marks up the design concepts bordering the room. It didn't take him more than a minute tops to grok the whole user experience and then cut it all in half."

He's intelligent, articulate, but he laughs a bit too loud at his own jokes, and he's too earnest when he's serious.

I'm taking a sip when it hits me. He reminds me of Neil, the computer hacker I hired to backfill my position at Tomo, who went on to betray the company. I choke on my drink and start a coughing fit. Amber and Kevin pass me napkins and my glass of water, but I shake them off.

"A few drops down the wrong pipe," I manage to gasp. "I'm fine. Ignore me."

I clear my throat a few times as Kevin talks about designing for web and mobile. I try to ignore the comparison to Neil, because I know it will prejudice me against him, but I can't help it. Neil had the same ingratiating mannerisms, even though I only realized that in retrospect. Only after he'd screwed over Tomo.

He's not Neil, yet the vibe he gives off convinces me this is a setup.

I grab my phone from my bag and send Amber a text: Are you sure this guy is legit, and he is who he says he is?

A few seconds later, Amber slips her phone out of her pocket, glances at it, and looks at me like I'm crazy. She gives me an eye-nod that says, Yes, of course, and then goes back to paying attention to him.

"Excuse me," I say, and take my phone to the restroom.

I do a quick search for Kevin, find his online profile. Yep, that's really him. There's an interview on a prominent UX blog from his time at Braeburn. Same photo. I rub my eyes and stare at myself in the mirror. Am I going crazy? I scan my body, as though the evidence of mental instability might be located somewhere on my extremities. I feel okay, though he gives me the heebie-jeebies. Did Tomo hire him to spy on us?

Wait, this is me, isn't it? I take a deep breath. I'm having a panic attack for no reason. It's PTSD, that's all. I wiggle my toes, feel them in my shoes. Focus on my pants, the feel of them hanging on my waist, the fabric brushing my knees. I squint in the glare of the light above the mirror. Someone walks into the restroom. I ignore them, concentrating on my grounding exercise.

PTSD or not, there's no way I'm hiring him. Kernighan, Ritchie, and Thompson could all show up and praise him as the next God of all things software, and I wouldn't let Kevin be any part of Tapestry. The thought of sitting at the table with him has me in a cold sweat.

Shit, I can't stay in the bathroom for the whole meal. I reluctantly go back and gingerly take my seat. The food still hasn't come.

"Feeling better?" Amber asks.

I nod.

"Maybe you could tell Kevin about your vision for Tapestry?"

Kevin turns to me, a gentle smile on his face, his blue eyes focused on me in a trusting gaze.

Neil had that gaze and he stole the company data. That fiasco got me placed on a leave of absence, nearly got me fired. I went back to work months later full of self-doubt. That's when I met Jeremy.

A single drop of sweat runs down my forehead. I can't do it.

"You know what?" I say. "I'm not feeling well. I need to go. Sorry." I grab my bag and turn to Amber. "Can you Uber home?"

"Uh, sure," Amber says, looking back and forth between us. "You okay?"

"Yeah, no. I mean, maybe it was something I ate at lunch. Good to meet you, Kevin." The words taste like ashes as I force out the bare minimum of politeness.

I nearly run outside to my car. Sitting inside, I rest my head on the steering wheel.

I screwed up, didn't I? Like Emily said I would because I can't handle being in the same place with a man. All the therapy in the world didn't stop a panic attack.

The thing is, that doesn't feel like the right explanation. It wasn't like a panic attack, it just felt *wrong*. Crap, make one, two really bad decisions in your life, and you spend the rest of it doubting everything.

I lean back in my seat, keys still in my hand. There didn't seem to be anything wrong about Jeremy when I met him. He was funny, charming. I was stressed about work and my life, and it seemed the only escape from that feeling was when I spent time with him. He was always concerned with my health, looking out for me. "Quit your job if they don't respect you," he said. "You're worth more than that."

It seemed like a good idea at the time. When you're stressed, and financially privileged, you take time off work. Totally logical. I had money saved up, and Jeremy had a great job at one of the investment banks. Income was irrelevant.

It was a relief in the beginning to move the focus off me. Too long I'd been at the center of everything at Tomo. I let Jeremy be the center of attention for a change. It was so easy to go to his events, see his friends, be in the periphery without any pressure.

Why would I even want to be at Tomo anyway? Not to hear recurring suspicions voiced that I purposely hired Neil and split the money with him.

Then as the tech world heated up again, Jeremy got busy, too busy for social events with me. Cooped up in the house, I read about the next generation of hot startups that needed talent. I had skills.

I started to look for my next job but Jeremy said talk in the tech world was people all through the community thought I had something to do with Tomo's stolen data. All the Bay Area startups knew about it. I should wait a while until things died down a bit.

I wasn't happy about it, but it seemed like good advice, so I went along with it. When Jeremy proposed to me, I wondered if he was purposely distracting me, though he seemed so excited about the prospect of getting married. Money was good then, valuations increasing, and he bought us a new house. We moved in right after the wedding. It was a little further out, a little harder to see our old friends, but Jeremy said it was a good idea to escape the craziness of the valley. Everyone was going nuts, and we needed a retreat, someplace away from all the hubbub. He wanted peace and quiet, so we ditched the Internet and phones at home, because people were trying to reach him all the time.

The more disconnected we got, the more angry and tense he became. I did everything I could to help, the dinners, keeping the house perfect the way he wanted. Somehow I'd become this domestic appendage, the exact opposite of everything I'd imagined for myself, and I wondered how I'd gotten where I was.

The pressure kept building up, all the time, so much strain. One of his big clients failed, a huge investment, the bank was out tens of millions. He came home in a rage, clearly drinking on his drive home, because he was unsteady when he walked in the door. I tried to help him, and that's when he—

A jabbing pain in my leg breaks me free of my thoughts. I'm still sitting in my car, parked across from Morton's. I'm stabbing myself in the leg with my car key. I feel cool wetness around the hot ache in my leg, like maybe I broke the skin.

No, I will not think about Jeremy. I reach around, shove the key in the ignition, and slam the car into gear. The street is empty, so I jam my foot on the gas and speed down the road.

I take the corner too fast, my tires chirping slightly before I climb the onramp to the bridge. Directly ahead, the primary steel girder of the bridge protrudes up from the deck, dividing the left and right lanes, only a small metal guardrail to keep a car from hitting it. Something comes over me, and I floor the gas, racing toward the heavy steel divider. I jerk the wheel at the last minute, getting the car over into the right lane, weaving back and forth before I regain control.

I slam on the brakes, bringing the car to a complete halt. I'm gasping, my fingers coiled around the steering wheel so tightly it's shaking under my grip. For a minute all I can see are the concrete columns of the underpass, and Jeremy passed out, drunk, next to me in the passenger seat. It was so easy, just a tiny press of a red button, and his seatbelt was undone. Maybe I would die, too, but I was beyond caring. Anything was better than my miserable existence. The underpass loomed large, the concrete column almost—

A car horn honks, and I look up, realize I'm stopped in the middle of the Hawthorne bridge. I glance right, the passenger seat's empty, although for a second I glimpse Jeremy's body there, the way it was in the crime scene photographs. I can't remember anything between releasing Jeremy's seatbelt and waking up in the hospital, my arm gone.

The guy behind me lays into his horn again.

"Fuck you, asshole," I yell, and give him the finger.

The horn falls silent.

I take my foot off the brake, and carefully step on the gas and drive the rest of the way home.

ʊ

I call Charlotte's emergency number when I arrive home, only to get an answering service. "I need to speak to her as soon as possible."

They promise to send the message to her.

She calls me back fifteen minutes later, but by then, sitting in my living room in the glow of the moonlight, the past has loosened its grip on me. She agrees to see me early tomorrow morning, before her other patients.

I grind my teeth on the drive over the next morning, angry I'm reliving these old events. By the time I take my seat in her office, I can barely stop myself from slamming my travel mug onto the side table.

"I came in here last week, you got me talking about Neil and how I met my husband, which I didn't want to do. Now I'm losing my mind. I want my past buried away where I don't need to think about it."

"How's that been working for you?" Charlotte asks.

"What?"

"The strategy of burying things. It's really a good short-term strategy. When we experience trauma, the mind needs to protect itself, and which it can do by focusing attention elsewhere, *trying* to ignore those memories. It's only effective temporarily."

"It's worked fine for five years."

Charlotte waits.

"Mostly fine," I say. "I work, I have a relationship."

"I beg to differ. Your personal strength keeps you functional in spite of trying to bury those memories. You're brave enough to place yourself in terrifying situations again and again, dealing with your male coworkers, surrounded by men in public spaces, even being touched by Thomas. There is an alternative in which you aren't afraid, where life isn't an ongoing battle between what you want and what you fear."

She stops and takes a sip of her tea.

I fiddle with the edge of my shirt, not wanting to accept what she's said.

"You wouldn't be here unless you believed that on some level," she adds.

I nod. I pretend the room is empty and I'm talking to myself.

"After Jeremy became abusive"—abusive is an hollow word that can't encompass what it's like to be belittled and broken down by the man you love, a word that doesn't evoke in the slightest way the terror of never knowing when the next outburst is coming or what might happen as a result, or the self-loathing that suffocated me when I lay there in pain knowing I hadn't defended myself yet again, and this is why abusive is a safe word, because I don't have to think about those things—"he didn't let me talk to my family."

I shake my head. "No. That's not true. It didn't start then. It was earlier he cut me off from my friends and family. I'm not stupid, I knew my situation was twisted, but I couldn't find a way out. I was confused all the time, like someone had convinced me up was down and left was right. In theory, all I had to do was walk out the door. But a thousand things kept me there. I didn't have anyone to call, I had no money, I was convinced Jeremy would kill me or himself..."

I'm losing my thread. I wanted to talk about my mom. I draw my knees up in the chair, wrap my arm around my legs, so I'm sitting folded up as small and cocooned as I can be.

"There was this room Jeremy called his office, with a deadbolt on the door. That's where everything important was, everything Jeremy didn't want me to get my hands on. Bank paperwork, my license, the phone. One day he went to work, and after he left, I found the door unlocked.

"I waffled, afraid to go in, but I eventually did. You know what I did? I looked through the mail. Such a little thing, but I hadn't had the feeling of rifling through the mail in so long. There was so much mail! Buried in the stack was an open envelope from a New York lawyer, addressed to me. The lawyer's letter was regarding the disposition of *my mother's estate*. I had no idea she was even dead, or that she'd even been sick. Jeremy hid that from me, the bastard!"

"I'm sorry," Charlotte says.

"It wasn't until later I discovered how much he'd kept secret. When my mother was diagnosed with cancer, she hired someone to track us down. They never figured out where we lived, though they discovered where Jeremy worked. My mother flew out to California, confronted Jeremy at his work. You know what that asshole did?"

My eyes focus on Charlotte momentarily, then I let her fade away. I'm in an empty room.

"He called the police, and convinced them to haul my mother away, when it was *him* that should have been arrested and locked up," I half yell, half cry, my voice ragged. "She never left. She spent the last months of her life looking for me, and failed. She died less than ten miles from where I was."

I don't tell Charlotte the next part, although it's connected, intrinsically part of the gestalt. That was the day I decided to kill Jeremy. It took me a while to figure out how to do it in a plausibly deniable sort of way, and I waited still longer for the opportunity to present itself. In the end, my plan didn't survive the first encounter with the police. It's why I'm so careful now. I can't afford a second mistake.

CHAPTER 28

THIS MORNING I MET WITH THE MORTGAGE BROKER, and we began the process of refinancing. Even with 100 percent loan-to-value, I only have enough equity to last a few months. The thought of using what little financial safety net I have makes me sick, though the idea of failing is worse. I hound Mat for introductions to more angel investors, force myself to make cold calls, and work through the weekend.

Thomas texts to ask me out to dinner on Saturday.

"Only if you're buying," I tell him, which he does, of course. We laugh about it, and for a few minutes on Saturday, with a glass of wine in me, I'm... well, maybe not relaxed, but not exactly on the edge of my seat either. We go back to his place, get busy in his bed, and an hour later I'm headed back to Amber's. She's surprised when I show up, but I sit alongside her and we crank out code until two in the morning.

I've got angel investor pitches lined up for Monday, Tuesday, and Wednesday, all by videoconference.

Including the work we do over the weekend, we now possess a working demo showing six different components working together: friend management, friend finder, status updates, notifications, news feed, photo upload, and selective sharing. This last piece is a huge deal. Up until now, if you want to share everything publicly, the existing, open IndieWeb movement could give you most of what you wanted simply by publishing content via your blog. If you want to share to a single person, there are dozens of texting and messaging apps, even email. Yet if you want to share privately to a group of people you select, then Tomo is the only real option. By supporting selective sharing of content, we're on equal footing with Tomo.

On Monday morning, I'm waiting in line for a coffee at Coava, stressing about the two investor pitch meetings scheduled that day, when my phone buzzes. I look down to see an email. The from: line says "Lewis," no last name.

I try to swallow, my saliva sticking in my throat as my heart pounds. I abandon the coffee line and look for something to lean on as I open the email.

From: lewis (lewis@tomo.com)

To: angie@angieb.me

```
Hey Angie,

I hear you're working on some interesting stuff.`
We'd love to have a look, maybe help you with funding.

  - L
```

Lewis is the CEO and founder of Tomo. I panic and half-run for the exit, pushing my way rudely though the line. Outside I take gulps of air, but I'm afraid I might be sick. Lewis Rasmussen is literally the last person on Earth I want to know about Tapestry. He has bought, crushed, or rendered obsolete every company that has in any way competed with or threatened Tomo. In my car, my heart pounds as I read the message over and over. Why this message, why these words? He didn't mention the non-compete, which isn't in their database, but he'd certainly know it should exist. He could have threatened me. Of course, that is never his way. He doesn't need to do anything like that.

He can afford to be nice. He paid billions for Picaloo, because why not? He'll offer to buy me, give me all the money I need to succeed, maybe even offer me a pick of staff from Tomo. I knew this message would come some day. I didn't think it would happen so soon. I imagined it occurring when I had a product and users, millions of users. It is inevitable we'd eventually go head-to-head, only I imagined that would be when I was on equal footing, with an army of lawyers and executives on my side.

To attract his attention now means he believes I'm dangerous. Powerful people don't like dangerous things around them.

When I call Emily it goes to voicemail. I hang up and call back. It takes four tries before she answers.

"What's up?" she says, the urgency in her voice making it clear she's in the middle of something important.

"Lewis emailed me. He knows about Tapestry."

She sighs. "It was going to happen sooner or later."

"Why so quickly?" I say. "Why Lewis and not a flunky?"

"He knows you. You were an early employee and a veteran of the company. Seems natural they'd keep track of what you're doing. Maybe he's paying you the respect you deserve by contacting you directly."

How does Lewis even know what we're doing? Is he spying on me?

"Who'd he find out from? Practically nobody knows."

"There's only so many people in tech," Emily says. "Maybe those new employees you want to hire said something?"

"Maybe he's reading my emails."

"That's paranoia talking," Emily says, her voice suddenly stronger, like she's paying attention to this conversation for the first time. "Look, there's no point in worrying about any of this. You don't want to hear Lewis's offer, right?"

"Right."

"Then ignore the email, and go about life like you didn't receive it."

We hang up a few minutes later, Emily's reassurances failing to convince me. Lewis must be keeping track of me to know so soon, and with such perfect timing. Of course he'd approach me when I'm most desperate for financing. There's an obvious answer: hack Lewis back and check all of *his* messages. Find out what he's doing.

☊

Lewis is on my mind as I go through my morning investor pitch. My delivery is off, and the investor knows it. We've scheduled a twenty-minute videoconference, yet after a few minutes all I receive are distracted nods while the investor does something else on his computer in the background. At ten minutes he says he's not interested, and we end early.

Amber hears my cursing and comes running from the living room. I quickly recap the call without saying anything about the email from Lewis. I'll take care of that myself later.

"Let that one go," Amber says. "Let's get you back in the game before the next pitch and grab some lunch. Boki Bowl?"

I love the noodle shop, but it's expensive for noodles. "Let's do Thai." Though I'm not sure saving five dollars on lunch makes a real difference, I feel sick with every extra dollar I spend.

We eat, then Amber suggests walking up Mount Tabor. I huff and puff my way to the top, and we spend a few minutes circling the crest and gazing out on the city from several hundred feet up.

By the time we head back down, I wouldn't say I feel good, but I feel normal enough to function for the second pitch. I handle the call better, and the investor asks me to send her the rest of my slides. That's at least a little promising.

I leave after the call and head home. I grab an extra laptop from our office, then image the laptop with a clean operating system. I drive across town to a dive bar on Alberta I know has deep booths. It's early and the place is almost empty. I take a dark booth in the back, order the burger because it's one of the least expensive items on the menu, and pull on my headphones. I'm not listening to anything, but it should keep the waiter from interrupting me too often. I pull out a little USB wi-fi adapter about the size of a deck of cards. It's got a directional antenna in it, nothing as effective as a Pringles can or any of my good electronics gear, but it's enough to acquire the open wi-fi of a coffee shop a block away.

I pull down an encrypted disk image off an old website. Decrypted, it gives me enough basic tools to do what I need. After rerouting through a public VPN, I connect into Tomo's network. Reading Lewis's email and Tomo messages, stored on the Tomo network, couldn't be easier. Of course, Lewis is a CEO, and his inbox is massive. He receives more email in a day than I get in a few weeks. I want to search his messages for any mention of me, but I can't resist peeking through his inbox.

His email is a gold mine. He's got messages from everyone on his executive team, detailing plans for the next several quarters. He's running a whole bunch of secret projects, PrivacyGuard being only one of them. I'm reading about their plans for providing free Internet access when I feel vaguely disgusted with myself.

The net effect of Tomo is evil, but is Lewis Ramussen himself a bad guy? Is it right for me to read his email? I want to beat Tomo so bad, but what I'm doing essentially amounts to corporate espionage. I have no problem reading some asshole abuser's email, but this feels dishonorable. I shake my head and take a bite of my cold hamburger. No. How can it be inappropriate? What Tomo does is unethical. Aren't I justified to use any means possible to end their abuse of their users? I waffle back and forth, unwilling to look at any more of his emails. Why does this feel so wrong?

I want to win fair and square, that's why. If I beat Tomo by reading Lewis's emails and spying on their plans, then anything I ever achieve with Tapestry will forever be tainted by what amounts to cheating. Though I've done much that needs to be accounted for, Tapestry is my chance for a fresh start, untarnished by my history. *All* my history. The killings, the hacks, the secretiveness. All of it. Leave the past where it is. It's time to move on.

I sit for a long time staring at Lewis's inbox. Then I close the windows, disconnect from the network, and run the script that will wipe the hard drive. When it's done I close the lid and put it back in my bag. I feel strangely numb, half certain I'm making a bad decision, and half certain I'm doing the right thing.

I pay and go home, still in some strangely detached mental state. I slip Metallica's Black Album into the CD player and zone out.

ʊ

1985, Brooklyn, New York.

The shaggy-haired blonde guy in combat boots is the only real metal-head in graphic arts shop class. "You listen to Metallica?"

I nod. "*Kill 'Em All* is brilliant."

"You ever listen to them on 'shrooms?"

Sean turns every conversation to drugs. Usually he likes to impersonate both sides of a conversation between a person on 'ludes and another person on speed.

"My roots!"

We both turn to the only other rocker in the room, the platinum blonde girl whose name I've never bothered to learn.

She's holding a compact in her hand, and points to her forehead. "My roots are showing."

True enough, her dark hair is growing in. I never quite know what to say to her, in part because nothing she says is ever more intelligent than what she's said just now.

Sean and I turn back to each other. He silently mouths, "poser."

I giggle.

"Metallica's playing a secret show in New Jersey next weekend," Sean says. "Want to go?"

I tilt my head and look crooked at him, trying to decide if this is him asking me out.

"How'd you find out about the show?"

"A post on a BBS."

"Bee Bee Ess?"

"Bulletin Board System. You use a computer and a modem, and you can call all these different places."

My cousin has a computer he plays weird games with, but I've never used it. "What's a modem?" I ask.

"A thing you connect to the computer so it can talk over the phone to other computers."

"What do you talk about?"

"Anything. Music. Drugs. Mostly I hang out on DDial."

I shake my head in puzzlement again. "Dee dial?"

"Diversi-Dial, a chat system," Sean says. "You can talk to other people."

"A DDial is a BBS?"

"No. Look, come to my house after school and I'll show you. It's cool."

Now is he asking me out?

I have nothing to do after school and my mom won't return until after five, so I walk home with Sean. He offers me a Marlboro Red, which I accept eagerly. I can't afford to buy my own. He flips a brass Zippo open to light me. We argue about whether Metallica or Slayer is better, and he tells me stories about doing mushrooms with his ex-girlfriend.

When we get to his house, he yells that he's home, and we go up to his room without waiting for a response. There's a faint yell of his mother's response, which he ignores. Once in his bedroom, he locks the door. His room is overflowing with dirty clothes, metal posters, and random shit. Other than my cousin's, I've never been in a boy's bedroom before. He sits in front of his computer at a desk.

"Grab a seat," he says, gesturing to his messy bed.

I tug at his covers to make a flat spot and gingerly sit on the edge.

He turns on his computer, and opens a drawer to reveal an ashtray overflowing with butts. We light up again, and when the computer is on, he types some stuff. Suddenly there's a shrieking, warbling noise from the computer, then it goes silent.

"See, these are all the other people who are online." He points to scrolling green text, a bunch of lines that are some variation of "Hi Ruger!"

"Who's Ruger?"

"I am," Sean says. "You need to pick a handle. What handle do you want to use?"

"How do you pick a handle?"

He shrugs. "Pick anything you like."

I look at other's people's handles. Malek Resr0n. BTS. Cyclone. Blue Adept.

I have no idea what they mean. Choosing a handle? What does it say about me? I watch Sean chat with these other people, most of whom seem to know him. Finally, I'm done with my cigarette, and I stub it out in the ashtray.

"Angel of Mercy," I say. "That's what I want to use for my handle."

"Okay," Sean says. He types a message into the computer.

```
#4[T1:Ruger) Hey, my friend is here. This is her
first time on DDial. Her name is Angel of Mercy. Say hi
to her.

#3[T1:Blue Adept) Hi Angel!

#2[T1:BTS!) Welcome AoM!

#6[T1:Malek Resr0n) Greetings, Angel of Mercy.
```

Sean stands up. "Here, you sit and type."

"I don't know what to say."

"It doesn't matter. Say hi."

I sit in his chair, and because I don't know how to type, it takes me forever to hunt and peck "hi everyone" A few people ask me questions, which I answer with the shortest responses I can, and then I see a new person suddenly appear.

```
#0<T1:> (dragon) Welcome, Angel of Mercy. Enjoy
sanitarium.
```

"Why does his name look different than everyone else?"

"He's the sysop, the system operator. He owns this."

"Owns it?"

"Yeah."

I keep chatting with people online, while Sean lies on his bed and chain smokes, and calls out comments on what people are saying from the bit of the screen he can read. All of a sudden, I remember to check the time and discover almost two hours have passed. "Holy shit, I have to go. If I'm not home before my mom, I'm gonna be in a heap of trouble."

I don't want to leave. DDial is awesome. It's talking to other people without judgement of who you are or where you're from. My mind spins with new ideas, new names, new friends. "Hey, would it be okay if I come over again sometime?" I hold my breath hoping he'll say yes.

"Yeah, course."

I jog home, narrowly beating my mom there. I lie awake in bed that night, fantasizing about being online.

The next morning I see Sean in the hallway after first period, and ask if I can come over that afternoon. He says yes, and I end up visiting his house after school every day that week.

On Saturday morning, my mom wakes me up just before she leaves to go grocery shopping. "Get started on your chores," she tells me, once I nod to indicate I'm awake.

I lie there in the bed for a minute, hear the front door slam, and then I race into top gear. By the time she comes home, I've vacuumed, dusted, cleaned the kitchen, and I'm starting in on the bathroom.

"Help me unload," she yells from the entrance.

"I'm almost done with the bathtub," I call back.

A few seconds later, she appears in the doorway. "Since when do you clean the—"

I make the mistake of looking at her. She gets one glance at my face, which betrays my hopeful excitement.

"Uh oh. What do you want? If it's to go to that CB whatever music place, the answer is still no."

"CBGB, and no, that's not it."

"Is it a boy?"

I inadvertently think about Sean, and when he—

"Ah, it is a boy. Who is he?"

"No, mom. It's not. I want…" My stomach is trying to climb into my throat. I've never desired anything so much, never felt so much riding on a single decision from my mother. "I want to buy a computer."

"A what?"

"A computer. It's like a typewriter that connects to a television."

"I know what a computer is, honey. I've seen them at work. Why do you want one?"

I launch into a mile-a-minute explanation of bulletin board systems and DDial. At some point I become aware I'm still wearing yellow rubber gloves, and take them off. "So I'd also need a modem to be able to dial these BBSes."

"How much does it cost?"

"Six hundred and fifty dollars." I'm asking for more than twice what we pay in rent.

"I'm sorry, honey, that's out of the question." She shakes her head and walks out of the bathroom.

I run after her. "Please, mom. Can I borrow the money and pay you back? I can earn it."

"I don't have that kind of money."

"I'll get a job. I'll babysit or work at the grocery store. You don't understand. I really want this."

She reaches up and runs her fingers through my hair. "I see you do, but there's no way we can afford it. You know that. Plus you have to be sixteen to work."

"Not to babysit."

"You hate babysitting. You sat the Serrano kids once and came home crying."

I loathe watching their bratty kids, but I'd do almost anything to afford that computer.

"Fine, I'll save up the money on my own." I cross my arms, and then give up and run off to my room. Even if I babysit several nights a week, and spend absolutely nothing, it's going to take me most of a year to save the money.

My mother follows me to my doorway. "Come sit with me at the table and show me how much everything costs."

KILL PROCESS | 159

In the end, it takes three months of babysitting almost every night to save up a quarter of the money. My mom buys day-old bread and dented cans, and somehow scrimps up most of the rest. The night before my sixteenth birthday, we count up what's in the jar and we're still short.

There's a heated argument by phone with my uncle, and the next thing I know, my mom's taking the subway to my uncle's house, and returns later that night with the rest of the money.

The next morning, a Saturday, we take the bus together the computer store, and carry the box back home between us. Sitting on the bus on the way home, the box clutched tight in my lap, I'm nearly bursting with excitement.

Having my own computer, I spend most of every night online. I type up my school assignments so my mom thinks there's some educational value. Soon I have dozens of new friends. Most I never meet, yet from behind the safety of the screen, I share my hopes and dreams with them. Others I do hang out with, and Ruger, dragon, and BTS become regular companions on adventures around the city.

For some reason, my best friend since first grade, Emily, never quite approves of my new computer friends. As I spend more time with them, both online and in endless meet-ups and parties, Emily and I gradually grow apart. During my second year of college, I'll be back home during a holiday break, and realize I haven't seen her since before I left for school. When I think back to when I last saw her, I realize we never said goodbye.

CHAPTER 29

ON TUESDAY, I RECEIVE A TEXT MESSAGE from Owen, the angel I pitched to last week.

"Have time to meet again?"

"Sure, when?" I reply.

"Tomorrow morning at 11"

"Let me check my calendar."

I'm busy then, with a phone call set up to pitch to another VC. I call Mat for advice, and he urges me to reschedule the other call and meet with Owen instead.

I go to his office this time, in a building along the park blocks near Portland State University. I peek around the small suite of rooms curiously as one of the employees walks me over to Owen's office. The windows overlook the park outside, where a group of college students sit on the grass, having what appears to be a serious discussion.

"Thanks for coming, Angie," Owen says. He shakes properly, touching his right elbow to mine. "This is Stella, my legal counsel, and Todd, my business manager."

Whoa. I thought maybe Owen wanted to learn more, but this is another step up.

Stella greets me with a warm smile, and Todd waves one hand at me.

I repeat my dog and pony show, glad to show our progress with the new selective sharing feature.

Todd comes and leans over to look at my laptop, placing one hand on my shoulder. I freeze mid-sentence, my vision narrows, and I try desperately to remember what to do.

"Angie?" Owen says.

Todd's hand is gone, though I'm still frozen in time. Owen could be a thousand feet away. I'm having a panic attack. At an investor meeting, no less. I'm going to screw it up.

Then I remember my therapist's advice. The feeling of being in danger is a symptom, like having spots in my vision. It's not truly reality, not even useful to me now. I'm afraid. It's okay to be afraid. I can be afraid and still function, like I could have a toothache and still do what needs to be done, even if I'm uncomfortable and in pain. Panic will not kill me. Todd's hand will not kill me. Todd is not trying to hit me or control me.

I can breathe. I take a few deep breaths. I concentrate, move my pinky, then the rest of my fingers, then my arm. The worst is over.

I swallow and say what Charlotte told me to say in this situation. "I'm sorry. I was totally lost there for a second. What were we talking about?" Act like it was no big deal, Charlotte said.

Todd repeats his question, and the meeting goes on like nothing happened.

We had an hour planned, but it's going on two when Stella grills me on intellectual property.

"You're sure there's no non-compete with Tomo that can affect you?"

"None. I never signed one."

She shakes her head in disbelief. "I know they have them for other employees."

I shrug. "Maybe it was after my time."

"Some of this is based on published open protocols," Stella says, looking at Owen. "IndieWeb. It's going to be hard to lock it up."

"The point is not to lock it up," I say. "We want it to be open. The more participants the better."

"Open is good," Todd says. "You want contributions. On the other hand, you don't want to be so open that Tomo comes along, replaces your role in the ecosystem, and you disappear."

"We're the accounting backbone in the system. We track which components are involved in which interactions, and credit them with fractional payments. Without us in that role, nobody can process payments. That's our control point."

"That's a powerful place to be," Stella says. "Although alternative app stores have sprung up on mobile OSes. If anyone can find a way to insert themselves into your system, and substitute themselves in that role, they'll do it."

A vague ache spreads from the back of my head. I wish I could walk into these meetings and understand what people want. Technical discussions are so much easier. Do they want to invest or don't they?

"Don't worry," Owen says, catching my expression. "I'm investing. There are still major challenges for you to figure out, though. That's why, in addition to these terms..." He withdraws a sheet of paper from a folder and hands it to me. "I want a seat on your board. I can help you solve these problems."

I look over the term sheet. Enough money for four months, including our growth in headcount and the hardware Igloo needs.

"You'll want your lawyers to look this over," Stella says.

I clear my throat and try not to sound like I'm desperate. "Once we sign, how long until we receive money?"

"We can cut you a good faith check immediately to cover any short-term expenses, and you'd get the balance once we've concluded the legal restructuring."

Holy shit. I won't need to refi my condo. We can hire Kevin. The company can keep going. Someone believes in us!

Part Three

CHAPTER 30

Six months later

I SCAN MY BADGE at the door and step into the office with my bag slung over my shoulder and a coffee in my hand. The door pushes open in both directions, a two-thousand dollar extra the building management company was happy to tack on to our move-in cost. It seems expensive to make a door open two ways, but after an entire career of juggling my coffee cup and badge every time I enter an office building, I've earned it.

The lights are already on, so I'm not the first one here. It's mostly an open floor plan, with conference rooms and a handful of offices, including mine, around the edges, so it takes only a second to spot Igloo in her corner. All these months later, Igloo's real name still escapes me. Our finance guy must know her real name.

I'm shocked to see Igloo in this early. She routinely works late hours. On top of that, she uses a conference room as practice space for her band, so most days she has two or three hours of practice after she finishes work.

I set down my coffee and wander over. "What's got you up so early?"

"Early?" Igloo's voice cracks, though she doesn't look up from her screen or take her hands off her keyboard.

Uh oh. "It's a little after seven."

"Oh shit, seven already?" Igloo glances up at me, her eyes bloodshot. "Microfinance transactions and service records. I'm post-processing the log data to figure out which components are credited for each view. I have to tie the aggregation back to the original records in case of audit or if the service wants detailed usage metrics."

"This is related to Kindred?" Our new name for the chatbot, which now has two personalities: Jake and Ada.

"Yeah, I found discrepancies between Kindred's built-in usage metrics and the aggregated service records, and there was no way to correlate them."

I nod, only half grokking, and look around. "You've been here all night?"

"I guess. We had band practice until two, and I figured I'd work a few hours before bed."

I remember having that kind of energy. Must be nice to be young. "Go home and get some sleep."

"There's no point now. The new hire arrives at ten. I'll just grab breakfast."

Igloo turns back to her screen, grabs a box of Lucky Charms from her desk, and shoves a handful into her mouth.

"Are you sure—" I cut myself off before I can comment on her food choice. It doesn't matter because she's not listening to me, anyway. I'm not her mother, even if I feel that way. Of our twenty-one employees, seventeen are in their twenties, and I constantly remind myself not to parent them.

Overall, I'm proud of the employees. Fifteen are women, more than 70 percent. That's probably a record for a tech startup. A part of me wants to hire only women, but my conversation with Emily haunts me. With each new position, I wonder if I'd accidentally miss the best person for the position by excluding men. In the end, we have a good balance. Thanks to my ongoing therapy with Charlotte, I've never had a day in the office when I've been uncomfortable or had to check where the nearest door was.

Every employee is on board with Tapestry's mission, not only to build a credible competitor to Tomo, but to fundamentally change the power relationship between companies and users.

℧

The new employee is Keith. We hired him away from a late-stage Portland startup that's having an IPO in six months. "We spend all our time chasing the next buck," he told Amber and I during lunch a few weeks ago. "I want to actually build new stuff."

Igloo shows him around the office and gets him set up with a desk and a laptop. They finish in time for our staff meeting. We're crowded into the second biggest conference room, because the big one is full of band equipment. With the brand new employees, we're cramped in here, and I can barely hear myself think.

"Igloo, you've got to move the band into a different office."

Igloo's leaning back in a chair in the corner, eyes closed, her trademark white hoodie pulled over her head. Apparently she's finally succumbed to sleep.

"I'll send her an email," Amber says.

I nod and grasp my stump in my hand. "Let's start, people," I yell.

Everyone quiets down.

"A key part of our strategy is to build a social network that encompasses multiple companies. We can't build it all ourselves. If we did, we'd end up replicating Tomo, which doesn't differentiate us in the eyes of the user, and doesn't prevent the accumulation of power that comes with monolithic tech giants. We need partner companies to build diverse services and flesh out Tapestry."

"Indie partners," Igloo yells out without opening her eyes.

Figures she was faking.

"Yes to indie partners. Definitely we want indies on board. The more the merrier. We also need a few big players to give us distribution, and we finally have one of those. We signed a business relationship deal on Friday with CompEx."

Igloo, who was part of the technical evaluation of CompEx, and knows about the deal, boos from the back of the room.

I raise my eyebrows at Amber, and she grabs her phone. As I continue, I see Igloo pick up her phone, and she nods at me. I don't know if Amber texted "be quiet" or "humor the old lady," but as long as Igloo lets me finish this presentation, I'll be happy.

"CompEx will implement a Tapestry storage service, single-sign-on, and a PC reader app. The out-of-box-experience for new CompEx tablets and PCs will include Tapestry signup. They're taking a small ownership stake in the company, and it'll give us several months of cash in the bank. That will tide us over until we close our VC funding."

There are cheers from the room, although Igloo and Amber are quiet. I thought I was maniacal about the power relationships between companies and their customers, but Igloo and Amber can't tolerate getting in bed with what they see as a dominant corporation.

"Igloo doesn't like that we're dealing with a big company, but in this case, it's a good deal. CompEx has stayed free of social media. They have no big partnerships. As the number three PC manufacturer and number four mobile phone manufacturer, they're eager to make something happen, and they see us as the path to be a serious player in social media. I'm fine with taking their cash to do that, especially since they're also on the hook to give us those services. Any questions?"

"What's the timeline?" our Director of Quality asks. "Are we going to do this before South By?"

Tons of companies launch at SXSW, the big interactive festival that draws thirty thousand attendees. Amber's got a keynote address on IndieWeb and returning power to the user, and Igloo will be moderating a panel composed solely of AI chat systems: our Ada chat personality, IBM Watson, and Bina-48.

"No, CompEx wants to announce at ITX in January."

Groans erupt from the crowd.

"That's two months ahead of schedule," someone cries. "We'll never be ready!"

"Nobody goes to ITX except industry people," says our social media manager. "We need a promotion plan outside of ITX."

"Yes, although nobody can talk about it ahead of time. We can mention the investment, without any specifics about the CompEx integration. I trust all of you to keep this confidential. A different company might keep this secret from their employees, but that's not the way I run Tapestry. I'm telling you and trusting you not to talk about it outside of here, neither officially nor unofficially. Not with your friends and not at any meetups. The day Tomo finds out, they'll use their leverage to stop CompEx from investing in us."

The room is sober for minute.

The newest new guy, Keith, raises his hand. "What prevents CompEx from building a silo on top of our service? Why stop at the services they've agreed to? What if they build all the components? Their users won't ever know they've got other options."

"Every client application has to provide access to the user settings app that only we provide," I say. "It's the equivalent of a mobile OS app store."

"Multiple app stores have shown up on AvoOS."

Igloo nods. Luckily she's in the back of the room where nobody notices.

"Then they lose their ability to interoperate with any non-CompEx components."

"What if they don't care? If they have 95 percent of Tapestry users, they might decide controlling their ecosystem is more important than remaining open."

I take a deep breath. I'm the one who chose employees who think through implications and challenge people. Mat once said there would come a point when I'd want people who put their heads down and do as they're told. At moments like this, I see his perspective.

"Open solutions work out the best. The IBM PC. You can argue IBM lost control over the PC, but the PC won because it was open. Avogadro's mobile OS has eight times the market share of their competitors, and yes, they might lose control, but the platform is open and winning. If we lose control, but Tapestry stays open and beats Tomo, I'm happy, even if our investors aren't."

"Allowing Tapestry to turn into a CompEx silo... I wouldn't do the deal if I thought that could happen. Still, if we want to avoid letting them gain control, we must keep planning our public launch, building our user base, getting indie partners to build components, investing in Kindred, building the reference service implementations. That strengthens our core so CompEx can't cut us off."

The questions go on for forty minutes, and by the time we break, I'm exhausted. It's still not over, as I'm intercepted by multiple people on the way back to my desk, fielding questions about the deal, database fields, and the user interface. By the time I sit down at my computer, I've got a hundred new emails and voice messages.

"Help. Need break from work," I message Thomas.

He comes by in thirty minutes. I grab a sweatshirt, and he drives to the park. He even has a sandwich from Elephant's Deli for me.

One-handed sandwich eating can be messy.

He catches my expression at the food. "Sorry about the sandwich, but I figured you'd be hungry and I grabbed something portable."

"No, it's great." Mostly it is.

He takes me to Laurelhurst Park. "Want to talk about it?"

"Not really. I'm exhausted from talking. I want to eat my sandwich and sit with you. Is that okay?"

"Just fine."

We find a bench overlooking the lake. It's a crisp, sunny spring day. Thomas bought himself a sandwich too, so we sit side-by-side and eat. When I'm done, I lean my head against his shoulder and close my eyes. I hear the ducks at the lake, which sound almost like dog barks. There's the distant sound of a mother talking to her kids, and the kids squealing.

It is fantastic to sit and not have anyone asking me questions or forcing me to make decisions about stuff I don't have any expertise in.

"Can we live in the woods?" I ask.

Thomas chuckles. "You'd hate it. Away from everything and everyone and with a shitty Internet connection to boot. The first time the power went out or the net went down, you'd flip out."

"Shush. I want my fantasy. They deliver sushi in the woods, right?"

He kisses my forehead. "Yes, sushi, Thai, tapas. It's all available. Also drones deliver packages in under thirty minutes."

"Oh, perfect."

"Let's get a cabin this weekend," he says. "I'll find something for Saturday night."

"I can't. I need to prep this weekend for an investor call on Monday."

I blink my eyes open, the sunlight startling me. A rude return to reality, investor calls.

"How about next weekend, Saturday night?"

We go back and forth, checking calendars and availability until we settle on a Saturday four weeks in the future.

"I'll even bring you home by noon on Sunday, so you have the afternoon to work."

"Deal. Now kiss me."

We spend a minute making out on the park bench, and it feels good. Then Thomas pulls away. I open my eyes to see him gesture with his head toward the lake.

There's a little kid, maybe three or four, holding half a slice of bread and staring at us with big eyes. Two ducks slowly waddle after her, following a trail of breadcrumbs.

"Come back here, Ella," yells the mom. "Leave those people alone."

"Come on," Thomas says, grabbing my hand. "Let's go before we're arrested for indecency."

I'm a little late, a little sweaty, and my hair is messed when I return to the office for the API meeting Amber leads. But I'm a lot less stressed. A worthwhile tradeoff.

Amber shakes her head even as she smiles.

CHAPTER 31

Chris> What's up?

Joe> The client who wanted the data on Angelina Benenati. Now they want her out of the picture.

Chris> Wetwork?

He doesn't usually do that sort of thing. But if the price is right, he could. It's what he had trained to do before everything went digital. She's a woman, and a powerful one. It would actually be enjoyable.

Joe> Jesus, no. You scare me. She's started a company. They want the company to go away. Maybe she's

```
found embezzling, goes to jail, that sort of thing.
Discredited, not disemboweled.
```

Well, that's vaguely disappointing. Still, she's successful. He imagines the fall would be pretty painful.

```
Chris> Give me a few days to dig, see what I have
to work with.
```

Daryl is out for a few hours, which means Chris Daly has time on his own to research. He goes downstairs to the basement. They're in another short-term rental house, in Seattle this time, which makes Daly happy, because he'll see the waitress tonight.

Daly unlocks his computer into his secret partition and goes back to his files on Benenati. Back when the client first asked for a data dump on her, he'd pulled down everything. Modern detailed data such as web history, email, and phone records goes back about ten years, although everyone has financial and credit data, arrest records, tax filings as far back as the eighties in most cases, when computerization of records began in earnest.

Thing is, there's a lot of data on Benenati, although only in certain areas. Her online profile is ten times the average size. He'd glanced through her browser history one time and been bored to tears. Six hundred web searches on a single day, all related to aspects of programming.

Outside of work, she watched a hell of a lot of movies. Mostly popular stuff, yet it wasn't unusual for her to stream movies for hours on end. 95th percentile for hours of television watched, more than a bit odd for a computer programmer. The psych profilers even mentioned it when he asked them to take a pass through the file.

She also had a lot of VPN traffic. Fact is, that was the number one thing that stood out about her. On the other hand, it was a VPN into her work, not any of the bit torrent obfuscators. Still, a lot of network traffic. A lot of it happening at the same time as she was apparently watching television.

And she spent a lot of money as cash. Big, regular cash withdrawals, not in the realm of blackmail, yet still a lot more hard currency than the average person.

And yet, she has almost no social data online. Few Tomo posts of substance, no Picaloo account, few connections to anyone else.

Problem is, none of these pieces of data individually mean anything. Put all together, it points to something more, but neither he nor the data geeks at Central had come up with anything conclusive.

↺

Chris Daly doesn't go into the office often; then again, he doesn't need to. He has his burner phones, and encrypted connections for when he needs to talk to Enso. Normally, he and Daryl spend all their time operating in the field, taking care of Enso's most sensitive, most politically deniable stuff.

The only time he sees anyone from BRI is when he calls in a crew for a temporary base of operations, cleanup, or if they need a bit of wetwork.

But now he needs to see the data boys, the analytic geeks that crunch the data, profiling people and digging up dirt. He needs to put the fear of God or Enso or something into them, which is why he took the redeye last night from coast to coast, and this morning he's heading for the Hopper Information Services Center (HISC), part of the Office of Naval Intelligence.

BRI is a modern ghost organization, which means BRI doesn't exist. Not only are there no public records, there's also no actual organization or budget. Their data arm is twenty-odd staff paid for and housed by the Navy, and armed with data by the big fat Naval data center.

The psych arm of BRI is run out of Military Information Services Organization (MISO), part of the U.S. Army. Chris himself is technically part of the FCC's Enforcement Bureau in the Investigations Division. He visits FCC headquarters once a year to renew his badge. Everyone is in a position where their BRI work is plausibly consistent with their day jobs.

Only Enso reports to the NSA's Signal Intelligence organization, where he is a Division Chief, with a regular NSA team, working on mundane intelligence. BRI is his second job.

Daly enters the Suitland Federal Center, which houses a dozen different government agencies, including the Naval Intelligence Center. He's on the permanent access list, in theory having something to do with investigating pirate radio stations operating in international waters, and they allow him into the parking lot.

Lieutenant Jessica Plaint, U.S. Navy, is in charge of the team of mixed naval staff and contractors. She's not happy to see him when he plants himself in her office at 8:45.

"Daly." She drinks what appears to be the last sip of coffee in her cup, and does a double-take at the empty mug. "I've got a meeting in five minutes."

"Really?" He glances at the wall clock. "You schedule meetings at ten before the hour?"

"Don't be a dick. What do you want?"

For some reason, he and Plaint never get along. He suspects Plaint only likes mining data, and doesn't want to think about what's done with it, which is what he represents.

"I need to work with your team."

"Obviously." She leans back in her chair, arms crossed. "You didn't come for the company. What for?"

He doesn't know why she has to be so goddamn antagonistic. "I have a person of interest, maybe connected to a suspicious death."

"Yeah, we already got your request through Enso. The team investigated, found a few anomalies. Cell phones in the vicinity that weren't usually there. License plates caught by traffic and security cameras. They dug into each, ran them by PsychOps, and none match your person of interest."

"Maybe the team overlooked something or PsychOps profiled wrong."

Plaint's face tightens and her voice gets frosty. "Or maybe your person of interest had nothing to do with it."

"There's got to be something. I want to spend the day with them."

"Come on, Daly. You're going to annoy them. It does no good for someone to watch over their shoulders."

"I want to spend the day with them." Chris enunciates each word forcefully.

Plaint glances at the clock. "Jesus, Daly. You're a pain. Fine, spend the day with them."

"Thanks, Jessica. You're a sweetheart."

She raises her eyebrows at that. "Get out."

He puts up one hand in submission and lets himself out.

↻

The investigation team works down the hall from Plaint's office, in a room whose door won't open to Daly's badge. He settles for knocking.

The door opens a crack and a young kid (they all look like kids to him these days) blocks the path. Chris pushes his way in, and the kid protests.

"You can't come in here."

Chris is on the verge of telling him off, when a familiar face from across the room hurries over.

"It's okay," Pete says, "Daly is one of us."

A handful of analysts around the room look up and nod in Daly's direction.

"Oh, you're Mr. Daly," the kid says. "Sorry. It's, er... Nice to meet you." He retreats to a dark corner.

"How are you, Pete?" Chris says as they shake.

"I'm fine. Sorry about this case. We're not turning up anything."

"Show me what you have."

He follows Pete back to his desk. The team of analysts are spread around the perimeter of the room, about twenty people, each with an eight-foot wide swath of desk covered with monitors. Most ignore him and Pete.

"We pulled all camera and cellular data, and wi-fi connections for a two-mile radius, from 1 A.M. until four on the day in question. There's a lot less people out and about in the middle of the night, so the search results were small. After we excluded the people who live in the neighborhood, we turned up less than twenty anomalies. Mostly out-of-towners vacationing, but a few were folks from other parts of town visiting friends. We cross-checked with email and cells records, and all appear legitimate: they made plans in advance and had consistent electronic trails. We flagged them for ongoing monitoring, and all of their subsequent electronic activity is continuing within statistical norms. Your person-of-interest, Angelina—"

"She goes by Angie," Chris says.

"Angie was on Mount Hood, at Timberline Lodge, the entire time. Definitely not in Bend. I've got her cell phone there, cell phone activity. Her vehicle never showed up on any street cameras. She was watching TV like usual. She watches a hell of a lot of TV."

"We can make a false electronic trail to pass that level of inspection. She could have taken another car. Any chance of either?"

Pete shrugs, doubt on his face. "In theory, yes, but that's a lot of work, and harder still without backdoors into the telecoms to insert the data in the first place."

"What about the cookie?" Chris asks.

"Please don't tell me all this is based on that cookie."

The browser cookie is all Chris has. The day after the death in Bend, which is now months ago, there was a news story on the Bend Bulletin website. Tens of thousands read the article, their web browsers automatically sending tracking cookies so that advertisers can know who they are regardless of what website they visit. The NSA has those cookies, of course, and can map them to people's identities as easily as the advertisers can. One of those visitors, according to the cookie, was Angie.

"It doesn't show up in her browsing history," Chris says. "And there's no trail of how she got to that story. She didn't hit the Bulletin landing page and there's nothing in any of her social media feeds about it. No one hits a deep URL without some trace of how they got there."

"She was still at Tomo then." Pete shrugs. "It's a huge company, really complex network. Lots of mixed hardware and software. Maybe she bounced a connection through routers in a way that we missed. The logs aren't perfect. For all we know, the story was linked from another site, and we don't know."

"Something doesn't add up here," Chris says. "Why doesn't it show in her browser history?"

"Plenty of people clear their browser history. Plus, in her case, she's a programmer. They clear out everything on a regular basis."

"There's something weird about her, and something fishy about the death in Bend."

"I don't know about her, but you're right about the death. The field team got the firmware back from the furnace last night. It differs from the factory code, and it was flashed the night of the death."

"We can tell when something was flashed?" Chris is impressed.

"Yeah, something about half-life decay of electrons from atoms," Pete says. "I'm not sure how it works. Anyhow, the evidence is clear someone modified the software, which is almost certainly what caused the carbon monoxide poisoning. Whoever it was left no record. They came in clean, no electronic devices, and probably used a directional antenna only the house wi-fi would pick up, and not any of the neighbors. You know what that means?"

Chris shakes his head.

"Whoever altered the furnace firmware might know we've compromised the consumer wi-fi access points to report on which MAC addresses show up. Nobody's leaked that yet, which could mean they've got a source in the government."

"Or they've read the leaks and assume we can track everything." Chris glances at his watch. He can't afford to be completely sidetracked by this personal job. He still needs to take care of his official BRI work. "Keep Angie on active monitoring, and let me know if anything pops up."

CHAPTER 32

FOUR GRUELING WEEKS OF WORK fly by in a blur. The deal with CompEx turns out to be bigger than anyone expected. They've suddenly decided they want in on our Series A round of financing.

On the plus side, it's vastly more funds raised, their participation giving us industry acceptance, and the terms we've negotiated bring hundreds of millions of CompEx customers directly to Tapestry as part of the new product purchase experience. They're such a conservative investor that merely including them in the investment round has upped our valuation.

On the flip side, their entry, along with the terms they want, dilutes my ownership stake under 50 percent, the point at which I lose total control over the board of directors, and therefore the company. This is exactly what I sought to avoid.

Still, Owen is convinced CompEx is a friendly investor. They have neither the desire nor the mettle to interfere with management of the company, and he asserts we can count on them to vote with me.

I've talked it over at length with Emily, Thomas, and over two sessions with Charlotte. None of them can offer a crystal ball. Worse, the negotiations are causing delays, and we're already two weeks behind when we should have closed funding. My CFO begs me daily to close the deal so we can make payroll.

I desperately want to cancel the trip with Thomas. On Thursday night we grab dinner a little after nine, the restaurant nearly empty because this is late for Portland dining. Although I want a drink, I reluctantly skip the booze to save my clarity of thought for a call scheduled for later tonight.

I almost tell Thomas we need to reschedule. Looking at him, considering everything I've made him go through the last year, I realize I can't do it. I've missed too many things, forced him to bear the burden of my stress too many times. It's obvious the weekend is important to him. I must follow through regardless of what is going on at work.

On Saturday morning, we drive up to Timberline Lodge. It was cold on Thursday night, and there are a couple of inches of fresh snow on the mountain. I spend the first half of the trip on the phone as Thomas drives, exchanging messages and jumping on a call with the investors who are questioning our burn rate.

Not only has CompEx thrown the investments plans into chaos, they've also destroyed my spending forecasts. I've been forced to rapidly staff up our biz dev team to procure us a full complement of partners in time for our new ITX launch date. Hiring faster than planned has messed with our financials.

I spend the call defending my actions and juggling various factions. While most of the investors want to slow hiring and spending, one urges us to run an incubator program to bring smaller, more innovative partners onboard, which requires more money and people. Meanwhile, CompEx wants us focused on their integration. Everyone's demanding more information, more data, more answers. My head pounds trying to keep track of it all. Balancing everything is critical to closing the funding round.

In the midst of this, Lewis Rasmussen comes to mind. He sent that email right before Owen gave us our seed funding, and then another a month later, congratulating us, despite the lack of any public announcement. Since then, nothing. It's been six or seven months. If he was paying close attention before, why hasn't he been in touch? It's too much to hope we fell off his radar. I made a mental note to ask Owen if he's heard anything the next time we meet in person.

I spend an hour arguing with the investors and ironing out details while Thomas patiently drives, only occasionally raising an eyebrow at my end of the conversation.

We're passing a small town on Highway 26, when Thomas squawks. I glance over at him, and he smiles at me.

I shrug back at him and mouth "what?"

He makes more pretend static noises until I clue in. He's been pretty patient so far.

"Hey guys," I say, and it is all men on the phone besides me, because, despite my best efforts, I haven't been able to find any female investors, "I'm heading into the mountains, and I may lose you. I'd better hang up here. I'll have answers for you by Monday."

I disconnect, and stare at the phone in my hand for a moment. The battery is hot from non-stop usage. Screw it. I turn the phone off, and turn to Thomas. "Sorry about that."

"It's fine," he says. "I'm signed up for the package deal. Everything okay?"

"Good enough for now. Please, let's not talk about it. What are you working on these days? I have no idea."

He tells me about his cases, his new automated legal discovery software, and before I know it, we're turning up the seven-mile long driveway to Timberline.

It hits me as we pass the waterfalls along the road. The last time I was up this way was almost ten months ago, the summer of last year, when I faked a vacation and actually took a trip to Bend to kill some guy. To *kill* someone. I'm a murderer. I put that part of myself away when I left Tomo, and I've been living a whole different life since then. The old me, is she even in there anymore?

What happened to my old values? This new life might be too easy. I actually like running a company.

Maybe I'm addicted to power. Running a company is another form of dominion. I've gone from killing people to a more socially acceptable way of being in control.

And yet I'm creating Tapestry to stop people like me from being in charge.

I rest my head against the window. I don't know if I can trust myself.

"Everything okay over there?"

"The snow is pretty," I say.

"Yeah, it is."

Unlike Emily, whom I could never fool with such an easy distraction, Thomas takes everything at face value.

"Did you pack boots?" he asks. "We can go for a walk tomorrow morning, up to Mirror Lake."

"Yup," I say. "Though you need to feed me before we can even talk about anything active because I'm starving."

He chuckles. "Don't worry, we have a dinner reservation at the lodge."

We check in, and make our way up to our room with our luggage.

"Our reservation is in twenty minutes," Thomas says, stepping into the bathroom.

"I'll need a minute to freshen up when you're done in there."

The wood-paneled room is dark at first. I open the shades and light from the setting sun streams in, turning the room golden. I lie on the bed while Thomas uses the bathroom, just for a minute to rest, because I'm suddenly exhausted. The next thing I know, I wake up, the room dark. Thomas is curled up next to me, his arm wrapped around me. Once it would have made me scream, now I gently push his arm aside.

His eyes open immediately.

"You're not sleeping?"

He shakes his head.

"Why didn't you wake me?"

"You were tired. I moved dinner back an hour. I'm keeping an eye on the clock."

I lean over and kiss him. "How much more time do we have?"

"Enough."

One thing leads to another, and soon we're naked. Thomas goes down on me, and I wrap my fingers in his hair and bite my lip to keep from crying out. I'm melting into the bed as he climbs on top of me.

"Apparently the antidote to work stress is sex," he tells me as we finally make our way to the dining room half an hour after our second reservation time.

"Yes, but if you don't feed me, I'm really going to die. My stomach is trying to digest itself."

"Hah. They have ribeye on the menu. Will that do?"

"If it comes with a honking huge potato it will."

When we arrive at the dining room, it's nearly empty, a few wait staff cleaning up and a single table of diners eating dessert.

"We had a reservation for eight o'clock," Thomas says to one of the staff who's walking by with a tray of glasses. "We're a little late."

A hostess walks up from behind us. "Sorry, the last seating is at eight. We're closed now."

"It's only eight-thirty," Thomas says.

"The Ram's Head Bar is open until eleven, and they have food."

"I want to eat here," Thomas says.

"It's fine," I say. "Let's go to the bar."

Thomas stares forlornly at the dining room.

"I can live without a steak. I'm sure there's something good upstairs."

The Ram's Head is crazy busy, a whole different atmosphere from the fine dining experience we missed. Even at this late hour there are families with kids of all ages running around, and layers of wet snow clothes draped over everything. We manage to grab a table by the window. When the waitress comes with menus, I don't let her leave until we've both ordered food and drinks.

"I want to—" Thomas begins.

"Wait," I say. "I'm too hungry. No talking until the food comes."

Bread and olives and our drinks finally arrive together. Buttering bread is not one of my fortes, so I plop a slab of butter on a slice and try to shove the whole thing in my mouth at once, which is, by far, too much food. I'm like a chipmunk, my cheeks puffed out and so full of bread I can't even properly chew.

Thomas laughs, which makes me laugh, and I blow little chunks of crust onto the table. Soon we're both laughing so hard tears are pouring down my cheeks. "Sure, laugh at the one-armed woman trying to eat before she dies of hunger."

"I'm sorry," Thomas says, still laughing. "Can I give you a hand?"

"Sure, I'll take the right one." I rip a smaller piece of bread.

"You'd look funny with one hairy arm."

Finally, food makes it to my stomach and the frenetic hunger dissipates.

"I want to ask you something," Thomas says.

There's something in his tone that makes me look up from the olives. Nothing prepares me for what comes next.

He carefully places a box on the table and pushes it toward me. My mind can't make sense of it at first, and then I realize.

"Will you marry me?" He opens the felt box turned towards me. There's a ring inside.

Oh. My. I nervously giggle, then cover my mouth with my hand. I take a deep breath, then a swallow of my drink. I breathe deeply a few more times and fan my face. I'm burning up in here.

"There's no rush," Thomas says with a smile. "But I guess I'd like some inkling of what you're thinking."

"I wasn't expecting… I mean. I'm so honored. I…"

"It's our two-year anniversary. I hope it's not too much of a surprise."

Cue the record screeching effect. Holy shit, our anniversary? Two years? I'm stunned, too shocked to say a thing.

Thomas's smile is a smidgen smaller than it was a minute ago. "You said you wanted to wait, and I have. But not forever. I want to live with you, spend our lives together. Do you want the same? We don't need to do anything right now, though I'd like to know if you at least have the same vision as me."

When we last skirted around the topic of getting married, I was still leading a double-life, working days at Tomo, and killing assholes by night. Back then, I'd said no, still too traumatized by my past experience, and unable to imagine marriage with the secrets I needed to keep. How would I have snuck out of the house to kill people? What would I have said about the VW bus? That's my secret lair, don't get any DNA on it?

There's no VW bus anymore, no sneaking out of the house, and while there are secrets, they're now about the past. If anything I'd done was going to be exposed, it would have happened by now.

There's no reason not to marry Thomas except that I'm in the middle of starting a company, surrounded by venture capitalists and investors and hounded by my employees and work at all hours of the day and night. Damn it.

"Yes, I'll marry you."

I lean across the table to kiss Thomas.

"Excuse me, hot plates," the waitress says just before our lips meet. She pushes her way in between us, setting food down on the table.

I laugh as we wait for her to leave, then come around the table to kiss Thomas. "I love you."

CHAPTER 33

ON MONDAY MORNING, I stop at Coava for a pour-over on my way into work. I'm in the office crazy early and spend a couple of hours catching up on emails and code commits. Between our night on the mountain and investor calls yesterday, I'm way behind on the actual running of the company. Still, I've reviewed every git pull request since I brought Amber on board, and I'm committed (pun intended) to continuing. I start off by approving an expansion of the beta program from five hundred to a thousand users, then get into code changes.

My eyes glaze over when I review the presentation layer changes, a mess of Javascript in what passes for one of the new presentation frameworks the kids like these days.

I scrutinize the ORM commits twice as hard to make up for my cursory skimming of the Javascript. There are countless queries I know could be written better in pure SQL, but I hold myself back from recommending changes. I'll drive my engineers crazy with that level of attention. I single out one schema change I know will come back to bite us later, and comment on it. Otherwise I settle for merely reading the changes.

Shit. When was the last time I actually wrote code? I check my own git history. It's been six weeks and two days since I pushed code, and that was a mere fifty-line Python script to query cloud server usage and predict future costs.

Is there something I could add to, where I could work a few hours a week and make a useful contribution?

Everything changes so fast, and the demands on my time would make it so—

"Boss? You coming to staff?" Amber gestures toward the conference room. "It's ten now."

Exactly my point. There's no way I can do anything without getting interrupted. "Be right there."

Amber nods and leaves.

I shove my laptop into my bag for the short journey to the conference room to free my hand for my coffee cup, and make it halfway to the conference room before I realize I've forgotten the coffee. I go back for my cup, and arrive to find the conference room full.

Igloo must have had the band in over the weekend, because we're in the big conference room, and there is space for us all now.

I set my laptop down and connect wirelessly to the big screen. I look up at the room, and the talking dies down.

Wow. There are forty-two of us here. I only know the number because head-count growth came up in the investor briefing yesterday. Technically we don't have employee numbers, because Igloo complained that monotonically increasing identification numbers contributed to the male-dominated, hierarchical management paradigm, so we all have SHA keys instead.

"Where is Igloo?" I ask Amber.

"Not here," Amber says.

"Igloo's never missed a day before."

"She's probably hungover," a friend of hers calls out.

That might be, but still, Igloo has never missed a day. Oh, I've discovered her on the couch in the break room, reeking of alcohol and pot, but actually not in the office is disconcerting. Still, everyone gets sick eventually.

The meeting passes without incident, and I give the presentation about our plans for the next couple of weeks, including our major development themes. I introduce the new guy, our third business development hire. Afterwards, I'm sidelined into a debate over third-party testing and validation, which goes right through lunch, which I'd planned to use for a series of phone calls, and then I'm into a string of afternoon meetings with marketing.

Dinnertime comes, and half the employees are still here. A call goes round for Mexican takeout orders, and they make the new guy go pick up the order. When the food shows up, everyone gathers in the break room. I grab my burrito and make a hasty exit. I hear the distant thud and the sound of laughter as they try to load a new keg into the refrigerator. I wonder if Igloo's band has been taking advantage of the free beer. If so, that might be pushing things a bit. I'll talk to Igloo about it when she gets back.

I think back to the commits I reviewed this morning. I didn't see anything from Igloo in the last few days. It was the weekend, but this is Igloo we're talking about. She must be really sick.

I grab my phone, hesitate a second, then dial Igloo.

The phone rings and rings.

"This is Igloo. If you are not the man, leave a message."

"Hey. This is Angie. I wanted to check to see if you were okay."

I send the same message by text.

☻

I show up on Tuesday morning, a bit late after meeting with Mat. I've got a heavy buzz from an over-caffeinated coffee, and I'm hyper when I arrive at the office. I greet the first few employees with way too much enthusiasm.

"We IPO already?" Amber asks. "You're sure excited."

"No, I just drank a mutant coffee bean."

"Eat some protein. There's fried chicken in the fridge."

"Will that help?"

"Not really. I was mostly suggesting it for the placebo effect. Also, I wanted to see if I could make you eat fried chicken for breakfast."

"Is Igloo in?"

"No."

"Have you heard from her?"

Amber shakes her head. "Give the girl a break. She works twelve, sixteen hours a day, seven days a week. Everyone needs some time off."

I nod and head to my desk. I send another quick message: "Hope you're feeling okay. Send me a message and let me know you're still alive."

It's another grueling day at work. The Series B funding is in the last stage of wrapping up, with everything in the lawyers' hands. There's nothing I need to do, but knowing what's happening in the background doubles my tension.

In the late afternoon, I go for a walk, and when I come back, the smell of leftover fried chicken is overwhelming. I check my messages again. The lawyers are waiting on one last set of supposedly minor tweaks from CompEx, then we'll have an agreement to sign.

I pace back and forth in my office, still worried about Igloo. I can't do this. I need to get out of here.

Sitting in my car, I tether my laptop to my phone, and check HR records to get Igloo's address. She lives in an apartment complex on the East Side, off Sandy Boulevard. I drive over and park outside her building, feeling foolish, like an overprotective mother.

She's an adult, right? She doesn't need me watching her. It would be a great way to spoil a perfectly good employee relationship if I act weird. Still, my gut aches.

I shut off the engine, brainstorming excuses for why I'm visiting her at home. For all I know, I'm breaking some employer law. I hit the intercom for her apartment, and wait without getting an answer.

I stare at the front door, noting the lock mechanism and intercom model. I'm fairly certain I had some exploits for this model, back when I had my… hobby. My tools are backed up, heavily encrypted, sitting on random hard drives, including a server in Germany, in case I need them again. Not easily accessible at this moment.

I hit buttons for other apartments. It's a modern system that uses an auto-dialer to ring their phone, and can only dial one person at a time.

"Hello?"

"It's me, I'm at the door."

"Me who?"

"Sorry, wrong button."

It takes six tries before someone buzzes the door open.

I find Igloo's apartment on the second floor and knock. No answer. I knock louder, my knuckles complaining. Still no answer.

Ten minutes later I'm back in my car, still staring at the apartment building.

I drive along Burnside, looking for an open coffee shop. I park outside one, and take out my laptop. I change the MAC address, using a bit of shell script to store the old one and generate a new one. I shut down everything I can that might connect to the net and leak any data about who I am. No browser, no email widgets, no Dropbox, no software update tools. When there's nothing left except Firefox running in incognito mode, I connect to the wi-fi, and download TOR. It's compromised, but better than nothing.

I make a couple of configuration changes from memory, and log into A Dead Channel. I page sysop.

```
SysOp> Back from the dead?
Angel> Long story. Been busy.
SysOp> I know. Been watching. You want a locate on
your friend?
```

I know Nathan keeps tabs on me, and I'm fine with that. We've been friends a long time, and it's good to have people watching your back. I didn't realize he was keeping *that* close a watch, though. He is blind, so at least I don't need to worry about him watching my video feeds. But if he can do this, who else can?

```
Angel> Yeah, her mobile geo would be nice.
SysOp> Hold on.
```

Two minutes go by. A few people go into the coffee shop. A cop drives by.

```
SysOp> In her apartment, in the SW corner.
Angel> You sure? I was just there.
SysOp> Yes. You want history?
```

Nathan could tell me everything about what Igloo's done online and in the physical world, probably inside of ten minutes. Is it worth that level of intrusion into her privacy? I can't operate that way anymore.

```
Angel> No, I'm good. Thanks. Owe you one.
```

I disconnect everything and power down the laptop. It's not perfect, although it's the best I can do without other tools handy to ensure no traces of my connection to the board is in memory.

Back at Igloo's apartment, I do my thing at the door again, starting with apartment number seven, until someone buzzes me in. I go back to Igloo's, knock on the door, and then text her. "I know you're inside. You don't want to open the door, you don't reply to messages. I'm worried about you. I'm not leaving until you tell me what's going on."

I sit down on the floor, wrap my arm around my chest, and wait.

A few minutes later I hear footsteps near the door, but it doesn't open.

"I'm still here," I call out loudly.

"Go away, Angie." She talks through the door, her voice muffled.

"I'm worried about you and I don't want you to be alone."

"I'm fine."

"You haven't committed any code in five days. You're not fine."

"Can you please leave?"

"No. Let me know what's going on. We can talk."

"I'm sick. I don't want to infect you."

"I've already lost an arm. I'm not afraid of germs."

Nothing. I keep waiting.

"Are you still there?"

"Yes."

The deadbolt turns and the door opens.

"You can come in."

I practically jump to my feet. At least, what counts as jumping for a forty-five-year-old, out-of-shape computer programmer. I inspect Igloo's face. It's red, and she's got bags under her eyes. Nothing I can see looks like bruises, although she's mostly covered up as usual, under layers of clothing and regular baggy white hoodie.

I couldn't admit it to myself before, but I was worried she had gotten into trouble with a man. It doesn't appear that way, at least not obviously. I let out a small sigh of relief.

I follow her into the apartment. It's small. A tiny, gloomy living room and kitchen, and through an open door, I see a bedroom, brightly lit.

Igloo turns on the living room light and clears her throat. "See? I'm fine."

"I thought you were sick."

"I am."

"You look okay."

"You're not my mother. I didn't want to come into work, okay? Is that such a problem?"

"You've never not come into work before. I wasn't even sure you had a place to live outside the office. Why don't you tell me what's really going on?"

We're standing awkwardly, facing each other across the living room. In the kitchen, dishes are piled up, garbage on the counter.

"It's nothing you can help with."

There is something. I knew it.

"Is a guy bothering you?"

She shakes her head.

"A girl?"

"No. It's not about me. It's my sister, Claire."

"What's going on?" I take a seat on the couch, hoping Igloo will follow suit. She slumps into a chair across the room.

"She, ah…" Igloo runs her hands through her hair, then pulls apart a greasy tangle. "Aw, fuck. It's complicated."

I nod and wait, suddenly feeling like my therapist.

"Claire took pictures of herself and her girlfriend. My mother doesn't know about the girlfriend."

I'm confused about where this is going. "How old is she?"

"Fourteen."

"Your mom saw the pictures?"

"No." Igloo takes a deep breath, and I realize she's on the verge of crying. "Someone messaged Claire. They hacked her phone and had the photos. They threatened to share the photos with everyone. You know what it's like? When you're different, and everyone gossips about the slightest thing."

Now Igloo does cry.

"What'd they want?"

"More photos. Naked pictures."

Oh, crap. I know where this is going. "Did she?"

Igloo nods and wipes her face with her sleeve.

"And then they wanted still more," I say, "and they used each new round of more compromising photos to blackmail her."

Ratters, possibly the most villainous scum on the net this side of Mos Eisley, use remote access tools to invade their victims' phones and computers and toy with them. A subset of the more manipulative and cruel assholes keep escalating their demands, obtaining ever more incriminating photos and videos, until they turn their victims into their personal online sex slaves.

"They won't stop," Igloo yells, her voice choked up. "Why won't they leave her alone?"

If they've taken it this far, they will never leave her alone, not until they run out of ways to torture her (unlikely) or become bored of her (somewhat likely) or she kills herself. It's not going to help to tell Igloo this.

"Why are you here," I ask, "and not with her?"

"I thought I could find them, figure out who's doing this. She sent me their messages. They're coming from an IP address range in Sweden that belongs to a VPN provider."

"You're not going to be able to trace them." In fact, it's more likely they'll find Igloo and threaten her too.

"No, but they're using a tool called Mole to take over her phone. Because they know things she's only talked about, like they're listening to her all the time, even when she's not on the phone. I found a darknet forum where Mole was created and I'm pretending to be a teenage guy."

"She should turn her phone off," I say. "Not give them anything else to use against her."

Igloo shakes her head. "They told her she's not allowed to turn her phone off, or they'll share the photos." Her voice catches. "They created a whole website under her name, password protected. They keep threatening to turn off the password."

"Is she likely to hurt herself?"

Igloo wipes her face on her sleeve. "I don't know."

"You should go home right away, be with her."

"I'm going to find the assholes who are doing this and fucking kill them."

"I will take care of it," I say, my voice firm.

Igloo looks up at me.

"I have contacts from when I used to work in security, white hats. They'll find these guys quickly, faster than you. They can take care of the website, and destroy all the photographs."

Igloo stares. I'm not sure if she's even seeing me.

"What did I tell you your first day at Tapestry?"

"Never get coffee or fix the copier for a man."

I come over and sit next to her. "True, but not what I was thinking. I also said I would take care of my employees, and I will. Go pack right now. I'll drive you to the airport. Whatever's the next flight home, take it. Be with your sister. She needs you in person. I'll take care of these scum."

↻

It's almost one in the morning by the time I see Igloo off at the airport. I solve one small mystery when I watch her pack. I often wondered how her sweatshirt stays clean, given she never takes it off. Half of her closet was white hoodies, one after another hanging in a row.

I've been up since five, and I'm exhausted after fourteen hours of work and tonight's drama. Still, there's no way I can sleep. Every hour that passes increases the chance of irreparable harm. If the scum post photos or videos publicly, there will be no way to scrub them from the Internet, despite Tomo's pretend version of privacy. Whether anything is released or not, the odds are high Igloo's sister may harm herself.

I need my tools and a place to work.

There's a storage facility off I-84 I chose specifically for its location and 24-hour access. I drive there now, park in a corner out of range of the security camera. With my laptop bag over my shoulder, I skirt the parking lot to enter through a side door, my hand over my eyes as if to shield them from the light. I have a soft RFID transmitter that can mimic different RFID keys, and in this case, I have the codes of several different tenants I stole over the course of a few months after I got my own storage room. The reader rejects the first code, accepts the second, and the door unlocks with a click.

I make my way to my storage room, an eight-by-ten cinderblock box at the back of the building. I enter the room and switch on the single fluorescent tube that spans the ceiling. It blinks and buzzes, and then settles into an uneasy light. The room is half full of furniture, with a stack of cardboard boxes along one wall. I pull out a folding chair and card table, set both up, and start my laptop.

In the 1800s, railroad companies criss-crossed the United States in unbroken lines spanning thousands of miles.

In 1865, the Southern Pacific Railroad formed and, over time, acquired other companies, peaking at 14,000 miles. Their right-of-way encompassed the railroad line and a swath on either side of the tracks. Southern Pacific built a nation-spanning communications network along those tracks using microwave transmitters run by a division of the company called Southern Pacific Communications.

In 1972, Southern Pacific Communications began leasing extra capacity on their network to large companies as private long-distance phone lines, skirting the existing telephone monopoly. Then in '78, MCI won the right to provide switched-telephony services to compete with AT&T. Southern Pacific also sued, and, in the Execunet II decision, was granted the right to offer their own switched telephone network. They needed a new name and chose SPRINT, an acronym for Southern Pacific Railroad Internal Networking Telephony.

That brings us to the modern day, and the fiber optic switch station located on the other side of this cinderblock wall.

A couple of years ago, I broke into a Sprint supply truck and replaced a stock blade server with a customized version. I was back in touch with Nathan9 by then. Still the master, compared to me, he connected to the Sprint network switch station and faked imminent failure messages from a blade server. The monitoring team received the messages and routed the truck to the station, where the blade was replaced with my compromised version.

Now I enjoy direct access to Sprint's Internet backbone through my blade server plugged into their slot.

Years ago I compromised a server cluster in Germany, and it, along with a few other servers around the world, have been unwittingly hosting backups of all my tools for years. I download a compressed virtual machine, or VM, image from the server. The VM runs on my Mac, insulating the host operating system by running a simulated computer within the real one. If someone tries to attack or profile me, they'll only penetrate as far as the virtual machine. The VM is preconfigured with all the tools I don't want found on my computer because merely possessing them is a crime.

It's not as perfect as my preferred setup, which would require completely scrubbed physical hardware, but then I'm deeply paranoid. No matter how good you are, someone else out there is better, and playing in this space is as likely to attract unwanted attention as it is to achieve the goals you want in the first place. When camping, you need twice the warmth under you as you do above you. In hacking, you should spend twice the energy on avoiding being detected or traced as you do on the hacking.

Well, enough foreplay. Time to get to work.

Ratters use remote access tools, originally designed for sysadmin-type work, to remotely install software, monitor computers, and fix problems. That same set of tools, applied to more evil purposes, can be used to watch your every keystroke, record your webcam or phone camera, or change what you see on your screen. Since the ratters are behind a virtual private network, as Igloo said, I won't be able to trace their IP packets directly back to them, which would be the easiest and most direct way to identify them.

Nathan could probably do it, because he'd possess the tools to intercept all the traffic going to and from the VPN data center. I'm dead set against asking. If he does all my work for me, I'm no longer an equal trading favors, but a supplicant begging indulgence. We have a long history, and he wouldn't turn me down, but I'm afraid of changing the nature of our relationship.

I consider the tools to hide my point of origin. Do I still trust my own backdoors into Tomo? How about my onion network? The last time I used it, I lost a few nodes. I can use a VPN, but that only goes so far. I could compromise a few systems and set up a temporary routing network, but my tools are a year out of date, which means I won't have as many zero day exploits. I decide to VPN first, then take my chances with my old Raspberry Pi network. Either the nodes will be up or they won't.

A few minutes later, I'm reconnecting to the old network, the nodes coming online one by one. Each node reports a last use date consistent with my previous usage. Some of the nodes chosen at random don't respond, about par for the course, given that those rooftop boxes are two years old now. Surely some were discovered and thrown away, had their solar panels covered with leaves or other debris, or otherwise failed due to exposure. Soon enough my packets are routed through eight nodes.

A custom search tool connects in parallel to all the darknet forums I have access to. There's a bit of sadness when I see two of my old favorites are gone. The search tool scans the ones left to find any mentions of Mole, the RAT software Igloo detected. A few minutes of reading uncovers that Mole is newish, about four months old, based on an older RAT. The source code is available.

I think of three basic strategies I can exploit: I can try to reverse engineer Mole, looking for undiscovered exploits that would let me tunnel back into the hackers' computer from code I'd run on their victim's phone. It would be powerful because it would allow me to identify them and counter-attack in one. Unfortunately, it requires finding and using an exploit in software that's presumably been peer-reviewed. If there is a weakness, it could take days to find. Backtracing their VPN connection is another option, though perhaps beyond my abilities.

Lastly, I can search the forums themselves for something to identify the hackers: a brag mentioning the victim's name or an image file matching a known photo from the phone. This is the simplest approach, and costs me very little. I configure my spidering search tool to find the closest matches to the messages I received from Igloo. Then I sit back to wait, because the process isn't fast.

Thirty minutes later I'm regretting I stopped for that coffee on the way back from the airport and don't have a bucket in my cinderblock box. I make a mental note to never again own a villainous lair without a toilet. I'm older and richer, and frankly, too tired and grumpy to rough it. On top of that, I wonder if I'm starting menopause. I'm forty-five. Could it be happening?

With a sigh, I turn to the stack of boxes. I have no idea what's in most of them. I acquired them at an auction at another storage facility, and moved them in here for show. The second box I open has a men's felt cowboy hat. I turn it over in my hand. What the hell, it'll hold liquid for a little while, at least.

The search returns, and I'm staring at the phrase Hitler's Mustache. What the hell? Am I dealing with a neo-Nazi group? It's bad enough I have to handle misogynists, now I'm getting into Nazis? Frak me. I shouldn't have this much responsibility.

A few minutes and web searches later, and I laugh in relief. Apparently a Hitler's Mustache is the Brazilian term for sculpted pubic hair, or what the rest of the world would call a Brazilian wax job. My attacker is merely Brazilian, not a Nazi.

I spend the next couple of hours researching different Brazilian underground forums, and getting access to them. I pass their quizzes to keep out the riffraff, and know the right names to throw around. Although it's four in the morning here, it's mid-morning in Brazil. By the time I should be heading into work, I've gotten accounts on four of the biggest Brazilian hacker boards. I reconfigure my spider search tool to use my new forum accounts, and redo my earlier search.

It's going to take a while, so I use the opportunity to decamp the storage facility, walk a dozen blocks away, and leave a message for Amber, asking her to take over my meetings. My throat is hoarse from the all-nighter which adds legitimacy to my "I'm sick and can't come in" plea.

I stop at another coffee shop, which has just opened for the day, and buy pastries and coffee and use the restroom. There's a little hardware store down the block, so I purchase a bucket and a padded furniture blanket.

Back at the storage facility, my search results have returned, and I've received several matches on Claire's photos. The downside is her photos are leaking into the wild, the upside is now I have a line on the person who's doing this: a user named Titereiro.

Things become a little tricky, because the posts are in Portuguese, which I don't speak. Online translate is my friend, but I must keep it on a separate network connection from my other work. I take the necessary precautions, and cut and paste forum posts, beginning with the ones surrounding Claire's photos, and expanding to everything posted by Titereiro.

His profile photo is a football club logo of a team in São Paolo. Occam's Razor says he lives in São Paolo. The forum posts from Titereiro came in from various hours of the day, not an isolated few, which suggests he's not doing this from an Internet cafe but has steady net access, probably from home. I spend the next hour scanning forum posts, trying to discern patterns. He's been online for a year. Longer posts and photos are posted at night and on weekends. There are no photos or long posts between 8 A.M. and 4 P.M. In fact, those daytime posts are short, with even more text-speak. So he's posting by phone during the day. He's at work, or more likely, school.

Even if I could compromise the message board and either find a log of IP addresses or start monitoring every connection, there would be no point. If he's smart enough to disguise himself behind a VPN when he's attacking these girls, he'll do the same when visiting the message board.

Instead, I download all his posts in raw Portuguese and connect to Tomo's network. Access to my backdoors at Tomo was part of my ongoing exchanges with Nathan9, and even though I left the company, he would've kept them open. He's not half the coder I am, but maintaining an existing exploit is easier than engineering it in the first place. Most of my changes were not obvious, and only Nathan and I use them, which means the chance of discovery is exceedingly low. If something breaks, it's more likely to be a random side effect of code changes.

I write a quick Ruby script to break Titereiro's posts into individual sentences. The script then takes each sentence and searches Tomo's database of message posts, filtering by those messages posted in San Paolo, by someone of high school age, and ordering by closeness of match. There's more than five thousand sentences, and what I'm hoping will happen is one user will bubble up, one person in San Paolo who talks about the same sorts of topics, with the same patterns of language usage.

It takes nearly twenty minutes because the API wasn't built for this type of bulk query, and logging directly into the database isn't a risk I want to take. When the query is done, one person rises to the top, nearly forty percent ahead of the second closest match. His name, his phone, his high school, all the data is mine. A few searches later, and I flesh out the rest of the picture.

Theo. Seventeen years old. Not a nice person, if he's the one doing this. Before I burn him, I must make sure. I don't want to wreck the wrong kid's life.

I'm not familiar with Brazilian ISPs or Internet records, but what I want to know is easy for someone who is. I connect to a darknet board running on a pirate server on a Scandinavian ISP. There's a chat room there, busy all hours of the day or night, where people trade favors. Like any modern social media system, of course, reputation is codified, the favor economy measured and meted according to contribution. In short, I've got credits to spare, and it takes only a quarter of an hour from the time I post my request with a bounty until I've got Theo's home IP address.

I could trade in another favor to reset the router, but a quick test shows I don't need it because the router is still configured with the default admin password. In a few minutes I'm on Theo's machine, a Windows computer. He might have known enough to use a VPN, but he wasn't smart enough to store all his compromising pictures and videos on a separately encrypted volume. There are thirty-odd folders, each labeled with a girl's name. I spot check a few files. A video starts with a girl, eyes red and puffy, and Theo's voice, speaking in accented English, telling her to take off her shirt. The bastard.

I stop and rest my head on the table, feeling sick. Afraid and angry at the same time, I'm divided between wanting to crawl into a corner or punching something. I don't dare open Igloo's sister's folder, although I see her name there in the list of folders: Claire-14.

I sit up, and breathe in and out through pursed lips. I need to take care of him. But how? He's seventeen. Can I kill a child, even a monstrous one like Theo? Maybe I don't need to. Unlike in-person abuse, there's a solid trail of evidence of Theo's crimes. Here in the U.S., what he's done is a significant crime, and with the right tips, the government would investigate and deal with him accordingly.

Will the Brazilian government treat online blackmail with the same seriousness? I don't know what current Brazilian policies are. However, every government can be counted on to give the utmost consideration to the safety of their leaders. I spend a few minutes searching the Internet, and soon I find my answer. The Vice President of Brazil has a daughter.

I make a new folder on his computer: Juliana-14. I populate it with a few public photos of Juliana, then grab one clear shot, and feed it into Tomo's image recognition algorithm. A few minutes later, it spits out a matching Picaloo user: xJulie02x. As I figured. The government probably won't let Juliana create social media accounts as a semi-public figure. But then she's a clever girl, under peer pressure like everyone else, and she found a way to make an account on Tomo's companion photo sharing network.

The key thing is she's in Tomo's database, and she's running the Picaloo app, which means I can grab her phone's photos. I start the process.

It takes a while, so I use the bucket and clean my hands with a wet wipe. I eat half a scone I bought earlier. A few crumbs drop to the floor, reminding me of the accumulating DNA evidence in this room. I used the van for a long time, and before that, I had other blind offices. The problem, of course, is if someone finds this place and my DNA in it. My connection into Sprint's backbone might be off the radar at present, but an NSA-level investigation would turn it up. If I'm caught now, it's not only my fate I'm affecting. It's the future of Tapestry and Thomas.

Is there any reason to believe anyone would be suspicious? How many times can I get away with this?

The upload is done. This part I feel a little queasy about, yet if I want to protect Claire, I can't take the chance Theo will suffer anything less than prison. I pick a few of Juliana's photos taken in her bedroom. They're completely innocent: in one she's making a funny face while she works on her homework, and in the other she's holding up her dog and taking a picture in the mirror. But both are undeniably private, and that's what will guarantee Theo goes to prison.

I add these photos to Theo's hard drive. Then, working from Theo's computer, I publicly post the photos on Tomo as Theo, and brag about breaking into Juliana's home computer. I make sure his social media profile is up to date with his home address. No point in making the police work harder than necessary. To add as much pressure as possible, I submit a tip to Folha de São Paulo, the largest national newspaper, with a link to Theo's profile.

One last task: I examine his browser history, find the sites where he's been uploading photos of these girls hidden behind password-protected pages, and destroy all the sites. I'd like to remove the photos of his victims from his computer, but then I'd be destroying the evidence the police will need to put him away.

I disconnect and clean up after myself. It's afternoon and I've been up since yesterday morning. There's a nugget of satisfaction that I've taken care of Claire's problems, wrapped in a thick layer of exhaustion, surrounded by a crunchy shell of worry. I have more than myself to consider now: my employees, payroll, our board meeting, Thomas.

I have work to do, both Tapestry work, and cleanup work here. I imagine the DNA, fingerprints, crumbs, footprints, and other records of my existence that place me here in this room. I'm too tired for any of it. I'll come back and do it later. I need sleep.

CHAPTER 34

SOMEONE YELLS AND I STRUGGLE UP, fighting bedcovers, until I'm sitting, my heart pounding and throat sore. It was me, screaming for help. The room is silent.

I rub my face and stare at the clock before I piece together the time and realize it's the middle of the night. I have barely enough time to think I haven't had one of those nightmares in months before I fall back to sleep.

When I wake in the morning, I find I've slept for almost fourteen hours, not counting my nighttime waking. I vaguely recall the nightmare, a nameless, faceless terror touching me as I lay paralyzed, unable to move or do anything. I feel dirty, like it wasn't merely a dream, but someone actually violating me. I can't wait to shower.

I glance at the urgently blinking light on my phone, which turns out to be a mistake. Too many guilt-inducing missed calls, screenfuls of text messages, and triple-digit new emails. I swipe the notifications off the screen. I can't deal with all that. I take a long shower, forcing myself to stay in and ignore the psychological pressure of the demands on me. I'm toweling off when my phone rings with a call from Thomas. I place him on speaker as I finish getting ready in the bathroom.

"Hi, I'm getting dressed."

"I like the sound of that," he says, "but what the heck happened last night?"

"What do you mean?"

"We planned dinner and I was supposed to stay over. You never showed at the restaurant, and I called and texted a bunch, and never heard back."

Oh, shit. "I'm so sorry. Work was crazy. When I got home, I took what I thought would be a short nap, and only woke up a little while ago." My heart twinges at this lie. Crap, I hate being forced into this position. For a moment I'm furious at him for even calling, even asking me about yesterday. I don't want to be accountable to anyone for how I spend my time. This is why I kept him distant, back when my social work was an everyday occurrence.

"Work, huh?" Thomas says.

"Yeah. There's a lot going on."

"That's funny, I talked to Amber, wondering if maybe your phone had died or something, and she said she hadn't seen you and you'd missed the board meeting."

Oh, crap. The board meeting. The funding paperwork. Shit.

Whoa. Thomas was calling my coworkers?

"Why are you checking up on me?" The words come out of my mouth reflexively. It's not until they're out in the air that I realize what I've said. Those are the same words I said once before, before the whole world went to hell. Thinking of it, my skin crawls and my bowels weaken. The room spins and the left side of my face burns for no reason other than my memories.

Thomas talks, although I can't make out his words over the pounding in my ears.

I gradually sink to the floor, my legs giving way as my mind fills with heinous thoughts. The walls close in on me, and part of my mind screams. Everything is numb and distant.

I look up to the counter, a million miles above me, where a corner of my phone extends out over the counter, a lifeline thin as a strand of spider silk, the other end of which is tied to an abstract concept called help. I fumble for the phone, hang up on Thomas, and hit the button for Emily. She answers, and I try to speak, but my voice has vanished, and nothing comes out. I want to ask for help, ask to be taken away from it all, but she is too far away.

↺

I'm on a cold floor when there's a distant pounding on the door. I hear it, but I can't stand. Emily lets herself in, finds me in the bathroom.

She gets my bathrobe, wraps me in it, and urges me up. I follow her directions without conscious thought. She brings me to bed, gets me in a sitting position, tucks me in. I'm not crying, not thinking. I'm just nothing.

Some time later she comes back with a cup of hot tea, brings it to my lips, and holds it there. "Sip," she says.

It takes a few moments for me to process the instructions, remember what that means, command my body to obey the order.

The sickeningly sweet tea brings back memories. This is not the first time Emily has taken care of me.

She sits next to me, makes me take more sips.

Her phone buzzes inside her purse. It stops, then buzzes again.

In my head, I form a thought with some difficulty, find the words to match the thought, send the words to my lips. "Get it," I say, though by the time the words come out the phone has stopped ringing.

"It's not important," Emily says.

"You are," I say, meaning she's important, and the people who are trying to call need her, because there are things only she can do, but I can't possibly say all those words.

"Nothing they need is as important as being here with you."

Tears run down my cheeks as I silently sob.

Emily strokes my hair.

When I can finally speak, I give voice to my darkest fear. "What would I do if you weren't here?"

"You are strong. If I wasn't here, you'd call Thomas..."

I urgently shake my head.

"Or your therapist. Even if no one was there, you know what would happen?"

I shake my head no.

"You might have sat there on the floor for a while. Eventually, you would have gotten up. Even without me, or anyone else, you would have done it. You're strong, Angie. The strongest person I know."

"I feel like a china cup that broke and was put back together wrong."

Emily takes my hand. "The Japanese have a name for that, when they repair pottery with gold. They say it makes the pottery even better."

"Kintsugi."

"There you go. But I'm not talking about your cracks. I'm talking about you, Angie. Remember in the fourth grade, when James was picking on me, and you stabbed him in the hand with your pencil to protect me? That Angie is still there, inside you, and she will always be there."

I wipe my face with the back of my hand. "I twisted the pencil so the lead broke off in his hand. It's still in there."

"Believe me, I know. Every couple of years he posts a picture and tags me." Emily sighs. "What brought this on today? You haven't had an attack in…well, a long time."

"I missed a date with Thomas last night. He called this morning to ask me where I was." I stop, take a sip of tea. "He talked to Amber, found out I wasn't at work yesterday. I asked him why he was ch…checking up on me."

"Ah," Emily says. She knows the story well enough, how the abuse started. "Thomas is a fine person. Besides, if he ever hurt you, I'd kill him. Maybe he was worried about you."

"Maybe this is how it begins. Maybe today he's asking where I was, and tomorrow he's telling me I can't go out."

Emily takes a deep breath. "It's hard to trust people."

I nod.

"He asked you to marry him. Is that what's bringing this on?"

Somehow I'd forgotten about his proposal. That wasn't it. "It was him asking me where I'd been."

"Try to see it from his perspective." Emily's phone buzzes. She ignores it. "You had plans for dinner. You forgot?"

I nod.

"He doesn't hear from you, so he calls you. Did you answer?"

"No, my phone was off."

"Did he email you?"

"Yes, although I didn't see the messages at the time. I wasn't checking email."

"Jesus," she says, laughing. "That is reason for concern. Since when are you not reading email?"

"I was busy."

"Well, if you had plans, and you don't show up, and don't answer your phone or email, then isn't it logical he might be a little worried?"

"Does that mean he should contact my coworkers, asking them where I am?"

Emily shrugs. "Maybe, maybe not. It depends on where you set your boundaries."

"I've been pretty damn clear about where I set my boundaries."

"Agreed, but he can still be worried and forget about those boundaries."

"He's not allowed."

"He's a human being," Emily says. "He loves you. Hell, he may be worried you'll change your mind about getting married. Who knows what's going through his head? He's a man, after all. They're all sports and cars and sex up there. Can you imagine being in a man's head?" She makes the universal sign for crazy, and I laugh. "Look, if I was suddenly missing, you would stop at nothing to find me."

She's right. When Igloo was missing, I called in a favor from Nathan9, and didn't leave until I knew she was okay. Thomas is entitled to the same. I don't know what I'm going to say if he presses me on where I was.

Her phone buzzes again. She must have received at least a dozen calls since she got here. "You going to be okay? Because you're looking better, and I walked out of a client meeting, so eventually I must answer the damn phone."

"I will survive."

"Good. Go get dressed. I'll take this call from your living room. I'm not leaving until I see you on your way to work."

"You don't need to."

"Yeah, I do. Now go powder your nose." She swipes at her phone and lifts it to her ear. "This is Emily."

I finish getting ready in the bathroom to the distant sounds of Emily arguing on the phone. It's comforting somehow, like rain pelting against the roof.

She's on the phone literally the entire time, and we walk out of my condo together. She sees me to my car, gives me a quick peck on the cheek, and mouths "Love you, girl," before she turns and walks to her car.

ʊ

On the way into work, I leave Thomas a voice message.

"Hey, I'm sorry about this morning and last night. I'm not even sure what I said before. I had a mini-freakout until Emily talked me down. Yesterday, I needed a day away from it all. I'm sorry if I worried you. I love you." I waffle back and forth before I hang up, first thinking I should say something about being excited about getting married, then thinking maybe marriage will never work— I'll never totally be able to give up my side work, because who knows when something like this will happen again. The pause goes on too awkwardly long even if I knew what to say, so I hit End.

I walk into the building and make a beeline for my office, hoping to sneak in so I can catch up on all my messages. I walk in to find Owen and his lawyer, Stella, having a conference call in *my* office.

Owen says, "Let me call you back, she's here," and hangs up.

"We need to talk about the offer."

CHAPTER 35

OWEN'S WORDS RING IN MY EARS. "The offer? What offer?" I can't imagine what he's talking about. Owen knows no part of my plan includes selling Tapestry. Even so, the next words leak out. "From who?"

"Before we discuss that, where the hell were you yesterday? The entire board and everybody's lawyers convened to sign the financing paperwork. In sixteen years I've been in the business, never has a founder failed to show up to sign their own paperwork."

I'm vaguely aware this is the second time today someone has questioned me about where I was, but that takes back seat to the money and getting the funding. So it's damage control time. What the hell do I say?

"I had a critical emergency to take care of."

"What kind of emergency?" Owen asks.

"A personal one."

"Dammit, Angie. That's not good enough. You make me look bad, you make the company look bad, you make yourself as CEO look bad. What was it? Someone die? Gimme something."

The best lies are partial truths, Repard always said.

"A close friend was in an abusive situation and I had to drop everything to help her."

"Jesus." Owen swallows. "Sorry. Is she okay?"

"She is now."

He shakes his head. "Well, maybe it's for the best the signing got delayed. There's been a development, and you need to know about this new information before you do anything." He nods to Stella.

Stella stands up from where she's sitting at my desk and passes over a sheet of paper. "First thing this morning, the board of directors received an acquisition offer. It went to everyone, including the would-be new director appointed by CompEx. In other words, it probably went out based on the assumption we signed the paperwork yesterday, which is not finalized because we don't have your signature."

"It's an exceptional proposal," Owen says. He sits on the edge of my desk facing me. "The investors want to accept. The terms generously represent the current value of the company and compensates everyone for their risk and involvements, generating a significant income event for every employee, especially you."

Nowhere in what they've said was the name of a person or company, and that can only mean one thing. "There is no damn way Tomo will get their hands on this company."

"They're offering three hundred million," Owen says.

Stella nods to confirm.

"The investors get the return they want, and you walk away with sixty million. We haven't even launched yet. Do you know how insanely great this deal is?"

"It's not about money!" I'm yelling and belatedly turn around and slam my office door shut. "The whole point of this is to compete *with* Tomo, to give people an option, a way out."

Owen looks at me like I'm crazy. "It *is* about money. That's why investors invest. Boulder wants to take it. CompEx wants it. *I* want it. You'll walk out with enough to self-fund your next company. Your next two or three companies. You'll never need an investor again. You know how many entrepreneurs would kill for that?"

"I'm not engaging in a debate with you. This is not open for discussion. The answer is *no*. I don't care what their offer is. The point of this company is to give people the ability to walk away from their relationship with Tomo. To give them a safe haven where their rights are respected, they own their own data, and possess full agency over what happens to them and their data and their relationships with people."

Owen waves a hand at me. "I understand, I do. I get the whole social mission part. It's compelling. That's part of the reason why I invested, and why I pulled the Boulder investors in on the Series A funding. You must see it from our perspective, though. Your vision is ambitious, almost to the point of being impossible. We believed and invested anyway. But here's the thing. Nobody has any idea what's going to happen at launch. Tapestry could utterly flop. A month after launch it could be a ghost town, and your valuation could drop to zero. If we look at three hundred million in our pockets now, prior to that inflection point...no risk-adjusted valuation could equal that."

"It's not about the fucking money!" I'm losing my shit. Owen knows it, and from the glimpses of my employees through the interior window in my office, they know it. I clench and release my fist several times. When I try to take a deep breath it catches in my throat and almost turns into a sob. Almost. I will not show one scrap of weakness. Do not betray me now, body.

I turn around and face Owen. "I don't care whether you and the other investors want the offer. I will not accept the offer. The amount of money is not part of my decision process."

Owen gazes down at his shoes, and when he looks back up at me, he seems genuinely sad. "I figured you would say as much, but I had to try. I'm sorry it's come to this. Excuse me."

He walks past me, opens the door, and leaves my office.

What the—? Where is he going?

Stella clears her throat, reminding me of her presence, sitting quietly in my seat at my desk. "Why don't you take a seat?"

She talks rapid-fire in dense legalese.

"Stop. Just give me plain English."

She sighs. "If you sign the contract paperwork enabling the funding round to close, the other investors will vote to accept the offer and you don't control enough votes to stop them. If you don't sign the paperwork, then the funding round doesn't close, and you don't get any money."

"I can't make payroll. I need that money."

Stella closes her laptop lid. "Sorry, Angie. I really am. The investors want to act in everyone's best interests."

"Get out." I point a finger to the door, in case she's forgotten where it is.

"It would be best if your counsel responds within twenty-four hours. I'm on your side in this, really."

She's face to face with me now, and I don't know if she's telling the truth or not. She seems earnest enough. Then again, I trusted my husband, and look where that got me.

"Maybe you are, maybe you aren't," I say. "For now, I want you out of my office, okay?"

She nods and leaves. Before I've even reached my chair, Amber walks in.

"I can't talk right now," I say. "I need to call Schwartz and Associates. I'll debrief you later."

"What should I say?" Amber asks.

I look out through the window and every employee of the company is staring at me, identical anxious expressions on their faces. For the second time since coming into the office, I want to cry. I clear my throat and force some rigor into my voice. "Tell them to please get their work done, and I'll hold an all-hands meeting as soon as I have something to share."

ↄ

I call our lawyers, explain to the receptionist what's going on, and a minute later I'm talking to an associate partner. I relate the situation again, and five minutes after that, in what little capacity I have left in me to be surprised, find I'm speaking to the head of the firm, David Schwartz.

"This offer is counter to everything I believe in and what the company stands for," I say, when I'm finished retelling the story for the third time. "But I must get money in the door, and soon. Do I have any options?"

"Let me review everything," David says. "I'll need to go over the contracts with a fine-tooth comb."

I'm immediately soothed. I've got somebody in my corner.

"Can you give me some indication of how serious the situation is? Should I be worried?"

"I don't want to give you either false hope or worries," he says. "I'd rather read through everything first, and give you a definitive answer."

"How about a number on a scale of one to ten, ten being everything is okay?" I need some sort of reassurance.

"Every contract is different, but it's unlikely you're going to be able to obtain the funding and also stop the acquisition. If that's the only outcome you consider success, then I'd give you a two."

"*Two*? Damn it," I say. "I'll panic then."

My mind races. How much is left? Can we move funds around to make payroll this week? Even if we do, what happens in two weeks?

↻

I lean back into my chair, utterly drained. It's barely been an hour since I said goodbye to Emily at my condo. Shit, Igloo and her sister. Theo the bastard. What's happened to him?

Checking the news from here would leave a trace back to me. Really, how likely are they to investigate a scumbag like Theo deeply? He'll confess to blackmailing the rest of the girls under that much pressure and evidence, even if he denies any involvement with the Prime Minister's daughter. I'm too tired to hunt down an anonymous network to read the news.

It's been twenty hours since my tip to Folha, so I go straight to their website, hoping for an article. I can't help smiling when I see a front page picture of Theo, side-by-side with the photo I planted on his hard drive of the Vice President's daughter. I click on the article and let my browser translate it to English. The second paragraph says the Departamento de Polícia Federal are holding him in custody. Problem solved.

I need to let Igloo know and make sure she keeps quiet about the whole thing. Unfortunately, I don't have a secure way to communicate with her. I tap my fingers on my desk. Actually, there is a way. I could use her public key from Github with rsutl to encrypt a message. Alas, sending an encrypted message is like firing off a flare gun to the NSA. It'll increase the likelihood of the NSA monitoring me. Still, I don't have much choice. On the other hand, I have no idea what security she's using for her private key, which means I really can't trust that at all.

Fudge. I send a chat message to Amber: "I want Tapestry to support encrypted chats and voice calls with 3-layer encryption. Encrypt everything." That'll piss off the NSA. I ignore Amber's reply.

I install Redphone, a fairly well-regarded encrypted telephony app, and send an invite to Igloo to connect with me. I stare at my screen until I receive a notification she accepted my invite. I establish an encrypted call with her.

"Hey Igloo, we fixed your image retrieval bug in the codebase."

"Uh, okay?" She sounds confused, but I don't want her to say anything incriminating.

"It's probably safe now. Nobody will hold it over your head anymore. All the same, it's best we don't talk about it. Let bygones be bygones."

"I can come back?" Igloo asks. "Everything is okay?"

"Yup. Totally taken care of."

"Thank you so much."

"No, it's fine. Please, *don't mention it*. I need to go deal with some other issues. Take care of yourself, Igloo."

One small good deed done. Now back to work. I've got to talk to everyone in the office, tell them something of what's going on. I catch myself grinding my teeth. I'm wound so tight and for a brief moment I daydream of a cigarette and the rush of nicotine from that first hit. Oh God, that wouldn't be good. It took years to quit. I'm not going to restart now. I jot down a few notes, then gather everyone in the office together in the largest conference room.

I stand there looking at a sea of expectant and worried faces. I never learned what the deal would have offered my employees, although from a guess at our stock distribution, the deal might be in the ballpark of a million dollars per employee. The investors might not be the only ones who want to take the deal.

Everyone I hired was in line with our values, but that's a lot of money, especially to everyone here that's a year or two out of college, struggling to pay their student loans and Portland's astronomical rents. I'd better not say anything about amounts.

"I'm sure you all saw, and probably heard, the scene in my office this morning. Tomo made an offer to purchase us. Our investors want to take the offer. I do not.

"Tomo has no interest in Tapestry the federated social network. They want to buy the company because that's the easiest way to gain control. They want control because they're scared of how Tapestry decentralizes power. Consider this validation of everything we're doing—our privacy and data ownership features, our partnerships with other companies in the industry, the control we're delivering to the customer. Tomo knows all of this threatens their way of doing business.

"If we sold to them, we'd give up everything we've worked for. I told the investors we will not accept any offer from Tomo. Unfortunately this means we can't close the funding round. Our lawyers are currently investigating to determine our options. That's what I know. Any questions?"

One of the marketing employees raises a hand and shouts out, "How much is the offer?"

Of course. First question. "Sizable enough the investors want to take it. It still isn't a good deal for us. It's counter to our values."

I field a few more questions, then send everyone back to work, telling them I'll let them know when there's more information.

I return to my desk, my head whirling. How much is at risk? Could I really lose the company after I've worked so hard, not only to build it, but to ensure I would keep control? This is the very thing I did my best to guarantee wouldn't happen.

I call Emily, who surprises me by picking up on the first ring. Then I realize she probably assumes I'm still a mess from my breakdown this morning, which feels like it happened months ago.

I relate everything that's happened.

"Sounds serious," she says. "What does your lawyer say?"

"I actually talked to the founder of the company for once, although I'm not sure that's a good thing. He didn't say much, except that he'd investigate and get back to me."

"I don't understand the timing. You closed your funding round yesterday."

"No," I say. I can't explain it all fell apart because I was holed up in the storage center pursuing Theo. "The funding round didn't close, which is the reason why I'm still in control of the company. Had I signed the paperwork yesterday, I'd be outvoted by the other investors."

"Well, that's suspicious," Emily says. "You're about to pick up a new investor, and the next day there's an offer which they know you wouldn't accept, but the investors will."

Emily is a lot of things. Powerful, strategic, occasionally manipulative, an overachiever, and highly competitive. Kind to the few people she cares deeply about. Overly prone to suspicion is not one of her qualities, however, not the way it is for me. If she believes this is suspicious, then it almost certainly is.

I recall Lewis Rasmussen's first offer, almost a year ago. The Tomo CEO is influential and powerful enough that if he wanted CompEx to become a stakeholder in Tapestry, thereby shifting the voting control in the company, it wouldn't take him more than a phone call or two to make it happen. The CompEx deal came together so quickly. I assumed it was a logical fit, two companies who could help each other. Maybe there's more to it.

"I need to go, Em."

I pack up my things, including an extra laptop, to head back to the storage facility, where I'm going to break into Lewis's email and phone records and find out exactly what he's been up to.

CHAPTER 36

CHRIS DALY GOES BACK to the restaurant at eleven, when the waitress gets off work. He wears a gray business suit, in keeping with the story he told her about traveling for work. It's funny, him being single but claiming to have a wife. It gives him a ready excuse to avoid all the pesky phone calls and text messages between visits. Things are simpler this way. Friends in every town, no complications.

He knocks on the locked door. She opens it a minute later.

"Give me ten minutes," she says, then kisses him quickly.

Chris sits at a table by the door where he can watch her work, clearing the last few tables. He admires the curve of her waist, the tight fit of her skirt. Dish washing and other noises come from the kitchen as the crew finish up their last tasks for the night.

As she passes by his table, Chris grabs her by the waist and pulls her down into his lap. She laughs at first, then tries to push him away as he grabs her tit.

"Stop, I'm at work," she says, but there isn't much strength to it. Still, he lets her up. They'll be back at the hotel soon enough. Chris likes her because she's compliant. He can take what he wants from any woman, but over the years, he's found it's easier with the ones who don't create a fuss. It's easier to keep a low profile if there aren't police artists sketching your face in every town.

The cues are so easy to find: a slight inability to meet his gaze, a hesitancy to their speech, the way they hold their shoulders.

Later, they're in the hotel room. She's tied to the bed with cotton cord. It's a lot of waste for one night, but zipties are so uncivilized. He's got three strands of cord around her neck, his right hand in the loop, twisting to restrict the carotid arteries. Her face turns that lovely purplish tint as she thrashes harder under her bonds. Chris is close to release when his phone buzzes, the double short buzz of his *work* phone.

He should answer that, but...

He finishes with her, then releases the neck rope and climbs off. She gasps for breath, a pleasant background noise, while he checks his messages. The origin is masked, though he can tell from the fake caller ID it's got to be Pete in Naval Intelligence.

"The parts you asked for came in."

The only thing Pete's working on is Angie, so there must be a breakthrough.

Crap. He was looking forward to hours more fun. He slips his Benchmade folder out of his pants pocket and flicks the blade open with one hand. He sits on the bed next to her, and caresses her face and neck with the outside of the hand holding the knife. She's sweaty, merely panting now, as her color returns to normal.

"I'm sorry. Something critical has come up."

She flinches as the blade nears her eye and tries to pull away.

Chris laughs and cuts the rope from her neck, then frees her wrists and legs.

She pulls the sheets up to cover her body, then turns onto her side. Her mouth twitches like she wants to say something, but whatever it is, she can't bring herself to speak. He sees this in them sometimes. The regret, the self-loathing. It's good the call came when it did. It'll spare him having to listen to whatever it is she wants to unload.

It takes him a few minutes to clean up and dress, and still she doesn't get out of bed.

"Feel free to hang out, use the hotel room. I won't be back tonight." He walks to the door. "I'll come by the restaurant tomorrow night, if I'm free."

℧

Chris briefly wonders what the waitress gets out of their rendezvous. Some weird combination of attention and validation. Probably the boys in psych could tell him, although he doesn't care that much.

He pulls up outside a chain hotel, piggybacks on their wi-fi signal, and calls Pete on an encrypted channel.

"Daly here, what do you have for me?"

"I'm fine, thanks for asking," Pete says. "Hope you are well, too."

Chris is silent. Best to wait him out.

"Your girl, Angie. She's in the middle of a funding round for her company, and her company received an acquisition offer from Tomo."

Chris mentally reviews what he knows of Angie and her work, and doesn't see why this is worth calling him. "So what?"

"So she takes the time out of her busy, busy day to visit the website of a Brazilian newspaper this morning. She clicks on one and only one article, about a teenager named Theo, arrested in São Paulo for breaking into a number of women and girls' accounts and blackmailing them into sending him sex videos. Then she installs an encrypted voice calling app on her phone, and calls one of her employees."

"Could we decode it?" Chris asks. Considering all of Pete's resources, he bets Pete has the sex videos from the Brazilian. Would it be too weird to ask for them? Probably.

"Of course we can decode it," Pete says. "Don't interrupt. Anyhow, she tells the employee 'she's fixed the image acquisition bug' and it's safe to come back. Then she goes back to dealing with her investors and Tomo offer, then disappears off the grid."

"What?"

"Exactly. It gets better. I go backwards in time. Is there any previous connection between Angie and the teenager in Brazil? No. On the other hand, there is between the employee she called and Theo. In fact, Theo has photos of the employee's sister on his computer. Two nights before, Angie goes to the employee's apartment, spends a couple of hours there with her, then disappears off the grid."

"Where does she go when she disappears?" Chris asks.

"Are you gonna let me tell the story?" Pete says. "The first time she disappeared off the grid, I wasn't watching too closely. I figured maybe stress from the job drove her to turn off everything electronic. This time around, I thought something she was doing something connected with the kid Theo. I check all the incoming traffic into his computer for the last two weeks."

The breadth of data they're recording impresses even Chris. The odds of them singling out some random teenager in Brazil for observation is minimal, so the implication is the NSA has historical records on every data connection over every router on the planet. How is that even possible?

"I found an inbound connection that retrieved the photos from his computer, and then, a few minutes later, added photos of the Vice President of Brazil's daughter."

"That wasn't Theo?" Chris asks.

"Nope," Pete says. "He was in school. I've got complete logs for his phone's data traffic and geocoordinates, and I've got him on a school security camera at the time the connection was live. It definitely wasn't him."

"Who was it? Where was the connection from?"

"Ah, that's where the story becomes interesting," Pete says. "The connection is a dead-end from a coffee shop in Amsterdam."

"Why a dead-end?"

"Because there was no traceable client data. We couldn't track the browser back to any known person. No tracking cookies. Someone connects with a burner laptop, uses the coffee shop wi-fi, connects to Theo's computer, and then no evidence of them again."

"Do we have video for the coffee shop?"

"Doesn't matter," Pete says. "The coffee shop wasn't open at the time of the connection. It was eight at night. The coffee shop closes at 4 P.M."

"Street cameras pick up anyone nearby, using the wi-fi?"

"No, although there was an oddity about the network traffic. The connection was really slow, consistent with an onion routing network."

"NSA has TOR logs, doesn't it?" Chris asks. "Got anything matching your profile?"

"No, I checked. She's using a different onion network, maybe even something she built."

"She? You're convinced it's Angie?"

"It's too much of a coincidence," Pete says.

"I need more than coincidence," Chris says. "I need proof, and I need to figure out what else she's doing. If she was involved with the kid, it wasn't a solitary activity. She has to have done more. Can't you correlate her data traffic with other wi-fi access points? Find other routers sending the same data at the same time? Back track that way?"

Pete's quiet for a moment. "Oy. I know what you want, but it's hard. That query doesn't exist in any good form. We need to brute-force it. Compare all the routing data to all the other routing data. It's how we used to break TOR before we compromised the network itself."

"Then do it."

"I'll need NSA compute time to correlate the data on a billion access points and routers. There isn't enough computing power here. You'll need Enso to approve it."

"I'll get the approval."

"Then I'll start work on the query."

ↄ

The NSA has more computing power than God, unless you believe the universe is a simulation, in which case there is still someone out there with a bigger supercomputer. Chris has no idea what the exact numbers are, but he's heard they're running somewhere over twenty million servers.

The Utah Data Center stores more data than has ever been stored in one location before. Huge pipelines feed it information from around the world, particularly through backdoors in virtually all industry communications, from telecom companies to social networking to email. Taken from the best practices of the day, it has also been designed for parallel data retrieval. When records need to be correlated across massive data sets, the entire facility can operate simultaneously to search for the data, each of the millions of computers searching a subset of data, bubbling up results which are correlated to be organized at higher levels. What might take Naval Intelligence a year to search for will be accomplished in minutes at the NSA's data center.

Of course, there are only so many minutes in a day, and so any extensive requests require approval.

Asking Enso for dedicated NSA supercomputer time could, in theory, be a problem, because his investigation into Angie with the goal of developing leverage against her isn't government business. The client pays Daly, not Uncle Sam.

The thing about an organization like BRI is that it's so dark, so far off the radar or from any sort of oversight, it's difficult to tell what might be legitimate or not. Had Enso asked him to distract the Congresswoman because of some official charter, or was that Enso's prerogative? Nobody knows but Enso. If there were records of what they were doing, they couldn't be dark. People in the government require plausible deniability to take care of the things that need to happen.

The system that allows the President to influence, as a hypothetical example, the vice chancellor of Germany to ensure a particular trade vote and yet remain blissfully ignorant, works in Chris's favor when he needs NSA computer time.

Chris waits for East Coast business hours, then calls Enso on a secure channel.

"What's up?" Enso sounds distracted, rapid-fire background typing audible over the connection.

"I need dedicated supercomputer time for an investigation into a woman—"

"How much time?" Enso cuts him off. "I just got out of a department meeting and I've got things to do."

"We're not sure. Pete needs to run a brute-force—"

"Yeah, okay. I've got an approval number for you."

Enso reads off the query request code, which Daly writes down on a slip of quick-erase paper. Anti-climatic, even by Chris's standards. He didn't even get to use any of the multiple justifications he'd fabricated. Chris makes a note of the time. If Enso's usually busy and distracted at this time of the week, Chris can use that to his advantage the next time he needs to make a request.

"Thanks," Pete says when Chris calls him back with the number.

"No biggie," Chris says. "Query done?"

"Not yet. I'm going to test it in the simulator. Make sure it works before we burn through a tanker truck."

Chris chuckles. The Utah Data Center's backup generators burn a tanker truck's worth of fuel every minute. Not that they've ever had to use it, since there's plentiful grid power, but it's still their unit of measure for the enormous power of the NSA.

"Fine. I'm going to Portland, check her out in person. I'll be in touch later."

Chris leaves his government work in his partner's hands, and takes their scrubbed, tracking-free car on the four-hour drive from Seattle down to Portland. Once there, he gets an AirBnB, and spends an hour making sure there's nothing to track him. The owner of the house has a few security cameras. Chris re-angles one on the front porch so it's staring at the ceiling, and inside he covers the Nest thermometer with a throw blanket so it won't sense when he's there or not. He's got a little travel kit for secure communications, and he uses the directional antenna to find good wi-fi half a mile away on the nearest busy street.

He initiates a video conference with Pete.

"Anything?"

"Not yet," Pete says, smiling.

"What are you so happy about?" Chris asks.

"The largest computer on the planet's running my code. Half a billion processor cores in parallel. I don't experience this every day."

"We'll be sure to withdraw the cost of the electricity from your pay."

Pete's eyes go large. "There's goes my paycheck for the rest of my career."

"How long will it take?"

"Ten minutes, max. We're loading the traffic metadata from every router in the world to find another router that sent the same sequence of packet sizes as the coffee shop router."

Eight minutes later, the answer comes back: another IP address in Amsterdam.

"Well, what is it?"

Pete types at his keyboard and curses.

"A coffee shop on the next block over."

"What the fuck? That's a hell of a search to find a coffee shop two blocks away."

Pete initiates screen sharing, and his video cam is replaced with a live stream of his desktop. "Look at the path here." He mouses over a network trace route. "Angie hooked up a repeater connected to both business's wi-fi networks at once. The data comes in at the first coffee shop, Filter Cafe, to a device on their network, and forty milliseconds later, a slightly different packet goes out over EcoGreen Coffee's wi-fi, before hitting our boy in Brazil."

"Why's the packet different?"

"Onion routing and obfuscation. Each node decrypts, removes address information, then pads with random data to change the length of the packet and re-encrypts. If she's smart, she's doing this specifically to make the analysis we're doing far harder. I was one step ahead of her, figured she'd try that and so I created a statistical search model adjusting for data permutation. Now, here at Filter Cafe, we see an actual Internet connection, a VPN connection originated at a coffee shop in San Diego and terminating at the same MAC address as the device that sent those packets. You know what this means, right? We're going to have to run the whole shebang again, because there's no way this connection originated in San Diego. We have to keep going backwards." Pete smiles. "Get me more compute time. You might want to ask for a few hours, because this will take a while."

Chris shakes his head. "I can't go back to Enso twice in one day. Can't you do the search at ONI, and assume you're looking for another endpoint within a few blocks?"

Pete hems and haws, but agrees to try.

Thirty minutes later, he finds the matching node, a hotel in the Gaslamp district. Pete passes the information on to Daly.

"You ought to send a team out. There's a device somewhere within signal range of each of these access points. You might be able to track the hardware back to Angie."

"What do I tell them to look for?"

"It could be anything from a laptop to a box the size of a deck of cards. It'll need power. They'll need to triangulate the wi-fi signal of every device that's connecting to the access points of these coffee shops. I'll give them the technical details."

Chris nods. "Give me a bit." He disconnects from Pete and wonders if he's getting in over his head.

His typical private job was easy. The customer wants data on someone, Chris pulls their complete file from the central database, analyzes it himself, and turns over what the client asked for.

Angie has proven vastly more difficult. So far, he's involved Naval Intelligence, the psych arm housed in the Army, and the NSA. He wonders if it's time to go back to the client for a higher fee. Not yet. It might be better to trade for a favor.

He makes a call to his liaison at the FBI, and using his official FCC identity, claims he's investigating a pirate radio station. He gets the FBI to deploy a tech team in San Diego to find the hardware connecting the coffee shop with a hotel bordering the Gaslamp District.

He reconnects with Pete. "Listen, I want someone on Angie full-time. Let's compromise her phone, her computer, her office. I want every email as she's composing it, see every photo she takes, I want her phone mic on 24/7 and a transcript of every conversation, and I want to know what she eats for breakfast."

Pete shakes his head. "We still don't know for sure she's done anything."

"Let's make damn sure of it then. If she doesn't have anything to hide, fine. We can discontinue after a week."

"We'll need a rotating team then, three analysts around the clock if you want that level of observation."

"Do it," Chris says.

Pete sighs and types something into his computer only he can see, then turns away to talk to someone off-screen. "Done," he says, when he comes back in front of the camera. "It'll probably be eight hours or so before we've compromised everything."

"What's next on backtracking the onion network?"

"I go home," Pete says. "I've got dinner with my kids. I'll finish it tomorrow."

"Come on, I need this now."

"The data's not going away. The search could take days."

"Backtrack one more node for me."

Pete stares at the floor for a minute. "Fine. Let me call my wife." Pete leaves, probably so he can call from outside the secure environment of their office. When he comes back a few minutes later, he bangs on the keyboard harder.

Chris ignores the passive aggressive behavior. Pete's working, and that's what matters.

Except soon Pete stops typing.

"This stuff has an impact, you know. My kid's got a homework project I'm supposed to help her with."

"This is government business," Chris says. "We're tracking down a potentially dangerous computer criminal. You can't compare that to a homework project."

"Except there's always someone. A terrorist needs fact-finding, or a politician might be corrupt. It doesn't ever stop. My daughter, she only gets so many homework projects. If I don't help her now, I've missed the opportunity for all time."

Daly stares at Pete through the video connection. "What is wrong with your priorities? A woman running a soon-to-be influential tech company may be a major computer hacker. Have you read her chat messages? She told her employees she wants them to encrypt every message sent over the system and specifically tells them not to use any of the protocols we've compromised. Do you know what this could do to national security? This isn't a run-of-the-mill investigation of some freak halfway around the world."

Pete leans in close to the video camera. "I get it, and that's why I'm still here. You and Enso come in with these urgent requests all the time, though. I've missed every one of my kids' performances this year. You two need a little more respect."

Chris leans back in his chair. One of the things that makes him so effective in his job is that he's just as innocuous as can be. No matter where he goes, people see him as a pushover. He's deliberately cultivated what he's come to think of as negative presence. Where some people use their walk, posture and stance to command people's attention, when Chris walks into a room, everyone's eyes wander past him, and they wonder why they even looked up in the first place. The downside of this is even nerds like Pete think they can boss him around. Of course, if he rose to the challenge, it would defeat the whole purpose of cultivating negative presence in the first place.

He falls into the chair a little deeper and says "Of course, Pete. I'll talk to Enso about it."

Pete nods, and goes back to typing.

While Pete's staring off at another window on his own screen, Chris stares at Pete's brachial plexus, where the bundle of nerves exits the spinal column near the neck and feathers into the separate nerves controlling the arm. He'd strike Pete there, stunning him and leaving him without use of his arms for a few minutes. Then he'd leisurely strangle him. Kind of hard to do through the video camera though.

Mastering negative presence requires channeling his proclivities more deeply. Daly leans back in his chair and waits.

An hour later he's deep in meditation when Pete breaks the silence.

"Damn."

"What?"

"I traced her back through two more nodes. This isn't easy. It's not like we have metadata for every single transmission in the world. I need to compensate for missing nodes, correlate across records, and account for the fact she's transmogrifying the data at each node. Working backwards from San Diego,

212 | WILLIAM HERTLING

the data originated from a hospital's intranet. I had to compromise their firewall so I could access the router's logs, which they fortunately preserved, to
find a doctor's computer, and then back through this same doctor's home PC,
which was accessing the work computer through LogMeIn, and from that
doctor to a server in Sweden. Luckily we compromised the Swedish ISP's
trunk line way back, so we have all that data. Then we run into a problem."

"What?"

"The Swedish connection originates from a node in the Russian botnet."

"Damn."

"Exactly," Pete says. "They've got their own onion network. We've partially
compromised it, but our coverage is spotty. The NSA has the records, but it's
under the jurisdiction of the Department of Justice Computer Crime division.
You're going to need to their permission."

Chris had no contacts at DOJ. Enso could make it happen, and even then,
only with a lot of questions.

"Okay, look. Forget about backtracking the connection to Brazil. What
about pattern matching the size and timing of packets? She's here in Portland.
Do we see data traffic originating from anywhere in Portland, similar to what
you've found between the nodes in her network?"

"I'm going to need another NSA search."

"Goddamnit, I can't, not today."

"That's okay. Because I'm heading home." Pete gets up his chair. Peers
down at the camera. "I'm going to see my kid before she goes to bed. You can
send me the NSA search approval tomorrow."

Pete disconnects the video conference.

The little shit! Chris hurls his phone at the wall, glass splinters, and it falls
to the ground.

Chris takes a deep breath. This bitch is making his life miserable. She's
going to pay for it, one way or another. Time to take a look up close and
personal.

CHAPTER 37

ON THE WAY TO THE STORAGE FACILITY to break into Lewis's email, I call Thomas.

"Thomas, there's some crazy shit happening at work. The financing didn't
close, and Tomo is trying to buy us." I fill him in on the details. "I'm sorry

about yesterday and this morning. I want to set your expectation: I have no idea what I'm going to be doing or where I will be until this all gets resolved. Don't freak out, okay?"

I have to admit, a hostile takeover of your company is a pretty good get-out-of-jail-free card for ignoring your boyfriend and being MIA for twenty-four hours.

"Holy cow," he says. "You need anything from me?"

"Understanding and patience."

"You got it. I'm sorry about this morning. I had no idea all this was going on."

"It's okay. I'll let you know as soon as I learn anything significant."

I hang up and realize that was easier than expected. Granted, I've got a killer excuse, but still, now I don't need to worry about being incommunicado and Thomas being worried. There's part of me that's pissed about the whole dynamic, and why I should be accountable to Thomas at all. A different part of me says Thomas deserves nothing less than the full truth.

"Stop!" I yell at myself. Great, I've become one of those crazy drivers who talks out loud to themselves. "Be quiet. I need to think."

By the time I enter my storage room, I've created a plan. Lewis is no dummy. He won't have left a record on Tomo, or any phones with Tomo installed. He'd know enough to use a burner phone, or an unassociated computer. I need to treat him as an aware adversary, not your typical clueless computer user.

I do all my usual setup: secured machine images, VPN, onion routing using my boxes.

I won't be caught unaware of developments this time: the spare computer is set up with my email and usual stuff, going through a different trunk line on the fiber optic connections I've hijacked from Sprint on the other side of the cinderblock room. From there I VPN right back in to my home network through a neighbor's Internet connection. To anyone else in the world who's spying on me, I'll appear to be working from home.

On my hacking computer, I download all of Lewis's records. His email, chat records, and his text message, of course. I also grab all his metadata: the IP addresses he connects from, the geocoordinate history of his Tomo-connected phone, and his website browsing history.

On my local machine, I set my software to search for patterns, the same sort of data crunching I do to identify asshole abusers, but in this I'm looking for any interesting patterns.

While that's working in the background, I connect to Dead Channel. Nathan's already online waiting for me.

```
Angel> Am I suddenly interesting or something? Why
are you always watching me?

SysOp> Because someone is watching you.

Angel> Yes, you.

SysOp> No, a different someone. Department of Motor
Vehicles. Purchasing history. Emails. VPN history.
```

My mind nearly falls out learning that Nathan knows all this. It's one thing to obtain access to the raw data. That's relatively easy. You only need either a backdoor into the system, or a user login, or access to someone who has one of those. To know when other people are accessing the data implies something far greater: it means you've compromised their system to install these little alerts. Or you're watching traffic over the network and see the requests as they go over the wire. Or, and this is even crazier, you've compromised the watchers themselves: the people and software that exist to detect any compromise in the system.

I wonder whether my relationship with Nathan goes deep enough to ask Nathan how he's monitoring data access at that level. Then the bigger question hits me.

```
Angel> Who's watching me?

SysOp> You tell me.
```

Argh. That's just like Nathan to pull his Zen master philosophical bullshit.

There's really only three basic possibilities. First, the government could be watching me, either because they know of my murders or because my online behaviors triggered counter-terrorist detection algorithms. Second, Tomo is investigating me because of my role in Tapestry. Third, a random hacker is trying to figure out who Angel of Mercy is.

I work my way through the options backwards. The odds of an errant computer jock tracking me down is low, probably the lowest it's ever been since I've kept such a minimal profile for so long. Still, it's not zero. Sometimes people try to track down old hackers, to figure out if they've given up the trade, been caught, or what.

If Tomo was investigating me, they could use an employee to track down my internal data. They might hire someone for a bit of corporate espionage, to access my Tapestry email and files. It would be a little unusual to look up my purchasing history, but maybe they're blindly trying to discover something compromising they can use as leverage. On the other hand, DMV records would be pretty meaningless. What would they do, blackmail me for a speeding ticket? I've heard of people being caught having an affair when they're pulled over with someone else in the car. It's a long shot though, and I'm not even married. Maybe it's Tomo.

The only other option is the government. It seems a little silly. On the one hand, I doubt local police would know what a VPN is, let alone be able to break the encrypted connection to access the underlying data. Not that I'm trying to toot my own horn, but only a federal agency with a three-letter acronym would possess the ability to track me. This hypothetical TLA agency would have access to the centralized intelligence databases created by the NSA. There'd be no reason to pull DMV records or purchasing history because they'd already store that data in their own database. It would be a waste of effort.

Hmm...

```
Angel> Was the first thing pulled the DMV records?

SysOp> :)

Angie> The government then. They fetch the same
data over and over again, rather than trusting what's
already stored.

SysOp> Bingo.
```

Knowing the government was investigating me didn't make me feel any better.

```
Angel> Why?

SysOp> That's not the right question. Think who,
not why.

Angel> I don't want to play your games now.

SysOp> Chill. I promise this is interesting.
```

If they were on to me for the murders, it would be the FBI.

```
Angel> FBI?

SysOp> Try again.
```

If I triggered counter-terrorism detection rules, then the NSA. Or was it DHS? I can never remember who handles that.

```
Angel> NSA or DHS?
SysOp> Nope.
```

Well, that was interesting. What was left?

```
Angel> Secret Service?
SysOp> Now you're just guessing. Office of Naval In-
telligence.
Angel> Joking?
SysOp> Serious. ONI, "America's premier maritime
intelligence service" according to their own site.
```

What could I have done to merit involvement from Naval Intelligence? Had I killed any sailors or officers? I ran through the last year in my head. I couldn't remember all the details of every asshole I've killed, though I'd surely recall if they were Navy. I stayed clear of military systems because there are too many cyber security grunts guarding against the inevitable Chinese attack to make that worth the risk.

```
Angel> Any other requests from ONI?
SysOp> Thousands. Here are some interesting ones.
Governor Whitmore, who suddenly decided not to run
for reelection. Pierre Martin, CTO of the number two
French telecom company, fired after a newspaper re-
vealed he spent company funds on prostitutes. And this
one: Congresswoman DeWalt, who was investigating black
intelligence organizations before she spontaneously
dropped it to focus on gun control.
```

A mushroom cloud of an explosion goes off in my head. Nathan's found a black agency. I back away from the computer, suddenly nauseous. Public government agencies at least pay lip service to things like laws and people's rights. The deeper and darker those agencies get, the less such niceties are observed. Nathan's excited about his discovery, but my life is evaporating before my eyes. I could cease to exist at a moment's notice.

↻

Nathan and I agree there's nothing much to do about the government observation, except to be ten times as cautious about my digital tracks.

SysOp> You can't trust anything, not even your
hardware, no matter how well you scrub it.

I'm prepared to hear they'd track my email and web browsing, though I'm surprised Nathan believes they'd compromise my physical devices.

Angel> My phone and computer are always with me.

SysOp> Right now? They'll track you to the storage
facility.

Angel> I bagged them both. EMF-proof.

SysOp> They only need a few seconds. You know about
Avogadro and China, right?

Angel> No, what?

SysOp> When an Avogadro Corp employee goes to China, once they come back they take the employee's phone
and laptop and stick them in a giant shredder. The
laptops are so thoroughly compromised with malware in
software, firmware, and even hardware bugging devices
they can't ever be trusted. The laptops are typically
out of employees' hands for less than ten minutes as
they go through customs. If that's what China can do
in ten minutes, what do you think the U.S. government
can do while you're looking the other way?

There's a chasm in my stomach threatening to swallow me and I can't help but look behind me even though I'm in a locked cinderblock room at the bottom of a secured storage facility. There's nobody in the room. Is there someone outside the door? In the parking lot? Someone with a frequency scanner monitoring my transmissions?

Angel> You think I'm being personally monitored? People stalking me?

SysOp> I don't know. Two weeks ago you weren't being monitored by the government, and now you are. Does pulling DMV records equal total surveillance? No. But the odds of you being surveilled jumped at least a thousand times higher.

Angel> Wait. Back when I had to get rid of the VW van, someone compromised my onion network. Do you think that was the government that far back?

Long seconds go by, and I wonder if Nathan is going to reply. I place my hand on the keyboard to type.

SysOp> That was me.

Angel> WTF? You claimed to know nothing about it.

SysOp> I thought maybe you needed a nudge.

Angel> You manipulated me?

SysOp> I couldn't watch you throw your life away killing people.

To say my mind reels doesn't begin to describe my emotions. I'm like a skyscraper toppling in slow motion after having its foundation washed away by a tsunami.

Angel> You don't get to decide somebody else's life.

SysOp> I don't regret it, and you shouldn't either. Look what you've built since then. Isn't it all worthwhile? Besides, you spent plenty of time changing other people's lives.

I rub my head, kneading my skull with my fingers. I...I just can't deal with this right now. I'm not sure whether to feel betrayed or saved. Both are true. Fuck.

Suddenly, I wonder if my connection to Dead Channel is secure. Nathan set up the encryption. It's running Threefish over Serpent, and even that runs through my onion network, which is Twofish over AES. The keys were generated from space telescope white noise. The whole thing should be secure not merely against the NSA of today, but even the global computing infrastructure of 2045. Yet I'm still looking at text on a screen. If they compromised my hardware, all is mute. The keys, the passwords, all irrelevant. They could intercept my video signal on the way to the display. I can settle up with Nathan9 later. For now, I've got to figure out my government problem.

```
Angel> What do I do?
SysOp> Don't do anything that would compromise you.
Or me, for that matter.
Angel> I need data from Tomo.
SysOp> Not right now.
```

I consider the company's money situation.

```
Angel> I might need to run another financial crack.
SysOp> No way. You'd never see the light of day
again. There's nothing the government goes after hard-
er than anyone who messes with the sheep's confidence
in the financial system.
Angel> Fuck.
SysOp> Be an ordinary person, no more, no less.
I'll keep an eye on your records, and if we go three
or four months with no activity, I'll let you know
that it's safe.
```

Three or four *months*? I'll be lucky to keep Tapestry running through the end of this month with the tricks Tomo is pulling.

```
SysOp> And, I hate to say this, but just in case...
better not connect to Dead Channel.
Angel> Damn it. You're my lifeline.
```

```
    SysOp> I know. I'm sorry, you're a little too hot
right now. We don't want that kind of attention.

    Angel> We've been friends for thirty years.

    SysOp> We're still friends, but we're hackers first.
Hackers don't burn other hackers.

    Angel> Fuck you very much.
```

I disconnect. The goddamn shit. Wait until I need him more than ever, and then cast me out? I've done all the field work. Compromised every system at Tomo. Gave him access he never would have gotten otherwise.

I stare at my other computer. It's done pulling all of Lewis's records from Tomo. I carefully disconnect it, store all the data on a triple-encrypted file, and shut it down.

A tear falls, lands on the keyboard, and I wipe it away with a shaking hand. I lay my face in my hand.

This is how it ends for hackers. Alone.

I tried to pretend otherwise. I believed I could have a normal life. Marry Thomas, even.

How am I ever going to face him? What's he going to think when they take me away? He's going to realize he never knew me, the real me. He'll believe everything was all a lie, doubt the entire foundation of our relationship. I scream at the walls and pick up the laptop, prepared to smash it against the cinderblock.

Fuck! I don't even have the money to buy another. I set the laptop down carefully and kick the cardboard boxes in the storage room instead, pounding them with my feet until the room is in shambles.

My chest heaves when I finally give up and lean against the wall.

If the government comes for me, they're going to stick me in prison. Prison is a locked room. A locked room is unacceptable. The thought makes me shake in fear. If they come for me, I will kill myself. I can't survive being in a box.

That night, on the way home, I stop about a mile from my house, and park outside a church. It's a lame excuse if I'm called to account for my whereabouts, but it beats parking at a grocery store. The old church doesn't have any security cameras, whereas the grocery has plenty, not to mention all the other shoppers with their phones out and about, waving around cellphone cameras without a thought of who might be spying on them. It's a funny thing, people's blindness to their cell phone cameras. Maybe one in fifty people are savvy enough to cover their computer webcams so they aren't spied on, but fewer than one in a thousand take the same precaution with their mobile devices.

At any rate, I park by the church, leave my electronics in the car, then walk a few blocks to the garage I rent where I keep my electronics tools. It's here where I assembled my homemade onion router hardware, and where I've customized endless laptops and other electronics. There's very little left except a few partially assembled airborne drones and my locked tool chest. I grab a screwdriver out of the tool chest, and undo the cover on the electrical panel. Once open, I remove two screws from the back panel, and the whole box pulls forward. I hold it in place with my stump and feel behind the box for the leather package. I set it on the workbench with a small thump, and screw the electric box back into place.

I unroll the leather until the Glock 26 is revealed. I stare without touching the gun. It seemed like a good idea once, though I was wrong. There was no way I could ever use it to kill any of the abuser bastards I was going after. It was too close, too immediate, too loud, too violent. Pulling the trigger myself was out of the question. It was everything I was not. I would curl up on the floor in a ball before I could ever aim it at someone, and so it was useless to me.

Until now. I know for certain I could shoot myself before I would let myself be imprisoned. Oh, if it came down to that, to the choice between losing my autonomy again or dying, I would not hesitate.

I pick up the gun, feeling the heft of it. After a moment's hesitation, I turn the muzzle toward my own head and hold it there. A numbness passes through me in a wave, like some part of me is ready to vacate this body. The edge between life and death is imperceptibly thin, only a squeeze of a finger away. I take a shaky breath, lay the gun back down, and begin the tedious process of loading the magazine with one hand.

Part Four

CHAPTER 38

AFTER A NIGHT OF MORE NIGHTMARES than any actual rest, I come into the office in the morning like a zombie. When David Schwartz calls, my voice is raspy from lack of sleep.

"I don't see anything you can exploit in the contract. If you sign, they're getting control. Don't sign."

My addled brain tries to make sense of it.

"What about approaching other investors?" I croak. "Or getting a bank loan?"

"No, on both accounts. You'd need the existing investors to sign, and they're not going to do it, not if they want to force you into accepting their terms. You could secure a personal loan, not a business loan, and put your own money in."

The idea is absurd. A startup is a money-consuming monster. Our burn rate is four hundred thousand a month. My personal equity wouldn't cover a single payroll.

"Thanks, David. I'll figure something out."

"Sorry I don't have better news," David says. "Get some rest."

Of course I'm going to ignore his advice. I can sleep when I'm dead. For now I need to figure out some way to save this company.

As soon as Amber and Igloo are in the office, I grab them along with Harry, our finance guy, and convene a meeting in the one conference room without windows. I close the door and gesture for them to take seats.

"Harry, how much cash do we have?"

"Cash or liquid assets?"

"Anything. How much money we can access to pay the bills with, right this second."

"About ten k cash, and twenty-five in our line of credit," Harry says. "The transfer from our investors should show up the day the funding closes. When is that going to happen?"

"None of the funds from our investors are coming because I won't sign because I refuse to accept the Tomo offer."

"I told you CompEx was a bad idea," Igloo says.

Amber punches the table. "Corporate assholes."

"Shit," Harry says. He opens his laptop, stares furiously at the screen. "We're not going to clear payroll."

"I know. We need to come up with a plan. The four of us. We need some way to cover the next couple of weeks, maybe months, to keep us operating. A source of money that doesn't involve banks or investors."

The room is dead silent. Igloo and Amber exchange glances. Harry stares at me, his mouth hanging open. Nobody looks confident.

I sink into a chair along with the rest of them. "We have to figure out something. Harry, what happens if we don't pay our rent?"

"We're evicted." The expression on Harry's face is one of utter dread. I suspect no part of what he signed up for including running finances for a company without money.

"Yeah, but that can't happen immediately, can it? It's not like we're going to show up tomorrow and the doors will be locked."

"Eventually they'll kick us out."

"Okay, your task after the meeting is to stop our next payment from happening. Find out how long before they lock the doors. What about payroll?"

"We can go without pay," Igloo says. "If we tell people, they'll understand."

I feel a pit in my stomach at the thought. These are my people. Before we took on Owen as an angel, Igloo was living on ramen. I've failed my people if I can't pay them. I take a couple of deep breaths to keep myself stable.

I turn to Amber. "You know everybody's past employment the best. You think everyone can manage if we don't pay them?"

Amber shakes her head. "A few are coming from a successful exit. Most are limping along from one early-stage startup to the next and it'll be hard on them if we don't pay. We'll lose their attention pretty quickly once they're worrying about rent; and worse, if we miss payroll once, they'll assume it'll happen again and spend their time job hunting."

Fudge.

"How much do we need to make the next paycheck?" I ask Harry.

"Excluding us," Igloo adds.

Harry looks at me, and I nod.

"Excluding you three," Harry says, "we need about a hundred thousand."

Double fudge.

I glance at Amber. "I hate to do this to you, but can you talk to each person, one on one, and see if they're able to forego a paycheck? If they need to be paid, what's the minimum they can survive with?"

Amber rubs her face and lets out a sigh. "You really want to delegate that? You're the CEO. You're the one people expect to hold that conversation with."

"I have other things—"

"We all have a thousand other things," Amber says. "That's not the point. It's your job to conduct those hard conversations. If you're not woman enough to do it, then sure, I will. But it says a whole lot about how much you care about the employees."

My blood boils at her accusation. "Fuck you! I care. I have critical stuff I *have* to do."

"What stuff?" Amber says. "You keep disappearing for entire days for no reason. What is this stuff you're working on?"

"Can you two *please* not fight?" Igloo says in a tiny voice.

"I'm sorry." I settle back in my chair.

"It's like listening to my parents," Igloo says. "How are we going to handle this if you're fighting? Let's work together."

I stare at Amber for a few moments, and nod in apology. "I will talk to everyone about payroll."

"I can take half," Amber says, and now she looks a little like she regrets her outburst.

"That would be a huge help. Thank you."

Nobody says anything for a minute as we let the emotions settle down for a bit. Harry looks shell-shocked.

"Too much estrogen for you, Harry?" I say, hoping the atmosphere can handle a little joke.

He mumbles something, then stares off into the distance. "I've never worked with people who were so open about how they feel."

"I'll take that as a compliment," I say.

Harry points at his computer screen. "We're forgetting something important. Our cloud bill. It's about fifteen thousand, and gets charged to our credit card."

"We can make the minimum payment, right?" I say.

Harry shakes his head. "That's what we've done the last three months. We'll go over the limit if we don't pay the credit card bill before the cloud computing charge hits. I expected the investment money would be here by now."

"Switch the account to my personal credit card." I turn to Amber. "You need to keep the spend under my credit limit."

I stand to stretch my legs. "If that's it for the immediate expenses, then we're covered for the next couple of weeks. However, we need a long-term plan to bring in money. If we can't go to investors or banks that leaves one option. We launch."

"That's not for three and a half more months!" Amber says.

"No, we launch now. The beta users are happy, right?"

Igloo nods. "We have almost a thousand users. Engagement is high."

Amber looks at me and Igloo, slaps her forehead dramatically. "Please tell me you're kidding?"

"No," I say. "If we launch, we bring in revenue."

"Nobody is ready! Marketing and biz dev and tech all aligned on a plan to launch in January, a plan we just pulled up from March."

"Then we accelerate it some more."

"You're asking for the impossible," Amber says. "We can't solve this problem by launching! Even if we could somehow, miraculously launch today, we're not going to receive revenue for months, and not meaningful quantities for even longer, six months or a year."

"I know. We don't need to be totally profitable. We just need to change the game enough. Look, Owen says the investors all want to take the Tomo offer. But the moment we launch, everything changes. If there's dissent among the investors, maybe launching will change the dynamic and win one to our side."

"The number one killer of startups is insufficient funding," Amber says. "Launching will accelerate our spend. Without money in the bank, we can't run ads, can't scale servers, can't run a PR campaign."

"The sooner we're ready, the more options we have. If I miraculously drum up a few hundred thousand and we're ready to launch, we do it and spend the money to get the word out. If we're not ready, the money comes in, goes to pay the bills, and then we're back to square one. Find a way to be technically ready for a full public launch in a month. I'll convince marketing to develop a guerrilla marketing plan that doesn't require any spend."

Amber shakes her head in reluctant acceptance. "This is going to be a disaster."

↻

After our meeting, I go back to my office. I stare at my purse with loathing, then open it and apply more makeup. I'm putting on my jacket to go when Amber walks by and looks at me.

"I don't mean to be such an ass about it," Amber says, "but what is it that's so important that you have to do?"

I stare at her for a moment. "Swallow my pride and go beg every person I know for money."

"Oh."

The silence is overwhelming and awkward.

"I better get to it, then," I say, and edge past her.

As I walk outside my heart aches. Yes, I really am about to beg for money, and putting on makeup to do it is somehow doubly demeaning, an acknowledgement that at the end of the day, every woman has to decide how much to leverage her looks rather than only her brains. I'm so desperate right now that if I were a younger woman, and a whole one, I would consider sleeping with every post-IPO CEO in this town if it would keep Tapestry afloat. I'm filled with self-loathing at the thought.

That's not why my heart aches. It's because even though I'm really going to beg for money now, my answer was a deception, a distraction to keep Amber from asking more questions about where I've been in the past days when I've been at the storage facility.

I want to stop lying to the people I care about.

An old black Lincoln pulls up outside the building. I get in the passenger door.

"Hi, Danger."

"I didn't expect I'd be seeing you anymore. I gave you the last bitcoin payment months ago." He pulls away from the curb. "Got something new in the works?"

"Sort of." The car's cracked red leather interior tugs at my memory. "Isn't this the car from *The Matrix*?"

Danger smiles. "I never had much money until the Bitcoin run. Seemed like a worthwhile investment."

"You have any of that money left?"

"Are you going to do it again? I thought you'd gone legit. I keep seeing your photo next to articles about the secret startup in Portland."

"No, I can't do it again. I was wondering if you'd like to become an investor in my company?"

Half an hour later, Danger drops me off at Thomas's law office. I go in, talk to Thomas, wait a half hour, and then come out and go to another company in town. Finally, late that afternoon, I Uber back to our offices. I walk in and set my bag down with a thump on Harry's desk.

He stares at it suspiciously.

"For the employees who need to be paid, this is what you're going to pay them with."

"Please tell me that's not a bag full of cash."

"It was all legally acquired. I didn't rob any banks."

"This is not the normal way money comes into a business."

"Harry, please. Pay the employees. I borrowed from friends."

He reluctantly pulls the bag toward him.

"Oh, and Harry?"

"Yeah?"

"There's not going to be any more, so find a way to make that last."

Again, partial truths. Sure, the money from my boyfriend is a loan, one which he promised me doesn't need to be repaid. For all the rest though, I promised them stock. Handshake deals, cash now for some of my personal stock in Tapestry later. I'm sure I'm breaking some securities law, and I'm trading away the stock way below valuation, but now we've got cash, enough for critical expenses for the next few weeks or maybe a month or two if we eke it out.

It's not like I really needed the stock. I have no goal of getting rich out of this. Just keep this company alive, find a way to defeat Tomo, and in the process make the world a better, safer place. That's not so much to ask.

↻

It's midafternoon, and I've talked to all but a handful of employees. What I really want to do now is finally look at the data I got from Lewis's accounts at Tomo. I don't need to download anything or connect to any sites. It's all contained there on the encrypted hardware on the second laptop in my bag.

To appease Amber's concerns about my continual disappearances, I settle on examining the data right here in my office. However, before I turn the laptop on, I'm going to make damn sure it's isolated from the net. I flip it over on my desk and use a screwdriver to undo the back. After I take off the access panel, I remove the battery and hard drive, and remove the screws from the motherboard.

Halfway through my work, Keith comes in, our biz dev guy. He returned from a trip today, and I texted him to come straight into the office from the airport. Apparently he's already heard through the rumor mill I want to accelerate the launch.

"It's not possible to pull up the launch." He pauses, watches me take the computer apart. "What are you doing?"

"Fixing this laptop," I say. "We can't afford to buy a new one."

"The money situation is that bad?"

"Yeah. Did Amber talk to you about pay yet?" I lift the motherboard out, and find the connector that leads up through the hinge into the display.

"No..."

I stop for a second and look him in the eye. "You believe in what we're doing, right? We're not building another website here. We're trying to make a difference in the world."

"I know," Keith says. "To stop Tomo."

"Well, we've scared Tomo, so they're doing what they usually do: buy anyone who might threaten them down the road. I said *no*, but our investors, who aren't as principled, want to accept. Long story short, we have no funding. I really need help from employees that are financially able to do without their full pay. I'm not going to force anyone to go without pay, because I don't believe that's fair. If you're able to manage without a paycheck, or with a partial one, that would be a huge help."

In the end, he agrees to forgo his paycheck, and promises to figure out how to support a product launch in six weeks.

He leaves, and I unplug the tiny combined wi-fi and bluetooth module, ensuring the computer is totally isolated. It's the only way I can trust no one will see the information on the laptop, my final download of all the data on Lewis.

Before I reassemble the computer, I check the innards against photos of this particular model for surplus parts like government keystroke loggers that happened to fall inside and plug themselves into the keyboard connector. Fortunately, everything appears pristine.

I put the hardware back together again, which requires tediously positioning everything exactly right and matching screws—half of which roll away before I can seat them—to holes, and need to be found all over again. For all that, it's still easier to reconstruct computers than to take them apart, which has always puzzled me.

I finally boot the computer, but before I enter the first of several passwords, I examine my office. I make sure no webcams point in my general direction. Nothing the screen might reflect off. I have no idea what a physical government bug might look like, and in the end decide to take no chances. I grab an empty cardboard box from the lunch room, cut one side off with scissors, and place it upside down over the laptop so the screen can only be seen from exactly where my head will be. I'd like to cover the box in layers of aluminum foil, but the lunch room is out. It's not paranoia when they're really out to get you, right?

My absurd preparations complete, I finally decrypt the hard drive, and pray everything I've dumped will be enough to tell me Lewis's role in this. I begin with the obvious: searching his email for mentions of Tapestry and my name. Not surprisingly, there are many matches.

The oldest message in the search results is from January, when I began looking for angel investors. The email is from an angel investor, and he tells Lewis about my pitch. I don't even remember the guy. Although Lewis doesn't reply by email, I have a separate list of his text messages, and I see he sends a text saying thanks.

I switch to my regular computer, access my own email, and search for messages from Lewis there. The first message he sent me, back when I was looking for investors, was the very same day he learned about it from a guy I pitched.

I clench my fist and hold myself back from hitting the computer. That asshole betrayed my confidence. He never should have talked about my company to anyone, but he went running to Lewis immediately.

After that, there's nothing relevant in his inbox for a few months. Then an email from a mid-level Tomo manager whose employee is friends with someone we hired. Then a bunch of messages over the next few weeks from people all over the tech community.

While I thought we were keeping things quiet, the reality is everyone's been talking about us for months. Our use of IndieWeb, our partnerships, our revenue-sharing model, who we've hired, the top-secret chat system we're working on. Together, all the pieces add up to a complete picture of everything we're doing.

Still, there are almost no messages from Lewis on the topic. Then I find an email from Lewis's chief of staff with meeting minutes. They discussed an investigation into my non-compete agreement, and consultation with legal on whether they could win a case without the signed document. Four weeks after that, another set of meeting notes on ways to mitigate the threat of Tapestry. Notes from R&D on replicating our chatbots. Biz dev arrangements to lock up the top twenty content sites with exclusivity agreements tying them deeper into the Tomo ecosystem.

I jump at a sharp knock, and my heart races until I realize someone's merely at my office door.

"Come in."

It's Igloo. She sits in my spare chair, oblivious to the fact that I'm staring into a cardboard covered box like Spock monitoring his scope. She reaches under her hood and rubs her ears.

"I, uh, of course, can go without pay." She clears her throat. "I also asked my mom for some money. She's going to send us ten thousand."

That gets my attention. I didn't dig deeply into Igloo's family, but there's no way that's spare change for them. I abandon the computer and turn to her.

As usual, she's buried inside her hoodie.

"We can't take your mother's money," I say. "I'm totally committed to Tapestry, but the overwhelming likelihood is we're going to fail and we won't be able to pay your mother back."

"This is my dream. I want to make it happen. Since I was a kid I believed I could make a digital friend for people who have nobody. Tapestry is the best way of getting it out to everyone." She sticks her fingers in her ears, pulls them out.

Right now that dream feels like a million pounds weighing down on my shoulders. I have no idea of what to say to her. I want her dream to live just as I want my dream to live.

"Let's talk to the lawyers, and make an agreement so even if Tapestry goes down, you keep all the rights to your chat software."

Igloo's got her hands over her ears. "What'd you say?"

"I said we should... Forget it. Why are you covering your ears?"

"That heinous noise. How can you stand it?"

"What noise?"

"Like fingernails on a chalkboard," she says, "although much higher pitched."

"I don't hear a thing."

"You're really old. No offense, but you lose hearing at the upper frequencies when you're old."

Jeez. "I'm not that old."

"Old enough. Hold on, I'll show you on a sound meter." She leaves with her hands still over her ears.

When she comes back a few minutes later she's got earplugs in, and she's carrying a tablet with a fancy microphone plugged into the USB port.

"This is a sound spectrum analyzer. We use it when we're recording. This graph is by frequency along the bottom, amplitude vertically." As she speaks, the graph jumps up and down on the left hand side. "That's my voice. Now look over here." She pinches and zooms into the right hand side of the graph. "The area between twenty and twenty-two kilohertz is pegged," she says.

Indeed, the graph jumps up and down in that range.

"You can't hear that, most people can't. I'm pretty sensitive to high frequencies. This is right at the upper limit of what regular speakers produce."

She moves the microphone around and the graph jumps even higher as it nears my phone, and high again when it nears the cardboard box.

Oh, God. "Is there anything you can do so I can hear it?"

She nods. "A frequency shift. Hold on."

232 | WILLIAM HERTLING

A few seconds later I hear a warble similar to an old-fashioned modem. My heart jumps into my throat. Oh, God.

I grab my phone and hold the power button down until the phone does a hard shutdown, or appears to. The screen blinks and goes dark, but the sound meter is still active.

I seize my desk lamp by the gooseneck and smash the weighted base down on my phone, splintering the screen. I keep pounding until shards of electronics go flying.

"Holy shit!" Igloo ducks away, shielding herself from debris. Then she stands upright and turns the display toward me. The frequency meter has dropped to zero.

Igloo stares at me, then the desk and the remnants of my phone. She pulls back her hood. "That's, uh, weird, dude. What's going on?"

I'm breathing heavy, a rush of adrenaline kicking in from my act of violence.

"I isolated that computer," I say, pointing to the cardboard box, "so nobody could access the data on it. That sounded like an old acoustic modem. It must be an ultrasonic exploit to work around air gaps. I didn't think…"

I sink into the chair. I'm not merely being investigated by the government. I must be on active watch. There are probably agents sitting outside the building right now, waiting for me.

"Who would do that?" Igloo asks.

"The government," I blurt out.

"You think the government is spying on you?"

I nod, afraid she's going to conclude I've mentally lost it.

"That makes sense," Igloo says. "Imagine what a threat Tapestry would be to their ability to spy on us. Decentralized. Encrypted. Power to the people. Of course the NSA will be pissed."

"Oh," I say, suddenly feeling dumb. I assumed the government was after me for *killing* people. That's my guilt speaking. It makes more sense they'd watch me because I'm threatening their ability to monitor the population.

CHAPTER 39

CHRIS DALY PARKS A FEW BLOCKS AWAY and shoulders a large black back-pack. Angie's condo is a mid-rise building on a street straddling a residential neighborhood and a mixed-use district. Coming through the neighborhood, he's able to avoid the more prevalent security cameras in the businesses. The condo has a digital security card reader next to the door. Without stopping, he sticks a small scanner to the underside of the reader, and continues past the door.

The analysis detail started in on Angie this morning. Computers, phones, work security cameras, home network. They're all being cracked right now. Her security is good, her patches up to date, her accounts and ports all locked down, but there are ways in.

Her home has been particularly resistant. Despite several hours of trying, they haven't been able to connect to a single webcam or microphone.

He walks around the block, back through the neighborhood, and stops a block and a half away. He can see the entrance from here, where he won't be suspicious. He waits until someone enters, then walks back toward the building. Once there, he peels the scanner off the bottom of the badge reader, and gives it a squeeze. The door unlocks.

Inside, the building has its own security cameras, of course. The team back home assured him they'd erase today's footage at midnight and replace it with yesterday's footage. Angie's at work, so he can do anything he wants for the next couple of hours.

He doesn't know what security Angie has inside her apartment. That's why he knocks on the neighbor's place, which is guaranteed to be less secure than her place. No one answers, as expected, since the analysts told him one neighbor was traveling and the other at work, so he spends a minute getting the neighbor's door open.

He undoes the backpack, pulls out four devices on tripods, and stands them, evenly spaced, throughout the neighbor's condo facing Angie's. When he's done setting them up, he goes around to the neighbor on the opposite side of Angie's condo, and repeats the process with four more tripods.

He pulls out a small tablet and initiates the 3D scanning process. Each device sends out tens of thousands of pings at different angles and frequencies, while the others listen. Then the next device sends out pings, until they've all had turns to broadcast and listen.

Materials like wood, metal, plastic, and fabrics each block or deflect different frequency ranges. With the listeners positioned at many different places, they track every signal as it passes through the condo, bounces off materials. The massive quantities of raw data are sucked up into an array of servers that process the signal measurements and experimentally retrofit a three-dimensional model that best fits the deviations in path, intensity, and frequency shifts.

When signal capture is done, twenty minutes later, he packs up the equipment while the data is crunched in the cloud. By the time all the equipment is back in the car, he's got a 3D model of everything inside Angie's condo, accurate to within a few millimeters. The software continues to work, correlating patterns of shapes and materials against a database of known objects. As each object is identified, the model is updated. An outline of a pot in a kitchen cabinet is identified as an All-Clad Stainless Steel 2 Quart Boiler.

In the bedroom, her clothes closet is a haze, the soft fabrics difficult to resolve. The software can never match such soft items individually, though it incorporates her purchase history, and the vague confusion of clothing is overlaid with the constrained list of possibilities.

When the analysis is complete, Chris knows the model of webcam she has monitoring the front door and windows. Radio frequency monitoring identifies both the router talking to the webcams, as well as the wireless NAS hard drive hidden inside her IKEA hollow-core headboard, inductively charging off a power cord that passes behind the bed. He's startled by the appearance of motion inside the apartment during the scan, but it's only her robotic floor cleaner beginning its rounds.

The webcams by themselves indicate someone seriously obsessed with security, and the hidden hard drive demonstrates a level of paranoia typically reserved for criminals and crazies. Unfortunately, there's nothing in the apartment directly incriminating Angie. Crazy on the other hand…maybe.

When the FBI team dispatched to San Diego finally turned up the solar-powered Raspberry Pi router sitting on a downtown building rooftop, they had a courier take it directly to a lab. The lab technicians are still trying to recover the contents of the overwritten flash memory, but Chris has complete specs on the hardware. Nothing in the apartment matches. Angie has some electronics tools, but no soldering iron, and the techs were clear the onion router had been hand-soldered. There isn't any proof she fabricated them here.

At every step he becomes more convinced Angie is hiding something huge, even though they lack evidence tying her to anything specific.

The client paid him to derail Angie, and he has to deliver. However, there's an opportunity to make a genuine break in a previously unknown string of crimes, and he hates to pass that opportunity up. Imagine meeting the deliverable by legitimately arresting her? It doesn't get more elegant than that. Yet despite all the resources at BRI's disposal, he's been unable to make a connection.

That brings him back to the alternative. The psych boys say she's unstable, and it won't take much to push her over the edge. He'll need to resort to a smear campaign based on what they know about her past.

CHAPTER 40

THAT AFTERNOON, I CLEAN UP the splintered fragments of glass and circuitry from my smashed phone. Part of me wishes I'd taken a less destructive approach to shutting down the ultrasonic modem, though I was too panicked to think clearly at the time.

There are some older phones lying around somewhere. I rummage through my drawers until I find one. The SIM card from my broken phone is destroyed. Fortunately, my bin full of odds and ends has a few blank SIM cards and an old SIM reader/writer I built for a few bucks in parts from an electronics shop. A handy thing if you want to clone other people's SIM cards to make and receive phone calls as them. In this case, I restore my own backed up SIM card, and I've got a new working phone.

Defeating the ultrasonic modem is decidedly low-tech. Although the ideal solution would be a frequency limiter on the speaker and microphone, the phone's electronics are smaller than I'm capable of manipulating. Luckily, a layer of electrical tape over each is sufficient to attenuate the higher frequencies. It makes everything I say muffled, which is a bother, but I still feel clever for solving the problem.

I drive into work the next morning trying to put all that behind me and renew my focus on the work challenges ahead: finding some way to launch the company and bring in revenue in days rather than months. I'm mentally primed to deal with our employees' doubts and questions around the offer I turned down and the board of director's plan to cut off our funding.

As I pass the building to park at my reserved spot, what I'm not expecting is a little crowd of people standing in front of the office. Is that a...cameraman? At Tapestry?

Suddenly the hundreds of notifications on my phone I decided to ignore when I got up this morning seem a lot more ominous. I keep going, and pull over on the next block.

I swipe at my phone and expand the notifications to find the socialsphere has hundreds of broadcasts and mentions coalescing around one headline:

Tapestry CEO Killed Husband

Hacker Angie Benenati's New Company to Exploit User Data

The links all point to an article on TechnoWord, the blog that covers Portland startups. My hand trembles as I click on the link. What do they know?

Angie Benenati was one of Repard's White Knights, the hot-shot white hat hacker group he fostered at nineties powerhouse accounting firm Palmer-Cooper. The White Knights disbanded after Repard was charged in two indictments for breaking into a business newswire to steal unpublished press releases containing financial information used to make trades yielding an estimated $120 million in illegal profits.

Benenati resurfaced as employee number forty-eight at then-exploding Tomo. Benenati became chief database architect for Tomo from 2003 to 2009 when she left the company after marrying Jeremy Pearson. Three years later, Jeremy Pearson was dead.

An anonymous Wikileaks contribution contains previously sealed police records about the case. Until now, no one knew Benenati was the subject of an investigation by the Menlo Park Police Department on Pearson's death. An internal memo by the lead investigator says "There is no doubt whatsoever Benenati premeditated the vehicular accident [that killed Pearson] when she disabled the airbag system."

Two weeks after the accident, the District Attorney and lead investigator, citing extenuating circumstances, jointly agreed not to prosecute and sealed all records.

Benenati, who lost her right arm in the accident, was rehired in Tomo's Portland office in 2012 as a data analyst. Former colleagues claim she was involved in everything from database architecture to deployment infrastructure, far outreaching her official responsibilities.

She left Tomo last year to found Tapestry, a stealth mode company, self-funding operations for six months. According to emails exchanged with her accountant, Benenati paid all expenses and salaries in cash until she later secured angel funding led by local investor Owen Mitchell.

Tapestry was set to complete a new funding round on Tuesday of nearly $8MM on a post-investment $50MM valuation. The funding round was aborted without warning, leaving would-be investors literally waiting at the table to sign with Benenati a no-show.

Benenati leaves us with more questions than answers.

- Why was a former computer hacker, peripherally involved in one of the biggest scandals at the start of the new millennium, given complete control over Tomo's user data?
- Why was Benenati, clearly believed guilty of a premeditated murder, not prosecuted?
- Why did Benenati pay employees and expenses in cash for over six months? What was she hiding? Where did the money come from?
- Is Benenati still involved in computer hacking, and if so, to what end?

My blood pounds in my temples and my vision narrows. People are prying into my very private life, my history. Add this to all the other unsolvable problems I'm grappling with, and suicide sounds like a good option.

But, God, how many years of my marriage did I spend wanting to kill myself? I can't go back to that darkness. If I must, I will disappear and start a new life, or go live in Emily's basement and never come out. I have those options at least.

Still, my rage fades away and I'm left only with despair. I fought for so long to keep my past secret. The life I created for myself seems over now. I wanted to create something positive and the universe destroyed my dream.

I call Emily, and she miraculously picks up on the first ring. In my panic, it's hard for me to explain at first, but eventually I make myself understood well enough that she goes to TechnoWord's site to read the article.

"I don't see it," she says. "There's a post saying their site was compromised, they're investigating, and they'll update when they know more."

"What?" I hit refresh on my phone, the page updates, and the article is gone. I try to puzzle out what this means. The article was not legit. TechnoWord never found the information they claimed to uncover. Someone else published the article, knowing once it was released, the damage would be done. Whether TechnoWord retracts or not, you can't ever kill a meme, and *startup founder/hacker/murderer* is too much to take back. Worse, now that the truth is out, it's inevitable people will search for evidence to support it.

Somebody will pay. Maybe I won't be able to save Tapestry, but whatever bastard did this is surely going to rot in hell.

"I have to go, Em."

"You sure? You sound upset. I can come over."

"No. This is a smear campaign. I'll fight it."

I hang up and make a U-turn and head back toward the office. A half dozen or more people are still loitering around the building. Fortunately, there's no one blocking the parking lot, because in my current state I'd probably plow right through them.

Unfortunately, they see me pull in and gather around my car while I'm parked. I grab my shoulder bag and prepare to push my way through them. They're shouting questions at me through the glass. The cameraman is lining up for a shot through my windshield.

"Did you really kill your husband?"

"Where did the seed money for Tapestry come from?"

"Is it true Tapestry is a front for the Russian mob, that your real purpose is to steal financial data from Americans?"

"Do your employees know what you've done?"

I grit my teeth and open the car door.

I knew they were there before I got out of the car, knew I needed to push my way through them, but I'm not prepared for how closely they crowd me. They're all staring, yelling, touching me at the same time. My legs go weak with the office door a mere twenty feet away. I should be able to push my way through a tiny crowd of people, but I can't. One of the reporters shoves a smartphone in front of my face, and I flinch away. Someone else touches my shoulder, and I cower back. I want to push forward, but find myself involuntarily retreating back up against my car.

"Leave her alone!" someone screams over the din.

Igloo runs toward the assembly carrying a mic stand from her band's practice equipment. She slams it into the ground. The resulting metal ringing captures everyone's attention. She picks the stand back up and swings the heavy base in a wide arc. Everyone falls back, stumbling over each other in a panicked rush to escape Igloo's reach.

I'm distantly aware that if a photo of that makes it out on the news, it's not going to be good PR.

"What the fuck is wrong with you people?" Igloo yells. She grabs me by one shoulder and drags me toward the building.

I stumble along as best I can, my legs wooden, sights and sounds coming through a long, thin tunnel.

ʊ

Inside the office, what little strength I have fades and I sink to the floor, slipping out of Igloo's grasp.

My vision has narrowed to a little window. Igloo's mouth moves, but I can't hear anything over the roar of static in my ears.

Later, when I come to, I find myself lying on the floor in the lunch room. There's a female firefighter tending me, and two male firefighters on the other side of the room, one of whom is treating a nosebleed on the other. The woman next to me sees my eyes focus on her.

"You have a good left hook."

I don't know what she's talking about, but I've had enough dissociative episodes to know I've lost time. It usually makes everyone feel better and go away sooner if I pretend to have some idea what they're talking about, so I manage a little smile.

She helps me to a sitting position, then makes the other firefighters leave the room. For the next ten minutes, she asks me the usual domestic and work-place violence questions. Am I in danger? Am I safe at home? Am I safe at work? Is anyone harassing or threatening me?

Am I safe? What can I say? That the world's largest social media company is in cahoots with the government to discredit me and take my company away? If they don't succeed, there are agencies in the government that could make me disappear? I'd be in the psych ward in time to get lunch. Or dinner. Whatever time it is.

Instead I make excuses about PTSD from past abuse triggered by the stress of the morning and promise I'll call my therapist and take it easy. She lets Igloo back in the room and instructs her to keep me calm, and not to let me leave by myself. Then the firefighters go with all their gear, except the blanket they leave me wrapped up in.

Igloo kneels next to me. I ask for tea and honey, which she brings. I drink half the cup in silence.

"What's happened?" I eventually say.

"I'm not sure we should talk about it," Igloo says.

"I can't afford to not know. I promise not to faint or anything."

"Well, Amber is pretty pissed about the article."

"She believes the stuff they printed?"

Igloo shrugs. "I'm not sure. She saw they retracted it. I don't think she cares about that so much as the impact on the company. She believes you're to blame somehow."

"What else?"

"You gave Harry a bag of money yesterday."

I nod.

"He read the article, thought you had stolen it, and turned it all in to the police."

"What? The idiot." I try to force myself up.

Igloo pushes me back down. "I said we shouldn't talk about it."

"Why did he do that?" I realize I'm whining. "That's all the money we have. I borrowed it. I sold my stock for it."

"He thought he was doing the right thing," Igloo said. "You purposely hired people who would do the right thing, remember?"

"Help me up," I say.

I climb to my feet with Igloo's assistance and lean against a table for a while.

"Anything else I should know?"

"Everyone was distracted with the press and everything else, so most folks went home."

I look Igloo in the eyes.

"*You* haven't asked me if it's true."

"You were the one who took care of my sister's problem," she says.

I nod once.

"That's all I need to know."

I clasp her shoulder. "Thanks. Only some of it was true."

"That's the way it is. When they're not hiding the stuff that matters, they're making the stuff that doesn't matter sound worse than it is. It's the man trying to distract us."

My brain's functioning again, and I try to gather my thoughts. Tomo wants to stop me and the government is investigating me. Occam's Razor says the simplest explanation is the most likely one: these things are connected. The odds of both happening independently at the same time is unlikely, especially since I haven't gone after any domestic abusers in a long time. I guess the government doesn't yet have any idea of all the bastards I've murdered, because they didn't even hint at it in the fake article. Yet they discovered my involvement in the hacking community because they mentioned that. If I don't do something to level the playing field, this war will go on forever, and they're better situated to outlast me.

The main thing I need to know now is who in the government is pursuing me. Is it really this black agency that Nathan9 believes he discovered, or is it a legit investigation? How are they connected to Tomo?

It's far beyond my ability to figure this out, but I know one person who can.

"Help me back to my office."

ʊ

I'm running out of options to hide my network traffic. TOR is compromised, my own onion network is suspect, and sending packets through Tomo, when I know they're actively looking for ways to stop me, seems foolish. VPN only goes so far.

I find the most secure VPN host I can, install the software to connect to the darkest darknet there appears to be this month, and find a host that will packet forward for me. Then I connect to Dead Channel, half suspecting my account will be revoked, and ready to use one of the two backdoors I know of.

But my login still works, and I immediately ping Nathan9.

SysOp> I left your login as a measure of goodwill.
Your problem didn't go away in two days. Unless you
fixed it, you're putting me and Dead Channel at risk.

I want to brag that I don't need the login, but I must weigh the value of bravado against the likelihood of Nathan hunting for and closing the backdoors. I decide against mentioning it.

```
Angel> I can't fix my problem without knowing specif-
ically who's leading the investigation into me. I want
to know who.
SysOp> Ha. I would like to sit in the Oval Office.
Some things cannot be obtained.
Angel> The name of the agent would be nothing. It's
somewhere, on paperwork. Somebody had to sign off on
the investigation.
SysOp> It's a dark agency, one that no one has ever
even mentioned. I'm not sure those assumptions hold
true.
Angel> You could pull in favors to find out.
SysOp> Not likely.
```

I hate that it comes to this next step, I really do. I have to assess the continued value of our thirty-year relationship against the immediate dangers, and right now, the present trumps the future.

```
Angel> I have a complete dump of Dead Channel. I
will post it.
SysOp> Don't be ridiculous.
```

I wait without responding. Nothing makes people more uncomfortable than silence. Repard taught me that.

```
SysOp> You can't expose anybody. All connections to
Dead Channel are untraceable, and the exploits boards
is fully anonymous, even among the members.
Angel> You know it's not about the government ar-
resting them. It's about whether any of those members
will continue to come to the Dead Channel if all the
archives are dumped.
```

Everything is dead silent, my screen unchanging for a long time. I imagine I can sense the bytes flowing along endlessly complex connections into Nathan's computer, percolating up through network and operating system and application layers until they scroll across a screen he'll never see and into the text-to-speech module where they'll reconstitute into spoken words, which he will listen to, and then rage will spread across his face and through his body as he understands the magnitude of what I've threatened.

```
SysOp> Fuck you. I've spent my entire life building
this community.
```

Yeah, the threat is not about getting hackers arrested. We're not even talking about a lot of people. Maybe twenty people around the world that really matter. People who leave my modest skills in the dust. But hackers are powered by secrecy and a thin veneer of trust. Break their trust by exposing their secrets, and nobody will ever frequent Dead Channel or any other board Nathan runs. That's nothing compared to what they'll do to me. I know that, Nathan knows that, but desperate people are dangerous and Nathan knows I'm desperate.

```
Angie> I need to know who's leading the investiga-
tion, and not some code name. Hard identity.
```

There's another pause. I pass the long seconds by biting my nails. I need to find my enemy to fight them.

```
SysOp> You'll get your data in the morning.
SysOp> You understand it's over between us. You
don't burn your friends.
SysOp> Goodbye, Angie.
```

The connection terminates.

CHAPTER 41

DALY'S SITTING IN A RESTAURANT with a view of Angie's building when the call comes. He shuts down the tablet—not that there was anything useful on it after she encrypted her connection—and answers the call.

"I've got her," Pete says.

"Yeah?" This is the third time Pete's said this, except every time he thought he had a solid connection, it turned out there were more layers. Spending several million dollars in NSA compute time to break three-layer encryption on what appeared to be an important stream of traffic, only to unveil Angie's personal photos, did not make Enso happy. That the same exact photos were also posted publicly on Flickr did not help his case.

Chris was on the wrong end of a long lecture about BRI's need to maintain a low profile, culminating in all the BRI resources being yanked off Angie's investigation.

But Chris knows she's up to something, and she knows *they* are up to something. There is no other explanation for a forty-five-year-old woman taking a bathroom selfie with her tongue stuck out at the camera. She might as well have captioned the photo "Fuck you, NSA."

While, against all odds, Enso and the powers-that-be might not be convinced, Pete's finally convinced. Or maybe he's taken it as a personal challenge because Angie's made a mockery of his pursuit. Whatever the case, Pete's working on his own time, using ONI's smaller computing resources to continue the investigation, and hiding his efforts from Plaint.

"Analyzing the network traffic profiles got us to all these different wi-fi spots around the city," Pete says. "None of the surveillance footage has ever shown Angie in those places at the time of the encrypted traffic streams, although she visited some of the spots."

"We knew that a week ago."

"Yeah, but now I can tie her to those places."

"How?" Chris asks.

"I found every city street camera, every business surveillance, every personal webcam with a view of the street and sufficient resolution to do facial analysis of vehicle drivers. A hundred and ninety cameras, an average of three thousand vehicles per day per camera, about half a million facial analyses per day, two hundred million attempts in all for the last year's worth of data."

"And? What did you find?" Why did Pete need to draw everything out?

"Six photos of her driving a '77 Volkswagen Type 2 camper van."

"Placing her at the wi-fi spots?"

"Not exactly," Pete says. "Knowing the vehicle I was looking for, I re-did the image search looking for the van. There are a lot of cameras good enough to resolve a car, not so many that can make out the person driving it. Every day the van was out and about correlates almost perfectly with the wi-fi encrypted traffic streams, and in the majority of occasions, I can place it within long-range wi-fi distance at the time and location of her data streams. Unfortunately, the van disappeared about eight months ago. I'm guessing she switched vehicles."

Chris muses on this. Statistically speaking, the correlation ties her to the network traffic, and Pete's gradually turned up connections between the network traffic streams and several suspicious deaths, as well as the kid in Brazil. It's not the same thing as proof. That would require decoding the network traffic streams, which Pete has been unable to do because she's using multi-layer cryptography. After the photo fiasco, he's not going to be able to go back to Enso and ask for the kinds of resources it would take to break that encryption.

However, Chris is not a judge in a court system and he doesn't need proof. BRI's game is leverage, and this new information is leverage.

CHAPTER 42

I SPEND THE REST OF THE DAY in damage control, personally reaching out to every employee, explaining the article has been retracted, and it's clear this is a smear campaign, probably led by Tomo. The problem is most of the article is true, and there's much more, and worse, that could yet be uncovered. So I fess up a bit, and admit I've got skeletons in my closet, and if I could change the past, I would. All I can do is move forward. I tell everyone to take the day off and come in tomorrow prepared to kick butt.

I go easiest to hard, to give me time to refine my spiel, and so I've left Harry and Amber for the end.

I'm a bit tougher on Harry, both because I'm furious at him for giving away the last of our money, money I literally begged for, and because I know if I go in apologetic, he'll think I'm guilty. So I go in hard, put him on the defensive, and tell him it's his responsibility, as our accountant, to straighten out the mess he's created, otherwise every employee will be without pay and the viability of the company jeopardized, and he could be liable to the investors. In one fell swoop, I've applied personal guilt, tribal obligations, and legal ramifications of his job responsibility. Not surprisingly, he caves. Nathan9 said my social game needed work. Hah!

That leaves Amber. She's holed up in her office. We've avoided each other all day. The door's closed and locked. I know because I hear her turn the lock each time she goes in. I knock.

She unlocks the door, pulls it open a few inches, looks at me, turns and goes back to her desk.

I enter with confidence, determined not to walk on eggshells around her. On the contrary, my mind is in high gear, boosted from an hour of successful employee discussions, and I've planned my approach. She's going to make the same argument she did back when we were working out of the back of her house, about her limited time, and how I'm throwing away people's lives.

She pounds at the keyboard for a minute and I wait to let her have the first word.

"The thing is, I'm almost thirty years old," Amber says. "I only get so much time, so many companies I can incubate."

Inside I'm smiling. I know her, how her mind works. I own her.

"I don't know what you've got going on," she continues, "but no matter what happens, you keep coming back here, you keep pushing everyone to succeed. I don't understand you half the time and I don't like the chaos you've caused. I can't do anything about that. What I can do is sit here and code. Spare me whatever argument you've prepared, because I don't want to hear it. I'll be here until the police come and seize our computers. Go do whatever it is you need to do."

"I, umm…" Jesus. My mind is blank. Amber's gone way off script. This is the part where she's supposed to say I'm wasting the limited years she has available to change the world.

Amber turns back to her computer and thrashes her keyboard some more.

"Thank you," I say.

Her fingers pause her furious typing. "I don't need thanks. I don't even need your friendship. I need you to keep the company going, to figure out the revenue, and fix whatever the hell is going on out there, so we can focus on changing the world and stopping goddamn Tomo."

I walk out of the office knowing our relationship has changed. It's sometimes been stormy, but I thought there was a friendship, too. Whatever we had, it's lost now, replaced by an alliance made by two parties who find themselves reluctantly on the same side in a war that's bigger than them. Maybe I can count on Amber to the end, but I don't have enough friends that I can afford to keep losing them.

↻

As the day goes by, the press and bloggers outside gradually give up. When the door buzzer goes off in the afternoon, someone answers it. A few minutes later, one of our engineers comes into my office.

"Angie? You got a delivery." He shrugs sheepishly.

He's holding a single rose, the flower petals dyed black. "It came with this." He holds out the rose and a manila envelope.

I receive the rose with trepidation. It's the sort of portent we used back in the heyday. I lay it cautiously on the table and grab the envelope.

"Thanks," I say, then stare at my engineer who's waiting around hoping to see what's in the envelope. He leaves disappointed.

I grasp the envelope tight under my stump and rip the red pull-tab. I shake out a micro-SD card.

I stare at it, think back to that night at Death's party when I was fifteen. For all the years Nathan9 and I were friends, that was the last time I saw him in person. He's the idolized hacker the kid version of me looked up to, and his reclusiveness, his blindness, the way he reaches out and changes the world from wherever it is he hides out, it's all added to the mystique, my elevation of him onto a God-like pedestal.

For all that, he's the one person who's always known this side of me, held secrets no one else, not even Emily, can be aware of. He led me into this world, that day at the party, and I assumed he would remain constant.

To hold something he physically touched... No. My shoulders slump. He's never touched this. He sent the bits on to someone else, had them copy the data onto the SD card. I had hoped for a sign our friendship might continue.

I find a quarantined laptop and redouble my counter-surveillance precautions. In addition to my usual measures, and the electric tape on my phone to cut the chance of my phone being used as an acoustic backchannel, I also run a frequency jammer and white noise generator. Only then do I copy the data onto the computer.

It's the full deal. Names, aliases. Known phone numbers, email addresses, server logins. Associates. All used IMEI numbers. Hardware MAC addresses. All online profiles. Employee IDs and social security numbers. Nathan didn't scrimp at all: he must have traded in favors in a big way. Whoever did the work used extensive correlation to determine all the identities used by this man. Chris Daly is merely the current alias of the man trying to destroy my life. His last known location? Portland, Oregon. He's close, watching me in person, not only online.

There's more in the package. Messages between Chris Daly and someone named Joe, concerning the client who's hired Daly to investigate and destroy...me.

I try to remember to breathe. This is the proof I need!

Daly is not doing this on behalf of a government investigation. He's freelancing, selling his access on the open market, using his power and capabilities to earn a spare buck, and ruining my life in the process.

Who hired Daly? That's the question. If I can expose them, cut them off at the source, that's the power I need. But the identity of the client is not here anywhere. The "client" is all Joe and Chris Daly ever refer to. The client wants background info. The client wants Angie discredited. The client wants Angie to go away. Is the client Lewis Rasmussen? I never uncovered anything to prove Lewis's active malfeasance, and yet, who else could it be?

Daly has to know. There's no way he, with all of his government access, would not be aware of who his own client is. In fact, he even makes reference to the client having the money to pay more. He must know the identity.

I want to scream, but I'm conscious of my surroundings. I'm at the office, and there are people all around. I'm probably being monitored. I can't give anything away. A random outburst, if they're listening in, could give away the significance of the flower delivery, lead them to investigate even more.

I lean over, rest my forehead on my desk. I must stop Chris Daly and expose the client. Think, Angelina Benenati, think for all you're worth.

For long minutes, I sit there motionless. Suddenly I bolt upright, fear and certainty running through me in equal measures. There's something I can do. Something awful. Something that makes me want to puke right here, that has me shaking in my seat. But it will work.

☿

"You don't have to do this," I say. "Hell, I don't want you to do it."

"I can help, and I want to." Igloo's arms are buried somewhere deep inside her oversized hoodie. I'm afraid sometimes that if I blink, she might disappear inside it.

"You have no idea what risk you're putting yourself under."

I don't like it. I really don't. But Igloo is an adult, even if she seems like a kid to me. I can't stand in her way and decide for her. I was younger than her when I made bigger decisions.

"Fine," I say. "Go to the store and buy a dozen prepaid cell phones with data plans. Pay cash. I'll pack up the equipment here and secure us a ride."

Igloo leaves, and I prep a bunch of laptops, a mobile router, and a slew of chargers and spare batteries. Of course, I call Danger.

My preparations come to a screeching halt when a message from Thomas pops up.

Thomas> You okay? Read some news about you and the company, something about a fake article about you?

I've been focused on myself, the company, and our employees. Meanwhile, Thomas and Emily are my family, my support system. That means they're my vulnerabilities, and Chris Daly will certainly use Thomas and Emily against me.

Angie> I'm surviving. I'll fill you in a little later.

I need to squirrel them out of town without letting anyone know. I grab a spare hoodie from Igloo's desk. Even though she's half my size, the sweatshirt is baggy enough to fit. I stuff the sweatshirt and a random cap from the coatroom in a bag, then take a car-share downtown, which drops me off at a hotel. Once inside, I give my purse, with my cell phone and other electronics to the bell-hop. In an empty hallway free of cameras, I don the hoodie and hat, do my best to keep my face covered, and exit the hotel through the service entrance, squeezing my way past a delivery truck. I hoof it over to Thomas's office.

I sneak into his office and hold a finger to my lips when the receptionist spots me. She smiles and gestures towards his office with a nod. I feel ridiculous pretending everything is normal when I'm on the edge of panic. For the next twenty-four hours, though, there's going to be a whole lot of pretending.

I enter his office, and Thomas looks up from his computer. I keep my finger to my lips, and stay away from his webcam. I gesture for him to come to me. He's puzzled, but stands and walks over.

I pull his ear to my lips.

"We need to talk outside your office."

"What—"

I put my finger to his lips. "Shhh."

I turn and walk out of his office. He's in a third floor suite in an older mid-rise building. There's not much tech in the building, so I'm mostly concerned about the computers in his office. Unfortunately, he approaches with his phone in his hand. Careful to stay away from the camera, I take it from him and drop it on the receptionist's desk, then go back out to join him.

"Okay," he says, laughing. "Can you be any more mysterious?"

"I wish this was a joke of some kind, but it's serious. You heard about the article this morning?"

"Yes," Thomas says. "What is it all about? They retracted the article and said someone hacked their website. It keeps popping up in my feed, though."

"I know this will sound crazy, but it's part of a scheme to discredit me. Tomo hired a computer hacker to plant the story."

"Was that true? Your husband, the car accident?"

"That's the most insidious kind of lie, one blending truth and fiction. Because anyone who cares to investigate will find out he died in an accident, and once part of the story is confirmed, they'll believe the rest must be true, too. We're standing out here in the hallway right now because whoever they hired to do this is still out there, probably spying on our phone conversations, our computers."

"We aren't talking on the phone or the computer."

"It doesn't matter, a skilled intruder can listen using the microphone whether you think you're being watched or not."

Thomas raises an eyebrow, leans back an inch. "That's not—"

"It *is* possible," I say, raising my voice. "I worked in computer security for ten years. I know what can be done."

"Go to the police," Thomas says. "Surely they can figure out who is behind this."

If it was anyone else, I'd roll my eyes. That would be like asking a lawnmower mechanic to build an interstellar spaceship.

"No, I contacted some friends I used to work with in computer forensics, and they're investigating right now. But they said it was critically important to get you and Emily out of town and off the grid, because I'm close to you and the criminals might go after you next."

I've invented this third party, because it's a sad fact of life people are more likely to believe experts they don't know over the people they do. The lies roll off my tongue with ease, leaving behind a taste like burnt petrochemicals.

"I'm not leaving you," Thomas says. "I'm staying right here with you."

Here's the catch-22. If he hadn't said that, things wouldn't be right with the world. He loves me, he wants to protect me. Unfortunately, his presence is as much help as a load of bricks in the trunk of a race car. There are a dozen things I could say to distance him, hurt him, and make him leave. I'm not willing to take that approach anymore.

I grab his hand in mine. "If you could help me by staying here, I would keep you by my side. I need to work with my old coworkers on this. I'm not in any physical danger, but I must be able to concentrate. If you're here, the hackers will go after you, expose you and your work, for the express purpose of distracting me."

"I have nothing to hide," Thomas says.

"Everybody has something they want to keep private. Some website they've visited, some photo they've taken, some message they sent. Can you honestly say there's nothing embarrassing you've ever done online or that's been recorded on a computer? Nothing that, if it was suddenly shown in a courtroom in front of a judge, wouldn't discredit you in some way?"

He pauses, shrugs. "Well... Why do I need to leave, exactly?"

"Hackers like to taunt people. If you're online, if you're using your phone, if you're anywhere around your computer, they will know. They will spy on you through your webcam, talk to you through your speakers, and generally act like elementary school bullies. They'll call the police, claiming someone is being raped in your office. They'll dump all your case files on the Internet, every confidential file you've ever had, for no reason other than knowing it will annoy you and distract me. If you're not around, on the other hand, if they can't see the immediate effect, watch and rebroadcast videos of you crying as the police raid your office and take you away in handcuffs, then it takes away half the reason for toying with you."

Thomas runs a hand through his hair. "I don't know, Angie. This is all *strange*. I have work I need to bring with me, calls I need to make."

"No," I say. "Nothing electronic. No phone. You can bring paper files only." I give his hand a squeeze. "I'm in no danger, but I need to focus and know you're safe. I'm giving you the hardest job of all. Grab Emily from work and force her to leave her computer and phone. Stop at an ATM, withdraw the most cash you can, and after that, don't touch your credit cards again. Then take the train to Seattle with Emily."

"The train?"

"You won't need identification. Once there, find a cheap hotel or something where you don't need ID, and hang out for two days. Then you can call me and find out if everything is okay."

"There's no way Emily will go along," Thomas says. "She crushes mightier men than me."

"You've gone to trial and convinced judges and juries, you can work on Emily. You must do it, to keep her and her family safe."

He gently holds me by the shoulders, not in a harmful way, but to check in with me.

I flinch, despite my best efforts, and force myself not to pull away, even as my stomach clenches and adrenaline floods my system from his touch. Old habits and fears coming back...

"You're sure?"

I nod.

"Fine. I'll do it."

I lean forward, give him a kiss and a hug. "Thank you. I know it sounds crazy, but it's going to be a huge help for me to know you are both safe."

↻

By the time everything is prepared, it's late in the day and I'm exhausted. If I were twenty-five, I might choose to pull an all-nighter. Unfortunately, I'm not, and I need to be in top form. I confer with Danger and Igloo and we agree to start in the morning.

I head back to my place, acutely aware of the dangers surrounding me, and half expect I'll be swatted during the night: that Daly will call the police, report a violent crime in progress, and I'll end up spending the night at a police station without ever getting the rest I need. But a good torturer knows there's an ideal cadence to inflicting pain for maximum effect. Too much, too fast, and your subject goes into shock and isn't cognitively there to feel the pain. Too little, too slow, and they learn to tune it out. Watch a cat play with a captured mouse. They understand it instinctively. My gut tells me he won't swat me tonight. He'll have something planned for tomorrow, right when I think I'm getting a handle on this.

I lie in bed for a long time, alternating between trying to shut my brain off and trying to plan through all the contingencies. Every outside noise sends my pulse racing. I wish I had some magic drug to shut my brain down without any side effects. Finally, I turn onto my side and pull the pillow over my head to shut out any noises. If I die in my sleep, so be it.

CHAPTER 43

"EVERYBODY'S PHONES OFF and batteries disconnected?"

They both nod *yes*.

"Full gas tank?"

"Yep," Danger says from behind the wheel. "We're good to go."

"You've got all the equipment? Phones? Laptops? Spare batteries?"

"Everything," Igloo says.

We spent yesterday prepping, raiding the office for equipment, and sanitizing every machine. We're both sitting in the back for maximum working space, with Danger the designated chauffeur. A rat's nest of power cables and multi-plug adapters covers the front seat.

"Sort these cables out," I say to Igloo, "and duct-tape them in place on the back of the seat so we don't have to fumble for them."

"Be careful with the upholstery," Danger says.

My level of concern is with surviving the day, which makes Dan's concern laughable. If all goes to plan, the worst he'll experience is getting tape residue off car seats. If it doesn't, well…

I pass a smartphone up to the front seat. I preprogrammed a driving route with wi-fi access points this morning, and all Danger has to do is follow the plan for the rest of the day, or as long as it takes. "Follow these waypoints. Don't deviate."

Danger gets the car into gear.

"Now let's prepare these computers." Igloo and I plug in USB drives, loading clean virtual machines configured with the tools we'll need.

"I'm here," Danger says. "Now it's telling me 43 degrees."

"Here," I say, passing a long-range wi-fi antenna into the front seat. "Aim this at 43 degrees. It's got a signal strength meter on the display."

At the first stop, we lay the foundation. I want him cornered, unable to run.

It takes an hour perusing IRC and forums, slowly narrowing in on someone who can deliver what we want. Eventually we find a guy going by Devil's Snowball who looks like they could deliver.

Halfway through negotiations we need to drop off the net while Danger shifts locations. Devil's Snowball wants $10,000 in bitcoin. I can barely manage this by tapping, once more, into my emergency fund, but this certainly qualifies as a crisis, and grounding Daly is the foundation of my plan. I find someone I know, and confirm Snowball's creds via one of my alternate identities.

Devil's Snowball promises all of Daly's aliases and his associated metadata will be on the suspected terrorist no-fly list within an hour. Even if Daly shows up with an unknown fake identity, if he's carrying a phone with a known IMEI, Department of Homeland Security will pick him up. True, Daly is a government agent, and could eventually unfuck himself, but DHS is notoriously stubborn.

We move again and park outside a funeral home with open wi-fi. While people in dark suits and dresses go inside to pay their respects, we use my Tomo backdoor. Igloo lets out a small whistle.

"You have access to *everything*," she says.

I peer over at her screen, watch as she pulls up her own profile.

"All my web browsing, my purchases, my dating profile... How?"

"It's all tied together," I say, trying not to become too distracted by Igloo's first-timer enthusiasm. "Not everything has a solid one-to-one connection, but between cookies and browser fingerprints, we can build your profile over time."

"Browser fingerprints?" Igloo asks.

"Every website can query your browser to find out your operating system, screen size, browser version, list of enabled plugins, time zone, and available fonts. In theory, all of that is perfectly anonymous. The data is there so the website can customize your user experience. In practice, most people's computers suffer from a unique or close to unique fingerprint. The best you can do is try to blend into the crowd by installing the most common fonts and browser plugins, use the most common browser version, and configure it to report the most common screen size."

"That's why we're using these virtual machines," she says. "Got it. Wait, my sister still has a profile. That's not possible. She deleted all her online accounts after the kid from Brazil..."

I shake my head. "Sorry, no dice. All the profiles are still there. Nobody really deletes anything. Even if she'd never created a single account, we'd still have a shadow profile. Anyhow, you need to focus. Follow these instructions."

I share a document over our local network outlining what we need to do for the next phase. If we had time, I would have automated it. I never imagined pulling off an exploit of this magnitude.

See, Chris Daly is not going to run the Tomo app on his phone, not if he's got a shred of common sense around operational security, so I can't track his location directly. If Nathan was on my side, I'd ask him to track Daly's phone, as Nathan has back doors into all the cellular networks. I don't, so Igloo and I will do this the hard way.

He can't avoid the million other people in Portland who are running Tomo on their smartphones right now.

Step one is subverting Tomo's monitoring tools for the western coast so everything continues to report statistically normal data. Every Tomo server could drop dead right now, and nobody in Ops would know. This would make an excellent case study in why it's important to harden monitoring tools, but the truth is it's difficult to secure against the people who build the system.

Next, we use my existing backdoors into the provisioning layer, and without notifying anyone or allowing them to show up in any monitoring tools or logs, we allocate five hundred servers in the Dalles, Oregon data center to handle diagnostic feeds.

"Holy cow," Igloo says. "We'd really cut our hosting bill if we ran Tapestry on Tomo's servers."

"This won't last for long. What happens if someone tries to provision servers? The central database lists these machines as free. We can lose them at any second. Besides, if we keep them running at load for any length of time, it'll show up in the electrical consumption."

"Too bad," Igloo says. "I love the idea of free servers."

I nod in agreement, though the reality is I took them for granted when I worked for Tomo. I didn't realize what an advantage it was. I guess I had server privilege.

"How's that payload coming?" I ask.

"Ready for you to review."

Igloo and I go through the text file line by line. It will turn on debug mode for everyone within fifty miles of city center. It overrides the normal diagnostic server addresses, sending the traffic to the temporary server pool we created. Lastly, it uses the Tomo app's access to suppress data overage notifications on everyone's phone. They're still going to use up that data, but they won't know about it until the bill comes, and we'll be long done by then.

"Looks good."

I deploy the debug configuration file, the Tomo app pulls it down, and we watch as the data comes in.

What begins as a trickle turns into a flood.

"Server load is passing 1," Igloo reports.

Uh oh. "Craptastic. I didn't provision enough servers."

Sure enough, within minutes the five hundred servers crumble under the load of incoming diagnostic data. I allocate another five hundred, and loads decrease, but not enough. I add five hundred more. At this point, we're using every spare server in the data center. I can't even imagine what's happening to the cellular data networks right now.

This stream of unwanted diagnostic data is horrendous, yet it's intrinsically tied into debug mode. Nobody ever intended the diagnostic upload to be used for more than the occasional one-off case. They certainly didn't expect an entire city's worth of mobile devices to upload simultaneously.

"Last step," I say, "the binary package." It's compiled code that will use each mobile device's cellular radio to scan for all of Daly's unique IMEI numbers in the local vicinity.

"You're sure this will work?" Igloo asks, as we wait for the Tomo clients to download and begin executing our custom scanning code.

"In theory, it should," I say, wishing I felt more confident. "Nobody's ever tried anything like this before." If, or when, one of the millions of compromised smartphones in the city detects a sign of Daly's cell phone, it'll immediately use its GPS to determine the current geocoordinates, and turn on the camera and microphone to record and upload everything.

The Panopticon has been turned on Chris Daly.

Hours pass as we do this, and now it's past lunchtime. We stop for food and rotate through burner phones, keeping an eye on Daly's activity while we eat, and get snacks for the car.

Daly still hasn't come online; or if he has, he's strictly keeping to websites and devices and access points we're not tracking. That's okay, because we're not done yet.

After lunch I send Igloo back online to the IRC and forums, looking for someone to destroy Daly's credit rating and disable his credit cards and bank accounts.

While she's doing that, I focus on building a criminal history for him. I can't do much in the U.S. I don't have access to those systems, and I know from experience almost nobody does. Still, I can make him a fugitive wanted for murder, rape, and embezzlement in the Maldives, and the U.S. systems will cross-reference this data.

Danger keeps driving, moving us from spot to spot. I can't be sure if or when Daly will find out what we're doing, but when he does, he's going to be pissed. We're parked downtown now, near Pioneer square. This is a risk, because dozens of cameras can pick us up. But from here, without moving the car, we can piggyback on a thousand different wi-fi hotspots by refocusing the antenna. The best part is those hotspots are in tech companies with gobs of bandwidth. They're protected networks, of course, but Tomo's debug mode uploaded the SSIDs and associated passwords from everyone's phones, so we can access every network in the city now.

The thump of an approaching helicopter is audible even over the noise of the surrounding traffic and people on the streets. I look up, my pulse quickening. I can't spot it at first, then I see a black dot approaching.

"Get ready to drive," I say.

"Already?" Danger asks. "We're supposed to rotate between three more hotspots here before we go."

"Start the car."

He complies, and now we all watch the helicopter. I curse myself for not bringing binoculars.

"Kill all the connections," I say.

"Wait," Igloo says. "I've got someone who says he can cancel his bank accounts."

"No. Kill the antenna *now*."

Danger hits a switch, shutting it off.

"Shit," Igloo says. "Can I use a phone to go online?"

"No, nothing, no signals."

The helicopter hovers above Pioneer Square.

"It's only a helicopter," Igloo says. "They fly above downtown all the time."

She's right. If it had the insignia of a TV station, maybe I'd be willing to overlook it. But it hangs there, and I imagine men with directional scanners, telescopic cameras, maybe guns, all focused on us. I pull back from the window.

"Move. Just drive, normally. If they follow us, that'll tell us something. If they don't, we'll resume at the next waypoint."

Danger pulls out into traffic, heading south and then east toward the Hawthorne Bridge. The helicopter passes in and out of view as we pass behind buildings, but it doesn't appear to be following us. We cross the bridge, and on the east side, where the buildings are lower and we have a good view, we don't see the helicopter anymore. Still, I make Igloo wait.

We park at the Lloyd Center Mall, in a covered parking lot. I don't know how paranoid to be. Could he be watching us with satellites? The idea is so laughable I don't even mention it, though I really have no idea.

Danger gets an antenna fix, I reestablish an onion network connection, and we're back online.

"He's still here," Igloo says. "He goes by Holmes IV. He says he wants $25,000 to shut down all of Daly's accounts."

I glance away from my screen.

"We don't have that much." What can I offer him? "Offer him the full profiles with all shadow data for any ten people in the world. Make sure you say shadow data. Give him one or two as proof, and the rest after he delivers."

"Got it."

I lean over to show Igloo where she can find the tools to download profiles, but she's already figured it out.

"Holmes gave me the email address of some guy, and says he wants the profile for this person. I have no idea who they are."

"Perfect. Open my records database, add an entry for Holmes IV, then enter that email address under suspected family members."

"Why?" Igloo asks, then before I can respond, she answers her own question. "Oh…Because he gave me the email address of someone he knows, so he can validate whether I'm legit or not."

"Bingo."

It's been years since Nathan and I pair-hacked, and longer still since the early days working for Repard. It's nice to have someone helping me. I forgot what this was like.

His Maldives criminal record complete, I check back on the Tomo diagnostic data.

"He's online!" I yell. "Move the car, quick."

Danger jumps up.

"Wait!" Igloo says. "I have to close this deal."

"Switch to cellular," I say.

Danger pops a battery into another burner, and he and I watch anxiously for it to boot. Igloo's fingers pound on her keyboard. As soon as the phone's online, I initiate a data connection, and switch the onion circuit from one network to the other.

"Ok, drive."

Danger slams the car into gear, and we peel out leaving the garage.

"Why are we moving?" he asks.

"Just in case," I say, having no real concrete idea why. I'm afraid of Daly, afraid he's suddenly going to pop out from nowhere and corner us, leaving us no way to escape. Part of me says this is irrational, that if he only now appeared online, then he's busy doing something else, and this is the least likely moment of attack. I should have been worried more when we didn't know where he was.

"His banks accounts and credit cards are all shut down," Igloo says.

"He'll have cash," I say. "Assets handy, in case he gets cut off." I shake my head. Focus, Angie. This is no time for fear. "I can use your help with this next one. We're going to break into the FCC now, mess with his employment records."

If I had weeks or months and Nathan's help, I could probably penetrate the FCC's database straight from the Internet. But we don't have the time or the resources. What we do have is an FCC Resident Agent Office based in Portland, Oregon, and a pretty girl buried under a baggy hoodie.

"Skip to waypoint #12."

I grab a USB device out of my bag. It's still inside a Ziploc to reduce contaminants. "You're going to wear these gloves," I say, holding out another Ziploc containing a pair of thin leather gloves.

"I am?" Igloo squeaks. "I can't go in there."

"I've got one arm. You think they're not going to tie it back to me? How many one-armed programmers are there?"

"I can't," Igloo says, and there is pain written all over her face. "Make him do it."

"I don't trust him to do it right. I trust you."

"Gee, thanks guys," Danger says, "I'm right here you know."

I catch Danger's eyes in the rear view mirror and shake my head at him. Just let him keep quiet for a minute. "You *can* do this. Nobody is looking for you."

I can practically see Igloo thrashing inside herself, and a yawning chasm opens up inside me. I am the monster. Long seconds pass.

"Fine, I'll do it," she whispers.

"Good. Lose the sweatshirt and put this on." I hold out a blue button-down shirt and an electric company employee jacket.

More seconds pass while I hold the clothes out, my arm tiring.

Igloo sighs and takes the clothing from me. She reluctantly shrugs her way out of her white hoodie, a black Julie Ruin t-shirt underneath. She pulls the button-down on.

"Lose the t-shirt," I say, steeling myself for further objections. "Danger, close your eyes a minute."

"I'm driving!"

"Well, just look out the front window."

Danger shrugs and sighs. "That's the way I generally drive," he mumbles.

I ignore him and focus on getting my computer prepared.

"I'm ready," Igloo says, fidgeting with her shirt.

"Unbutton the top two buttons on your shirt." I want to throw up, telling another woman this.

"Why?"

"Because a little skin will make the difference between you breezing in and them questioning you. If it makes you feel any better, I'd walk in naked if it would help."

Igloo unfastens the buttons with shaking hands.

I rummage through a bag until I extract a hat and clear glasses.

"Put the hat and glasses on now. Leave the gloves until we park. Put them on without touching the outside, and don't touch the gloves to anything inside the car. When you leave the car, take the USB router out of the baggy, throw the baggy back in the car. Got that so far?"

I tug on her shirt to show more cleavage. Resentment flashes across her face, but she takes a breath, and afterwards she's resigned, her face emotionless.

"When you go in, say the electrical service reading shows spikes consistent with a transient electrical short, and you need to inspect the electrical service."

"They're the FCC. Won't they'd be able to detect something like that?"

"Good, you're thinking. I called yesterday to set up an appointment. There's only one actual agent for this office, and he's in the field today. The only people left will be administrative staff. I doubt they'll be electrical engineers. They *are* going to debate whether they can let you into the basement or not. While they're doing that, you move within arm's reach of one of their computers and plug the USB drive into the back."

"What if I can't get close enough?"

"Then you go down into the basement, visually inspect the electrical panel, and go back upstairs. Tell them you need to call another technician to come out, and ask them when would be a good time. All the while, keep getting closer to a computer, until you're able to plug it in."

"What if—"

"Look, make it up if you need to. Tell them their computer power supply is fluctuating, and you need to see their system settings. It doesn't matter what you say. If it's a guy, they're going to be looking at your tits. If it's not a guy, they'll assume you're an idiot because you're showing your tits."

"I can't…"

"I'm sorry, but you have to. In the jacket pocket is a salt shaker."

Igloo moves her hand to the pocket.

"No, don't touch it yet. Inside the salt shaker is dust and dirt from the streetcar, DNA from thousands of people. On your way out, you shake it discreetly, to leave a lot of conflicting evidence. Don't take off or touch your hat, it's keeping your hair in. Try not to look up. Cameras will be mounted high, aiming down. The hat and polarized glasses will be enough unless you look up."

"There it is," Danger says. "On the left."

We all look together at the building, a nondescript street level office.

"Okay, circle the block, then park at the corner."

Igloo is breathing fast, like she might hyperventilate.

"It's going to be easy-peasy," I lie. "You're up on stage when you play with your band, right? That's a performance in front of people. This is a performance, too."

"Nobody can see me in my sweatshirt."

"That makes this even better. We all know the girl in the big white hoodie is you. Now you're in a true disguise. You could walk through the Tapestry office right now dressed as you are, and nobody would recognize you."

Igloo examines herself and nods. "You're right."

Danger pulls over. The entrance is three doors down.

"Go."

Igloo opens the door, and walks down the street.

"What are the odds she can pull it off?" Danger says.

"Sixty percent. Don't tell her I said that. Look, nothing she's doing will appear to be a crime. It'll take a forensics lab to figure out anything is up with the USB drive." Who am I trying to convince? "Even if she totally botches it, nothing bad can happen."

I pull on a hat and long coat, don sunglasses. "If she's not out in ten minutes, I'll grab her."

Minutes pass. Danger bites his nails. Sirens sound in the distance.

I check the dashboard clock. Seven minutes.

The sirens grow closer. Nine minutes. I grab a can of pepper spray from the bag on the floor, shove it in my jacket pocket.

I put my hand on the door. "If she comes out without me, take her and go, okay?"

I give it a little more time. The dashboard clock ticks twelve minutes. It could take her longer than I thought. If she really has to go into the basement, who knows how involved that will get. The sirens are gone.

"I thought you were going at ten," Danger says.

"She can do it," I say, hoping it is true.

The clock ticks fourteen minutes.

"Fuck, fuck, fuck." I punch the seat in front of me. "I'm going."

I climb out of the car, and walk to the building, hand in my pocket wrapped around the pepper spray. I'm almost to the door when Igloo comes out. I catch her eye, and she nods at me with a big smile.

I gesture with a tilt of my head back toward the car, and keep walking without looking back. I stop at the corner, waiting to cross. Danger pulls up across the street, and honks the horn. Twice.

Jesus. I'm no secret agent, but it is possible to avoid being blatantly obvious.

Inside the car, Igloo is glowing and holds out a hand for a high-five.

I sigh and meet her hand.

"That was awesome," she says, a huge grin on her face. She leans back in her seat. "I went in, and it was like you said, there was a woman—"

"I want to hear all about it, *later*. Right now I need to get into his records. Danger, don't go far. We need to stay within a couple of blocks."

"Right," Danger says, and I see him looking around for a parking spot. "But I don't understand. You're trying to mess with this guy's employee records. How is a remote office going to help? Won't the data be back at headquarters?" He pulls into an empty space on the next block.

Danger's been listening to everything we're doing, an unfortunate but unavoidable consequence of using him as our driver. What happens if he gets uncomfortable? I meet his eyes in the rear view mirror. I think back to the bitcoin hack I did with him, and how I'd researched him before handing over the entirety of my bug-out cash. I trust him.

"We're on their virtual private network. Somewhere on that computer is a set of logon credentials. From there I can do an SQL injection attack. Internal systems are never secured as well as external ones. Perimeter security is a fallacy. Not only is it not secure, it actually worsens security because people learn to rely on it. I'll have root access to the database within ten minutes."

I find the employee portal login credentials Erik Wecks had emailed to himself, and run an automated suite of SQL injection attacks against the website until I find a compromised query. From there it's blind Boolean exploitation to figure out the structure of the database, until finally I insert a new record into the user's table, and grant the user every permission in the database. Then I log back in as my new superuser.

Igloo watches over my shoulder. "Amazing," she whispers.

"Hey, Angie, we've got company."

I jerk my head at Danger's tone. There's a parking enforcement officer pulled up next to us.

He shakes his head at us. "You need to pay the meter."

"I was on my way to pay," Danger says, opening the window.

"Sorry. Too late if I'm already here. I have to write up the ticket."

I glance around the car, which looks like we broke into an Apple store and stole everything in their inventory. Four laptops, three tablets, and an army of phones surround us, and enough cabling connects the devices to restring a suspension bridge. I keep my voice low so only Danger can hear it. "Let him write the ticket and give it to you. Don't provide your driver's license. It's just a parking ticket. If he tries to talk to you, ask him where the original hotcake house is."

Danger glances at me in the rear view mirror like I'm crazy.

Igloo's still sitting next to me dressed as an electrical company employee. We're so fucked.

The parking enforcement officer slips the ticket through the window, then gets back into his three-wheeler and drives away.

"Holy shit," Danger says. "Should I move the car?"

"No," I say. "You paid top dollar for this spot." I turn to Igloo. "Gimme Daly's employee number."

Igloo reads it off.

"What was that bit about the hotcake house?" Danger asks.

"Classic misdirection. Cognitive change, geographical redirection. Engages a different part of the brain. Now shh, I need to focus."

If I could, I'd delete Daly's record, make it so that he doesn't even exist as an employee. That's hard if I can't eliminate database backups. I settle for listing him as terminated. For cause of termination, I include a fake document that's been completely redacted. Yes, this seems a little absurd even to me, but this does happen in the government. Then I lock his personal record so only the FCC director can read or change it. I trigger the employee termination automation, which removes Daly's access to all systems, revokes his badges, and shuts down all his equipment.

Chris Daly now has no access to money. He can't fly. He has no job. He's got an overseas criminal record, and he's a suspected terrorist here in the United States. There are only a few things left to do.

CHAPTER 44

CHRIS DALY WAKES UP, brews coffee in the kitchen of the rented house, and pads into the basement barefoot. He logs into one of his two laptops, and searches the web for recent news on Angie. Most of the articles mention the retraction of the blog post he'd created, but even those cite facts that have been confirmed. The internets are now in a massive fact-finding hunt for Angie. Once unleashed, nothing can stop them, at least until everyone gets bored and moves onto the next thing.

He logs into the other laptop, does a quick check on her phone and finds she's at the office. Even though Angie's taking active counter surveillance measures, they're using two new zero-day exploits (the cost of which is billed back to Enso's department), and he can watch all the traffic to and from her computer and see her keystroke log.

From the network traffic and keystrokes, she appears to be coding. He shakes his head. How she could focus on the minutia of her product with all the pressure she's under is beyond him. Maybe she's trying to escape reality.

He checks in with the client directly, bypassing his agent. He's been going under the pseudonym Walter Williams.

```
Walter Williams> She's discredited, distracted.
Happy?
    R@2> This is good progress.
```

```
Walter Williams> The rest of the fee is due.

    R@2> Not until she folds or sells the company. You
promised results.
```

Chris squeezes his fist a few times. He guarantees results to his personal clients. Always.

That's his specialty, after all. BRI is a finely-tuned organization created to wield influence to achieve specific results, not cause chaos. As long as he's going to make a little money on the side, why not exploit the skills of this black government agency to their fullest?

In this case, he mostly wants to be done with Angie. Drug lords are less paranoid than she is. Oh, all the circumstantial evidence leaves no doubt she's guilty of some serious crime, but they can't prove anything, and he's over-extending his power and reach in BRI, pushing what he can get away with too far and for too long.

```
    Walter Williams> It's just a matter of time now.
Everything about her past will come out, and she'll
crack.

    R@2> Great. When that happens, you'll receive your
payment.
```

The nerve of this guy. Doesn't he realize who he's messing with? Maybe Daly can't enforce his agreement in a court of law, but he can make the client hellishly uncomfortable. Still, that's bad for business. He can't take out an ad in the paper, so he's dependent on referrals. Screw it. He's got a few more tricks he can use to increase the pressure on Angie. He can destroy her life the old-fashioned way.

```
    Walter Williams> I'll up the stakes with her. But I
want payment in 3 days regardless.
```

He disconnects, checks on Angie, and finds she's still coding. Seems safe enough to leave unattended while he gets breakfast.

He walks over to the biscuit place on Alberta. There's a line around the corner, and he's not much for lines. He scans the front of the line for a girl by herself, preferably one staring at her shoes and not too attractive. He finds a mark and walks up to her.

"Well, you're fucking adorable."

Whether the line works or not is irrelevant. If she talks to him, great. If he makes her so uncomfortable she yields her spot in line to him, that's fine too. Either way, he's not waiting like the rest of the sheep.

As soon as she looks up, the ever-so-slight flare of her nostrils gives away her anger at his intrusion. He keeps up the conversation, pretending she's taking part in it, edging his way into the line as she slowly backs away, until she's barely in the line at all. He could stop there, should stop there, because there are grumbles from the people behind her in the line, but now it's a game to see how far he can push her. She finally abandons the line altogether and stalks off as though she never wanted biscuits in the first place.

"You're an asshole," says a guy in the group of four now waiting behind Chris. "She's been waiting in line an hour."

Chris says nothing.

"You disgust me," one of the girlfriends says. "You shouldn't even be in this line. Go to the back."

"Or get lost entirely, you dick."

The trick, of course, is simply not to care. The sheep can bleat all they want, it doesn't change anything. He keeps his focus on the register, and politely orders when he gets to the counter. He was of half a mind to order to go, but now he's going to eat here on principle.

The breakfast sandwich is pretty damn good, the biscuit flaky and soft. At the end of the meal, he makes a point of standing so the group of four, sitting one table over, can see him leave without bussing his dishes.

"Douchebag," one of the guys mumbles.

"Hey, don't say 'douchebag'," his girlfriend says. "That's a sexist insult. It mocks women."

Daly shakes his head. He needs to escape Portland before the people here drive him crazy.

℧

Back at the house, Daly checks Angie's location again. Still at work, still coding. Not totally out of character, but surprising. She has an extensive background as a developer, but since they started actively monitoring her, she's spent most of her time in meetings or handling email and phone calls. Except for when she was completely off-the-grid. Where does she go during those breaks?

He messages Pete. Once people chose phone calls to avoid leaving a paper trail, but now that all the calls are recorded, text is better. There's language analysis that can suggest a sender, and typing keystroke frequency analysis that's as predictive as a fingerprint, but Daly uses software to buffer all his keystrokes, and none of that stuff is as damning as a single voice call.

    Chris> Any new developments on analyzing Angie's
    traffic?

    Pete> No, Plaint got wind of the time I had sunk
    into it, and ordered that I not do any more analysis.

    Chris> Not even a little off-the-record?

    Pete> There is no off-the-record anymore. She's
    watching all the computer time I use. Not unless Enso
    explicitly endorses it.

Normally he'd keep his private business off the radar, but he'd been able to leverage Angie's suspicious behaviors into cause for an informal investigation. Unfortunately, he's run out of rope. He's already been chewed out by Enso for the time and resources he's spent on this. And Lt. Plaint has hated him since the day they met, so she probably relishes his current doghouse status.

    Chris> Could you get another guy on the team to do
    it?

    Pete> Plaint told everyone not to work on your
    stuff unless it comes from her. Sorry.

    Chris> What if we bury it as part of another case?

    Pete> Jesus. What part of *no* don't you understand?
    If anyone works on Angie, it's got to be official. No
    more of this off-the-record stuff. I've done a ton of
    favors for you over the years, gotten you records you
    wanted without any connected case. I hate red tape as
    much as the next guy, but Plaint's pissed. I'm not
    sticking my neck out again. Make sure Enso vets it be-
    fore you make another request.

Pete disconnects, leaving Daly staring at a blinking cursor.

Plaint has a lot of nerve, trying to shut him down. The thing is, he can't go back to Enso, but he absolutely can't let her dictate the terms of engagement. She'd end up believing she could push him around.

He has leverage he can use on Plaint, but not long distance. It's got to be done in person. He hates to leave Portland when things are so close with Angie, but getting Pete's assistance is essential.

He logs into his travel app and grabs one of the last seats on the redeye flight for that night. He clicks Book Flight once the details are entered, and the screen refreshes a few seconds later with a credit card denial. Weird. He reenters the number and security code only to be denied again. He checks the card against the screen. No typos.

He grabs another credit card, enters the new information, and gets another rejection. He squints at the screen. It's impossible for his cards to be denied. They're flagged to approve all purchases. An operative in the field travels in a way that triggers fraud detection algorithms, so the agency preemptively disables them with the credit card agencies. Crap. He has another identity with different cards, but switching is a hassle.

He disconnects his computers, wipes them, and logs in with his alternate identity. He connects through an onion network. All of this so that there will be no connection between his two identities. Then he tries again to book a flight with a new credit card under this identity.

Also denied.

He checks online to see if any outages are reported for the airline websites. None.

A chill passes through him. Has Angie done something to him? No, she couldn't have. Even if she knew someone was monitoring her, messing with her, how could she ever trace it back to him? The most she could know was the article he'd posted, and that could have come from anyone. Not possible.

He checks a different reservation site, gets the same problem.

He has one remaining identity he can use. On the off-chance his location is blown, he has to make the attempt from somewhere else, rather than risk contaminating his last ID. He packs up his bags, loads the car, and checks the vehicle for transponders with a handheld scanner. All clear. He runs a surveillance avoidance route to a random hotel. Sitting in the lobby, using the free wi-fi, he tries the third identity. No luck. Tries again with an alternative credit card. Still can't book a flight.

Jesus H.

He grabs his suitcase and yanks it after him. He'll pay cash at the airport.

Thirty minutes later his car is in short term parking, and he's waiting in line at the airline counter with the rest of the sheep. He tries to channel non-presence to blend in with everyone else, but he mostly wants to scream. Two kids behind him keep bumping into him and after the third time, he abruptly about-faces.

After a glance at his expression, the mother blanches and yanks the kids back.

He doesn't think he would've hit them, though the idea runs through his mind in a pleasing way. Maybe he should forget the kids and take his retribution out on the mom. He takes a few deep breaths. Plaint will get a piece of his mind when he gets back.

The line moves with a frustratingly irregular pace, airline attendants occasionally calling over coworkers for help, sometimes three of them at a time working on one passenger.

At long last, he reaches the counter with his ID and a wad of bills. He expects problems paying for the flight with cash, but there's no law against it.

Things stall as soon as he passes over his ID. The attendant calls over another, apparently more experienced, attendant who asks Daly to wait.

He grits his teeth. This shouldn't be happening. He's not the first customer to require multiple employees, but he can't be sure if everyone here is merely incompetent or if there's something genuinely wrong with his information.

The mother and kids are now being helped at the next counter over. She's already getting her boarding passes.

Screw it. He grabs his bags, leaving his ID with the attendant, and walks away.

"Sir, please wait a moment."

He pretends he doesn't hear, and walks steadily toward the door.

Out of the corner of his eye, he sees a group of DHS officers, a few hundred feet distant, coming in the general direction of the check-in counter. He carefully keeps his pace steady. The doors are only a dozen paces away. As he approaches, he uses the opportunity to check behind him. The officers are double-timing it now, fortunately still focused on the counter, not the exit.

He walks out to the curb and scans the line of cars. Without breaking stride, he heads for an idling car three spots down, the driver hugging someone goodbye. He steps out between the cars, and his wheeled suitcase gets caught on the bumper of the car in front of him. No time now. He abandons the bag and keeps going, barely pausing. He pulls the door open, tosses his shoulder bag into the passenger seat, gets in and shifts the car into gear before he's even finished closing the driver door.

He peels away from the curb to the distant sound of yelling behind him. He speeds down the road and catches a glimpse of flashing lights in his rear view mirror. He pulls off at the next exit, a strip mall. His first thought is to switch cars, but he sees signs for a light rail station and abandons the car in the first parking spot he finds. He heads for the waiting platform, keeping an eye on the two police cars that pull into the nearby parking lot. A few minutes later, the downtown train pulls up, and he hops on.

He takes a long, slow breath as he sinks into a seat, now carrying only his shoulder bag. There's no doubt this is Angie's doing. She's found his alternate identities, disabled his accounts, and did something to trigger a security response at the airport. She not only discovered the general investigation, she also somehow pinpointed him and his alternate identities, despite his operational precautions.

Phones are the most likely culprit. He digs his current device out of his pocket and extracts the SIM card in case he needs it later. He does the same for the other phone in his bag. At the next train stop, he dashes outside, throws the phones in the trash, and reboards before the train leaves.

Fucking bitch. She's making his life hell.

He gets off at a downtown stop, finds a store to buy two new phones with cash. He's got a few hundred bucks on him, a small laptop, and now two burner phones. He left loads of equipment and his gun at the rental house, and there's a bug out bag in the trunk of the car he abandoned at the airport. Unfortunately, there's no telling how big the response at the airport will be, or what's under observation now. It won't be safe to go back to either spot for a few days.

That leaves him operating without backup, resources, or weapons. It's not so much that he gives a shit about standard operating procedures, but rules exist for a reason. Statistically speaking, operating without recommended resources could end up killing him.

He weighs his options. If he calls the office for help, it will trigger an investigation into his online profile and how he's spending his time. He plays it safe with his side jobs, but he can't withstand that level of scrutiny. No one can. The resources he's marshaled so far to investigate Angie are only a tiny percentage of what the government security apparatus could apply to him if they were motivated to investigate his activities in depth. How many side projects and clients has he taken on over the years? At least a hundred.

He's got to fix this problem on his own.

He lacks Angie's skills with computers, and therein lies his primary mistake. He's played so far on her battlefield, assuming his associates at BRI could match her skills. All they've done is gotten their ass kicked while they wandered around trying to find her.

The hell with that approach. Angie lives in the real world, not cyberspace. He doesn't have to beat her online. She lives, she breathes, she eats, and she shits. It's time to take the fight to the world he knows.

He thinks back to this morning. He checked on her three, four times, and every time she sat at her computer, programming. It seemed a bit funny then, though it's glaringly obvious now: she wasn't at the office. She couldn't have been programming all that time, not while she was completely fucking with his life. That was a ruse, some sort of trick. A script maybe, playing back some other day of programming. She was somewhere else. Maybe home, maybe not.

Eventually, though, she has to return home.

He'd been heading in the general direction of the local FCC office to see if he could pick up cash, a computer maybe. But he doesn't need those things. The bit of money he has will go far in a hardware store. He can't wait to see how a one-armed computer geek fares against two feet of steel pipe.

CHAPTER 45

"ARE YOU SURE ABOUT THIS?" Igloo says. "I don't like the idea of leaving you alone."

"I'll be fine. We've got trackers on his new phones. He's sitting downtown, probably grabbing wi-fi off that coffee shop. He hasn't moved in twenty minutes. The logical thing is he's going to go back to his car."

"I don't like it," Danger says. "Why don't we all stick together while you build the transceiver thingy?"

"Yeah," Igloo says. "I can help assemble it, then we can go to the airport together and disable his car."

"I want to cut him off from all his resources, not only his car. That means you guys go to the police station and report a man waving around a gun at his address."

"We can call it in," Danger says.

"No. Police won't bust into an empty house if all they receive is a call. Too much videogame swatting going on. If you go in person, they'll take the complaint seriously."

"Let me do it," Danger says, "and have Igloo stay with you."

"No offense, Danger, but I don't trust your execution. We saw how well Igloo did at the FCC. We need another performance just like that."

"Then why don't—"

I cut Danger off. Jesus, why can't they do as I want without all the arguing?

"I'm not sending Igloo into a police station by herself. Look, I'm a grown woman. I know how to enter my own house and lock the door. I can certainly put together a simple circuit and antenna. I'll call you when I'm done, and if you're still there, I'll join you guys."

Danger pulls up outside my condo. The old engine idles roughly, the car throbbing.

"Let us check out your place," Danger says.

Why does he pick now to become protective? "Go to the damn police station already. We want to cut him off before he gets anything from the house. If he picks up a gun or a wad of cash then we've lost half the benefit of what we've spent all day doing. Just fucking go!"

I get out, slamming the door harder than I need to, and wave Danger on. They both give me hurt looks, but he accelerates away.

I take a deep breath. Alone at last. I'm exhausted from a whole day in the car with both of them. An introvert's nightmare. I need to be alone for what comes next. There are certain things they're not prepared for, at least not yet. I let them in on the secret of the hacking because I required their help. I can't involve them in the killing. That risks too much.

I walk up to the building, a bag with two laptops hanging heavily from my shoulder. The rest of the equipment is still in the car with Igloo. Inside, I take the stairs to my floor, pull out my keys, and open the door.

From the corner of my eye I see movement, a flash of something coming toward me faster than I could have imagined.

ʊ

The world is fuzzy and gray. Something's wrong, but I can't put together the words for it yet. There's pain, pain everywhere. I try to protest but can't seem to speak, then I'm gagging, and my brain tries to put two and two together.

I'm staring at the dining room fan, trying to remember why I'm looking at the fan.

Oh, I was coming home. I entered the house. The movement.

I thrash around instinctively, trying to escape, though I only succeed in wrenching my shoulder. Something's holding me down. I try to scream, but gag indeed as I discover my mouth is stuffed with cloth. I try to budge my head at least, to look around, but the pain of my skin and hair pulling away stops me cold.

"Welcome back to the land of the living."

A face comes into view to my right. This is the face from the identity records for Chris Daly, and Matthew O'Donald, and Steven Morgan. My stomach clenches, and I try to shake my head.

"That's okay, don't get up," Daly says. He reaches out, and looks like he's going to caress my face. I try to pull away, loathing even the thought of his touch, but there's nowhere to go. Instead he jabs a finger in my eye. Shock and pain surge through me, but I struggle to no avail. Tears come, and I choke on the gag in my mouth, struggling to breathe through a nose rapidly clogging with snot.

"You thought you could mess with me. A federal agent. Did you think I was going to run home with my tail between my legs? Or that you could set me up to be arrested like the kid in Brazil? Are you kidding me?" He leans over, holds out a finger in front of my face again, and I flinch and cry harder.

He reaches out and panic lances through me, my blood pumping faster; my legs ineffectually flail, unable to break free. He strokes my face, wiping tears away. He dries his hand on my shirt and his hand creeps down to my breast.

I try again, every ounce of strength, to rip free, but I'm immobile. I gasp, trying to suck air through my increasingly clogged nose, desperately afraid I might puke with the gag in my mouth and choke on my own vomit. My vision narrows and my mind screams that I'm going to die.

"Don't worry, honey, you're not going anywhere. Duct tape. You know, they even use it on the space station. It keeps things where you want them. But I can see you're having a bit of trouble breathing. Would you like me to remove the gag?"

I nod the microscopic amount my head can move. In my panic, I couldn't figure out what had happened to me, since I can't see a thing except Daly's face, the ceiling, and the light fixture. But his mention of tape clues me in. He's taped me down to my own dining room table. My arm is taped off to the side, my fingers free, and now I recognize the feeling of the wood beneath my skin. Knowing what's happened helps the panic subside a tiny amount.

"Now, before I take that gag out, you must promise not to scream."

I nod quickly, as best as I can. There's little spots in my vision now. Give me back my mouth, you monster.

"If you scream, I'll put it back in, obviously. We could go back and forth like that all day. So I'm going to up the ante a little. If you scream, I'll put the gag in, *and* I'll break one of your fingers."

He's deadly serious, but I'm so desperate for oxygen that everything he says is a warble to me. I keep nodding, hoping that's what he wants.

He smiles at me, and that's worse. Even if I could appease his anger, he'd keep doing what he's doing for the fun of it.

"If you keep screaming, I'll cut off your fingers and throw them down the garbage disposal. You can't be much of a hacker without fingers. Are we totally, one hundred percent clear about the screaming bit?"

I nod again, my nose totally clogged. I try to blow the snot out, but I can't inhale, and now I'm left with nothing in my lungs. I thrash about.

He pulls the tape off slowly, purposely lengthening the experience.

Even when the tape is off, I can't draw a breath around the cloth packed tightly into my mouth. He pulls out the cloth and air, precious air, floods my lungs. My stomach heaves and all I can do is gasp until the spots leave my vision.

Still, my jaw aches, and my mouth is dry. I try and fail to form words. I distantly recognize the cloth as one of the dish towels Emily bought me for my birthday, and somehow my hatred for Daly grows for taking something valued and using it against me.

"Now we can talk like civilized people," Daly says. "Here's what I want. I want to know what you've done to my records, how you did it, and how to undo it. Before you even ask, of course I'm not going to give you a computer. I'm not even going to let you within sight of one. I'm not an idiot. You could probably kill me with my electric shaver if you had a computer."

My eyes refocus on Daly when he mentions the electric shaver.

He catches my look, and he's momentarily startled. "Really? An electric shaver. I'm curious, I am, though not as curious as I am about what you've done to me. Talk. In exchange for you talking, I'm not going to torture you. That's a good deal, right?"

I look away from Daly, toward my bedroom, and try to work some moisture into my mouth, then turn back to him. "Who hired you?" It's the only question that really matters.

He laughs. "You want me to fess up, catch me on camera naming names, and bring that to the police? It doesn't matter. The video cameras are recording to the hard drive hidden in your bed frame. Thought you were clever, right? That if we never saw the video streaming over your network connection, we wouldn't know about the cameras. We know everything. We'll wipe the hard drives."

"How much is Lewis Rasmussen paying you? Whatever it is, I'll double it."

Daly leans close. "You're broke, Angie. You've got nothing and your company is falling apart. It's not going to last the month. You can't match even a small fraction of what Lewis paid."

Daly shakes his head. "You turned out to be a lot more complicated than I expected. Thankfully, there are escalator clauses for that sort of thing. A powerful man owes me favors now. You don't have anything of comparable value."

He leans back. "Tell me what you did to me."

"I froze your bank accounts with automated fraud detection. The money—" I break off, coughing, my throat dry from being gagged. I continue in a lower voice. "The money is still there. I didn't touch a dime."

"How do I regain access?"

"Call your banks. I changed your address and secret questions, too. You'll need to know the new info or they won't let you restore access."

"What's the new address?"

"9800" I stop to cough. "9800 Savage Road, suite 6248."

"Very cute. The NSA."

"Can I get a drink of water? Please?"

"I don't know, Angie. How do I know you're not going to attack me when my back is turned?"

I stare at him dumbfounded.

"Oh, yeah, the tape. I guess I can leave you for a second. If you do anything you shouldn't, it'll cost you a finger."

As soon as he turns his back, I use every fiber of my body to pull against the tape. My legs, the strongest muscles in the human body, I can't budge them. My arm, I try tugging, twisting, pulling, bending. I ignore the pain of my hair being pulled, and strain every muscle in my neck trying to raise my head off the table.

Nothing.

I give up, breathing hard from my attempted exertion.

Daly comes back into view, and perches on the table next to me. "Well that was fun to watch. I went over there," and he points to a spot outside my field of view, "to see how hard you would work to free yourself." He nods his head. "You tried pretty hard. Good job, Angie." He leans close. "No, I'm not getting you any water. I don't care if you're thirsty. Keep talking."

I purse my lips, but my mouth is desert dry, not even the slightest speck of moisture. "Please, anything," I say, my voice hoarse.

"You want water?" Daly says. "Open your mouth."

I open, afraid of what's coming, yet willing to do anything to moisten my lips.

Daly spits in my mouth. "There's your water." He turns sideways and punches me in the stomach. All the air rushes out of me, and my body strains against the tape, trying to protect itself.

"That's for trying to get loose. Now quit stalling. What happened at the airport? Why did DHS come after me?"

I put my lips together, my mouth ever so slightly moistened by Daly's spit, and I remember Repard, the early days, before it all got so terribly complicated, and I whistle.

Daly hits me, pain blossoming across my face, but I don't stop. I whistle again. He hits me again. I keep whistling.

After the third time, I don't have it in me to fight anymore. Any will to resist Daly has left. The pain is vanishing, too, replaced by numbness. This is someone else's body. I'm not here. This flesh isn't me.

"Why did you whistle?" Daly yells. "What the hell was that for?"

He's loud, and I'm glad he's loud. I hope he keeps being loud.

He glances around, suspicious now. He lifts a length of steel gray pipe up over my legs, and there's an explosion of pain.

↻

A robotic home vacuum cleaner, even a top of the line model, is not fast. Yes, there are great open source libraries. Yes, you can build features on top of the mobile chassis completely unrelated to vacuuming. Still, speed is not one of its best attributes, and this particular robotic vacuum is heavily laden and driving all the way from the bedroom.

It's also not the best driver in the world. This one is both sound and motion sensitive, and at some point its primitive visual sensors will detect active movement and its path will become more focused, but at the moment it's trying to follow a 1300 Hz audio signal.

It bounces off the bed, reverses direction. It hits the dresser, backs up, angles off in a random direction. A particularly astute observer might wonder why the bedroom door doesn't close properly, why it tends to swing open and won't latch properly no matter how hard you try. It wouldn't take much to notice the top hinge is not in its original location, and the door has no choice other than to swing open when it leans that way. Fortunately, Daly wasn't interested in construction, and so the door remains open as it has been designed to be.

The vacuum passes through the doorway. The 1300 Hz signal is gone; however, once the robot is activated, it will continue its programming using only motion and sound detection. There's a lot of sound coming from the direction of the dining room, and so the vacuum heads that way after a false start toward the couch and a brief entanglement with the legs of the coffee table.

Eventually the visual sensors detect motion. This is a very exciting time for the program running on its little CPU. The robot switches modes, stops moving forward, and turns in a circle. It will stop when it reaches the point of maximum detected motion.

But these are very simple algorithms and the current programming is designed to turn only one way: clockwise. This it does, and after turning 360 degrees it figures out exactly where the most motion is occurring, and then it turns 330 degrees more, almost a complete second circle, and sends an electrical signal to the trigger actuator on the Glock mounted to its weighted top, firing once. The Roomba turns another five degrees, fires again, and repeats this sequence twice more, exhausting four of the ten rounds of ammunition.

After the code completes, the algorithm repeats again, first detecting motion, then firing four rounds at five-degree intervals around the center of motion.

With two rounds left in the magazine, the algorithm would run an abbreviated iteration, but when the motion detector runs for the third time, it fails to find any movement.

The vacuum waits. There is no activity. The algorithms tell the robot to recharge. It plays a short happy tune, and returns to its charging station.

CHAPTER 46

DALY HITS ME ACROSS THE THIGHS and agony shoots through me. With every fiber of my being, I force myself not to scream. I need to be silent. I pray he hasn't broken my legs.

Daly does a double-take at my lack of a scream or reaction. He raises the pipe back up to hit me again. Please, God, no.

Then he glances toward the living room, his eyes searching. I know what to listen for, and I barely make out the whine of little electric motors over the waves of pain coursing through me.

The shot, when it comes, even though I expect it, is deafening, and my bowels clench. More are coming, and I try, fruitlessly, to shrink smaller, knowing I'm close to Daly and could easily be hit. If a round strikes me, even a glancing wound, I'll bleed to death strapped to this table.

Daly's attention snaps to the robot with the first shot, and at first he's still, as though trying to come to terms with what he's seeing. There's a second shot, and from the way he jerks around, I know he's been hit.

"Fuck!"

He dives left, out of my field of vision, and for a brief moment my heart surges, because he's moved in the same direction as the robot turns, clockwise. It fires again, and there's another curse as he's presumably hit again. I can't see him now.

The fourth shot comes, and then there's silence. I know the robot's spinning around, crunching video data to find motion, computationally eliminating its own spinning motion from the equation. The fear comes again, because the next shot, the left-most one, is the one most likely to hit me.

I hear something crash against the wall, and Daly rushes by, his arm overhead as though he's going to toss the pipe at the little robot.

Then another four shots ring out, one after another. Metal clangs as the pipe bounces off the tile floor, and a few seconds later, Daly crashes to the ground with a thud.

A few seconds later the vacuum beeps and plays the returning-to-base sound.

I take inventory of my body. My thighs are in raging agony where Daly hit me with the pipe, and my stomach and face ache from repeated punches. There's so much pain, I'm not even sure if I'm shot. I'm as stuck as before. I make a feeble attempt to move, but I have no energy left.

I pray the robot sent its emails.

↻

I'm startled awake by pounding on the door. Someone yells, but I lack the strength to respond.

The front door opens with a crash, followed by booted feet running, and a bunch of radio talk that makes no sense to me. Soon two police officers in heavy combat gear are freeing me from the dining room table, while others secure the house and check on Chris Daly.

The police and paramedics are fighting over me, and I end up on a stretcher, being questioned as I'm strapped down.

"What happened?"

I can't tell which of the officers asks me. Only one thing matters.

"Is he dead?"

The officer nearest me nods.

"He forced himself in, attacked me. He says he was paid to do it, by Lewis Rasmussen."

"The CEO of Tomo?"

I nod. "I have a recording of him saying it, on a hard drive."

"A recording?" The officer looks puzzled.

A paramedic's arm passes into my field of view, and I flinch, trying to pull away. They're strapping me down, and I try to resist further panic.

"Surveillance cameras."

The officer raises an eyebrow and shakes his head, before he yells, "Sergeant, call the techs down here pronto. She's got the whole thing recorded."

The paramedics are in the midst of lifting me when Danger and Igloo rush in, trailed by yet another police officer.

"You knew!" Igloo's face is dark and accusing, then her eyes go wide at my appearance. "Jesus. Uh, are you okay?" She catches sight of the body on the floor and recoils.

"Bruised, mostly," I say, although the truth is my whole body is one mass of hurt. I hope there are strong painkillers in my immediate future. "If you'd been here, he would've killed you. He didn't need either of you, only me. He confessed. Lewis Rasmussen hired him."

"That bastard," Igloo says.

"The police will take care of him."

"Here we go, ma'am," one of the paramedics says, and they carry me towards the door.

"Thomas will call from a payphone," I say, on my way out. "Let him know it's okay to come back."

Igloo nods.

"Wait, please."

The paramedic facing me rolls his eyes.

"Come close," I say to Igloo.

She bends down, a few inches from my face.

"There's a second copy of the video on an SSD in the freezer. Leak it tonight to social media, BitTorrent. There's no telling how long the police will sit on it."

CHAPTER 47

I'M BLISSED OUT ON PHARMACEUTICALS when Thomas and Emily arrive at the hospital. I don't remember much, other than professing my undying love for them. Later they'll tell me it was four o'clock in the morning when they arrived, driving back to Portland in a rental. Apparently, I mumbled lots of incoherent things at them before falling back asleep.

When I wake, the intense pain of the night before has been replaced by the dull agony of aches everywhere. I touch my face and immediately regret it. My cry wakes Thomas, who was sleeping in a chair next to the bed.

"Angie." He snaps erect. "Are you in pain?"

I nod.

He presses a button next to me, and I hear a distant chime.

"The nurse will be back with another dose of pain relievers. Are you okay?"

What do I say to that? He probably knows better than I the extent of my injuries.

He reaches toward me, and I flinch. He withdraws his hand. "Okay to touch your arm?" he asks.

I try to speak, but can't open my mouth without choking up.

"You're going to be okay," he says. "The doctors say nothing is broken. Just a moderate concussion and severe bruising, especially on your legs, where..." Thomas's voice breaks. "I'm so sorry, Angie. I should've been there for you."

I swallow and take a few breaths. "You couldn't have done anything." Talking makes me realize how foggy I am. I vaguely wonder what drugs I'm on and how much more pain I'd be in without them. "It had to happen exactly that way."

"It never should've happened at all. I shouldn't have let you talk me into going to Seattle."

We'll be arguing this point for a long time, I suspect. I change the topic. "Did the police find the recordings?"

Thomas nods. "They did, and discovered something about Lewis Rasmussen hiring that monster. The detective told me the California police are bringing Rasmussen in for questioning."

"Already?"

"A judge issued a subpoena for Rasmussen's communication records already. They're looking for more evidence linking Rasmussen to Daly. The detective's here at the hospital, waiting to talk to you when you wake up. Which is now, I guess. You can wait, if you're not ready."

"No, it's fine. Send him in."

Thomas leans over to kiss me, and I turn away, afraid of his touch.

"Sorry," I mumble.

"It's okay," Thomas says, but my stomach says it is very much not okay.

Thomas goes out, and a woman in street clothes comes in and holds out a badge and photo ID.

"Hello, Ms. Benenati, I'm the detective working the Daly case. I'm very sorry for everything you've been through. If you're up to it now, I'd like to ask you a few questions."

I try to straighten out the hospital blanket around me, like it somehow matters how presentable I am in the hospital, but I'm too befuddled to do more than pull randomly on it.

"Call me Angie."

"Angie, did you know Chris Daly, the man in your apartment?"

"No… I never met him before today."

"Really? We've listened to the recordings from your apartment. You addressed him by name."

"I knew he was harassing me."

"Was he behind the blog post earlier this week?"

I'm impressed. The police did their homework.

"Yes, but that's not all he did. He broke into Tapestry's systems. He was reading our emails, tapping our phones."

"How do you know?"

"I worked in security for years. I found traces of him in our logs, in file change dates, in our network latency. I knew someone was out there."

"How did you know it was Chris Daly?"

This is where I must skirt a fine edge, and my head is still woozy.

"Anyone who works in computer security needs an alternate profile as a hacker. The only way to stay abreast of threats…to be where they're being discussed. Our company security is top-notch, and there are only so many people with the knowledge and skills to compromise it. I asked around the hacker community, got answers."

"You said to Daly, 'I hacked your bank accounts. Froze them all with automated fraud detection.' Why did you do that?"

I freeze, wishing I could remember exactly who said what. If only my brain wasn't so clouded with drugs.

"I should talk to my lawyer first."

"We're not here to arrest you. The video evidence clearly shows you were in immediate, life-threatening danger from Daly. The police found you still taped to the table. Daly was clearly a dangerous man, you must have suspected as much. Your actions likely provoked Daly into torturing you."

Are the things I say here admissible in court? I'm not sure, but I don't want to find out after the fact. "I don't want to answer that question."

"You were deliberately antagonizing and provoking Daly. We had your two friends down to the precinct, spent hours questioning them. Cyber-crime isn't my beat, I'm strictly homicide. Still, your behavior complicates things."

"We weren't antagonizing him. If someone attacks me with a gun, and I take the gun away, that's not provoking them. That's reasonable defense. Daly was attacking *me*, and all I did was take away his access to tools he could use to hurt me."

"Why not go to the police? Why take matters into your own hands and risk Daly lashing out at you?"

"What would the police have done exactly? Travel back in time and undo the damage done by the fake article on Monday? Why even ask me this? If you think I was in the wrong, ask Daly why *he* didn't go to the police."

"Daly is dead," says the detective, "and you are not."

"That makes me the perpetrator and Daly the victim?" I glare back at the detective.

"I'm not here to judge you. Just to discover the facts of what happened. Tell me about the robot with the gun. Whose robot was that, yours or Daly's?"

"I want to talk to my lawyer."

The detective sighs, looks off into the distance, then back down at me. "I've been up since midnight, Angie. I pulled your files, saw the closed records from California, made some calls. I understand you've been through tough times before. It must have made it even more difficult to go through last night. Help me understand why Daly singled you out."

"Lewis Rasmussen paid him."

"That's what you said last night. We're pulling records right now, trying to find a connection. You must have had a reason for believing that."

"Rasmussen has been interfering with my company, Tapestry, right from the beginning. He tried to buy us, and when I wouldn't sell, he tried to cut off our funding, and when that didn't work, he hired Daly to destroy me, to kill me if necessary. I had to do what I did to Daly to protect my life."

"Why does Rasmussen care about you?"

"Tapestry's existence is a threat to Tomo."

The detective shakes her head. "Not meaning any disrespect to your company. Tomo's the largest company in the world. It's hard to believe Tapestry is a threat to them."

I tug on the blanket. "Tapestry isn't a competing social network. It's a framework that prevents the centralization of power. Rasmussen wasn't afraid we'd destroy Tomo as much as he was afraid we'd destroy all forms of centralized power."

The detective scratches in her notepad.

"Tomo holds their users hostage," I say. "You can't leave Tomo without losing connections to your friends and family. Could *you* quit today? Ask them about PrivacyGuard. It's a hoax. A system designed to fool people into believing they have privacy. They track everything you do. Have you seen the data they compile on everyone?"

Of course she has, she's a police officer. Although it never seems crazy from their side of the wire. She ignores my question. I've wandered too far into the land of the paranoid even if I've avoided saying the word "conspiracy." Jesus, I'm talking too much. I need to stay on message. I blame the drugs they've given me.

Eventually she finishes her questions, and as she talks to me about what's next, I find myself unable to pay attention and gradually nod off.

When I open my eyes later, Emily is in a chair on the other side of the room, typing silently but furiously on a tablet.

"Em!" I feel truly joyous at the sight of her.

Emily starts and looks at me. "Oh, Angie." She sets the tablet down and sits next to me on the bed. "Why did you do this to yourself?"

"What?"

"You played me and Thomas. You knew this was going to happen."

Of course Emily can see through me in an instant. I continue the deception anyway. "I didn't know…"

"You knew. You lied to us. You lied to everyone. The police, your friends. You knew exactly what to expect, how everyone would behave. You engineered us. I'm afraid I can't let you do that, Angie." She stands, lifts a steel pipe over her head, and slams it down on my legs.

"NOOO!" I scream and keep screaming.

The room blossoms into light and someone in scrubs races into the room. I'm still screaming when the orderly takes me by the shoulders.

"You're okay. I'm here."

"Where's Emily?" I say.

"I don't know who Emily is. Your husband went down to grab some food."

"Emily's not here?" I'm so confused.

"I'm afraid not, hon. You were having a nightmare. You want me to page your husband?"

I nod and lean back in the bed. Emily has never threatened me, never been a source of fear in my life or dreams. But the nightmare seemed so real.

ひ

They dismiss me from the hospital the next day. They probably would've let me go earlier, but someone took notice of all the press waiting to talk to me and decided to let me have another twelve hours of rest.

I can walk, but barely, my legs pure agony. They bring a wheelchair and Thomas wheels me out to the elevator. Downstairs a few reporters are hanging around, working on their computers, probably second stringers who can afford to sit in a hospital waiting room. I don't recognize any of them. One stands and introduces himself as a reporter for a television station, another for a newspaper, and the third for a local blog.

I loathe the idea of talking to the press, yet I can't pass up this opportunity. It's too big a potential news mention for Tapestry, too big a chance to take a chunk out of Rasmussen and Tomo. I decide on the newspaper reporter: I want someone with more credibility, someone who's got enough space to report the story properly. I tell him I'll do an interview tomorrow.

The police are still investigating my place, and I've been told it's a disaster. Thomas inspected it, and pronounced that I'd be staying at his house. We drive back to his place, and he sets me up in his bed, then gets me the next dose of my pain medication. When he needs to leave for work, Emily comes over to take care of me.

She takes one look at my bruised face and grimaces.

"What the hell happened?"

"I didn't think it would be like this." I try to say more, but I'm too choked up to speak.

Emily holds me tight, and I rest my head on her shoulder.

Later she gets me tea and sits next to me on the bed.

"Angie, I have to say something. I'm not sure I want to bring it up, but I can't stop worrying about it." She shakes her head. "From what Thomas and your friends told me, you had to know this Daly guy was going to come after you. Why did you send us away?"

"Are you blaming me for a sick bastard coming after me and torturing me?"

"Not exactly, but…"

"You are."

"You could've handled it other ways like a sane person. Like calling the police or having Thomas and I stay with you or even leaving town with us."

I shake my head. "It was the only way to make him stop. If he exposed himself and I got evidence, I could go to the police. It worked. He confessed and admitted it was Rasmussen."

Emily takes my hand. "You could have died. It was too big a gamble. Jesus, did you set out to kill him?"

I stare down at where her fingers wrap around mine and debate what to say.

"I thought maybe he'd come to my house. I pictured he'd come to the door, accuse me of attacking him, and confess what he'd done in view of the webcam at the front door. I never planned to let him in. It's a Brumbie security door, for Christ's sake. The robot was a last-ditch backup…not for him. For me. If I had to kill myself. I couldn't stomach the thought of…"

"Shh," Emily says, as I cry. She leans over and hugs me. "I'm sorry for mentioning it. I couldn't put the thought out of my mind. I didn't understand how you, of all people, would put yourself at risk."

"I'm afraid of Thomas," I say in a tiny whisper. "Each time he comes close I want to hide. All my symptoms are back."

"Then you'll keep going to therapy. You kicked its butt once, and you can do it again. I'll talk to Thomas for you if you want."

I nod.

Emily strokes my hair, and eventually I'm done crying and wipe my eyes.

"I need to do a press interview tomorrow. Can you help me get made up?"

"Are you sure?" Emily says. "So soon?"

"While the news is hot, and before the police try to stop me from talking to the press."

ʊ

Emily brings my laptop before she leaves, and I spend the afternoon getting caught up with what's happened in the day and a half I've been out of things.

There are a dozen stories about Chris Daly's death, and someone has linked him to his official job at the FCC, who have made no statement except to confirm he was an employee. What's been reported are the facts: gunshots, Daly dead, me hospitalized. There are mentions of the fraudulent blog post from a few days earlier, and some conjecture wondering if they are connected.

Other articles reveal Lewis Rasmussen has been arrested and is in custody, but there's no statement from the police yet about why, or what evidence they've found.

Igloo retrieved the spare video recording from my apartment and leaked it, so the video is making its way around social media, everywhere except on Tomo itself, where someone cut in the censor filter to exclude the video. I briefly consider circumventing the censoring code, but there are too many eyes on me right now. Besides, they're making things look worse for themselves, which is better for Tapestry.

Lots of stories are connecting the two events, Chris Daly's attack and death, with the arrest of Rasmussen, thanks to the video.

The tightness with which the police are controlling the flow of information suggest the investigation is being run from very high up, which can only mean it's being taken seriously—and that implies they've found further evidence linking Daly and Rasmussen.

I'm distracted by the computer and the web, and I don't notice until too late my legs are throbbing and my face aching. The painkillers have worn off and I'm in agony.

"Thomas!" I try to yell, and stop short at the pain in my jaw.

Nobody comes.

"Thomas! Emily! Someone…"

I panic, wonder if Daly got to them after all, or maybe he was working with a partner I didn't know about. They could be dead, maybe lying in the kitchen in a pool of blood, while their killer makes his way upstairs to…

The door bursts open and I shriek and cower behind my arm.

"It's just me," Thomas says.

I'm so relieved, I don't know whether to laugh or cry.

"Sorry," he says. "I was on a work call."

"It's okay. But I need something, I hurt so bad."

He glances at a clock. "Shit, you're way past due." He disappears into the bathroom and returns with a glass and my bottle of medication.

It's such a little thing to travel fifteen feet away for water and a pill, yet I'm so grateful that I'm overcome again. I take his hand and pull him close.

He sets down the glass. "Okay to hug?"

"Yes, gently."

He wraps me very softly in his arms, and I rest my head on his shoulder. He's warm and his shirt has the familiar smell of his dry cleaner. I could stay there forever, but I give him a kiss on the cheek and push him away so I can take the painkiller from him.

"What was that for?" he asks.

"For being you," I say.

CHAPTER 48

THE NEXT MORNING Emily brings some of my things to Thomas's house, then helps me dress and do my makeup. I'm waiting in the living room when the reporter arrives.

Two show up instead of one: Brian introduces himself as a technology reporter, and Kristine works on the crime beat. I did my research last night, and recognize the names as two of the most senior staff reporters.

Brian asks easy questions, background about me and Tapestry. Based on what they're asking, they already know the answers. Either they're looking for a new angle, or they're trying to soften me up before we move into the tough stuff.

Then Brian nods to Kristine, a silent handshake between the two.

"Tell us about the events of two days ago," Kristine says.

"I went home," I begin, and "I don't know exactly what happened, if he hit me or drugged me."

Kristine lets me talk about the events of that evening, and then she asks me to start with the beginning of the day. "When you woke up that morning, did you have any idea Daly might come after you that day?"

ↄ

1997 — New York City

"In these situations," Repard says, "you're tempted to say as little as possible. The fewer details you provide, the less there is to remember. You can see why that's a problem?"

"They'll keep asking for more information," I say.

"Exactly, and they end up digging deeper in unwanted directions than you're prepared to go. The alternative is to provide a richly detailed story. This is just as wrong because you've got to remember all the details. If you prepare real hard, you can memorize all the details right, and tell them in the same order every time."

"Five minutes!" the guard yells.

"Fuck you," Repard says, and tries to give him the finger, but hits the limits of the handcuffs before he can raise his arm. He shakes it off and turns back to me.

"If the story is too complicated, too rich, you have no choice except to memorize it verbatim. Then what will everyone remember? That you tell the same story the same way every time. It will feel like a fabrication, regardless of whether it is true or not."

"You're saying leave out details even if they're true?"

"Jesus, yes. Even if everything is 100 percent true, you can't tell it like it is, because you have no control over how they interpret the story. The objective is to establish a narrative, not tell exactly what happened. You leave certain holes in the narrative, and that makes them ask questions to fill in those gaps. Questions you're prepared to answer, but, more important, questions to focus their attention where you want it, instead of where you don't. They can only spot those gaps if there's a structure to what you're saying. Only then are you controlling the message."

"I don't know," I say, and gesture at the visiting room with its bars and plexiglass dividers. "Isn't the *message* of your lesson somewhat diminished by the side of the table you're sitting on?"

Repard shakes his head and his lips spread in a small smile. "Open your mind, Angie. This is part of the narrative."

I try to force a smile to my face and fail. He planned to be arrested and spend the rest of his life in jail? Ridiculous. He's trying to fit his circumstances to the story he's telling himself.

He appears saddened by my reaction. "At least remember this: you need a manageable number of details, not too many, not too few. Enough that it feels like you're telling a true story, not so many that you have to memorize your recital. You parse them out economically, and make sure the story remains consistent with or without any individual detail."

I shake my head, unwilling to listen to any more of his advice.

"Your luck has run out, Repard."

"Luck is for fools," he says. "I—"

"Yeah, yeah. You make your own destiny. I've heard it a thousand times."

I stand, fed up with the whole situation, and leave even before the guard returns for Repard. He's losing touch with reality. Why do I continue to meet him? He wants to keep mentoring me, but what kind of mentor is someone in jail? I can't trust anything he says. I'm mostly doing it for him, to give him some motivation to keep going.

Half the White Knights are here too, rounded up in the biggest computer crime case the government put together since the new FBI chief committed to cracking down on cybercriminals. Now he has to make this case stick or he'll lose political face.

Repard and his cohorts are being held out as an example. If you total up all the possible crimes and run their penalties out consecutively, the worst case is three hundred years in prison.

I've had nightmares about being arrested. Even my mother knew enough to spot my boss's name in the paper, and asked me what I'd gotten myself into.

In the meantime, I've been leading Repard's section at the company, even though half the people left are senior to me, some by many years. Everyone knows I'm Repard's favorite, so I've become de facto team lead. They're all crazy, treating the situation like a temporary inconvenience from which Repard will return shortly.

Three months later, my coworkers turn out to be right. The charges against Repard and the White Knights are dropped, and they walk with a public apology from the prosecutor's office. The money is never recovered.

A year after that, Repard retires and disappears. I try to track him down, but he's totally off the grid. I don't hear from him again, but when I apply for the job at Tomo, a recommendation letter from Repard mysteriously appears before my first job interview.

ↄ

The news reporters continue their interrogation longer than I expected. I'm wearing out, and worse, I timed my medication for maximum lucidity when they arrived, which means now I'm in pain.

"Why would Lewis Rasmussen go so far as to attack you personally?" Kristine asks. "Tapestry has an interesting but completely unproven vision. Tomo has two billion users, the largest revenue of any Internet company, and they're sitting on a hundred billion in cash, a war chest they could use to fight you for years, maybe decades."

"We're the first truly credible replacement for Tomo," I say. "Not just an alternative. A successor with a fundamental approach that allows everyone to participate on a fair basis. People don't want to do business with Tomo. Sure, they may desperately need the traffic funnel Tomo points at them, but at what cost? Nobody can deal with Tomo as an equal."

"How many partners signed up so far?" Brian asks.

"Hundreds," I say.

"Really?" Brian raises his eyebrows, and flips through his notes. "Sorry, I don't mean developers signed up for your API. How many partners at scale that could bring you hundreds of thousands or millions of users?"

"The CompEx deal will bring on a hundred million users in the next twelve months. It doesn't get much bigger than that." When I return to work, marketing will kill me for stealing their thunder.

"That's one. Earlier you said you were worried Lewis Rasmussen influenced CompEx, in essence to buy voting power away from you, ensuring acceptance of his acquisition offer. Is CompEx even a legitimate partner in that case?"

"We'll see what happens. If they pull back now that Rasmussen is implicated, maybe they were a pawn. If they and the other investors are willing to negotiate an investment in good faith, without wresting away control of the company, then we'll know they're legit."

Brian nods. "Could be."

"I had a mentor who said you can only learn who your true friends are when you're in a jam with nothing left to offer anybody. Anyone who still shows up to help is someone you can count on."

CHAPTER 49

THE INTERVIEW COMES OUT on Friday. It's both the first piece on Chris Daly with any depth to it and yet still far shorter than I had hoped.

Still, the article is only the first in a series of investigative pieces, and it's clear they're working hard on fact-checking, only publishing what they can substantiate. They make the connection between Lewis Rasmussen's arrest and Daly's attack, and they've verified through "confidential sources" that Tomo did in fact offer to acquire Tapestry on multiple occasions and was turned down.

Daly turns out to be an enigma, a verified employee at the FCC with an electronic history turned up via a credit check that nobody can verify. Phone calls to past employers turn up employee records, but nobody remembers him. No neighbors know him at any of his previous addresses. The article includes a slightly blurry official-looking photo and a request for more information about him.

The article promises more details into Rasmussen, the struggle for control with the board of directors, and role of CompEx next week.

The article's been live for a little over an hour when Owen Mitchell calls.

"What the hell have you done, Angie?"

"Yes, Owen, I'm fine, thank you so much for asking. You probably want to know how you can help, right?"

"No, I want to talk about you going to the press."

"Really, Owen. Three days after I was attacked and beaten, and you never ask how I'm doing?"

"Hell, I've worked with Amber and Igloo every day since you were attacked, helping them run the company, and getting regular updates on you. I didn't want to bother you at home, not after what the board put you though. I'm very, very sorry about what happened, and also sorry we fell victim to Rasmussen's manipulations."

Oh. I didn't expect that reaction.

Owen keeps going. "However, that doesn't excuse talking to the press about the investors the way you did. CompEx has a substantial brand. They do not want to be connected to anything contentious. You've put them in an awful bind."

"They consigned themselves to that situation by taking orders from Rasmussen."

"You forced them to up their stake to appear clean. They feel manipulated."

"What are you talking about?" I say. "There's nothing in the article about them upping their stake."

"No, but the reporters asked them questions yesterday, and made it clear they would be watching to see what CompEx does. Today's article reinforced all of these issues will be exposed in the next week."

"What did CompEx decide?" I try to keep the question light.

"Jesus, it's not about what they decide, it's that they're a major player, and you've put my relationship with them at stake."

"It's not all about you, Owen. The world doesn't revolve around your relationships. You, CompEx, me, we're all pawns in this."

Silence hangs heavy on the line. Finally, Owen breaks the quiet. "We had an emergency meeting with the investors, including CompEx, this morning. Everyone has agreed to jointly honor their financial commitments while maintaining your voting power to provide a show of confidence. We're increasing the valuation of the company so we don't dilute your share. You still have control. All this is tentative obviously."

"That's great news." The statement is vague and devoid of meaning. The outcome is what I hoped for, but the victory is hollow. Superior ideas, management skills, and technical expertise should have allowed me to win. I imagined Tapestry competing head-to-head against Tomo, beating them by the superiority of our meritocratic design principles. In the end it came down to hacking the bad guys and exposing their foul behavior. I played a game and won because I cheated better than the other team.

℧

On Monday I return to the office.

Harry, our CFO, is the first to see me, and he apologizes at least three times before he even reaches me. I edge away from him, but he keeps coming, like he's going to hug me, and all I can hear is a hum in my circuits, like I'm about to blow a fuse.

"I got all the money back from the police," he says, hands up, trying to placate me.

I have no idea what he's talking about, until I remember the cash I had begged and borrowed from friends to keep us afloat. I try to walk around him, but he blocks my path, oblivious to my discomfort, or maybe interpreting it as anger about the money.

"We'll receive the next series of payments from the investors, on an accelerated schedule. By tomorrow we'll have enough cash in the bank to meet payroll for the next four months."

I'm still cornered in the entranceway. Amber hears him, grabs me by the arm, and pushes him aside. She escorts me to my office and follows me in, closing the door behind her.

There's a knock at the door before I can even sit down. Igloo opens the door a crack to sit her head in. "Can I come in?" She's got puppy dog eyes.

I nod.

She gives me a hug.

"Careful," I say, afraid she's going to press on one of my still-sore injuries.

She's gentle though, and then she takes one of my guest chairs. Amber remains standing by the whiteboard.

"You shouldn't go out without one of us," Igloo says.

I nod, feeling foolish now that I'm in my office, even though I was undeniably stuck out there.

"Did you see today's article?" Amber asks.

"Yes," I say. It's the second in the series, and this one focused on Tomo and its effect on mental health, and privacy; it includes blurbs from experts in the field as well as regular Tomo users. Tomorrow, the article promises to unveil a dozen emails purportedly exchanged between Lewis Rasmussen and Chris Daly.

"So far this morning we've had five thousand people sign up to be notified when Tapestry goes live." Igloo passes over a tablet displaying a graph of signups. It looks like a hockey stick. "Tomo users are eager to defect."

"That's great," I say. We usually average a hundred email signups a day. "We'll see a lot more before the week is out."

"We should launch right now," Amber says.

I shake my head. "Even our accelerated date isn't for five more weeks."

"The platform is ready," Amber stands and paces across the room. "All the beta users are happy. You know what conversion rates are like. Maybe 5 percent of the signups will come back later to create an account. If we go live now, at least half will make an account and use Tapestry right away."

Ugh. I run my hand through my hair. "Marketing is pushing back again. Now that we have money again, they want to do an organized launch to coincide with ITX."

"Screw their plans," Amber says. "We'll drum up more press this week than marketing could obtain for ITX, and you know it."

I do, but I'm glad Amber concluded it on her own. "Are we ready to scale? If all our incoming traffic turns into active users and invites their friends?"

"We load tested yesterday to ten million clients." Amber looks smug. "Just in case."

"Ten million?" I'm shocked. We've never tested more than half a million before.

"We worked around some bottlenecks," Igloo says, "and latency crept up, but we sustained that load for an hour."

"We're ready," Amber says. "As ready as we're ever going to be."

Igloo pulls down her hood, and shakes her hair free. "This is Tapestry's moment."

It's been a year getting to this point, more if you count the time I spent germinating these ideas. When Thomas encouraged me to leave Tomo and create a company, I thought he was crazy. From where I stand now, it feels like my whole life has been leading up to this point. Succeed or fail, I've poured everything into this business.

"Let's do it," I say. "We launch tomorrow."

CHAPTER 50

Five months later...

Local Startup Tapestry Valued at $2B

Fourth consecutive month of exponential growth

Local tech darling Tapestry, founded by ex-Tomo employee Angie Benenati, is now valued at $2B after an investment round led by Pinchot Venture Partners. Growing users tenfold for the fourth consecutive month, Benenati says the valuation is justified given their growth potential.

"We have a path forward to grow well beyond $200B," Benenati said, referring to the declining market cap of competitor Tomo. "Our approach is fundamentally cooperative and inclusionary, not exclusionary. All of our partners are committed to cultivating the Tapestry ecosystem."

Tomo's initial stumble with the CEO Lewis Rasmussen's arrest for the alleged attempted murder of Benenati has turned into a string of setbacks as further investigation revealed evidence he coerced more than a dozen industry leaders into backroom deals that may violate anti-trust laws. Tomo stock is down nearly 25 percent since Rasmussen's arrest. The company's own PrivacyGuard product, decried by computer security experts since its introduction as a fatally flawed implementation, has been removed from the market. Rasmussen continues to profess his innocence while he awaits trial, even as evidence against him continues to mount.

"If you're not paying for the product, you are the product," Benenati said to wild applause during a keynote address at SXSW Interactive. "The era of control by mega-corporations is over, and open platforms are back. This is how the web was meant to be."

Benenati may be right. Web traffic analysis firm Alexa reports Tomo web visits are down 30 percent since their peak. Tomo's fall from grace couldn't be better timed for Tapestry's own growth.

↻

The killing days are over. The scrutiny I'm under as CEO of Tapestry is too immense to take such risks again. In many ways, I'm glad. The temptation would always exist to help one more person, right one more wrong. One era ends so another can begin.

Thomas and I can move forward without any new deceptions. It's a relief, and not only because of my ongoing guilt about lying. I can bring my whole self to our relationship. That feels good. Well, my whole self minus my past. Let that remain hidden at least.

Tapestry's odds of success are higher than ever, though by no means assured. Our launch, fueled by the news coverage surrounding Chris Daly and Lewis Rasmussen, exceeded our best estimates. New users continue to flood in.

Igloo is beyond ecstatic that Kindred is hugely popular with kids under sixteen, who spend hours relating their joys and woes to our chatbots. We hired a new team of psychologists to bolster the chatbots' capabilities so they can help people develop better coping skills and alleviate social isolation. There's even talk of bringing in educators to develop tutoring bots.

Amid the controversy, Tomo continues to shed users. Many sign up with us, but they're losing users faster than we're gaining them. That's okay. I'd like Tapestry to succeed with our particular vision for decentralization of control, but it's more important that people wake up and see the danger of manipulative, monolithic Internet silos.

It's crazy that three years ago I was writing SQL queries sequestered in a corner, hiding from everyone as best I could, and now I'm helping topple one of the world's largest companies.

Still, one ever-present knot of worry has taken up permanent residence in my stomach: the government. I skated by with Chris Daly, his crimes sufficiently atrocious that the government chose to keep their distance. Unless he worked in total isolation though, somewhere inside that massive intelligence organization are people who are aware of me.

Even if my crimes remain secret, we cannot keep hidden the threat Tapestry poses to government surveillance. The dispersion of data and communication to a distributed network of providers is a nightmare for centralized spying. Where once they could have forced a wiretap on a single enormous company, now they must individually seek out hundreds of different providers who can come and go in a few months.

I know they're watching me. Some would say I need luck on my side. But luck is for fools. I make my own destiny.

↻

"A little higher," I say, from my perch on my desk.

"What's the point?" Igloo says. "2600 Hz phone phreaking didn't work when you were a kid, and you still want me to learn it? And even if it did, I'd make my phone generate it." She grabs a mobile device out of her pocket, and opens a music app. "There's no point in doing it Grandpa's way."

With a few taps she generates the required frequency from her phone, and the light goes off on my software meter.

"I see your point, although the whistle kind of saved my life."

"Still." Igloo crosses her arms. "It's an old white guy custom. I don't want my rite of passage to be defined by the patriarchy."

I nod. "Fine. We need some rite of passage. Lock-picking?"

"With physical keys?" Igloo graces me with an intentionally silly bug-eyed gaze. "They'll be obsolete in a few years, replaced with digital locks."

These last few months caused me to reflect on my relationships with Repard and Nathan9. Repard is gone, and I'm still persona non grata to Nathan, but it's time for me to be the mentor anyway. Igloo will be my first disciple.

I might be able to leave the world of killing, but I'll never be able to leave the world of hacking. There are young hackers, old hackers and hackers in jail. But there are very few ex-hackers.

Igloo and I will forge new ways. What worked for Nathan and Repard won't work for us.

"How about compromising cloud provisioning?" Igloo says. "By the time someone gets the server they requested, it's already undermined."

"Whoa." I hold up my hand. "The point of tests of ability is not to go to jail, it's to demonstrate inside knowledge, skill, and courage."

"And whistling 2600 Hertz does that?" Igloo shakes her head.

Working with Igloo isn't going to be easy. She pushes too much. Well, maybe I did, too.

"We'll figure something out," I say.

↻

Thank you for purchasing *Kill Process*. I hope you enjoyed reading it.

As an independent author, I don't have the support of a large marketing department at a major publisher. Instead, I'm dependent on readers like you to spread the word. If you enjoyed *Kill Process*, please:

- Write a review online
- Tell a friend or two about *Kill Process*, or post about it on social media.
- Subscribe to updates on my blog at williamhertling.com/subscribe to find out about future book releases.

If you are new to my books, please check out *Avogadro Corp*, the first of four books in my Singularity series. The Singularity series, set in ten-year intervals starting in current day, is about the emergence of AI and the subsequent transformation of the world. This series is endorsed by Brad Feld, Harper Reed, Gene Kim, David Brin, and many more.

- Buy *Avogadro Corp*, the first book in the Singularity series, today at williamhertling.com/buy

Thanks again,
William Hertling

P.S. Keep reading for a free preview of *Avogadro Corp*.

Avogadro Corp:

The Singularity is Closer than it Appears

Chapter 3

Gary Mitchell took the Avogadro exit ramp off the Fremont bridge and pulled up to the parking gate, headlights bouncing off the reflective paint on the barrier in the early morning darkness. He waved his badge at the machine. The gate rose up, and Gary drove into the empty garage, a hint of a smile on his face.

It was two days before the deadline to pull ELOPe off the server. David and Mike hadn't done anything to drop usage. In fact, he woke up to blaring alerts from his phone. There'd been small CPU spikes all night long, and a big one this morning about five, right around the time the East coast workday was starting.

The idiots came within a hair's breadth of overloading the whole system. AvoMail adapted dynamically, cutting back polling frequencies and slowing the delivery of mail, but they'd been close to a full outage.

Gary alternated between anger and glee. He'd never had significant downtime on his watch, and didn't plan to. But this time David came so close Gary could justify sending the email he'd been wanting to write for months, letting Sean Leonov know he was going to kick ELOPe off production.

He would have liked to pull the plug first and then sent the message, but that was pushing the line with Sean.

It was the first time in a while he'd arrived at the office this early. Gary found the empty building disquieting. He pushed the feeling aside and thought about emailing Sean, which brought a smile back to his face. A few minutes later, Gary walked past his secretary's vacant desk and into his own office. His computer came to life, and Gary went straight to AvoMail to compose the email to Sean.

From: Gary Mitchell (Communication Products Division)

To: Sean Leonov (CEO)

Subject: ELOPe Project

Time: 6:22am

Sean, just to give you a heads up. I have no choice but to pull production access for the Email Language Optimization Project. They're consuming 2,000 times the server resources we allocated, and spiked usage this morning, causing degraded service levels for ninety minutes.

We gave them carte blanche when we had excess capacity because it's your special project. However, they consume so many resources we routinely dip into reserve capacity, and service degradations like the one they caused today lose us commercial accounts every time.

I spoke to David and Mike about their server utilization many times, but they did nothing to get usage down. I gave them a final warning two weeks ago and I've seen no improvements.

Effective tomorrow at 9am, I'm revoking production access for ELOPe.

Email finished, Gary sat and stared for a minute. Was he too obviously gloating? He didn't think so. He hit send.

Time for coffee. He sauntered down the hallway whistling.

↻

John Anderson let his heavy messenger bag slide to the floor and shrugged out of his wet raincoat, hanging it behind his desk. Dropping into his chair, the pneumatic shock absorber took his weight without complaint. He sighed at the thought of another day in Procurement processing purchase requests. Tentatively peeking at his inbox, he saw more than a hundred new emails. His shoulders slumped a little and he reached for his coffee.

This week John had the kids, so he had to drop them off at school before work. Portland's crazy school system meant the best public schools were all elective. He and his ex-wife had to choose among a dozen different schools. They ended up with the Environmental School. John's kids loved the school, and so did he. Unfortunately, they lived in Northeast Portland, the school was in Southeast, and work was across the river in Northwest. His normal twenty-minute commute turned into an hour-plus on the days he dropped the kids off. He'd arrive late at work, his smartphone beeping and buzzing as emails piled up. He loathed the backlog he started his day with. The consolation prize was that the kids' school was right next to a Stumptown Coffee. John sipped the Ethiopian brew. The dark, bittersweet warmth brought a smile to his face.

As the coffee kicked his brain into gear, he regained his will to tackle his inbox. He was brought up short by a puzzling email from Gary Mitchell. Sent earlier this morning, the email asked him to divert five thousand servers. John read the email three times in its brief entirety.

```
From: Gary Mitchell (Communication Products Division)

To: John Anderson (Procurement)

Subject: ELOPe Project

Time: 6:22am


Hi John,


Sean Leonev asked me to help out the ELOPe guys.
They need additional servers ASAP, and we're running
out of extra capacity here. Please accelerate 5,000
standard servers out of the normal procurement cycle,
and give them to IT for immediate deployment. Assign
asset ownership to David Ryan.
```

Thanks,

Gary Mitchell

John thought about the exception process. Normally when a department wanted new servers, they put in a purchase request. Parts were bought, shipped to Avogadro data centers, assembled into the custom servers Avogadro used, and installed onto racks. Then another group took over and installed the operating system and applications used on the servers. Depending on the size and timing of the order, it would take anywhere from six to twelve weeks from the time they were requested until the servers were available for use.

When a department needed servers in a rush, they requested an exception. That process would take servers already purchased for another group and in the pipeline, and divert the servers to the department that needed them urgently. Replacement computers would be ordered for the first group, who would have to wait a little longer.

Diversion requests weren't uncommon. No, the puzzling part wasn't the request, but that Gary would send an email. Only the procurement app could be used to order, expedite, or divert servers, a fact Gary should know since he routinely requested more servers.

He put his hand on the phone and then took it away. A call to Gary would eat up at least fifteen minutes. Regardless of what the procurement rules were, whenever John tried to explain them to anyone, they would argue with him. The higher up in the company they were, the more they would argue as though their lofty organizational heights carried potential energy that could override the rules. A quick email would save John from getting his ear chewed out.

To: Gary Mitchell (Communication Products Division)

From: John Anderson (Procurement)

Subject: Email Procurement Forms

Gary,

We can't do a server reallocation exception based on an email. I couldn't do that for 5 servers, let alone 5,000 servers. Please use the online Procurement tool to submit your request:

```
http://procurement.internal.avogadrocorp.com
```
or have your admin do it for you. That's the only process for procurement exceptions we can use. We can
approve your reallocation exception if you follow the
existing process and provide appropriate justification.

Thanks,

John Anderson

John continued to work through his backlog of emails. The hundreds of
new messages in his inbox would give the casual observer the impression he
had been gone from work for a week, rather than just the late start he had gotten dropping off his kids. He took another sip of coffee and continued to work
through emails. The rest of his day, like every other, would consist of endless
rounds of coffee and emails. Gary's message might have been a little unusual,
but it was quickly forgotten amid the deluge of other issues.

ↄ

A few hours later, on the other side of the campus from John Anderson, Pete
Wong brought his lunch from the cafeteria in Building Six, diagonally across
to Building Three, pausing briefly on the windowed sky bridge. The sun had
come out, and he raised his face to feel the heat for a few moments. Looking
down, he saw the light glisten on wet streets, perhaps one of his favorite parts
of Portland's climate. As a kid he would run outside on rainy days when the
sun broke through the clouds, pretending fairies had covered the street with
magic dust.

A crowd of laughing people, marketing folk from their attire, entered the
skybridge, distracting him from his memories. He continued through and
then went down four flights of stairs to his office. Out of the daylight and into
the fluorescent gloom of basement offices.

At one department meeting after another, Pete had been assured his Internal Tools team, responsible for delivering business applications used inside
the company, would be relocated just as soon as above-ground space became
available. Pete shook his head at the thought.

It was no surprise that the company had stuck the Internal Tools team in
what amounted to the dungeons. Everyone at Avogadro used their tools to
get their daily jobs done, from ordering office supplies to getting more disk

space to filling out their timecards. But because Pete's team didn't develop the sexy customer-facing products, they were the absolute runts in the corporate hierarchy. No executives or research and development engineers would ever be sentenced to the basement offices. The injustice made him gnash his teeth sometimes.

Back at his desk, Pete took solace in his lunch. His office space sucked and his team was unappreciated, but the food was good. Fresh gnocchi in a butter sauce and mixed salad greens. A cup of gelato stayed cold while he ate in a special vacuum insulated cup. All organic and locally sourced, of course. The coffee wasn't bad either, though it came from Kobos. Pete preferred Ristretto, but only a few of Portland's roasters were big enough to supply Avogadro's headquarters. Pete's wife, a tea drinker, couldn't understand the Portland obsession with coffee.

Pete ate with one hand as he looked over his inbox until a new message caught his eye.

```
To: Pete Wong (Internal Tools)
From: John Anderson (Procurement)
Subject: Email Procurement Forms


Hi Pete,


    This is John Anderson in Procurement. Even though
we've got a procurement web application from IT Tools,
we still get hundreds of email requests we can't han-
dle. Part of the problem stems from sales people in
the field who can send emails from their smartphone,
but have a hard time getting a secure VPN connection
to the internal web sites. Can you create an email-
to-web bridge to allow people to email us to get the
form, fill it out, and reply to submit the requisition?
I mentioned this idea to Sean Leonov, and he said you
guys could whip up something like this in a day or
two.

    Thanks,

    John
```

Pete stared at the strangeness. John Anderson, some guy in Procurement, buddies with Sean Leonov, cofounder of Avogadro? Sean was a living legend. Pete hadn't met anyone who knew Sean directly.

Pete pondered the email. Why did Sean think Internal Tools could implement this so quickly? Was he even aware of the IT department? How had Sean, or even Pete, decided to single him out? It all seemed so unlikely.

The request was a ten on the bizarre meter, but had a certain kind of plausibility. He imagined a salesperson working in the field, using their smartphone to access internal sites. Small screen, low bandwidth. The justification made sense, and if doing this impressed Sean Leonov, well, that couldn't hurt his career. This could be his ticket to one of the real R&D project teams instead of being stuck in the dead-end Internal Tools department.

Daydreaming of an office with sunlight pouring through immense windows, he spent a few minutes imagining his future workspace. Maybe he'd have a window overlooking the West Hills, or even better, the river.

With a start, he sat up straight. He would spend time looking into the request. He eagerly put his fingers on the keyboard and starting searching. His excitement grew when his first search for 'email to web service' turned up an existing design posted by some IBM guys. After reading through the article, he realized he could implement the email bridge in a couple of hours.

His other work forgotten, Pete started on the project. He created a new Ruby on Rails web application to do the necessary conversion of web pages to emails, and emails into web page form submissions. It was easier than expected and by mid-afternoon he had a simple prototype running on the department servers.

He discovered a few bugs in the software. Puzzling over the details in his head, he mindlessly rushed down the hall to the coffee station for a refill.

↻

Mike left his office, nodded to a few teammates he passed, and headed downstairs for the nearest exterior door. After banging his head against the same problem for hours and becoming increasingly frustrated, he needed to clear his mind. The performance issues had become an insurmountable obstacle.

Once outside, Mike wandered around Avogadro's South Plaza, an open amphitheater and park. Just one of the many corporate perks employed to keep everyone happy. Blissfully clear skies contrasted with still wet pavement from nighttime rains. He waved to a flock of engineers jogging by.

What he found this morning was far more puzzling than the issues he'd expected to run into. Mike considered the two distinct parts of ELOPe. Users saw the front-end process evaluating emails in real-time and offering suggested improvements. But the piece that troubled Mike today was the other half, the backend process for analyzing historical emails and generating affinity clusters.

While the performance of ELOPe stunk by anyone's measure, at least it had been predictably bad. In the course of attempting to improve efficiency over the past months, Mike learned each new email fed into the system required roughly the same number of processor cycles to process.

This morning, though, nothing behaved as expected. According to the application logs, nobody used ELOPe last night, and yet the load metrics had been pegged for hours — a sure indication of a ton of computer processing time being spent on something. But what? In closed prototype mode, only the members of the development team had access to ELOPe. That meant software coders, interaction designers, and the linguistics experts particular to their project. Everyone's activities were logged, but the records didn't show any activity. Yet someone had generated server load.

Mike hoped fresh air and a walk around the Plaza would help him figure out the problem. The last thing he wanted was additional performance problems when they were looking for a massive improvement. He sat on the amphitheater steps and rested his head on his hands. He watched another set of joggers go by. For someone who prided himself on taking things easy, the world weighed heavily on his shoulders right now.

CHAPTER 4

Pete Wong cut and pasted code he'd downloaded from a dozen different websites, creating a real kludge he wouldn't want to show off in a coding style contest. He ran the test suite one final time and smiled as the last finicky test passed. He'd implemented the email to web bridge in less than twenty-four hours! It worked, by golly! He tested the new service against the Internal Tools web service, Procurement application, and a handful of other sites. It seemed to work for everything.

He drummed his thumbs on desk in excitement. Using off the shelf libraries written for Ruby on Rails, he'd glued together the necessary pieces quickly. What once took weeks in old web development environments required mere hours in a modern, nearly magical language like Ruby. It was powerful tools like these that enabled startups to build products in a weekend and launch on a shoestring budget. He wondered for the hundredth time if he shouldn't leave Avogadro to start his own company.

Pete pulled his keyboard closer and started an email to John Anderson, the guy in Procurement. In a bold move, he cc:'ed Sean Leonov. No harm in a little visibility, right?

Pete explained the implementation and wrote detailed instructions on how to use the email bridge, a little more than five screenfuls of email. Woops. Perhaps the usage was more complicated than the folks in sales could cope with. Pete didn't know anyone in sales, but he suspected they might not have in-depth technical skills. Well, at least what he provided was complete, even if rough around the edges.

He clicked send and sat back in his chair, sipping his coffee and basking in the glow of his accomplishment. He had good coding kung fu.

Pete pondered bragging about his achievement to his coworkers. A dark thought occurred, perhaps there was something a little irregular about what he'd done. He sat forward and let his cup thump onto his desk. He never told the rest of the team about the project. This request should have come through the normal process like everything else. Not only that, but the code should have been peer reviewed by his fellow developers before he deployed. He'd been so concerned with impressing Sean Leonov he didn't stop to consider the usual process. Well, no one could blame him for taking initiative.

Despite this, some bigger issue nagged at him. What was it? He jumped out of his seat and pounded his desk with a fist. He'd just implemented an off-the-radar system that interfaced with a dozen different business critical web services inside the company, probably violating all sorts of security policies. On reflection, he definitely had. It suddenly felt hot in his cramped office.

Just as quickly as he had become alarmed, he relaxed a little and sat. If Sean Leonov thought the Internal Tools team could implement the request within twenty-four hours, he clearly meant they should pull out all the stops. Pete couldn't go back and yank the application off the servers, not after telling John and Sean the service was available. He shook his head, concluding he was worried about nothing. The bridge was invulnerable. His tool relied on email credentials to validate user logons, and if any product in the company was secure, it was AvoMail.

If he told his boss and the rest of his team now, he'd get his wrist slapped. The best course of action would be to keep quiet until he had gotten a response from Sean. Once he showed that to the team, any skipping of due process would be forgiven. With his plan in place, one in which he wouldn't take too much heat, he relaxed a little more.

A ruckus came from down the hall, rapidly getting closer. Had they already found out what he'd done? He grew alarmed until a group of his coworkers ran past his open door. A few seconds later, the Internal Tools technical lead stuck his balding head in Pete's doorway and said, "We got a hot tip the billiard room showed up on the fourth floor of Building Two. Coming?"

With relief, Pete smiled and leaped up from his desk. He'd never seen the mysterious Avogadro billiard room that roved from building to building. "Absolutely!" he called, as he ran from his office, following the gang of geeks.

Work forgotten, Pete joined the boisterous hunt for the billiard room. Laughter rang out as other groups heard the rumor and entered the chase. The room would only accept the keycards of the first sixty-four people to find the room's new location, adding to the urgency of the search. As teams ran through the halls, they told each other outright lies about the suspected whereabouts, all part of the game surrounding the mystery.

While people played and laughed, thousands of computers hummed and exchanged data. A few servers allocated to Internal Tools spiked in usage, but nobody was around to notice.

ʊ

Gene Keyes walked back to his office with another cup of coffee, grateful the campus had returned to a somewhat normal decorum after the insanity of the hunt for the billiard room. On some level, he was curious about the mystery of the moving room, but he hated the way the kids around him turned the puzzle into a superficial game, as they did with everything.

He searched the pockets of his suit for a note. His rumpled jacket and graying, disheveled hair was a stark contrast to the young, hip employees dressed in the latest designer jeans or fashionable retro sixties clothing. Nor did he fit in with the young, geeky employees in their plaid shirts or tees with obscure logos. Not to mention the young, smartly dressed marketing people in their tailored business casual wear. Fitting in and impressing others weren't high on his list of priorities.

As he approached his own office, he found a woman knocking on his door. "Can I help you?" he asked, halting the search for the missing note.

"I'm looking for Gene Keyes," she said in a bubbly voice. "I'm Maggie Reynolds, and I—"

"I'm Gene," he said, cutting her off. "Come in." Gene opened the door and walked in. She could follow him or not.

"Uh, my boss sent me because he's missing four..." She trailed off.

Gene put his cup down and took a seat. He glanced up to an astonished expression on her face.

"Wow, I didn't know anyone still used... Wow, this is a lot of paper."

Gene turned around, despite himself. Yes, it was true his office was piled with computer generated reports. Stacks of good, old fashioned letter-sized paper littered every flat surface. Oversized plotter printouts with huge spreadsheets and charts hung from the walls. The centerpiece of the office, the desk he occupied, was a 1950s era wooden piece that nearly spanned the width of the room. It might have been the only furnishing in the entire building complex manufactured in the previous century. Incongruously, the desk was far larger in every dimension than the door. The people with a good brain on their heads, often engineers, but occasionally a smart manager, those who trusted their guts, instincts, and eyes, but took little for granted, they'd come in and their eyes would bounce back and forth between the desk and the door trying to puzzle out the mystery. Sadly, she didn't appear to notice.

"Wow, I saw this in a movie once," she said, coming around his desk to fondle a stack of continuous feed paper. She pulled at one end, the green and white striped paper unfolding accordion style. Her eyebrows went up and her jaw down. "Hey, do you have any punch cards?"

It rankled Gene to hear almost identical comments from every kid that walked in the door. He sat a little straighter in his wooden office chair, the same seat he liberated from the army the day he was discharged.

"Some things are better on paper," he explained, not for the first time. "Paper is consistent. It doesn't say one thing one day and a different thing a different day. And, no, I don't have punch cards. I'm not preserving this stuff for a museum. This is how I do my job." Gene tried to work some venom into his voice, but what came out just sounded tired. Gene knew what she'd say next, because he heard a variation of the same thing from every visitor.

"You know we work for Avogadro, right?" Maggie said, smiling.

Gene knew. But he worked in Controls and Compliance, what they used to properly call the Audit department. When push came to shove, paper never lied.

"Uh huh," he grumbled, ignoring that whole line of thinking. "So, what can I help you with?"

"Well, I have a problem. The database says we're supposed to have more than four million dollars left in our budget for the fiscal quarter, but our purchase orders keep getting denied. Finance says we spent our money, but I know we didn't. They said you would be able to help."

Gene gestured with both hands at the paper around him. "That's what the paper is for. Believe it or not, there's a printout here of every department's budget for each month. So we can examine your budget before and after and see what happened. Now let's take a look..."

↻

"Dude, you're here," Mike said, plopping down in David's spare chair. "Where were you this morning? I couldn't find you anywhere. I need to talk to you about some weird behavior in ELOPe. Not to mention you missed the entire hunt for the billiard room." Considering that they worked in neighboring offices, and were in constant electronic communication, David's vanishing act was impressive.

"What kind of weird behavior?" David gazed off into the distance, ignoring Mike's question.

"I told you we couldn't find any more performance gains, but I couldn't help trying. I started by establishing a baseline against the current code, to have something to test against. I correlated the bulk analysis import with server cycles consumed and..." Mike stopped.

David still stared out the window, and appeared lost in thought.

Mike glanced outside. A pleasant sunny day, uncommon for Portland in December, but he didn't see anything other than the ordinary bustle of people walking about on the street.

He turned back to David. "Are you listening? Isn't it critical this be fixed before Gary's deadline?"

"Well, I do have some good news there, but go on."

"I tried to establish a correlation, but I couldn't find one. You know ELOPe takes a predictable amount of server resources to analyze emails. At least it did, until two days ago. Now I can't find any relationship at all. The CPU utilization keeps going through the roof even when the logs indicate nobody is running any tests. It's as though the system is working on something, but I can't find any record of what."

David was still staring outside. Mike felt his head start to pound. He'd been struggling with the damn optimization for days. "So then David, I slept with your wife. She said it would be fine with you."

"Yeah, sure."

Mike waited, grinning to himself.

"Uh, what? What did you just say?" David finally focused on him.

Mike planted his body in front of the window to block David's view. "Why don't you tell me what the hell is going on, since you're clearly not interested in the performance issues."

"Ah, come read this email from Gary," David said, appearing animated for the first time since Mike entered the office. "The message came in a few minutes ago. We were allocated five thousand dedicated servers by way of a procurement exception. Accelerated deployment and all that. We'll have access to the computing power by tomorrow morning."

Mike came around to peer over David's shoulder at his screen, and let out a low whistle. "Holy smokes, five thousand servers. How did you get Gary to agree to that?"

"I sent him an email asking for dedicated nodes for ELOPe so we wouldn't be in conflict with the production AvoMail servers."

"Wow, what a fantastic reversal," Mike said. "I never would have guessed Gary would change his mind. Any clue why?"

David got that distant look in his face again. "I don't know. It is a bit surprising."

Excited by the possibilities of the extra computing power, Mike paced back and forth in front of the window. "Five thousand servers... We can move on to the next phase of the project, and scale up to limited production levels. We could start bulk processing customer emails in preparation for a public launch."

"Well, let's start with Avogadro's internal emails," David said. "This way, we won't adversely affect any customers if anything goes wrong. If we can analyze company emails at full volume, I'll suggest to Sean we turn the auto-suggestion feature on for all employees."

"Good plan. I'll stop work on the performance issues and focus on importing the internal emails. This is great news, David!" Mike did a little dance on his way out the door.

↻

When Mike left, David returned to staring out the window. The server allocation was great news. So why were the hairs raised on his neck?

He had sent the email to Gary. That part was true. But he'd neglected to tell Mike about the minor detail of ELOPe's involvement. Of course Mike would uncover massive background processing.

ELOPe needed to analyze Gary Mitchell's emails to optimize David's message, which meant ELOPe also required access to the inboxes of everyone Gary had emailed with, and then the inboxes of everyone those people communicated with, a spider web of relationships spanning many thousands of people. David's usage and modifications caused ELOPe to import a massive number of emails. He'd obscured his work by ensuring the new behavior wasn't part of the normal system logs, but he couldn't prevent system monitors from tracking CPU load.

David didn't know what to say. Mike would figure out the mystery behind the CPU utilization eventually. He hoped the discovery would take place later rather than sooner, after they'd solved their resource problems. David didn't want anyone, not even Mike, to know he was using ELOPe itself to get the resources to keep the project running.

A bug in the software, deeply integrated into the mail servers, could bring down all of AvoMail. If anything bad happened, David would feel some serious heat from upper management.

But that wasn't the cause for the pit of fear in his stomach.

No, the real issue stemmed from the changes David made during his all-night coding marathon. David went deep into the code for language analysis and put in an overarching directive to maximize the predicted sentiment for any message discussing the project. When any email mentioned ELOPe, from anyone or to anyone, then ELOPe would automatically and silently reword the message in a way favorable to overall success of the program.

The resulting emails were indistinguishable in writing style and language from those written by the purported sender, a testament to the skill of his team, whose language assembly algorithm used fragments from thousands of other emails to create a realistic message in the voice of the sender.

David relished the success and wished he could share with the team what they had accomplished. The culmination of years of research, the project had started with his efforts toward the Netflix Prize before he was hired, although even that work had been built on the shoulders of geniuses. Then months of labor with Mike to prove out the idea enough to justify further investment, followed by two years of a full R&D team, building the architecture and incrementally improving effectiveness month after month.

The results proved, beyond doubt, the power of the system. ELOPe's language optimization had acquired thousands of servers.

The problem, the unsettling fear, arose because David didn't understand how. He couldn't examine the altered emails, an unfortunate consequence of removing the logging so others wouldn't discover ELOPe's manipulations. Had Gary received a modified email convincing enough to make him change his mind? Or had ELOPe changed Gary's response to something more favorable? David found the uncertainty unnerving, and when he thought about how little control he had, the pit of fear in his stomach throbbed.

But sure enough, his dedicated servers would arrive tomorrow, an outcome worth dwelling on. An email from procurement confirmed the allocation, and another from operations showed the time the servers would be available. Whatever ELOPe had done worked. It might be the most server-intensive application in the company, if not the world, but by damn, it worked.

All the hard work, politics, and sacrifices now seemed worthwhile. The project had become his life, and his little baby was all grown up now, doing what it was built to do.

Well, maybe a little more besides.

He hadn't realized what it would feel like to have ELOPe working silently, behind the scenes. He was perpetuating a huge deception, and if anyone discovered what he had done, it would be the end of his career.

He turned to the window again. Outside, in the momentary sunshine, people went about their business, walking, talking, jogging, blissfully unaware of what was going on inside the company. From his office window, they looked chillingly carefree.

ʊ

Want more? Pick up *Avogadro Corp: The Singularity is Closer than it Appears* at williamhertling.com/buy

Sign up for my mailing list at williamhertling.com to receive alerts about upcoming releases, get book recommendations, and learn about the future of technology.

ALSO BY WILLIAM HERTLING

Singularity Series:

Avogadro Corp: The Singularity is Closer than it Appears
A.I. Apocalypse
The Last Firewall
The Turing Exception

Tapestry Series:

Kill Process
Kill Process 2 (forthcoming 2017)

Children's books written as Will Hertling

The Case of the Wilted Broccoli

*Subscribe to my mailing list at williamhertling.com
to learn about upcoming novel releases.*

Acknowledgements

The longer writers stay in the business, the more people they end up interacting with and relying on in the course of working on a novel. Also, as the length of the novel increases, so too does the number of people involved. All of this is to say that I'm indebted to many people for their help on Kill Process. As always, any errors that remain are my own fault.

I worked with two editors this time around, Anastasia Poirier and Dario Ciriello, and deeply appreciate their assistance. Editing is a business where the work doesn't stop with just one reading of the manuscript. There are follow-up phone calls, questions by email, spot-checking of revised material, and emotional handholding. Thanks to their hard work, characters spring to life in more vivid detail, emotions are felt more keenly, and everything has more clarity.

Thanks also to everyone involved in the production of the novel. Proofreading is thanks to Kate Heartfield. The red-and-black cover on the trade paperback is thanks to Mike Corley. The hooded hacker limited-edition paperback cover is thanks to Adam Hall. Formatting for the print edition was done by Dario Ciriello, and formatting for the ebook was done by Rick Fisher.

Beta readers are invaluable for their feedback on the manuscript. These folks are the first to read the manuscript as a whole, with fresh eyes. Their job isn't easy. Often stuck reading the manuscript at their computer in Word, they need to wade through and attempt to ignore thousands of grammar errors and lazy word choices, in order to provide feedback on the more substantive content issues. I'd like to thank Gene Kim, Brad Feld, Bernie A. Hernández, John-Isaac Clark, Stacey Wransky, Barb Vostmyer, Stacey Stein, Mat Ellis, Mike Whitmarsh, Monica Villaseñor, Catherine Shyu, Reid Tatoris, David Mandell, Katie Carey Levisay, Danger Marshall, Lucas Carlson, Eliot Peper, Catherine Woneis, Grace Ribaudo, and Amber Case.

My critique group was essential in refining the beginning of the novel, especially getting deeper into Angie's character. Thank you to Catherine Craglow, Cathy Heslin, Shana Kusin, David Melville, and Amy Seaholt.

Dr. Kusin also provided very helpful medical expertise. Grace Ribaudo and Katie Carey Levisay provided valuable psychological expertise.

As always, the members of Codex, an online community, rendered assistance with countless issues. Actually determining who provided help is a forensic exercise that can consume days, so in lieu of appreciating individually all of those talented and wise people, I would like to thank Luc Reid, who created and hosts the community, providing a valuable forum for hundreds of professional writers.

I'd like to thank Sean Cordero for getting me involved in DDial, and Vito Masotti, Mike Jee, Bill Shamam, Grace Scaglione, and others for many fun times at an influential point in my life. Bill Shamam and I had a blast on rmac DDial recently when I wanted to check a few details of DDial usage. If you'd like to experience an authentic eighties Diversi-Dial for yourself, telnet to rmac.d-dial.com, which is running on a collection of original Apple //e computers.

Chris DiBona invited me to a dinner celebrating open source luminaries last year. When we all grabbed seats, I found myself in the midst of several women who worked in tech. This turned out to be one of those serendipitous occurrences. I was already interested in the experiences of women working in technology, and all I had to do was be quiet and listen to hear inside stories from women at different stages in their careers. I'm incredibly grateful for that dinner conversation. Thanks to Deborah Bryant, Cat Allman, and Karen Sandler.

I'd like to thank several people who shared their experiences with domestic violence and abuse with me. You know who you are. I especially apologize for any mistakes in the handling of this topic, which is a sensitive issue, and one I care deeply about. I had to take a few liberties for the sake of the story, including: Most abusers avoid social media and other communication tools to isolate their victims. Abusers and victims come in all gender combinations. Because I couldn't stomach writing about it, and didn't want to subject my readers to it, I avoided going too deeply into the particulars of abusive situations. On the other hand, statistics I shared about abuse are accurate, based on the best data I could find. A few beta readers questioned whether forty percent of police officers really have violence in the home. Studies vary in their numbers and methodology, but most agree the prevalence of domestic violence for police officers is much higher than the population at large, and at least two studies agree on the forty percent figure. This includes both violence directed at spouses/partners as well as children, and both long term and isolated incidents of violence.

I also want to acknowledge Eliot Peper's *Uncommon Stock*, a great startup thriller series about the founding of a financial fraud detection software company, which stimulated my interest in writing about a tech startup.

As usual, many characters are inspired by or tributes to real-life people whom I greatly appreciate. However, in the spirit of fun mysteries, I'm not going to tie them to any specific names. Ask me over a whisky.

I also want to extend a very big thank you to my backers on Patreon. In exchange for a small monthly donation, these folks get early access to my published novels, signed copies, and occasionally cut scenes. Their regular contributions help smooth out my writing income between books and defray costs associated with production of each novel. Thank you very much to Mike Doyle, Bernie Hernandez, John-Isaac Clark, Joe Ludwig, Brad Feld, James Anderson, Carolyn Stark, Addison Smith, Greg Roberts, Keith Nolen, Richard Sorden, David Mussington, Jon Guidry, Robert Miller, Peter, Jason Gardner, Jackie Tortorella, Ben Bieker, Caleb Johnson, Steven E. Burchett, Robert Solovay, Gerald Auer, Peter Soldan, Stephen O., Adam Colon, Adith Radityo, Robert Dobkin, B. Wolf, Jan Svanda, Felix Knecht, Tom Haswell, Vivek Bharadwaj, Ted Young, Larry Pearson, Jim White, Stephen Syputa, Karl Bernard, Jonathan Yantis, Nicole J. LeBoeuf, Jacob Perkins, Alek, Nima Bigdely Shamlo, Erin Gately, Eugene Epshteyn, Nils, and Craig T. Wood. If this is at all interesting to you, please visit patreon.com/hertling.

Lastly, thanks to you, my reader. Without you, there would be no reason to write.

<<<<>>>

CPSIA information can be obtained
at www.ICGtesting.com
Printed in the USA
BVOW03s1730180617

487204BV00001B/112/P